PILGRIMAGE TO HERESY

PILGRIMAGE TO HERESY

Don't Believe Everything They Tell You

A Novel of The Camino

Tracy Saunders

iUniverse, Inc.
New York Lincoln Shanghai

PILGRIMAGE TO HERESY
Don't Believe Everything They Tell You

iUniverse books may be ordered through booksellers or by contacting:

iUniverse
2021 Pine Lake Road, Suite 100
Lincoln, NE 68512
www.iuniverse.com
1-800-Authors (1-800-288-4677)

Because of the dynamic nature of the Internet, any Web addresses or links contained in this book may have changed since publication and may no longer be valid.

ISBN: 978-0-595-46912-3 (pbk)
ISBN: 978-0-595-70702-7 (cloth)
ISBN: 978-0-595-91199-8 (ebk)

Printed in the United States of America

To my "sister" Sylvia
In celebration of almost 30 years
of friendship,
love, and advice

Acknowledgements

Pilgrimage to Heresy began as a bubble in the mind which would not go away.

Somewhere in between Ponferrada and Cacabelos on the Camino de Santiago, my fellow pilgrim, and a Gnostic priest, Dr. Lance Owens, mentioned the name of Priscillian to me as a possible candidate for the silver embossed casket which lies below the altar in Santiago de Compostela. I had walked 700 kilometers by then. I said I had never heard of Priscillian. Lance countered that his name was only written about in scholarly texts, such as that written by Henry Chadwick, Regis Professor of Classics. But the details I was to learn later.

It took more than two years to get hold of Prof. Chadwick's book: *Priscillian of Avila: The Occult and the Charismatic in the Early Church* (OUP 1976). And Lance was right: it wasn't a book for the lay reader. However, as I read it through I realized that not only was Priscillian of Avila's story a fascinating one, but it was also one that had to be told. By me, it seemed, I reasoned once I had thoroughly researched various libraries, and later online, and come up with next to nothing.

It contained all of the elements of a best-seller: mystery; betrayal and persecution; a scandal or two; and finally, the first appearance of the Inquisition, long before the word "Spanish" had been attached to it. (Actually, the Inquisition began in 12th Century France, but that is another story … perhaps the next?) Last of all, it posited a cover up; a "conspiracy" of sorts. A grasping of a truth to which pilgrims aspire, but which may be no more than a well-concealed lie.

My local bookshop couldn't find it. Amazon, even, didn't manage to locate it, although I waited a year. Finally, my good friend, Sylvia, managed to locate a copy for me. I read it and was enthralled. My instincts were right: not only did Priscillian's charisma last through the ages, but his story–which had been totally obscured by the Roman Catholic Church–was worth the telling: even if I had to make a lot of it up!

Make no mistake: Priscillian was real. In the course of my research, I made a visit to the town of Avila in central Spain. I asked a priest at the cathedral there about Bishop Priscillian. I was told that no such person ever existed. But he did! (And so did Saint Teresa–also from Avila, and the second Patron Saint of Spain, after St. James–even her burial place is hidden in obscurity ... that too is perhaps another story?)

First and foremost, I want to thank Sylvia Baago. I have followed Sylvia like the little dog following the Fool in the Tarot pack since 1979. She is my best friend, my "sister", and my Muse. Without her encouragement and growing fascination in what has become "my" Priscillian, I doubt this page would have been written, let alone the rest. I also want to say a big thank you to David and Rebecca, my grown children, who have put up with their mother's flights of fancy for many, many years. As the book was developing, I bounced my ideas off many of my friends. The ones which spring most to mind are Lance and Helen Hurst who countered my arguments with other, sometimes better arguments, and good wine. I would also like to thank Andrea Nobis–my "Angel of the Camino", who suggested that I not write about the Camino in case I spoiled the Pilgrimage's immediate and personal effect. Well, I did it Andrea, but perhaps in a different way from what you imagined. I hope you like it. It'll bring back some precious memories, that is for certain.

If Lance and Helen listened to the preamble, it was Colin who endlessly listened to the comments from the computer as I was editing. I want to thank him for that ... and well, everything else. Lastly, I would like to offer my thanks to Goddess Gladys. She's not only good for parking spaces, but works her magic with life's unexpected events too.

Many others have helped me along this written Pilgrimage to Truth. And you know who you are. Thank you to all of you.

Tracy Saunders,

Marbella, Spain, 2007

PROLOGUE

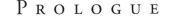

It was a Gallego welcome. That dark and secretive land of our ancestors. And in some ways, I suppose we should have expected it. The gentle easterly breezes that had brought us this far from Burdigala in Gaul had disappeared ever since we entered the seas off the Coast of Death. Now, buffeted by the fierce westerly winds, we clung to the boat, strong and seaworthy though it may have seemed to us when we chose it. Now, it was thrown helplessly from side to side, and we were forced to cling to anything that would keep us from being swept overboard. The sails were minimal now, and draped in near rags off the masthead. And I, Herenias, from land-locked Lugo, and never much of a sailor, would have gone below long ago, with my companion, Donatus, had not Galla insisted on remaining on deck with the casket which was bound securely enough.

She had not moved more than ten paces from it since we had left Treveris. I was in no state of mind to be indignant. Especially not now; it was too late. Wasn't I the one who had suggested that we transport the body overland? Followed the Old Road? Of course, it would have taken longer, but the danger was minimal, and the road paved by the Romans comfortable and safe. Once we entered Spain we would have had helpers a-plenty. And did it matter? They wouldn't have interfered by now—those Roman churchmen who understood so little, and denied even more—even had they wished: we had supporters enough, perhaps more than when he had been alive. If the Emperor wanted to dispose of the body in any other way, he had three years to do so before we came to claim it. Now, even he has gone—as have been so many who had claimed the purple before him. Decapitated they say; legal assassination say I. Still I am not sorry. He was no friend to us.

To my shame, I had been sick so many times, throwing my head over the side in self-pity and desperation that I almost felt that it no longer mattered. The Master was dead. Had been for too long. It was only my loyalty to the true religion, and my love for Galla that had sent me on what some had called a fool's errand. To bring the Bishop back to where he had started, and to where many awaited his return. Where his teachings had retained a foothold, albeit in secret now. That was what we had pledged, and now we were at the mercy of the gods he, and I, had denied. There were no signals on the headlands. Nothing but dark cliffs, ominous in the semi-light of the intermittent moon. No sign that we were even awaited. But still, despite the starless, treacherous night, and the bitter, frigid cold, I knew that I had made the right decision. My life was worth little in this world where I was not supposed to be, especially compared to those who had given theirs; but I was certain my soul would be saved if I could bring the Master back where he belonged. I knew it in my heart, though my stomach disagreed. And what was this discomfort, this fear, compared to what the Master, Euchrotia, who loved him and whom we had left behind, Latronianus, and the others had suffered for their beliefs?

All at once, there was bustle on the deck.
"What is it? What's happening?" I said to the captain as he brushed past me.
"We are at the river mouth," he said, and he hurried on. There was nothing in the darkness to distinguish between the depths we had been traveling and this moment, but I was no mariner, that much was certain. Galla, her face white with fear, looked up to mine and said: "It is over." This was her land, and the Master's. Mine too, though it had been long since it had welcomed me home.

Then all was activity. Donatus, green with the sickness, appeared at my side. "Our task is nearly over, my friend," he said, as he put his hands on my shoulder to steady himself.

Little by little, the nightmare abated, even if the winds did not. The port appeared like the answer to all our prayers, but it was too dark to see much. Just a few dim lanterns flickered to show us the way in. We were expected, but no-one knew exactly when.
We were in just as much danger in the estuary as we had ever been, and we knew it.

This town of Iria Flavia was the most remote of all Roman bastions, but their stamp was on it still, and strongly protected. Formerly the centre of the worship of Isis, the port was now a Christian community since the Emperor Constantine had made Christianity the state religion, for his own purposes. Iria Flavia may well have been remote, but it was crucial to the Romans—they used it to transport iron from the inner lands of Iberica, and they had built it as perhaps only they could. The port was well-situated and well-tended, though many thought of it as a backwater and a hardship post, and it was; but being at the river mouth it was treacherous to enter without a good pilot and even then, with bad weather such as this, a safe harbor was far from certain, as the sands were treacherous.

The harbor had welcomed ships for as long as the Romans had occupied this part of the world. **Finis Terrae**, they called it: the very end of the known world. Yet there were worlds beyond, occupied by the greatest power anyone had ever known. Marine traffic had plied this stretch since well before they had named it in their language. The Romans were followers, not conquerors only. Before they had become Christians—by their reckoning—they had borrowed their gods from who knows where, the Greeks mostly. And the Phoenicians—those great secret voyagers and explorers—had known it on their way to the Tin Islands, and the Carthaginians after them. They had shown the way long before Rome had made it their business. Still, it had taken the Romans to make it known to the world—their world, the only world now, to incorporate it into their vast stretch of Empire. In name, I was a Roman, but I was Iberian first.

The wind had dropped, not much but enough. The captain, a man from the coasts of Africa who had sailed these waters many a time, said to those assembled:

"We are at our destination, yet we will wait for the sun to rise. In the morning, you may all feel your feet on land again. But that time is not yet come. Go below and get some rest while you can. We will need everyone's hands once the morning comes."

We were glad to hear his words: "The journey is over," we thought. "Soon we will be on our own land once again." And all went below.

Except for one: Galla, drawing a breath of relief, still did not move. "I will sleep here," she said. And she put her head against the marble casket, as I had seen her do, so many nights before.

With sunrise, they awoke us. What awaited us was as familiar as anything any of us who had traveled the Roman world had ever seen. Iria Flavia glistened in the clear light of dawn. It was nowhere near as grand as most of the Roman cities, but it was a *welcome sight. Yet we were anchored a ways off from the docks and it was obvious to all—sailors as well as landlovers—that we were too far from the land to make transfer easy. And our cargo was a marble sarcophagus, heavy and wieldy, and containing what had once been a man, powerful and precious beyond measure.*

"There is nothing for it," the captain said, "we are stranded here on a sandbar newly thrown up by the storm. We will have to effect transfer in another way. Last night while you were sleeping, I sent a message into the town. When the tide is at its lowest, they will send an ox-cart to meet us. I will need all hands to transfer the cargo to the cart. From there, they will take it ashore, if the gods are with us." And with his words, I knew that Rome, those so-called Christians with their hierarchy of priests and bishops, they had not been as victorious as they liked to believe.

I looked at the water surrounding the boat, not deep seas now, but fixed firmly in the mud which surrounded us. I doubted the captain's conviction, but who was I to know? Now, more than ever, after all that we had been through, I knew that the true God was with us, in this, the final stage of our journey.

It was clear from the outset that the beasts, stupid though they may have been, had other ideas about entering the sludge and swirling waters at their feet as the tides retreated. But the driver's whips were persuasive and they did as they were bid. We set about moving the heavy marble casket—it seemed that we were woefully few. Galla would have helped us, but she had been pushed—roughly, since she was but a feeble woman—aside: this was men's work. Women, to these crude sailors, were for bedding, birthing, and mourning: nothing more. We managed to shift the sarcophagus to the side, and were ready to lower it upon the ox-cart, when the ropes began to stretch:

"Careful!" shouted someone. "We need to balance it! It's tipping beyond our control!" And it was true. Our Master was in danger of falling into the mud. We were losing our grip, and it seemed that his only resting place was to become the bottom of the river estuary, after we had come so far.

Suddenly, just as we had almost exhausted our strength, we were distracted by a loud splash from the river bank. A grey horse—almost silver in the early morning mist—and his rider leaped from the side into the waters, deeper and more dangerous there. It was long tense moments before he appeared on deck, though in reality no more than seconds. In that time between, we thought that we would lose not only our Master, but the rider and his horse too. But then he was with us.

He was massive. He looked to me like a gladiator of old, before the Christian empire forbade such things, and rightly. He took the ropes on his broadest of shoulders, and almost single-handedly slipped the casket—effortlessly—over the side onto the waiting cart. Then, before we could thank him, he jumped over the side, mounted his horse, shining golden now in the slanted dawn, and wading through the sands and tide, he was gone.

The sides of his horse were covered with weeds, and veiras: *cockle shells. It seemed to us, almost broken as we were, that a miracle had saved us.*

As the ox-cart reached the shore, we also jumped into the mud. I would have helped Galla, but she said: "I have come this far." On the dock, we gathered together, we three:
Donatus, Galla, and me.

Priscillian, Bishop of Avila, had come home.

PART I

▼

PILGRIMAGE TO HERESY

*   *   *   *

Our birth is but a sleeping and a forgetting;
the soul that rises with us, our life's star, hath had elsewhere its setting,
and cometh from afar; not in entire forgetfulness,
and not in utter nakedness,
but trailing clouds of glory do we come from God,
who is our home.

*   *   *   *

William Wordsworth (1770–1850)

"When the Holy Spirit breathes, the summer comes"

*   *   *   *

Nag Hammadi Gospels

CHAPTER 1

▼

ARAGON, 2000 CE

"What do you mean: 'Not there'?" Miranda wasn't sure she wanted to know the answer. In fact, she thought that by now she had heard quite enough.

"I suppose you believe in crop circles too?"

She stopped walking as if she had walked into a wall, as well it seemed she had. She stared at him with what Gothic novel writers might have called "barely-concealed loathing". She was in no mood to be patronized by anyone, especially by this man whom she had met only that morning, and he had talked her head off for the last three hours. Her feet were blistered and her poncho woefully inadequate to keep the incessant rain off her backpack. It wasn't that she didn't find what he had to say interesting. Far from it. He was clearly knowledgeable about a lot of things, most of which had never occurred to Miranda to question. It was just that she drifted in and out. She could just as easily have been walking alone. The route wasn't hard to follow—the yellow arrows were there for that. She had, in fact, resigned herself to solitude while preparing for this Pilgrimage: training as best anyone could in downtown Toronto for an 800 kilometer walk without heading up Yonge Street never to be heard of again. She had come a long way to do this, she had a long way to go, and she still didn't know why she was here. Now, sodden and more than a bit dispirited. The least he could do was keep quiet for a bit and let her feel sorry for herself in peace. Kieran walked a few paces beyond her, and then stopped and looked back, realizing he was walking alone.

Looking at the indignation on her face, he at least had the good grace to realize he had gone too far, in more ways than one.

"Look. I'm sorry. It was only meant as a bit of a joke. It's a favorite topic of mine: the history of the *Camino*. I guess I can go on a bit."

His apology was genuine. He had been enjoying her company and had taken her interjections as some sort of interest.

Miranda still looked as if she would have liked him to have elected to throw himself off the mountain path they trod and left her to have figured it all out for herself.

The rain hadn't let up since they left the small *Pension* in Canfranc. It was not raining hard enough to take shelter, not that there was any. Just enough to get down necks, and sleeves. Just enough to soak tomorrow's underwear, buried in the depths of her backpack—and God knows there was little enough of that. Just enough to take any pleasure of walking. Enough to make you forget that there was a reason why you came here, no matter how insignificant and ill-placed it may seem now. Enough to necessitate placing your feet more carefully, avoiding looking at the scenery—which must have been stunning: but how to know? It was raining just enough for self-doubt, which came to Miranda easily enough. Just enough to make leather permeable, preparation insufficient, and cheap ponchos—purchased in a last minute budget-conscious fit at the bargain shop—of no use at all. Dangerously, just enough to feel like tears of self-pity, though even now, she knew it was much too early to wish she hadn't come.

"But I meant what I said." Kieran still showed no sign of backing down regardless of Miranda's expression of contempt as they resumed their walking. "There is no evidence whatsoever to connect St. James to the Camino, or to Compostela. The sad part is that although it is common knowledge in Galicia, and the Catholic Church is more than well aware of it, no-one wants to admit that the bones in Compostela are those of someone else. It's more than pride or dogma: it's big business, and in all honesty, it always has been. And it's not just that these are the remains of just anyone else. No, that's the irony. It's that the body—or what's left of it—in that beautiful silver casket, is that of a heretic. That's what the Romans called him, and that is what he is considered by the church in Rome, even today, over 1600 years later. He was the first Christian to be martyred by the Christians themselves."

Miranda paused to survey her sturdy and classical but useless—on this sopping path—leather hiking boots and compared them to Kieran's impermeable and no doubt expensive Gore-tex ones. She had even considered hiking in sandals—it had seemed romantic and traditional. *"With scrip and sandal-shoon."* Now, she wouldn't have admitted that to anyone. He seemed to have this whole pilgrim-business pre-ordained, rationalized, and well-prepared. She, on the other hand, wasn't sure she wanted her mythology altered. She hadn't really been listening after the first hour anyway. It wasn't whether she cared whose bones were in the casket (it seemed more and more morbid, the more she thought about it, anyway); it was just that, having decided upon this Pilgrimage of sorts;—she liked to think of it capitalized otherwise it was hard to justify, even to herself— she wasn't yet prepared to be told that all the information in her guidebook and on the official web pages had been nothing more than a glossy deception. All of that history, painted with such certainty, in such glowing Mediaeval colors— beautiful, intricate, meaningful, like the ancient glass in a cathedral—now she was being told by a stranger that this was nothing more than a drawn out and economically expedient falsehood which had successfully drawn pilgrims—religious tourists really—to Galicia for the better part of 1200 years.

"Look, what makes you say this?" she said. She wasn't ready to be defeated within three hours of walking this morning. She had walked almost 20 kilometers the day before, alone, too. She had the blisters to show for it. "It's not called the way of Saint James for nothing," she continued. "People have been walking this route across the Pyrenees, as we are doing now, for hundreds of years. And not just this one. This is just one of the back roads from France. In the Middle Ages there were pilgrims from all walks of life: kings, knights, poets, even criminals seeking to avoid prison. They came from all over. You can't tell me all of them were wrong."

"It depends on what you mean by wrong," Kieran said, starting the pace again. "Pilgrims set out along this route from many points in France, as you said, and not only France … They called the route which crossed from Saint Jean-Pied-de-Port,"*El Camino Frances*". They came from the north by sea and landed in Galicia; they came from Portugal. Along with Jerusalem and Rome, Santiago de Compostela was a major holy site: the burial place of Saint James, who came to Spain shortly after the death of Jesus and converted the heathen souls. They all came to ask for absolution at the gravesite of St. James who was buried there, just as many do today—even though they may deny any religious connection; people hope to somehow find themselves in Saint James. The trouble is, it isn't true."

"Oh come on …" Miranda said. She just couldn't be bothered to listen anymore. This was too bizarre. A strap on her shoulder was too tight, but Miranda didn't want to go through the trouble of putting it down. It was not improving her mood any.

Unaware that he was in danger of losing his audience, Kieran continued:

"Seriously, if St. James came to the north west of Spain at all, he had very little success. If he converted a dozen, then that's the best he did. And there are reports that he converted two, or nine depending upon who you read; but there was no mass preaching upon the hilltops, I can tell you. So he left Spain and returned to Jerusalem, where he met with an even worse welcome: they decapitated him and left his body to be picked clean by the ravens. Eventually, when it was safe to do so, his followers took his body—what was left of it anyway, and you know, of course that there are supposedly bits scattered throughout France, supposedly— and buried it there, in the land of his birth, or some say in the north of Egypt. There's no evidence that he was brought back to Spain. And when you think about it: why would his followers have brought him back to a place where he not only had little success but where there was not even a welcome place for his burial?"

Miranda, looked at him, with wider, expectant eyes, as, in all honesty, he had hoped, having come this far. Neither of them was comfortable with this situation, but the story at this point was too important to drop now. She said nothing.

"O.K. That bit I'll explain that part later;" Kieran continued," but, you're asking, why did pilgrims come here from the 9th century onwards, at first in a trickle and later in a flood of souls? Why in the Middle Ages? Why after the supposed "reap-pearance" of Santiago at the Battle of Clavijo?"

"*Santiago Matamoros*," Miranda butted in,"I've never liked him."

"Not surprising … So why did they come …? Because they were told to, that's why. For some, for the wealthy, it was the fashion: the cult of relics was springing up all over. For some, they were in such terror for their souls, they were too afraid not to. For others it was an excellent opportunity to cash in—sure it might have meant their souls but a quick return is a good bet against the Devil. And as more and more pilgrims followed, more and more merchants came to fleece them, or accommodate them, in one way or the other. Did you know that in one town, they had to pay a toll or carry a rock to Compostela to add to the masonry for the building of the cathedral? They came in their thousands during the Middle-Ages. There were advantages to it: economical as well as saving souls. But what no-one wants to talk about is that the road from Gaul to Galicia was a site of pilgrimage long before Pelayo claimed to have seen lights and heard heavenly voices.

"I read about Pelayo," said Miranda. "Didn't he hear singing and see a star over a wood? He reported it to the bishop—I can't remember his name—who ordered the place to be dug up? They found bones there, and he said it was a holy place: the grave of Saint James. I think I read there were three bodies, and that the other two were Saint James' companions who brought his body from Jaffa to Spain. They were buried there later because it was such a holy site. Isn't that where the first church was built, and later it became the cathedral of Compostela? They called it The Field of the Star, just because of that."

Kieran stopped to take his water bottle from his backpack, which involved a good deal of unstrapping, putting down, and pulling out; pilgrim rituals were complicated sometimes. He offered a swig to Miranda. The rain had eased to just a trickle now, mostly off the trees, and there was clear sky on the southern horizon. The clouds were dispersing and the panorama of the Pyrenees was unpacking itself for their pleasure. A blackbird perched itself upon a nearby poplar and began to preen its feathers, attempting to dry off just as the pilgrims were. Miranda wiped out her hood, which was wet both inside and out, and made some efforts towards drying off both her backpack and her dark blonde hair— "dirty blonde" Jonathan called it, which always sounded to her like an expression of envy invented by mousy brunettes. Either way, the intention to dry out was less successful than the blackbird's who could, at least, ruffle his feathers.

Kieran seemed to watching her with amusement. Finally he said.

"The Bishop's name was Theodemirus, and the date was somewhere between 820 A.D. and 830. Although some documents give a more precise date, they are not sure exactly when. Most of Spain was overrun by the Moors—except Asturias, and that's another, related story. They were claiming almost all of the Peninsula as their own, and their strength was that they claimed the True God was on their side, with Mohammed as their prophet. Discovering the bones of one of the most important disciples of Jesus was—if you'll excuse the expression—a godsend to Spain, or rather what was left of it, which at that point, wasn't much. The bishop immediately claimed, upon very flimsy evidence—mostly based on miracles (which I'll spare you), and the Spanish were pretty short of these at the time—anyway, it was said—most expediently—that these bones were indeed those of Saint James whose remains had been said to have been brought by his own disciples in a stone boat, blown on the winds of God, without benefit of sails nor rudder. Their reception by one Queen Lupa was pretty frosty and she sent a cart pulled by wild bulls to pull the body to pieces. Instead, at the sign of the cross, the bulls became as docile as sheep and quietly conveyed the body right into the middle of Lupa's palace. The queen was so impressed by this little bit of miracle work that she consigned her men to building an impressive mausoleum, and the rest, as they say …"

"… is history. Really Kieran, how can you sound so glib? It sounds almost, I don't know, sacrilegious …"

"Only if the legend is true, and honestly, do you really believe it?"

They were walking again by now and Miranda's pack much more comfortable now that the offending poncho had been removed and the strap tightened. She actually was beginning to enjoy walking, listening to Kieran, and inhaling the peaty smell of the mountainside. It lifted her spirits. Kieran paused in his narrative to give her chance to reflect. "And what exactly do I believe?" she thought and stopped to push a stray strand of hair out of her eyes. I am a philosophy professor with no particularly religious beliefs except a fascination for the Eastern religions and the occasional attendance at the Unitarian Church uptown. I am a sort of hybrid who doesn't really care if God exists, but spends a lot of time with people who are trying to prove, or disprove his existence. And I am on a Pilgrimage.

Finally, she spoke: "I don't know. I guess I believed what I read. I didn't really question it. I doubt if many who walk this path do. At some level I guess that if you are going on a Pilgrimage culminating in visiting the grave site of Saint James,—which technically is the whole point—it is a bit disconcerting, to say the least, to hear that neither is he there, but that he probably never was. But, when it comes down to it, maybe, to modern day pilgrims, it makes no difference. It doesn't really matter who is buried there. Most pilgrims today walk to find out who they are. To what extent they can stretch themselves. They walk to form new friendships, to see new perspectives based on a simpler lifestyle with fewer necessities. Maybe I just didn't want to know anything else."

"I know what you mean, but not being interested in the truth is quite different from blinding yourself to it. Once when I mentioned to a friend something about Jesus' brothers he said that Jesus couldn't have had any brothers because Mary remained a virgin. When I said that it was written in the New Testament he said, 'Even if it is, I don't want to hear about it.'" Kieran left the rest of his views about his friend unsaid.

"So St. James became 'Santiago Matamoros' when Spain needed a hero to rival Mohammed? To inspire the soldiers to fight for Christian Spain? I suppose that makes sense." Miranda had temporarily forgotten her indignation, and her blisters, as they skirted the railway track running from Canfranc to Jaca on what had once been the border between Spain and France.

"Not a very Christian symbol, is he? There are many paintings where he is mounted, a sword in his hand as he reaches down to cut off the heads of the Moors. You'd think since his own head was cut off, he would have had more mercy."

Miranda stopped again. He was being facetious, and she felt like she was being taken in.
"Is this a joke to you? Because I don't find it very funny. Maybe you think I am näive. Maybe because you are a priest …"

"That isn't what I said …" interjected Kieran.

"Whatever, I don't care … Maybe you think I don't know anything, and maybe in some ways you are right. But I know that something told me to be here. You know what? Until the day before yesterday, I had never walked more than five miles in my life. I've never worn a backpack, and it's obvious I'm no weekend hiker ..."

"How's the blister ...?"

"It's obvious, I'm no weekend hiker," she continued, ignoring him and his Gore-tex,"but something—I don't know ... "—there were no words for it and it was infuriating in the present context—" ... something called me here."

Miranda stopped in utter frustration. Enough was enough. He was looking at her. What for? Just keep walking. I don't have to justify myself to you. She had had this conversation before she left Toronto. Why would anyone leave a good teaching job with the university to go gallivanting on some—for God's sake—"Religious Quest" in Spain? What an anachronistic idea. O.K. so she had some savings, and she didn't have to sign on, and summer students paid well, but more to the point, she didn't have tenure, and probably never would. Her attempts to publish had not had sufficient exposure in the journals that counted. This whole "Camino-business" made her friends and colleagues uncomfortable. And it wouldn't reflect well upon her professional career, that much was certain. There was little room for orthodox or even unorthodox religion within the walls of her department: rationalism and deconstruction was the current dominant world view, although a little Eastern emphasis was accepted as long as it wasn't taken too seriously. She had given up trying to explain to her colleagues why she needed this time for herself. How explain the inside, in terms of the outside? She knew it could not be done. Not in terms of the logic which dictated—which she had been taught in her undergraduate classes—that she had to play the game to give an answer. Because only the game—having the right words at the right time—dictated the terms of play. Plato said to know was to be able to give a reasoned account, but really, there was nothing reasoned about what she planned to do for the next six weeks, just a feeling that it was somehow "right"; almost a feeling that she had been called.

"But why you?" asked Jonathan, her live-in boyfriend of a bit too long." You don't even go to church on Christmas Day, and you couldn't navigate from King Street to Dundas."

There was no point in trying to explain, Miranda knew it. She had outgrown Jonathan and hadn't the guts to admit that having him around wasn't even worth half the rent any more. Leaving was easier, and there was something snail-like about having everything you needed down to eight kilos and carefully stuffed away in your backpack.

Simple. Pilgrimage: the 51st way to leave your lover!

Very few clouds remained, and the warmth on the hillsides had caused steam to rise from the trees. It wasn't hot by any means, but there was no wind as there had been yesterday, and the path had begun to descend towards a stone bridge they could see in the valley below. They had reached a yellow arrow. These arrows, painted at intervals, she had read, would keep her pointed in the right direction

"O.K." said Kieran, seeing it as a natural halt. "Lunch is for sharing. What have you got?"

Miranda happily spread her poncho on the ground, drier side up, and dumped the few contents of her backpack on it. She proceeded to remove an offending boot.

"Don't!" said Kieran,"You'll put me off, and you'll never get your boots on again either. Here: apple or banana?"

Both looked a bit sad, but Miranda took the banana and offered some sticky Camembert in exchange, and a couple of rice cakes.

"What do you know about the Camino?" said Kieran after a while, licking his fingers.

"You know what? I don't feel now as though I want to display what I know, mostly because it feels woefully inadequate. You are the expert, why don't you tell me?"

Kieran had the decency to look contrite.

"I suppose I have come across that way."

"Indeed you have."

Kieran's eyes focused on a hovering kestrel before he spoke. The bird had spotted prey and was waiting, you might even say, deciding, what to do next. Kieran seemed to be gauging his response by the raptor's next move. Miranda got the distinct feeling he would have preferred to have kept his thoughts to himself, for the first time since they had set out that morning. He suddenly looked distressed, a lot more vulnerable than she would have expected given his former verbosity. He seemed to be wrestling with what to say, and when he did speak, it all came out in a defensive rush:

"Stop, no, stop for a minute, and ask yourself just one thing before I say any more." The pause was too long. Was he hedging his bets, like the bird above while he spoke? "You say that I can't understand why you are here, what called you; but I am here too, no? Doesn't that tell you something? Perhaps, I don't know any more than you do. What if I am following a mystery, a hunch, just as much as you are?"

Miranda stopped—stopped nibbling at her pilgrim lunch, stopped trying to block out both him and the pain from her heel, stopped asking herself why she had ever thought of walking over 800 kilometers when the first twenty-five had just about done her in. She looked at the mountains around them. She took in his face: how old? Mid-late-thirties, maybe? Enough lines to make his face inter-esting. Some grey in his otherwise nondescript reddish-brown hair, not much; blue eyes, neither vivid nor vapid: just blue. He was medium everything: weight, height, looks. Not unattractive, just a little bit ordinary. But suddenly she wanted to listen; maybe being with him was part of the experience. She knew that most of the time she was anti-social: too solitary, too. One of the promises she had made to herself was that she would be more tolerant, less judgmental. Open to the lives and experiences of others. And Kieran's way of speaking said something more than just someone knowledgeable: this man knew secrets. Sure, perhaps it was just her imagination. But in places such as this—what is imagination for? When he spoke, the animation in his voice was compelling, and now she wanted him to tell her more.

She took a big bite of her rice cake and said: "I'm sorry. Go on."

CHAPTER 2

▼

"Most people believe that the Pilgrimage to Galicia began in the 9th century," Kieran began to warm to his theme once he had assured himself his audience wasn't just being polite. "With the discovery of the bodies, Pelayo contacted the Bishop, and the Bishop consulted with the Asturian king ..."

"Why the Asturian king?"

"Because at that time, politically, Galicia was part of the kingdom of Asturias ... anyway, the king, Alfonso the Second, seemed to think that this was the best news he had heard for a while. He traveled from Oviedo to see for himself. Pronouncing the body to be undoubtedly St. James', he gave permission for the construction of a Sanctuary: it covered three hectares and was comprised of two buildings: the episcopal ..."

"Meaning?"

"Having to do with the Bishop; and the monastic—where the monks were to live ..."

"I get that bit."

"Anyway, they were both enclosed by a defensive stockade. The episcopal buildings comprised an early, very simple church of St. James, and a cemetery. The cemetery was nothing new and had in fact been in use since Roman times, possibly since even before—but that has always been downplayed. The important thing to remember is that the body they discovered was not alone. He, or she, was buried with two others in close proximity, but there were many other remains situated close by."

"Followers of St. James?"

"Unlikely: you have to remember that before the discovery, although there was some mention of St. James in Spain, there was nothing to tie him to Galicia in particular, and certainly no reason for him to be buried there. He made almost no converts, and what's more, he was pretty unwelcome. Let me go back a little. James was said to have been decapitated in Jerusalem in 44 A.D ..."

"Back from the 9th century? That's hardly a little, Kieran, don't confuse me."

"Are you going to keep interrupting? Because if so you can get your official version from your Official Pilgrim Guide ..."

"Sorry. You don't have to get huffy."

"Hmm. Where was I?"

"44 A.D."

"Right. Supposedly, as I have already said, his disciples recovered his body, and brought it from Jaffa to Spain with a fair amount of miraculous intervention. On disembarking, the disciples presented themselves to Queen Lupa—whom some folk say was the grand-daughter of Julius Caesar—she referred them to the Roman legate, but he ordered them to be imprisoned. Shortly after, they were freed by an angel ..."

"Oh, the old 'set free by an angel' excuse. That one I have heard before." Miranda was brushing rice cake bits off her shoes.

"You know ... you might not be a lost cause after all."

"Thanks. Keep going; I'm getting interested."

"Hallelujah! Anyway, Queen Lupa tried to trick them again, this time by sending them wild bulls, supposedly to transport the apostle's body. I've told you that bit already … Her ploy didn't work, she converted to Christianity, and she gave them the place now called 'Libredon', at the foot of a small iron age hill fort (called a Castro—there are lots in Galicia) for his burial.

"Now, whether he had converts at the time or not, logically, as the number of Christians grew over the years, and especially when the Emperor Constantine proclaimed Christianity the official religion …"

"When was that?"

"337 AD."

"No more throwing Christians to the lions then?"

"No, although it wasn't until 380 that all other forms of religion were actually outlawed."

"Like worshipping Apollo and Diana and Minerva and stuff?"

"Yes, although they did a nice sleight of hand to persuade the people that their gods were just forms of the Christian story, and the dates were moved accordingly—like Saturnalia and Christmas, and so on. And, of course, many people, especially in rural and remote areas, still believed in the old gods. The Romans had tried to stamp out Druidism for many, many years, but they weren't successful. It's much easier to keep the Old Ways alive at night and in the woods, and Galicia was known for its Celtic vestiges. That will become more and more important … But I'm getting ahead of my story." He stopped for a minute and tried to backtrack.

"As the number of Christians grew …?" Miranda showed that she had been listening intently.

"Right. Where were all the believers flocking to the grave of one of Jesus' most important disciples? With the growth of Christianity, and especially its official sanction, you would expect Iria Flavia to have become a known site of Christian pilgrimage, and in fact it was. But why wasn't this place mentioned much earlier as the resting place of St. James? Even during Roman and Gothic times. After the Romans withdrew, Asturias and Galicia were overrun by the Sueves, a Gothic people. They were Christians. In fact they followed a particular type of Christianity called Arianism, which involved much more freedom of choice than the Roman church allowed, and which was branded as heresy very early on. But the known burial place of St. James would have been equally as important to them as it subsequently became in the 9th century. Yet they make no mention if it. None at all. Not one dicky bird was said about it before the "discovery!" Kieran paused in triumph. He knew his argument carried weight.

"Wasn't it?"

"No. There were pilgrims, lots of them, but it wasn't to St. James they were flocking. You see, you have to view this discovery within the religious and political context of the times … This has got to be boring you?"

"Actually, no. I am enjoying it. But I do think we should be getting on. We still have a couple of hours to go before Jaca."

Both stood up at the same time. Miranda noticed that it took a feat of anti-gravity to swing Kieran's pack up onto his shoulders.

"What have you got in there? A church bible?"

"Better," said Kieran, mysteriously.

Although there were muddy stretches along the pathway, the sky had cleared brilliantly. It was even warm and Miranda draped her poncho over the top of her pack. Walking comfortably was still an impossibility, and although she couldn't hear it, she imagined her feet squelching inside her boots. But she was beginning to enjoy the walk. More than that, she felt a delightful freshness, a freedom. Absolutely no-one knew exactly where she was. She didn't have to call anyone to say what she was doing, or when she expected to be home, or whom she was with. It was delicious.

At this point, a silver Maserati swept by them. They were close to the road here and the expensive car brought them back to the twentieth century. To the driver they didn't exist, and both realized that had they hitched a ride, they could have been in Santiago for supper that day. Kieran couldn't help but be impressed.

"Cool," said Kieran.

"So?" said Miranda.

Kieran picked up exactly where he had left off. "The idea that St. James had preached in Spain had been in the wind since the 6th century, and even more in the 8th century when it was very much in the interest of the Kingdom of Asturias to demonstrate powerful associations. In 718, a vision of the Virgin Mary appeared to soldiers of King Pelayo ..."

"Pelayo? Not the same one who discovered St. James grave?"

"No, interesting coincidence. Asturias was the only province never to be fully conquered by the Moors. And this was attributed to the timely appearance of the Virgin. A tiny Visigothic army was overwhelmingly victorious against much greater forces. There is an impressive shrine there in a cleft in the mountains in Asturias, if you have time. No, this was about 100 years before *'Santiago Matamoros'* but you can imagine what went through their heads: you never know, if it works once ..."

"A worthwhile gambit. There's nothing like having God on your side. Especially when the odds are against you."

"As I said earlier, after the discovery, a small but potentially powerful stockade of buildings was constructed in Galicia. Spiritually isolated from the outside world. But by the end of the 9th century, the bishop thought that the complex should be more accessible and the building of a new church was ordained. Gradually a small town began to grow up around it. It was called *Villa Santa Jacobi*. Defenses were added due to the threat of Norman attack. They were successful, but, in 997, the town was sacked by the Moorish ruler Almanzor and the bell was carried off to Cordoba where it remained for many years."

"So the Moors got their own back on St. James."

"Precisely."

Since they had left Canfranc after breakfast, they hadn't seen a single soul except the goatherd at the stone bridge who had murmured something which sounded vaguely like "*Un abrazo por el apostol*". A hug for the saint? On occasion, they thought they had caught sight of backpacks disappearing around curves in the distance ahead, but for the most part, they had enjoyed their walk alone.

Now, for the first time, another walker approached. He had dark skin—weathered and lived in. He wore a short black beard, and sunglasses. His open jacket and shorts were military khaki, and his pack looked like it could easily have contained the kitchen sink. He had a most determined look on his face, the sort you see on long-distance runners and cyclists nearing the tops of mountains, and he was moving at a fast clip: twice the pace of either Miranda or Kieran. Although neither could have identified it at the time, both later felt like he was bearing down on them like the TGV train, and instinctively they stood on opposite sides of the narrow mountain path to let him through.

"*Buen dia,*" he said, as he swept past, looking neither left nor right.

"Phew!" said Miranda, after he had trundled on. "If that's the way the professionals do it, we'd better get a move on!"

"Water first," said Kieran. "I feel like I've just been sandblasted!"

They walked in silence for several minutes after that. Since they had set out, the landscape had been alpine: pinnacles of rock and the occasional goat to justify them, pine trees, singly for the most part, and growing at vertiginous heights where nothing ought to have been able to establish a foothold; holly bushes, groves of spruce. The river Aragon always to the left—as at first, or later, after they had crossed the Villanúa Bridge, to the right as they also began to follow the main road. Villages at first seemingly deserted; derelict churches with crumbling Romanesque *porticos,* and doors which looked like no-one had opened them for 200 years.

Now they seemed to be descending, at last. Copses of birch and beech began to replace the coniferous trees. They passed a small village topped by castle, and then only a steep climb down and a steeper climb up separated them from Jaca and a hot shower, please God.

"We're not quite there yet," said Miranda. "The last few kilometers are always the longest. Finish the story ... please," she added, modestly.

"O.K. But I may get sidetracked, thinking about putting my feet up and having a beer!"

"Now that's something to make us speed up a bit!" Miranda laughed.

"I'll skip a few centuries. With the reconstruction of the city of Santiago de Compostela, a new cathedral was commissioned. And an amazing piece of work it was too."

"Is that the Cathedral you see today?"

"Well, yes, and no. The outside, that famous front, is Baroque, belonging to a much later period: the 17th and 18th centuries. But the inside is one of the most beautiful examples of Romanesque architecture you will ever see anywhere."

"So, you've been there before then?"

"Oh yes, when I was attending the Seminary. A group of us went. I'll never forget feeling intoxicated by the warmth of the stones inside such a vast edifice. The smell of thousand year old incense. The sense of personal security, the light of votive candles and the hope going along with each and every one; and I think I know every face on the Portico de Gloria; I sat on the floor inside the doorway and looked at them for so long ... very early one morning, before the tourists arrived. I was the only one there. I felt like it belonged to me. Kieran smiled almost beatifically at the memory.

"This time, I will feel even more at home. Now that I know ..."

"Stop teasing me!" Miranda said in frustration; he kept dropping hints as though the best was yet to come.

Kieran looked surprised," But I'm getting to that. You can't condense two thousand years of conspiracy down to an hour and 20 minutes."

"Conspiracy?"

"Mmm. So be quiet and listen."

"By the thirteenth century, the pilgrims were coming along the paths to Compostela in a flood of souls. This was when the traditional pilgrim's garb—wide brimmed hat, cloak, gourd for water, wooden staff, leather satchel—these were the standard uniform. Unlike today, the pilgrim received his scallop shell when he arrived at the most western point in Galicia. At the cape of Finisterre. It was proof to everyone that you had completed your pilgrimage. The first Pilgrim's Guidebooks were written about that time: one called the *Codex Calixtinus* is today kept in the Museum at the Cathedral. Relics—even an elbow joint—were big business, and not surprisingly, Compostela became a thriving commercial centre. From the 15th century onwards, pilgrims arriving at the sanctuary were presented with a *Compostelana*—a certificate on the completion of their journey. It helped to ensure them hospitality on their way home, and remember, many of them had come 1000 kilometers and some double that. Those who came in a Holy Year ..."

"Sorry, what makes a year especially holy?"

"If the Saint's day falls on a Sunday—every 4th and 11th year—it's called a Holy Year. The main door is open all year and pilgrims receive a special indulgence, valid for all their sins.

"By the 16th century, the flood had slowed to a trickle. Spain was threatened by its enemy, England, and a great prize would have been the abduction of the country's Patron Saint. Such a threat to national pride was unthinkable, and so the remains were hidden behind the altar stone. Then one day in 1879, a workman making repairs discovered the body. In 1884, Pope Leo XIII was consulted as to its authenticity; a sliver of a skull which was also claimed to be that of St. James was procured from another church in Italy and lo! It matched a missing piece. The Pope said that the discovery was very useful "in these days when the church is particularly tormented," and with remarkable archaeological insight, he proclaimed to all the world that this was indeed the lost St. James."

"Hang on. Hang on. Back up a minute. They hid the body whereupon it disappeared from anyone's memory, and they didn't find it for over 200 years?"

"Yeah. That's about the story. And pretty fuzzy it is too. You find a lot of so-called History's get awfully quiet and obscure about this time."

"So the body is identified, and the pilgrims start flocking to Santiago once again?" asked Miranda.

"Actually no. The Way of Saint James, as a route of pilgrimage as such, was virtually unused, lost, overgrown for most of our own century. As recently as the mid-1970's, the number of pilgrims along the way was minimal. And even today, there are a number of routes—older ones and with better claim to antiquity than the Camino Frances …"

"Such as?"

"Well "The *Camino Primitivo*": The Original Way for one. It went through Oviedo and Lugo, a walled city in central Galicia much older than Compostela, and it's rarely traveled today. Just as old is the "*Ruta de la Plata*": The Silver Route. It went from Italica—an important Roman city just above present-day Seville—directly north through Merida, which in Roman times was called *Emerita Augusta*, for your info, to Astorga. All are important names from the story of Priscillian …"

"We go through Astorga, don't we?" Miranda interrupted. "That's where Gaudi's Bishop's Palace is. I'm looking forward to seeing that."

"Yes, but I was talking about an older bishop."

"So the Camino we are walking today is a recent discovery?"

"Well, I suppose you could say that. Re-discovery is a better word."

As they entered the city of Jaca, at first it seemed like the outskirts of any small city in Spain. On top of a hill and easily defensible, it was compact. Parts of the old Roman walls were still standing in places. The mountains surrounded the city in virtually every direction, giving onto flatter areas abruptly as the river made its way first south and then west. But the modern and rather dreary blocks of breeze-block apartments gradually gave way to dark, stone buildings, much older, some mildewed, some closed up and rotting: cats and newspapers visible through broken boarding. Scaffolding buttressing vacant lots, replacing dwellings which had fallen down, overnight, maybe 50 years ago; maybe last week. Narrow alleys running off to turn abruptly at right angles. It was 3:00—the sacred hour of the *Siesta*—and the streets were all but deserted. Kieran and Miranda, between them, had vague directions to the pilgrim's hospice where they hoped to stay the night. But after more than seven hours walking, disorientation had set in with exhaustion. By a curious and military-looking walled complex, which seemed to be in a sort of star shape, they consulted Miranda's map. It wasn't a lot of help since it had no compass. And they knew at the very least that they were in the northern outskirts. At the approach of a taxi, Miranda, without thinking about what she was going to say, flagged the driver down:

"We're pilgrims," she said, perhaps a bit too loudly, indicating their packs and stating the obvious. "We need to find the *Pension*," and she pointed to her guide book.

The driver gave her several clipped words in Spanish and pointed both to left and right.

"No," Kieran interrupted," that was last night. This is the official place we are looking for this time: the pilgrim Refuge. Here, let me try." And with that, he grabbed Miranda's book, open to the map, thrust it inside the open window and asked the driver in almost too-perfect and accented Spanish:

"Por favor, Señor. ¿Se puede usted mostrar donde está el refugio de peregrinos?"

With this, the driver turned the map to a different angle, gestured along the street they were on, twice; gestured again to the right and then the left and circled an index finger in the middle of the map. And off he went.

"Easy," said Kieran with a self-satisfied grin. "Follow me."

And Miranda did.

CHAPTER 3

▼

There is an odd feeling of both exhilaration and disappointment when one enters a new *refugio* on the Camino. Miranda noticed it straightaway in Jaca, and was to experience it often as she walked the next few weeks.

"It is as if one part of my life has been left behind forever," she said to Kieran, just after they had produced their *Credentiales* and signed in, paying the small fee for accommodation levied for genuine pilgrims who carried the pilgrim's passport. Miranda noticed there were only six other names: Margaret and Elizabeth Hooper from Salisbury, Viveke Dykstra from Rotterdam, Dominic Guzman from Valencia, Maria Carmen Perez Sanchez from Madrid, and Felix Stephenson from Bristol.

"What do you mean?" said Kieran, adding his indecipherable signature, and noting Dublin as his place of residence.

"Well, you know, like, I'll never do that again—for the first time, I mean."

Yes, and …? So? Kieran had to give that a bit of thought.

"I think I know what you mean," he said after a while. They were looking around for the dormitories by now, longing to put their packs down.

"It's like the Buddhist "moment": for some that's all there is; for others even that doesn't exist because it passes too quickly into the next one. I've heard lots of people say that the Camino is a microcosm of life. But we don't, in normal life I mean, very often say: 'I'll never experience that—whatever—thought, event, time, meeting—again'. We are far more likely to miss it completely, thinking about our next move, or what just might be around the corner. We hardly ever really listen to what other people are saying before we give our answer. All the time they are talking, we are thinking about what we are going to say in response—and so we miss their whole point."

"And we miss the 'right now'," added Miranda. "That's it exactly."

"You know Paulo Coelho says that just before you are approaching something you have been waiting for, looking forward to, you should slow down as much as possible and anticipate it; think about what impact it is going to make in your life."

A big ginger beard accompanied the speaker, whom Miranda had not seen before. For a minute, it took her aback.

"Felix!" Kieran cried. "I thought you were going to take the bus to Pamplona!"

"A man can change his mind, can't he?"

"I'm delighted to see you again! Felix, this is Miranda. She's Canadian, but other than that she's pretty normal."

Miranda gave him a sour look. "Gee, thanks a lot!" she said, "20 kilometers, two blistered heels, and one downpour and he thinks he knows me! Pleased to meet you, Felix. Don't pay any attention to him. He's had centre-stage all day and thinks he's something special."

"Right," Kieran was not about to acknowledge nor deny sainthood, not yet, so he turned his attention to the newcomer: "You look like you've been here a while. How did you manage that?"

"I took the bus from Pau, stopped off in Oloron-Ste-Marie. Beautiful church there, by the way. Very atmospheric with lovely music. Carried on through to Canfranc, on the bus, and then took the train. While I was en-route I was so taken by the scenery that I thought maybe I'd give the Camino a try from here. I know you told me the *refugios* were few and far between, but, hey, I didn't come here for a walk in the woods did I? Well, not those woods."

Miranda was intrigued, but thought the questions could wait until later. She followed the two upstairs since they were still talking. There were several empty bunks. Kieran took the one next to Felix, beside the door. Miranda, in a fit of self-consciousness and unexpected shyness, bagged a lower bunk in the corner. But, a bit later, so as not to seem rude, went back to talk to the other two. Felix had gone into the showers. Kieran was turfing things out of his pack, setting up his sleeping bag, putting his alarm clock beside his pillow; aligning a book, or rather what looked like a photocopy of a book, alongside all of this.

"What's that," Miranda asked, though by this time her curiosity was waning.

"That, is a copy of a book, written in Greek round about the first century. I am translating it. It's very rare."

"Where did you get it?"

"Well that is quite the story. I have a friend who works in ..." and here, although there was no-one around, he lowered his voice. "Where do all the lost holy—or not so holy things end up ...? Never to be seen again by scholar or saint? No don't say it; I can tell by the look on your face that you know where I mean. Anyway, my friend came across it in an Index one day—one he was not supposed to have seen. So he checked it out and couldn't believe it. This book could change history. He managed to make a copy of it and then smuggled it out to me, because he knew of my interest in the subject. It isn't very long really, but it is undoubtedly one of the most important finds anywhere. How long it's been hidden is anyone's guess, although it has long been suspected to have existed."

"Looks pretty heavy to me. Why did you bring it with you? I mean, there are people who are tearing out and throwing away pages of their guidebooks to keep the weight down." Miranda had made enough sacrifices that day and couldn't see the value of making more.

"Well, maybe I'll tell you more about that as we go on," said Kieran. "I'll see you later, probably. You look beat. Get some weight off those feet."

Meanwhile, a woman in her 50's drifted by in a towel wrapped strategically and paid no attention to the newcomers whatsoever. Miranda found this a bit strange. Another week would need to pass, before she too would take no notice. But a lot would happen between now and then. Eventually she would realize that everything included men and women together it seemed, but that was perhaps the most asexual of arrangements she had ever come across. It was the general order of the day, and no big deal: The Camino came first. (Well most of the time. As a titillating aside: she was to find a very small, very lacy black bra on top of her sleeping bag one early morning after almost everyone had left in Sahagun some weeks later. Not, incidentally, Miranda's. Furthermore, she had been sure the top bunk had been occupied by a man. But that is another story—and that not Miranda's either.)

Now, she couldn't think of anything much: nothing beyond cleaning up, sleep, maybe food later, but even that wasn't so important. She didn't want to talk about anything at this point.

Kieran and Felix, however, seemed to be in an animated conversation: Miranda was so tired. She didn't think she had anything to add. Still though, she had a feeling which said, as she fought off her weariness: Hey, you guys. Don't forget me. And from that moment, certain points that had been percolating throughout the day, arose: you've been talking about a bishop, someone important, yes? Who was he? Tell me later. You promised to tell me, but you didn't. Who was he? I still want to know, but I have to rest now … She rummaged through her backpack and wrote this up on a piece of paper—sort of. She thought she could have just slid this into their conversation, but they were so involved, and she was so tired.

She couldn't decide whether she first wanted a shower or a sleep. Walking further was just not an option. While she was ruminating on this, another woman drifted through from the showers with a large bandage on her big toe:

"Lost it!" She said, noticing Miranda's look. "Somewhere between here and the last place. Oh well, it's a small sacrifice." And with that she plonked herself down on the bunk beside Miranda's. "But it's still an impediment!" she said; Miranda suppressed a smile. Her bunkmate covered herself with her sleeping bag, and was asleep within minutes.

Lost a toe? And Miranda was worried about blisters? What had she let herself in for!

(It turned out later in conversation with Liz—she of the bandage—that it was the toenail which had been lost.)

The showers were empty; luckily the water was still hottish and Miranda experienced, perhaps for the first time of many, the absolute joy of running water—hot or cold—which normal mortals take for granted, and pilgrims anticipate and in longer stretches, positively dream of. In doing this she learned the first lesson: never take anything for granted!

When she came back into the dormitory, she noticed that although "Liz the Toe" was still snoring happily, most of the rest of the bunks remained unoccupied. Kieran and Felix had both disappeared (he might have waited, thought Miranda, perhaps unreasonably), and there was no sign of the woman in the towel, although another bunk was taken just four away and much covered. Directly opposite, in another, darker corner, on a lower bunk next to a writing desk, was another large and heavy backpack. A crimson sleeping bag was rolled out on the bunk above. There was no sign of the occupant.

Since neither he nor Felix had reappeared, Miranda slid her note—the one she had written earlier—under Kieran's pillow: "*Hey, so who was in the grave in Compostela, anyway, hot shot?*" And she tried not to feel sidelined. But as it was, exhaustion claimed the better part of her.

Desire to explore vs. need to sleep fought briefly, and rest won on a technical knockout. Miranda decided that she had walked quite enough for one day, and crawling into her sleeping bag in T-shirt and underwear, was dreaming within minutes.

＊　　　＊　　　＊　　　＊

When she awoke, no-one was around. The light had dimmed a little, she thought, and the street below was noisier.

"Hey!" a voice and a red beard poked its nose into her lower bunk. "Aren't you coming out to discover the fleshpots of Jaca?"

"Hmmm? Go away!"

"No, come on: Earth to Pilgrim. It's time to get out there and see what you are walking through. Use, by all means, the Prime Directive."

"Huh, you're nuts. Walk, you mean? Put pressure on these poor tired feet and actually do it for fun? What kind of sadist are you? Bastard." She put her little pillow over her head," but she was laughing, and did, in actuality feel like she had perhaps indulged herself quite enough. She sat up. Slowly, and with degrees. "O.K. What's going on?"

"Well, there is a concert in the Cathedral at 9 o'clock. Some male group from France, singing sacred stuff. They're supposed to be good. There is food to be had, in the general vicinity and new scenery to be seen, and lucky for you, it's not even dark yet. Get up. Up!"

"Bully! O.K. MacDuff, lead on, but please turn your back first. I've only been a pilgrim for two days and I have to put my shorts on."

"Always the soul of chivalry, I. 'Vest thyself with confidence, my lady'," said Felix, and turned away dramatically, covering his eyes.

"Where's Kieran?" she asked as she painfully put on her boots.

"Perambulating," said Felix.

*   *   *   *

You cannot walk very far in Jaca. It is an ancient city, and still small. The Romans knew it as one of the passes over the Pyrenees. The Goths knew it. Charlemagne knew it. And the Moors would have liked to, but they didn't get far.

Felix walked along with his guidebook open. He looked like a tourist, Miranda thought, and then realized that that was exactly what they were: religiously sanctioned tourists, who hoped to get out of Purgatory at the end of it. Silly, when you thought about it.

"It says here," he said as they were walking, "that Ramiro the First made this city into the first capital of the Kingdom of Aragon, in1035, and that the cathedral is the oldest of its type in Spain."

"On the way in, we saw some fortifications, with very distinct walls. Does it say anything about that?

"Yes, It's called the *Ciudadela*,"—that's 'Citadel' to you—"it says here: It has a pentagonal floor-plan and is built on a flat surface ..."

"Great tourist info. I could see that for myself."

"It was built in the late 16th century and was declared a National Monument in ..."

"O.K. Enough! D'you know what? I'm not sure I care about history at this point. Does your guidebook say anything about cheap places to get a beer?"

As they were walking close to the Post Office, a corner bar appeared like the answer to a prayer: with bright umbrellas, and a cultural-looking view:

"This'll do," Miranda said, and they ordered.

Shortly after, when the beers and the olives were on the table, Miranda asked:

"Where did you meet Kieran?"

"Are you two, like ... you know, friends?"

"I only met him this morning. He's been talking my ear off all day, and ... I guess, I don't know, he kind of ... grows on you. That's why I asked."

"I see."

"No, Felix, believe me, you don't. But answer the question anyway."

Felix looked a bit put out. He was the sort of person who liked things to be nice and tidy without grey areas. But he thought back to her question and said:

"It's a long story, but we were in Lourdes together."

"Lourdes?"

"Yeah. We both stayed there in a small 'hotel', if you can call it that. It was pretty crappy, but cheap. Man, France is expensive!"

"I know, I made the romantic mistake of flying into Paris. Anyway, tell me more about Lourdes."

"Fantastic," said Felix.

"Oh, come on. You're joking. Everyone I met told me to avoid it like the Plague. They said it was tacky …"

"And they were right … How's your beer?"

It was such a Canadian question that it threw Miranda off at first. "Oh, it's fine, no …"

"*Otro, por favor*," said Felix carefully flashing two fingers at the waiter. "Go on"

"No, it's your turn. You agreed with me."

"About?"

"Do you have short-term memory problems? Bloody Lourdes, for God's sake! Tacky?"

"You're right. I can't drink, never could. Anyway. The one thing you have to keep in mind is that there are two sides to Lourdes, and both are very different. I think—and this is a very personal thing, mind—that the rivers separate them. You can be in the commercial town: more Plastic Virgins than you can shake a stick at. Lots of Irish doing some very serious shopping. And then you cross the bridges—there are two, I think, and a tremendous calm descends on you. Really. You don't have to be religious to feel the power. It's almost in compensation, but that's a very personal observation. But I challenge anyone: go down to the Grotto when there are few there; go past the candles—smell them, feel their heat, smile at the men employed to clean them up and feel their smile back; it's international, that smile. Go across the river by the small bridge and just sit and observe. Most of all, attend a candlelight procession. You don't have to be a Christian. You don't have to believe in what they say Bernadette saw, or heard, or said. You don't have to believe in the Immaculate Conception: I guarantee you that when you see those people in the processions, with their candles, with their hopes and prayers and faith, you will be impressed. Such a movement of feeling creates a power. I've been there twice, and I'm not even a Christian!"

"Wow! Just listening to you talking about it gives me shivers. Were you alone when you saw this?"

"Not this time, no. Kieran was with me. Afterwards, he said the same about the power of faith, and how it can work miracles."

"I don't know, Felix. I feel, I can't say … I'm a bit away from miracles right now."

"Maybe you've never needed one," he said enigmatically.

She was tired. Miranda had so many questions, she didn't know where to start, and so she decided, as many have, to keep them to herself. Sometimes, the problem isn't knowing the answer—which is clear enough—it is the correct phrasing of the question. But she didn't know enough to know that yet.

After their third beer, Miranda looked at her watch. "What time was that concert?"

"Nine o'clock, in the cathedral."

"It's a quarter past seven now. That's a while to wait."

"I've had enough culture for one day. I think I'll go back and change and maybe look for a bit of nightlife. Interested? I disco well."

"Thanks, I'm sure it is a command performance, but I'll pass."

"O.K. I'll see you in the morning, probably", but before he left, he asked her, in a fit of conscience, if she knew which direction to take in order to go back to the *refugio*:

Miranda was a bit offended: "Of course I do, round the Market Area, south of the Cathedral and … Don't worry, it's in my head."

When she got to the cathedral, she realized that, although she and others had been using it as a landmark all afternoon, actually seeing it had not been part of her itinerary. Nothing in Jaca is very far from anything else. The cathedral was very central, but although you couldn't have picked it out as a landmark, as such, and isolated it, in fact it was squat, and square, and unless you were beside it, you could have missed it easily. Almost out of obligation (something she was to overcome with her own will as the weeks went on) she went in.

It was quite dark inside. There were animals and vegetables on top of the capitals. Miranda thought it was a bit freaky. It goes without saying, that churches are old, but usually there is nothing to remind us of this: there is always a small army of cleaners—usually female troupes of the Lord, to keep the house "Cleansed and Garnished". Jaca is different. First of all, it is not grand; but what is perhaps more noticeable—it is dirty; the word "dusty" does not do justice to the experience: everything of importance is covered in a layer of centuries old dirt, and, far from taking away from its significance, it enhances it. Jaca is ancient: and its dust announces it. And oddly, gives it much greater authenticity. Make no doubt about it, the Cathedral says—I have been here a long time, and seen many things: nothing you can do or say will surprise me. And it defies you to make argument.

After a short circuit, she went into the cloisters, which were, her info sheet told her, much more recent than the cathedral itself. The garden was somewhat overgrown and blousy; but the smell was heavenly: lavender all the way around. Unlike the interior of the church, the atmosphere was quite comforting. She paid a small fee to look into the museum. There she discovered frescoes, cut wholesale from surrounding churches. Miranda disliked museums intensely in general, like zoos, and this was no exception. Why this well-meaning gathering together of walls when they would have had so much more effect *in situ?* She left feeling a little bit robbed of atmosphere and thought that the spaces, or reproductions, on the original walls must be a very depressing sight indeed.

She cheered herself up by thinking about Felix. Miranda was amused that Felix wanted to check out the discos, (there were quite a few, apparently), but then he hadn't walked yet. She was only interested in getting a feel for the city, but didn't intend to walk far. She wondered who would have the more authentic experience in the long run. It did not take very long before she began to feel tired, fatigued, wanting only solitude and comfort, and a new perspective for the day ahead: so she wandered along alone for the first time that day, and it was a welcome change.

She circled back around the south side of the cathedral. The *refugio* wasn't very far from there, and Miranda thought to go back to invite Kieran to come to the concert at the Cathedral that night. But as she passed the restaurants, she saw both Kieran, and the bearded man they had seen on the Camino that day, earlier on. They seemed very caught up in conversation, as if in disagreement. There were papers and what looked like a dictionary along with Kieran's book on the table. The bearded man was gesticulating with one hand, and aggressively tapping the book with the other. Their voices were raised: it was impossible to say if they were arguing or debating as they spoke only in Spanish. The feeling Miranda had was uncomfortable; threatening. In any other circumstances, she would have gone over to speak with them, pulled up a chair: "May I join you?" but it was very clear that such an action might not have been welcomed. This is what Miranda felt, though she couldn't explain why. And it made her feel uncomfortable. She moved out of sight.

It was night now. She had probably missed the concert anyway, and Felix was no-where to be seen. She went back to the *refugio*—so easy to find it now—but she was not feeling easy. In a few short hours, everything had changed.

She climbed into her sleeping bag. It was only 10 o'clock but seemed later. The lights were not yet out; people around her were occupied with their own individual things.

Miranda at once felt very far away from home.

What am I doing here? she thought.

*   *   *   *

Oddly, despite all the sensory input of the day before, Miranda accomplished a dreamless night, and woke feeling quite refreshed and ready to start again. The first thing that she noticed was that the sunlight was streaming through the side windows. The second thing was that it was remarkably quiet–none of the rustling of plastic bags she was beginning to get used to. She began to crawl out of her sleeping bag.

The dormitory was deserted.

"Oh, you've finally decided to re-join the world, I see." Felix was coming through the door, toothbrush in hand.

"Oh, my God! What time is it?"

"Nearly lunchtime I think!"

"What!" Miranda sat bolt upright and hit her head on the side of the bunk above,"Ow!"

"No, seriously, it's only 9 o'clock, but everybody left two hours or more ago. Kieran left you a note."

Miranda struggled into her shorts and stuffed her sleeping bag into its holdall.

"What note? Let me see? Where?"

"On top of your backpack. He put something in it too"

DEAR SLEEPY HEAD, the note read:
HAVE BEEN PERSUADED TO WALK UP TO THE MONASTERY OF SAN JUAN DE LA PEÑA. IT'S A BIT OFF THE CAMINO SO DIDN'T THINK YOU WOULD BE INTERESTED. WILL TAKE A TAXI DOWN AND MEET YOU GUYS AT THE REFUGIO IN PUENTE LA REINA. YOUR WAY LOOKS A BIT BORING AND THERE ARE SOME INTER-ESTING STORIES ABOUT THE MONASTERY—HOLY GRAIL STUFF. I

HAVE LEFT YOU THE FIRST FEW CHAPTERS OF A BOOK I AM
WRITING ABOUT PRISCILLIAN OF AVILA, SINCE YOU ASKED. I
THINK THIS IS PARTICULARLY CLEVER OF ME SINCE NOW I
DON'T HAVE TO CARRY THEM, AND YOU DO!
BUEN CAMINO,
KIERAN

"Well, what does the boyo have to say?"

"Great! He's gone detouring off to see the monastery at San Juan de la Peña. It's
that one we saw the picture of last night–the one underneath the overhanging
rocks. He says he'll meet us at the next *refugio*." Miranda felt a bit put out: first at
the desertion, and second at the imposition. But she had never been a morning
person and figured her grumpy-ness would rub off with her first coffee. Felix
went back to finishing his teeth. She fished the manuscript out of her backpack:

Pilgrimage to Heresy, by Kieran O'Donovan, she read:
It was a Gallego welcome, and....

"Hey! Were you planning on getting to Santiago anytime in this century?
Because time's running out you know."

"Sorry. You're right," she said, replacing the book and noticing that it almost
doubled the weight of her pack. "Do you have any Band Aids?"

CHAPTER IV

▼

GALICIA 380 CE

"And here am I, Priscillian of Lugo, as I have always been: once Senator of Rome, listened to before by how many studious pupils in the art of Rhetoric, and believed too—for once was my power. Talking to you, Cerberus, about what once was, and what could have been. Had it not been for the loss of my beloved Cecilia, much more could have been brought to my door. How is it, that when love is taken from you, the Muses depart? Why is it, too, that where once I thought in terms of universal understanding, I can have been brought to such a fragile and personal perception of my life, and life in general?"

Cerberus, as usual, said nothing, as I had expected. But looked along his long muzzle with such sympathy and understanding that I knew at least I had a willing ear.

"Are you not impressed, old friend, that my father, Gaius Aurelius, was a Senator before me, equally in the Capital of the Empire? Whose properties and investments brought him riches beyond measure and a voice before Rome?

Cerberus smiled, as was his habitual face. This sort of thing did not impress him, and I could not trust him to be objective anyway: he loved me too much.

It was our habit, now. Walking the walls of Lugo in the late afternoon. Impregnable walls built and announcing the power of Rome—challenged by only the most fool-

hardy. Inside these walls I have my home. Not so impressive now, perhaps, with fewer to serve me. But that is my choice. When Cecilia died, no earthly possession meant much: only that which ensured my relative comfort, and that of our daughter: little enough. I had shunned the world that I once had dominated. And who cared if my name had disappeared from the tongues of the mighty. Priscillian the Speaker, Priscillian the Wise, Priscillian, who opened doors to understanding most of our young men dared not dream of: He was gone. And after all his medical attempts ultimately proved fruitless, Priscillian the Doctor no longer cared to practise. Yet he was content. I stroked the dog's wiry coat. To you, I am but a man. A Master, perhaps, in your own limited world. It is enough.

We have taken this walk, sunset by sunset, for over a year now, Cerberus and I. And little by little, those we meet have ceased to say: "There goes Priscillian. He used to be … "Now, we were avoided. Grief can only be approached once or twice. After that, it cannot be discussed, even less, expiated.

All I needed these days was to see the apple trees below our town, in all their forms, but now, in the spring, most of all. To grow old and wait for my grandchildren. I am approaching my middle age and ready to grow old thus. The blossom now sent waves of heady scent towards my nose—our nose, for Cerberus had a greater sense for this than I. We were both satisfied with each other's company. And as his coat grew the grayer, so my need for others' acclamation grew the less. Cecilia had gone—taken much too soon, despite my prayers to any gods that listened, and my spirit, though only 40 years grown, grew fainter with every spring and every autumn. The world would never be the same. It had taken me less than two years to see it thus. Caring for her during her long illness. In the end, using the folk medicines dear Flavia had taught to me in my boyhood and adolescence, for nothing else had worked. Flavia—also gone. Now, I felt diminished—without hope. Nothing either my father or I had ever believed in had served me.

We sat, at this time, on the same rock, below the walls. Below us the fields spread, and those who inhabited them seemed further and further away from us. Their lives were simpler than mine; most followed the gods of their fathers, secretly these days. I no longer believed in any, but for the sake of my wife, and my public face, I had agreed to accept her God. Cerberus didn't care. He would have followed me to the gates of Hell and barked at them in defiance. Guardian he? Yes, but of Priscillian his Master. And woe betide any who interfered with that contract. But I had investigated those gates in detail, in those early dark days, and now did not acknowledge them at all. If they existed, they were present every day. And I had lived them. Day after tortuous night. Yet, in spite of all, I still believed that some purpose was to be demonstrated to me, and in vain I waited for it to be shown.

"Will tomorrow bring it any closer?" I asked my wolfhound, daily and seemingly without hope, and he turned to me with his gentle face and his far-seeing eyes, failing a little now. Blessed animal, not knowing truth from falsehood.

And thus, each day passed. Priscillian, the Orator, had nothing meaningful to say to himself, even less to others. Yet the day was grand, was it not? Believer in God? The gods? Or not. Perhaps there was something still to be salvaged? Something we could not explain?

Cerberus began to bark. It was his greeting, not a warning.

"My Lord! My Lord!"

My introspections were shattered. Helvias was at my side, and gasping.

"Relax, my friend! What can it be which brings you here so breathlessly? Sit with us." I am a creature of habit these days. Surely you must know ...?

"My Lord. My Lady sent me here without space for pause. She says that I am to convey to you a message that there are two visitors at the house: a man in sober clothing, and a woman ..."

"And who are these people? Creditors? Then pay them. We may be less than visible in society these days but we still pay our bills."

"No. They come from further than here. The man, by his looks, is from the Aquitaine, and the Lady ...? Her dress is rich and, well, not from these parts," he ended lamely.

"Well, it shall not be said that the house of Priscillian shall reject its visitors," I said. Though I would have preferred to have been left alone. "Tell my daughter that I shall be there presently and that she shall entertain our visitors as is our custom in Galicia." And Helvias, my faithful servant, departed in the manner in which he had come.

Well, I shall tell you, and to you only, that we did not rush, the wolfhound and I. Indifference and sloth are hard fellows to be set aside once they have established residence. But curiosity was born with my mother's milk: my father entertained all types of folks as I grew, and, as visitors had become scarce of late, I nudged my companion into a standing position and said:

"We are awaited, Cerberus. And who knows what adventure sits upon the day?"

Our city was compact and it took small time to enter my house. Even now, I remember it that day: the olive orchard, grey leaves with promise, and the herbs inside the gate; the flowers just appearing to show the approach of spring. All mine. But the pools in the courtyard showed no signs of life yet. The nights were too cold. In summer we entertained here, but now, I knew my visitors awaited me within:

Galla was waiting for us. Preoccupied, as her mother had taught her, to make a good impression. In the receiving room, on the table, were olives and wine, cucumber, and good Galician bread.

"Father. Your guests have traveled far to speak with you, and one, I think you know already."

The fire was drawn; it was not summer yet, and I bade Cerberus to sit beside it. Then I had the luxury to look upon my visitors:

One was short, bearded, older than I: perhaps 50 or more. His face was familiar but I couldn't fit it to his being present here. My expression must have shown it.

"Forgive me. I know you, stranger, but I know not from where?"

"I am Elpidius, my lord. When you were a student at the Academies of Burdigala, I was one of the assistant professors."

"Assistant to …?"

"The Lord Delphidius, Sir. My name is Elpidius," he said.

Recollection grows short as we grow older. "Did you assist my Master in procuring students? If so then I recognize you, though I do not recollect your name?"

"I am Elpidius, Lord," he repeated. And it was if as he could not believe that I could not recall his name, and thought my brain addled. But in truth, many years had passed.
I remembered my student years at the Academy: days of study, and nights of drunken debate and debauchery; not surprising that I had suppressed them.

"Of course," I said, still politeness kept me from the truth, though it came closer as I robbed him of his beard, "and how many times did you keep us students out of trouble! Woe to me that I should have forgotten such a worthy friend! And how is my old Master? It has been years since my thoughts have strayed to him. Truly it is a shame to me as he was the architect of my career."

"He is well my Lord," and then as in reflection, "Though, not so well. The years have not been kind to him and every year he sees himself more and more subject to censure, and the ill health of age."

"Ah, yes. Now I remember well. He was a Pagan, and his father was a Druid, was he not?"

"Yes, but it does no-one well to speak of it. Not now."

And now I remembered my manners and I turned to his companion.

My daughter was ahead of me:

"This is the lady Agape, she has traveled far to speak with you."

I now realized that I should have turned my attention first to her: she was tall, taller than most Roman women; she wore a tunic of green gathered at her waist, and her hair was of the color of those barbarians to the west of the Tin Isles, caught up so as to draw less attention but in doing so, failing: so bright as to have been made of strands of copper—no, something between the copper of the north, and the saffron of the south. The style defied comparison. Her eyes, now that they turned directly to me, were like the rarest emeralds of the emperor's jewels and for a moment, I thought I must have been mistaken. How could I possibly have seen anything in my life to compare with those eyes? Surely their like could not have existed anywhere in the world?

"This is Agape" said someone, my daughter, or my visitor.

"Agape." I said, turning all my attention to her. "'Charity': The most precious of the loves. You are surely most welcome in this house, where all four have been celebrated."

I paused, feeling that I had said overly-much, and for a moment, forgot where I was, and who I was.

"The hour is late. Shall we take refreshment?" said my daughter.

Thus I was brought to my senses. The day had begun in its normal way and I had not been prepared for this. Such was the labor of habit.

"Yes, yes, of course. Forgive me. Amantia, call for Herakles. Our visitors must have traveled much to be here with us." There were those, who to this day, called our part of the world: Finis Terrae—*the end of the world. And that was how it seemed to most.*

Sometime after she had gone Elpidius said: "Amantia?" Your daughter told us her name was Galla?"

At this point, she re-entered the spacious salon and hearing the question said directly:

*"It is my father's special name for me. I blush to say that it means "beloved", but perhaps only one or two—can call it so. I am proud of it, if a little embarrassed at times." And she looked at me—*keep it between us, father, please. It is not for others to hear.

A minor feast was brought before us: trout from the rivers, garlic, chestnuts, steamed with water sprouts, and almonds, and ginger: sweet root, the many uses of which mean little to most, mushrooms; and steamed figs to follow, cream. There was more ...

My guests were delighted with what was brought before them, but what was obvious, at least, looking at Elpidius' expression in particular, was not what was presented, but the presenter himself. I, myself, had gotten used to it.

It is true, he is not what one would call ordinary. Least of all in the salon of a Roman notable. He belongs in the gladiatorial ring. But he, by time and political circum-

stance, had missed all that. Had he not, he would have been acclaimed, or killed, for such were the politics of the Circus.

After he had departed, Elpidius said, half-jokingly: "Your slave? I didn't know they grew that size!"

Galla answered for me: "After my mother died, my father freed all of our slaves. They were given their option to leave, or to stay here with us. All chose to stay."

"Your mother was an amazingly insightful woman. Only now are her ideas being listened to."

"She was a Christian," I answered. I felt that the response was mine only. "It was very clear to her that we had no right to own others."

"And you, now?"

"Have followed her."

"It was my mother's wish. On her deathbed," said my daughter. It was true. But I wished I had not had, then, to admit it. I was still unsure in myself. It was a private thing, not explored or discussed even between Amantia and me.

"And so this giant? What do you call him?"

"Herakles. Why not? But for me, I am content to call him friend," I said, unhesitatingly. "Do you remember the scandal of Theophilas?

"Who does not! No-one ever expected the mighty could have fallen so far."

"Herakles, was his bodyguard. He saw and heard things that Theophilas would not have wanted spoken abroad and so he had his tongue cut out. After Theophilas was exposed as a traitor and a usurer, there was no place for his slave. But I believed he was loyal, even before, so I bought him. This was in the Capital, many years ago. Later, I gave him his freedom. But there was no-where for him to go. So he stays."

"And his name?"

"Was lost, if he ever had one. Well, what would you have called him?" I laughed.

"All our former slaves have stayed;" said my daughter, loyally, "they know they are cared for and respected."

"It's a terrible drain on my finances," I said. And I knew that no-one in my company took me seriously.

CHAPTER V

▼

Later, over fruit, and pastries, and more sweet wine, we were seated in the tri-clinium *in the last rays of the spring sun. Agape turned to me and said: "Do you remember a young man called Ausonius?"*

"From Burdigala?" I asked.

"Yes. You were students together."

It was a vague echo of the past. So many years ago. It was so competitive, that time. The only way to Rome was through the walls of the Academies. And not only for us students: the Masters themselves relied on their pupils to bring others to them: often, for some it was the only way to pay their fees. I, at least was spared that. I came from a rich family. But there were others—at least the system allowed those with sufficient intelligence and drive to gain their education by honest industry.

"It would help me if I knew more about you, and your interest in this young man," I said.

"His name was Ausonius;" she repeated, "he was my cousin, and he became my hus-band."

"Ausonius from Tarragonensis?"

"The same," she said.

As on awakening from dreams sometimes, with great concentration, we can gather all factors together, I suddenly recalled:

"Of course I remember! He was a year ahead of me. A brilliant student. His father was quite high placed as I recall."

"Dead now," she said, sadly.

"I'm sorry. I never had the honor of meeting him. He retired before I went to Rome. His son and I became friends over ...?" and here the memory escaped me, perhaps for good reason, given my audience. I didn't want my daughter to learn too much of her father's student days! "Anyway," and now it came flooding back: "Do you remember, Elpidius? We were studying Aristotle's Politics, and there was a passage—I don't remember what—we were supposed to translate it, but I missed the lesson. He told me it had to be translated into Coptic and I stayed up all that night, only to find the next day that all that was necessary was to translate it into Latin! At the time, I was furious, but later I could see the joke. Ausonius thought I was a good sport and he took me to the tavern for supper. We were all so competitive in those days. Success seemed the only way to preferment in Rome. Ausonius became a great poet and I ..."

"Became a great speaker, and philosopher and statesman. But you remained friends?" Agape asked.

"Of course. I had missed the class out of laziness ... but the lesson was a good one!" I strove to remember why in fact I had not attended, but memory has a habit of obscuring what we would rather not remember.

"And you remained friends?" she repeated.

"Of course. I probably would have done the same to him, and in the same humor."

"Your friendship went deep, did it not?"

"For my part, yes."

"Good, because he did not forget you, and that is why I am here today."

*   *   *   *

"Shortly after our marriage, Ausonius and I went to live in Alexandria." Agape began.

"A beautiful city," I mused aloud. *"Forgive me, I interrupt you."*

"Yes, we thought so, and our first years were happy there. We made many friends, amongst them was a man called Marcus, born in Upper Egypt near Memphis to parents from the Etruscan Hills. He and Ausonius bounced ideas off each other. Sometimes I thought our house could not hold both of them, and me, at the same time. It was not that I disliked him. Not at all for we enjoyed each other's company, though he was more flirtatious than I would have liked. Ausonius often teased me about it. He said I was too sensitive, or alternatively, would say that I secretly enjoyed the flattery, which incensed me: I had eyes for no other than my husband."

Or he for you, I thought, though I did not say it.

"Anyway, as the years went by, and I remained childless, my husband would spend fewer and fewer hours at home, preferring instead to travel with Marcus. One day, he told me that they were going to a monastery near Diospolis Parva, which as you may know is a garrison town. Ausonius had a friend there, a Centurion in charge of the soldiers, most of whom were from Asia Minor. He said he would go there afterwards, as Marcus planned to stay at the monastery. Apparently, he said, they had a marvelous library of rare books in Alexandria, and of course, that was something that Ausonius could never resist. It was part of the reason we had moved to Alexandria.

"When he returned a few days later, I had never seen him so excited. But he would not share his experiences with me: 'It is a secret,' he said. "You shall know soon enough.'

A month later, he went back, this time alone. He was to meet Marcus there at the monastery."

"Do you remember the name of the monastery?" I asked.

"Yes," she said, *"It was the Monastery of St. Pachiomus."*

"Ah, yes, I remember: 'Pay no attention to the loveliness and beauty of this world, whether it be beautiful food or clothing, or a cell, or an outwardly seductive book.' *They were bookbinders, those monks. They tanned the hides with which the Codices were bound."*

"Well, he never returned. I went to the monastery and all was in an uproar. Marcus told me that some soldiers had come and arrested my husband as he was packing to leave. They took him away, but would not say where they were taking him. They searched the monastery from top to bottom, but they didn't seem to find what they were looking for. Well, of course, I went to the garrison and spoke with the Centurion. Yes, he said, Ausonius had spent a night there a while ago. They had stayed late talking of old times. He had had another visitor at the same time, a deacon of the church, he said, from Alexandria, he thought, who had seemed fascinated with the conversation. The next day both left, in different directions. This was all he could say, and if he could be of any help in the matter further …"

"Do you think he knew more that he would say?"

"Actually, no, but I know my husband, when he is excited about something he is not as cautious as he should be. He often does not read the expressions of others well; he will assume they share his enthusiasm. He is an innocent in many ways, despite his great intellect."

"You speak in the present tense. Did you find him then?"

"I did not. But when I returned to the monastery, Marcus chose to accompany me back to Alexandria. We traveled in a closed wagon, as the dust and sand were almost intolerable. After we had gone some way, he lowered his voice and produced a book. He said that the monk who took care of the cows had given it to him. It seems that for sometime, the monks have been secretly translating certain papyri and codices from Greek into Coptic. The Coptic codices were then transferred elsewhere, and the Greek manuscripts were smuggled out from time to time, though he didn't know where they went. In the meantime, they were hidden in a most secret place in the cowshed. The very last place that anyone would have looked, though humble places are frequent in the story of Jesus Christ. I think that Marcus may have known more about this arrangement than he was prepared to say, but I could get no more out of him.

"It seems that this particular book was hidden in the stable when the monk showed it to my husband, the first time he was there. They had struck up a friendship—you remember Ausonius, he talked with everyone regardless of their station. Why the monk should have shown him this particular book, I don't know. Perhaps he was particularly attached to it—I can understand that; perhaps he should have parted with it earlier, but didn't. I didn't know the content of the book then; in the later years, I hadn't shared my husband's interests. He was like a bee, you know, landing on this flower, and draining it, moving on to another ... Of course, he probably was not as guarded when he visited the garrison ..."

"You think the content was so dangerous that someone overheard him and reported him?"

"Yes, of that, now, I am particularly certain."

She handed me a wrapped parcel.
"Please don't open it until after we have left. Ausonius apparently had it on his person when they came to take him away, perhaps he had bought it, I don't know."

"But he had time to give it back to the cowherd, who hid it for him?"

"Yes, and he gave it to Marcus to give to me, with a message: 'Take this to Priscillian of Lugo. He will know what to do with it.' *I was lucky enough to meet with Elpidius on the ship which brought me back to Rome. I was distraught. I didn't know what to do. When he told me he had known you at Burdigala, I began to tell him a little of my story. And as we talked, I realized that he and my husband were of like mind. Once I read this book, I became convinced that what it contained was dangerous enough for men to be killed for it. I knew I could not do this alone."*

"And Marcus?"

"Arrested shortly before I left. On charges of sorcery. But knowing him and his smooth words, I have no doubt that they will let him go." said Agape, with perhaps a trace of irony.

"Tomorrow we go to Salamanca to see Bishop Instantius," said Elpidius. "He has ideas which don't exactly coincide with those of the Bishop of Rome, but he cannot be too open. Besides, he is a mild man, with much heart, but young and with little per-

sonality or experience. However, he is of an open mind and one thing that I can predict is that he will be contacting you soon. Expect it."

Amantia had almost fallen asleep, and the hour was very late by now. We said we would meet in the morning.

Just as we were retiring, I suddenly remembered a question I had not asked.

"Agape? An unusual name."

"I was born Egeria. I changed my name when I became a Christian."

"I see," I said. "May I ask where your home was, before you met Ausonius."

"Iria Flavia, on the western ocean. I am Galician, the same as you," she said, and she smiled. "Sleep well, Priscillian."

If emeralds have a scent, I believed it brushed past me as she left.

*   *   *   *

I went to bed with the wrapped parcel in my hands. What was it I held which was so important, so dangerous that a man had disappeared, perhaps been killed for it? But I knew I would have to wait for the morning before I found out.

My guests were up with the sun. As was I, exercising the wolfhound and he, I. We spoke little of what we had talked about that night. Over figs and cheese we talked of their journey: whom they had seen—I wanted to meet with Symposius of Astorga, Elpidius had said, but he was away at Augusta Emerita—and where they were to go.

Agape wrapped her soft woolen riding cloak closely around her.

"Will you return to Iria Flavia, or Alexandria …?" I asked as I held the bridle of her mare. Where is one's home after a loved one is lost?

"I shall go back to Egypt to look for my husband. I shall go to Syria, or Mesopotamia, or Jerusalem. I am now the possessor of secrets and want to seek out others who have the same knowledge as I."

"You will, surely, not go alone?" I asked, looking from her to Elpidius and back.

"Why not?" she said, "we all travel faster who travel alone ... oh, I see You think I can not take care of myself?"
No, I thought. That wasn't what I thought at all.

✳   ✳   ✳   ✳

Once inside, I carefully took the wrappings from the package. My hands held a small codex, very simply bound in leather, somewhat scratched and marked. I ran my fingers over the title. It read:

The Apocryphon of Jesus the Christ

and underneath:

Whoso seeks the interpretation of these sayings will not experience death

Between my trembling fingers, I held the secret last words of our Lord.

CHAPTER 6

▼

Miranda set the package down on the small table beside her shell. She had begun to read it almost as soon as she arrived at the *refugio*. For a while she had forgotten where she was, and how she had got there. Given the circumstances, that was by no means a bad thing.

It hadn't been an easy day.

Oh it had started out optimistically enough, if a little late. She and Felix had walked in companionable silence for the most part; sometimes with him ahead a ways, sometimes she was the faster walker. Compared to the scenery she had hiked yesterday with Kieran, this was not very inspiring. In fact they were rarely out of sight of the N240 highway, and on the occasions that they were obliged to walk on the asphalt itself, the heavy goods vehicles swept by them with no regard for their sanctity, although a few drivers did honk their horns in support.

They walked slowly. Miranda was still having trouble with her blisters (multiplying now), and Felix, who had not yet got his walking pace, was finding the going more tiring than he had expected.

After a while, Miranda told him about what she had seen the night before: the bearded man, and his aggressive manner. Out of some sense of protectiveness, she said nothing about Kieran's photocopied book.

"Odd that he would go off, just like that," she observed.

"I don't think that after a day's walking, Miranda, that you can predict what someone will or won't do."

At first she took this as a reproach, but then realized the truth of Felix's words.

"No, maybe not," she said. "You're right, I'm being foolish."

But as the kilometers slipped by, she still couldn't quite shake of a sense of fore-boding.

*   *   *   *

They saw no other pilgrims that day on the Camino, neither morning nor after-noon. Everyone else would have been either behind them, walking into Jaca, or ahead, with their early start. Even had the *carretera* not taken them relentlessly to the west, there were yellow arrows at intervals, and neither of them saw the need to consult Miranda's pilgrim guidebook. So when they finally appeared at the turning to Puente La Reina, what they saw was a bit of a shock.

"It's no more than a truck stop!" Miranda exclaimed in despair.

There were two hotels, one of which was closed up and looked as though it hadn't been in operation for a while. There was no sign of a pilgrim refuge, and the receptionist at the second hotel told them that there was none. The next ref-uge, it seemed was some 15 kilometers further west along secondary roads.

It was almost 7 o' clock. The sky was clouding over.

Felix went out of the hotel and walked up and down the road a little. There was no sign of Kieran anywhere. As he re-joined Miranda, who was scanning the hotel's guest register in the lobby, he said:

"Are you sure he said he would meet us here? He should have arrived ages ago."

"I'm certain," she said. "No, nothing, thank you," she gave the book back to the receptionist with a disappointed smile.

"He said he would meet us at the next *refugio* in Puente la Reina, look:" she handed him the letter, now somewhat battered.

Felix took a while to consider the script: "Well, he must have been mistaken since there is no such *refugio* here. Only one over-priced last resort which somewhat lacks in pilgrimness. And since there is no other *refugio* between Jaca and here, logically, my dear Watson, he would either have stayed here at the hotel to wait for us, or, he would have had the same reaction as we have, and walked onto the next one. No?"

"But that's" she consulted her map, "That's miles away! We can't walk there tonight. That's three hours solid walking at least!"

"I don't think I could manage a third of that, to be honest. My suggestion is we stay here tonight, and go on tomorrow. We'll catch him up sooner or later; he can't be very far ahead."

"No, Felix. It doesn't work that way. I saw pilgrims in Canfranc that I haven't seen since. People walk at different paces. It's easy to catch up distances by car, or even by bicycle, but on foot? Impossible."

Miranda stopped to think for a minute. She knew in a way that Felix was right. Maybe sooner or later they would catch up to Kieran. Maybe he might stay 2 nights at the next *refugio* and wait for them. But she knew that most *hospitaleros* were very strict about the rules, and one night was the maximum, unless you had a doctor's certificate.

"I'm going on," she said, finally.

"Are you mad? It'll be midnight before you get there. You can't walk in the dark on your own. You don't even have a torch."

"I have this," she said, and brandished a thumb.

*   *   *   *

In the end it was decided that Miranda would go on and Felix would stay. Kieran had to be in one of the two places.

"Pity I don't have my cellular," Miranda said. She had vowed not to bring it.

"And are you conversant with Kieran's number? If he carries a phone, and I know for a fact that he doesn't." Felix hadn't meant it to sound so sarcastic, but there was really no other way to say it.

Miranda admitted defeat.

"Look, if he shows up here later," she remonstrated with Felix," at least you will be here. If you two get a very early start in the morning we can meet up at Artieda. It's a short walk after that to the next place, and so we can leave later, after you arrive."
And we can both give him shit, she left unsaid.

And so it was a plan.

"Take care, and watch out for dirty old men," said Felix.

*   *   *   *

In fact, Miranda was a lot more scared than she wanted to admit. She had no idea how long she would have to wait, but consoled herself with the thought that if it got too dark, she could always walk back to the hotel.

As it turned out, the first car that passed her, as she was walking, stopped ahead fifty meters or so and waited. Miranda ran as fast as her, now heavier and bulkier, backpack would allow. She had an unreasonable vision of the driver speeding ahead just as she reached him.

And it was a "him". It was getting dark and there was no-one on the road. The old Ford station wagon was full of clutter and it was clear that the inside had not been cleaned in many a month, years even. It also had a very distinct smell of sheep. Miranda leaned into the passenger window and pointed to her map: Artieda? she said, and pointing to the sun, made a downward movement with her finger, and lifted her palms in a gesture of helplessness.

The old man leaned over to open the door, which almost fell off its hinges. He moved various papers and brown, dusty envelopes from the seat. He had few teeth and those he had were stained and crooked. Miranda tossed her pack into the back, and off they went.

Despite her age–after all she was well into her thirties–she had a vision of her mother having a fit!

Miranda managed to discover to her great amusement that her rescuer's name was Gabriel, and laughed. It would be, wouldn't it! The kilometers flew past as the sun descended beneath the clouds, and a cold chill breeze came through the open window. Miranda had the sense that it would fall down into the door well had she tried to close it. Anyway, the farmer lit one Ducado after another and as he tossed the ends out of the window, Miranda had a vision of them being blown back in and setting fire to the entire contents, her pack included.

Eventually, a village appeared on their left. Atop a hill.

"Artieda", toothless Gabriel said, and stopped at the next crossroads.

"Thank you so much," Miranda said, "Gracias mucho." She took her wallet from the front of her pack. He waved his hands at her: no. Instead, he pulled her across the seat and planted a big wet kiss on her astonished lips.

"Yuck!" she said to herself, after he sped off down the road," Why do men think they can **do** these things? Damn that bloody Felix!"

But as she spiraled up the hill towards the village, she thought it was a small price to pay for three hours walk.

*   *   *   *

She was so certain that the first face she would see would be Kieran's that she almost, and totally irrationally, disbelieved the *hospitalera* when she said that no one had given her that name and that, in fact, Miranda was the only guest that night. She tried to describe him as best she could, but it was a pointless exercise: the woman, though kind, spoke only a little English, and anyway, it was quite clear that nobody else was hiding under the bunks.

"Now what?" she thought, and feeling foolish, considered the uncalled for idea of Felix and Kieran enjoying a beer in the hotel bar. Considered herself. As in moments like this she had done before: "What a Drama Queen I am!" she admitted, and she had to laugh.

*   *   *   *

The next day she decided to take a bit more care of her feet. Around midday the two sisters she had seen in Jaca arrived. Margaret, the younger of the two it seemed, was very quiet and said little. Elizabeth, on the other hand, had become quite an expert on the subject of feet and their care.

"You should carry a needle," she said.

Miranda had some strange vision of anaesthetic, but Liz produced an ordinary sewing needle and a cigarette lighter, which she proceeded to use to sterilize her surgical instrument. Then she threaded it with cotton. Miranda realized that her trust threshold had risen somewhat.

"You pass it through like this," she said, and did, "and the liquid drains out. Now it can heel properly. Add a bit of Betadine and Bingo! This and some Neurophen are the pilgrim's secret weapons."

Margaret had taken her *bocadillo* outside while the operation had been in progress. Miranda guessed that she had seen and heard quite enough about feet the last few days.

"Thanks, Liz. I thought you two would have been ahead of us. I'm surprised to see you."

"Well, we decided to go up to see the monastery. It's quite something, I can tell you. On the way down we got a bit lost, and so we asked around in Santa Cruz de los Serós, and persuaded a woman who was watering her plants to put us up for the night. I think she was glad of the company. She said that pilgrims don't usually pass the night there as there's no *refugio*; it's off the main route for most pilgrims."

"So you went up to the monastery the same day as Kieran! Tell me, did you see a guy about this height … mousy hair, blue eyes?"

"No dear. There was a bus full of culture vultures at the monastery. But the only other person we saw with a pack was a scary-looking man with a black beard and very intense-looking eyes. He was walking much faster than us. We saw him just as we got to Santa Cruz, but I don't think he stopped there. Leastways, we never saw him again. Why? You lost someone?"

"To tell you the truth, I think it's probably me that's lost. No doubt he'll turn up today later."

*   *   *   *

At exactly 2 o'clock, Miranda saw from her perch on the wall, a man turn off the main road and begin the climb up to the village. As he got closer, she saw a familiar thatch of red hair. He was walking with a limp. And he was alone.

"No sign. Sorry," said Felix over his coffee. "I waited as long as I could and then some girls came in, we got talking and they offered me a ride to Berdun. Great place, very atmospheric. No *refugio* but one small pension offering rooms for pilgrims. I was pretty tempted, but, thinking of you waiting for me here, my lady, always the gentleman, as you know, I walked the last bit. It was longer than I'd expected. 'Specially that last bit. Why is it always 'up'? Boy, I think my knee's done in."

"It's just the stiffness from unused muscles. It goes away in a day or two. Here," and she gave him a couple of Elizabeth's Neurophens. "Did you check to see if Kieran had passed through there?"

"I did. But no sign of the bog dweller himself. Just a middle-aged couple in the bar holding hands."

"I told Maria Antonia, the *hospitalera*, that I was waiting for you. She's really nice. She will let me stay another night as the *refugio* is not used a lot. I think that walk up daunts people and they go onto the next one. You can rest up a bit, and we can wait for Kieran. Damn! Where's he got to? I phoned ahead to Ruesta this morning and they haven't seen him, so he must be still behind us. Maybe he went back to Jaca the same road as he went up, though I can't see why he would do that. You know, the last time I saw him, he was talking with that big man who had the bunk across from me? Did you see him: big, with a beard, very intense looking eyes?"

"The one who looked like he would knife his grandmother for her string of pearls? Yes, I saw him. I avoid big brawly Germans. That's how I stay alive."

"I didn't say he was a German. I don't know what nationality he was. I vaguely remember he may have been Spanish. But I didn't like the look of him. And I saw him with Kieran last night. They looked as though they were arguing too. Why would Kieran go off with him without so much as a word? I don't like it, Felix."

"Who knows the ways of Irishmen?" Felix said, with a painful shrug of his shoulders: "I'm going to take a *siesta*."

But the afternoon passed, and the night fell. And still, there was no sign of the missing pilgrim.

CHAPTER 7

▼

And neither was there the next night, nor the next, nor the next. Nor the next. And that was where the pilgrim roads met. And so did Miranda and Felix' final hope. For it was called Puente la Reina.

"Time to admit it," said Felix,"We've been idiots. Look Miranda. Look at the note. Does it say, the **next** refugio? No. It does not. That was just something that between us we had assumed. It says Puente la Reina. And this," he paused," **is** Puente la Reina; it must be because I've seen it on the T-shirts."

"O.K. But he said he would take a taxi!" Miranda said. It had been several days since Jaca, and she had become, well, perhaps emotional and suspicious about this whole thing. And partly she felt she wanted nothing to do with it. She rationalized that it was the investigative part of her, but actually, she felt that there was more …

"Thinking like a 20th Century indigent," said Felix as he tapped the side of his head. "Think like a pilgrim: for us four days walking. For him a few hours and then time to sit, and r–e–l–a–x—in the Parador, I'll bet …"

In fact, it wasn't part of the Parador network, but the point was made.

"Oh, Felix. I've been a twit …"

Always the soul of discretion her companion said nothing …

"Of course!" she said, expanding on her thought processes: "When people talk about Puente la Reina, they always mean where the 'Two' Caminos meet. The *Camino Frances*, from St. Jean Pied-de-Port, and our own *Camino Aragones*. He's got to be there, somewhere. Probably rested and laughing at us with all of his book translated."

"Translated?" said Felix," I thought you said he was writing one. Isn't that what you've been lugging (and complaining about for the last four days—though I have been chivalristic to comment, please note)".

Miranda realized that in her relief to acknowledge her own mistake, she had said too much. Odd that she should still feel the need to keep Kieran's secrets:

"Yes, of course, that's what I meant. When things are about olden times that's what I …?" And she suddenly wondered why she was at such pains to hide Kieran's original disclosures to her.

They reached the Church of St. Mary of Eunate at about noon.

"'*The Church of Saint Mary of Eunate is located in the middle of the Ilzarbe Valley* da di da di da … *the architectural whole stands lonely in flat and isolated landscape, with open sights that enhance the spirituality and charm of the monument. It is located on …*' Shall I continue?" said Felix, reading from the tourist literature Miranda had picked up at the last place.

"If it gives you pleasure," said Miranda, absently, although in actuality she couldn't give a damn. She liked Felix, but she couldn't help but wish, at times, that he would shut up.

"… da di da … right … '*located on and linked*'," he said with a wink, " '*to the road of Santiago de Compostela, that coming through Somport* … da, da, da … *meets the road from Vancarlos in Puente la Reina. The architectural* … bla bla bla … *makes it one of the most interesting works of Romanesque architecture in Navarre.*'"

"You know what?" Miranda said," It's crap like that which stops anyone from wanting to visit." Eunate came closer and closer …
"Wow! It's gorgeous!"

And it was true. The building was unlike any that Miranda had ever seen. First of all it was octagonal, and it stood out like the proverbial sore thumb from its surroundings of corn stalk and poppies. She had a real desire to investigate further and hoped that it would not be closed, as had been most of the churches they had passed along the way in Spain.

"Coming?" she said to Felix.

"No, thanks. I'll stay here and ruminate."

Inside, the building was a contrast in styles: utter simplicity combined with odd sculpting on top of the columns. The capitals were far from simple, representing animals, plants, masks, and human figures. If atmosphere had been missing from the cathedral museum in Jaca, it was here in recompense. Miranda found herself gazing with open mouth.

"Wow!" she said again, *sotto voce*.

"What does it look like to you?" a man with pebble-glass spectacles said to her.

"Sorry?"

"They'll tell you it's a hospital or a burial ground—and they have found a lot of graves around here—but the Templars built this, and they kept their secrets to themselves." He touched a finger alongside his nose. "It is named after Saint Mary the Virgin; but that's a later addition. This was named after Mary all right, but I doubt she was a virgin. There's more than one Mary in the Jesus story. Look at the stone struts overhead. What do you see?"

Miranda saw stone struts.

"They're irregular!" he said in triumph. "That's always the mark of Templar work. No central keystone either, and that's unusual. They did everything in code.

Buen Camino." He said, and with that he hoisted a backpack which looked like it weighed a ton and left her open-mouthed.

Later she joined Felix outside, who was picking poppies.

"They won't last the night," she said.

"Maybe not. But at least they will have had the honor of gracing Felix the Great's backpack for his last steps on the *Camino Aragones*. What did you find out?"

"That the more I learn, the less I know. Come on, we're almost there."

And off they went.

*   *   *   *

By the time they got to the *refugio* in Puente la Reina it was packed. They were unused to this as the road they had been traveling so far was still little used by pilgrims. Here, they met up with those coming through the Pass of Roncesvalles, from France. They were lucky to get the last bunks, and those were on the top, of three.

"Serious vertigo," said Felix from the top berth next to her. "Just hope you don't fall off in the night."

"Rather I hope that **you** don't," she said," I'll never hear the last of it."

The *refugio* seemed to be almost taken over by Brazilians. They dominated the showers and the kitchens with their chatter and their laughter, and their sense of *bonhomie*. Miranda was to see them everywhere as she continued to walk, but this was the first time she had seen them in such numbers. The closeness of the bunks, and the sense of crowdedness between them, falling over packs and feet everywhere, gave her a feeling of claustrophobia, and she decided despite her tiredness to go for a walk.

Now a week before, and she would have collapsed on her bunk in exhaustion and snoozed the afternoon away, but those times were no more. Her blisters had vanished (thank you, Liz), her muscles no longer intruded their painful way into every movement, and her feeling for adventure pushed out thoughts of seclusion. She went out to investigate the town.

It was small, but then everything on the Camino was small so far. She made her way down the main street, passing churches along the way, and ended up beside an old bridge, the very one that Puente la Reina had been named for. She met a man at the foot of the bridge drinking Coca-Cola and writing in a notebook. She smiled. He smiled back. He offered her another can and they sat there drinking quietly, looking at the river passing by. He spoke reasonable English and they got into what passed for a pilgrim conversation. He had walked from Paris, he explained. He was from Sao Paolo, Brazil. His name, he said, was Santiago.

"I go to pay my respects to my uncle," he said with a grin.

They each took another swig of Coke and watched the passers by.

"You? Why do you come this way?" he enquired, after they had been sitting companionably for some time.

Now oddly, although it was on everybody's mind, nobody had asked her this so far.

"I don't really know, Santiago. Actually, I wish I did know."

"Ah," he nodded his head sagely," you should know that you do not choose the *Camino*. The *Camino* chooses you."

It was not the last time she was to hear this, and it became more and more profound every time she heard it.

Miranda wandered back towards the *refugio* and on the way bought a cheap T-Shirt with the bridge on it and the words: *Puente la Reina: el Principio del Camino*. Hmm. She thought, perhaps not the beginning, but in many ways the beginning for me. But her tranquility was shattered when she went to check out the kitchen. There was a noisy group from Switzerland, boiling spaghetti. One woman was loud. Not only did she have a loud voice, but a loud personality which filled the small kitchen and made others stay away, which was probably her intention.

"They have the … *coche de apoyo* … " her bunkmate said. "They are not pilgrims *de verdad*," he said in disapproval. "Look at the *mocilas!* Little! They have the car," and he shrugged his shoulders. But what can you do? He seemed to say.

Miranda knew that the pilgrim hospices were nominally only for those pilgrims traveling on foot, or bicycle. Or, these days, the very occasional horseman, (or woman). But she was to learn about, and disdain, as the others did—that there were also groups who traveled with light packs between the *refugios*, accompanied by cars such as this, which carried their heavier things, and transported food and other provisions between stops, which they spread out on the available tables, mocking those who had only fruit and bread sticks. They were generally regarded with disgust by the walkers who, like Miranda, had only the very fewest of posses-sions with them. The bicycle pilgrims seemed a race of their own and the two groups tended not to mix, but at least they were self-sufficient in their own mys-terious way. These pseudo-pilgrims she saw in the kitchen simply took up the very limited sleeping space that there was.

She decided to go out again—Felix was fast asleep—to see the ancient monastery church she had passed. On the way she passed the reception desk, and realizing that she had almost forgotten about Kieran, looked in the pilgrim diary to see if his name was there.
It was not. But one name she recognized was that of Dominic Guzmann. "Mari-ana?" it said,"*Estoy aqui, ¿pero donde estás tu?*" *¿Estás aqui?*" She had not seen that name since they had halted in Jaca, and the date was today. She asked the *hospi-talero.*

"Him? I don't remember. He is not here. Perhaps he has gone to the other *refu-gio.* We are full."

Other refugio? She asked.

"Yes, on the other side of the town. Up the hill. Not so nice." he said.

But it was clear he was closing up, and he made it clear that he didn't have any more time for pilgrim questions.

Miranda was left to wonder: *Could this Guzmann perhaps tell me more about Kie-ran?*

*   *   *   *

She could not explain the sense of intrusion she experienced as she entered the Church of the Crucifixion. Afterwards it became clearer to her, but at the time, she felt like an interloper. There was no-body there. It was warm, warmer than a mere stone building should have been, and unbelievably simple and magic. She had become accustomed to Catholic churches, more or less ornate, some much, much more than others. All more or less intimidating. None which made her feel worthy of entrance. This one was so simple as to be decidedly welcome and she gradually, as she allowed herself to enter, began to feel that it had been put there just for her to find in this way: afraid, and then not afraid. At the end of each of the pews were small garlands of flowers, as though some special sacrament, perhaps a wedding, had taken place there recently. As she approach the—very simple also—altar, she noticed beside it a crucifix. But it was unlike any she had ever seen since it was in the form of a "Y": looking more like a tree branch than anything else. She sat beside the flowers for a little while, feeling self-conscious as she always did in a church, until a feeling of belonging almost swamped her. *Why are you so afraid?* It seemed to say. *Don't you know you belong in my arms.* However, this sensation, rather than reassuring her, made her feel edgy, as though she did not belong at all, there or anywhere, and that her being there was some sort of fakery on her part.

She got up to leave in a hurry. But on her way out she noticed a pile of cards. She had already been given two of these little cards, one in Jaca and one in ...? She didn't remember. This one was of Saint Teresa.

Teresa. Her mother's name. It said:

> *Nada se turbe*
> *Nada te espante*
> *Todo se pasa*
> *Dios no se muda*
> *La paciencia*
> *Todo lo alcanza*
> *Quien a Dios tiene*
> *Nada se falta*
> *e Solo Dios basta*

"Nothing disturbs you; Nothing causes you dismay
Everything passes
God is unmoving
Patience reaches all
Those who have God
Lack for nothing
Only God is enough"

She took it.

*   *   *   *

On her way home—odd, she thought that she should think of the vertiginous bunk where she would pass that night in that way—Miranda stopped for a beer and some *tortilla* in a small bar just around the corner from the church. A program was on the television (which like all Spanish screens dominated the corner) and there were some obvious pilgrims watching it. It showed a passage, a road, a pathway from the air, and then a city.

"That's it!" one of them cried in delight. That's Logroño. That's where we are going next."

And suddenly, Miranda realized why she felt at home. This was her road. These were her people.

She went back to the *refugio* and carefully climbed up to her bunk. Almost all the lights were out and there were only muffled pilgrim whispers and the—impossible to muffle—sound of plastic bags being stuffed into backpacks.

And Miranda went to sleep with this thought: I've never been more sure in my life that this is where I am supposed to be.

*   *   *   *

Felix hadn't really featured in her personal wanderings or wonderings of the night before, and she wasn't really surprised when he said to her as she was packing up the next day:

"Hey, Miranda. Do you remember I told you I had met a couple of girls in the other Puente la Reina? They gave me a ride to come and meet you?"

It seemed a century ago.

"Well, I bumped into them in a bar last night," (what a surprise, she thought) "and anyway, they are going back to Pamplona—you know for that 'Bulls' thing, you know,—and I thought, that … you know … I'm not much of a pilgrim, am I?"

"It's O.K. Felix," Miranda said, and she kissed him. "You go and do what your heart tells you."

"Thanks, I thought you might be …?"

"Mad? Come off it! We each have to 'Do our own thing', though don't you ever tell anyone I know I said that. Anyway. There are buses, you know. Do you think we might meet up somewhere along the way? If you do a bit of calculation (you can add and multiply, I take it?), we could meet up again along the way. If not …"

"You, my Lady, are a true Princess. If I didn't think your heart was already taken …"

"Get outta here, idiot. But for God's sake watch out for those bulls chasing you!"

"It's not the bulls I worry about." he said," It's the women!"

But before he left he gave her a very faded and limp bouquet of poppies.

*   *   *   *

Just before she departed, somewhat late, as always, the *hospitalero* gave her a package:
MIRANDA …? It said. SOMETIME IN PUENTE LA REINA, AND WITH SINCERE APOLOGIES.

"*Lo siento, Señora.* I should have given you this yesterday, but I couldn't find you. Your friend said it was for you."

DEAR MIRANDA, it said underneath the printed address on the paper label. I ONLY HOPE YOU GET THIS ...

The Apocryphon of Jesus the Christ

Whoso seeks the interpretation of these sayings will not experience death.

We were gathered together, that last night, the Twelve and Mary Magdalene who loved the Savior. We were to eat well in our upper chamber, and had already drunk of the sweet juices of the last grape harvest. But all knew that the events of the most recent days were portents of things to come. We knew that we were assembled maybe for the last time. And so I perhaps in particular—to my sorrow—knew the importance of keeping those things which were to pass that night, though why this task should have come to me and not the others, remains a mystery to me. Perhaps I knew they would take less notice of me.

These, then are the secret sayings of our Master which I wrote down as I was listening to them talking with one another. I hope and pray that they will come to the notice of those who will question and understand them, for they are the way to truth and everlasting life.

*   *   *   *

We asked him: 'Master, when shall the kingdom come?"

And he answered us straightways: It will not come by waiting for it. It will not be a matter of saying, Here it is ... or There it is ... Rather, the kingdom of the father is spread upon the earth, but men do not see it.

If those who lead you say to you, 'See, the Kingdom is in the sky." Then the birds of the sky will precede you. If they say to you, 'It is in the sea,' then the fish will precede you. Rather the kingdom is inside you, and it is outside of you. When you come to know yourselves, then you will become known, and you will realize that you are the sons of the living father. But if you know yourselves not, you will dwell in poverty, and it is you who are that poverty.

You must become passers by.

Those who say they will die first and then rise are in error. If they do not first receive the resurrection while they live, when they die they will receive nothing. They say: baptism is a great thing, because if people receive it, they will live, but they are in error. There is more to learn, but … (here I could make out little as the writing was obscured).

The world came about through a mistake. For he who created it wanted to make it imperishable and immortal. But he fell short of attaining his desire. For the world never was immortal, nor, for that matter, was he who made the world.
And the Lord paused as we pondered his words.
For things are not imperishable, but his sons are. Nothing will be able to become imperishable until it becomes a son.
The cup of wine and water is appointed as the type of blood for which thanks are given. It is full of the Holy Spirit and it belongs to the wholly perfect man. The living water is a body. And it is necessary that we put on the living man; therefore, when he is about to go down to the water, he unclothes himself, in order that he may put on the living man.
In perfecting the water of baptism, we empty it of death.

Those who were gathered asked him: 'Lord, what is the fullness, *and what is the deficiency?'* (the word here is p*leroma*, and this is closest translation I can make. K)
He said to us: You are from the fullness and you dwell in the place where the deficiency is. And Lo! His life has poured down upon you … (here again I could not read the text as the words had been obscured, though by a stain of some sort.)

And the Lord said: Blessed is the wise man who sought after the truth and when he found it, rested upon it forever and was unafraid of those who wanted to disturb him.

Judas asked: 'Why for the sake of truth, do we die and live?'
And the Lord answered him, saying: Whatever is born of truth does not die. Whatever is born of woman, dies.

I was disturbed, and asked: 'Lord, is there a place which is lacking truth? I want to understand all things, just as they are.'
He answered me straightway: The place which lacks truth is the place where I am not! He who shall drink from my mouth shall become as I am. I shall become as he, and all things that are hidden shall be revealed to him.

But Peter said: Let Mary leave us, for women are not worthy of life.

But Jesus said to him: I myself shall lead her in order to make her as male, so that she may too become a living spirit. For every woman who will make herself so will enter the kingdom of heaven.

But Mary was afraid of Peter for he knew that he hated her race and believed that they were incapable of telling the truth.

The disciples said to him: 'We know that you will depart from us. Tell us who will be our leader then?'
He said to them: You are to go to James the righteous, for whose sake heaven and earth came into being.

This is as far as I have got. Catch you later.
K

CHAPTER VIII

▼

LUGO 382 CE

Two years have passed since I first read those words. Two long years in which my life has changed immeasurably. In between I have read them over and over again, until I know them by heart. And not only these. With the help of others of like mind, who have come to seek me out, I have searched for, and found, other sources, almost as lost, and just as forbidden. But I am getting ahead of myself.

In the week following Agape and Elpidius' unexpected arrival, two more visitors came to see me. One was Instantius of Salamanca, as Elpidius had foreseen. The other was Salvianus, Bishop of Braga, who, though not a young man or fit, was eager to see for himself these words which our lord Jesus spoke. They came together which caused my household a good deal of fussing—unnecessary fussing in my opinion, but I said nothing. Visitors were, or rather had been, rather rare. It was time to revise our former hospitality. And in truth, our servants enjoyed it, as did my daughter.

Yet even before their coming, other events were to change the direction I had found myself taking; or perhaps more accurately, acted as a force upon my unmoving life. I was to perform two acts in an old capacity: according to the people of Lugo, I saved two lives, and perhaps I did.

As I believe I have already said, it had been my fascination since a boy to collect herbs, flowers, roots, certain nuts, and bark with medicinal properties. Sometimes I would *find these beside an old shrine, marked with stones. Often too they were beside mountain springs, similarly marked. One, beside a weathered statue of an older god, or perhaps, a goddess. There were many of these scattered throughout our hills. Sacred places, and not all abandoned. Some I would find bedecked with wild flowers, a clay pot, or a trinket or two. I paid reverence to them despite my conversion. It does not do to ignore power, regardless of one's own beliefs. Many of the plants I collected, it is true, were used to no more effect than to add flavor to our meals, but many I ground with mortar and pestle, or added to oils to make salves, or dried to make tisanes. I had learned this from Flavia, my nurse and first teacher. Flavia was a pagan, (as was my father, and I until Cecilia's death: we kept a household shrine still, for our servants, mostly). Flavia was one of the Old Ones: the* Meigas. *She had come to the house as a slave when I was very young. My mother had died when I was only two months old, and it was Flavia's milk I had fed upon as she had lost a baby when she had been captured, though I know neither the circumstances of her coming, or even where she was from. But again, forgive me, I digress.*

One such herb was one we used to heal burns, quite frequent in our kitchen where the girth of Herakles often reduced the working size to almost nothing. Our giant had a habit of flailing his arms in frustration sometimes when he was unable to make himself understood. The result was many overturned pots and minor, I am glad to say, scaldings. The ingredients for the salve were common enough in the countryside and often grew alongside nettles. I have often wondered at a god who, while thoughtful enough to put the antidote next to the cause, could have avoided the cause altogether. But these things are not to be wondered at for long. Life is too short.

Another ailment in our damp climate is a sudden and frightening loss of breath: I have suffered from this myself on occasion, and over the years have perfected a powder which, when inhaled, brings almost instantaneous relief to the sufferer. For some this is but a mild discomfort which passes, though it involves a strength of will to reduce the sense of panic it engenders. For others, not so fortunate, it can mean a painful and agonizing death.

This day, as I wandered, I had been pondering the writings I had read. Linking them to what I already knew; questioning them for what I did not. I have often, even in my days in Rome, sought out the wilderness and solitude to help me think.

And so it was that I was on my way back from such a gathering when I passed through the market place. Amantia had asked me to buy some food or item, I recall not what.

The townspeople were shocked at first to see the Master shopping like a common servant, but in recent years they had become accustomed to the sight and paid me little mind except to acknowledge me with a smile and a nod of reverence. The doings of our domus *had always attracted some attention as we were far from orthodox in our ways, even in my father's time. Today, a crowd had gathered, circling something or someone, leaving the stalls unattended for the moment. Curiosity has always been one of my failings, or perhaps strengths, and I went to investigate.*

A small man, one of the farmers I had seen with his produce passing through from time to time, was bent double in the middle of the townsfolk who surrounded him almost without exit. I pushed my way to the front: "Perhaps I can help," I said.

He was clutching his chest, searching for a breath which did not come. His face was rapidly turning the color of cocks' combs and I recognized the symptoms only too well. Afterwards, it was hailed as a miracle, and perhaps it was: that I was in the vicinity at the time of the attack, and luckily had just gathered some of the flowering herbs needed to alleviate just such a spasm. Though they were not completely seasoned they were dry enough as luckily I had gathered them in a sheltered spot. I took a bunch in my hand and plunged them into the brazier beside the chestnut seller.

Immediately they caught alight, but the flame died down straightaway and this was just the effect I wanted. I took them and gave them to the nearest person:

"Hold them directly under his face," I said, "Quickly, woman, there is no time to lose: now!"

While she did this, I helped the man into a sitting position leaning his elbows on his knees. "Try to relax," I said, "in a few moments you will be breathing easily again." He breathed in and out violently once as I stroked his scalp with one hand and supported him with the other, and gradually his color began to change and his wheezing started to give way to rapid but deeper breathing.

"Move back;" to the crowd, "give him room. The worst is over."

Two days later, the fellow came to our kitchen with onions, garlic, and wild carrots freshly gathered.

As it happened, I was peering in pots, annoying the kitchen maids no doubt, but they too were used to my eccentricities.

"My lord. You saved my life. It was a miracle!" he said, thrusting a bunch of carrots into my hand. And then, realizing his station, he blushed.

"What is your name, fellow?" I asked as he hastened to depart.

"Mathias," he answered.

"The name of one dear to our lord Jesus," I said. "Remember this and tell others: it is not man who performs miracles. It is the power of faith."

The farmer touched his heart and once again turned to go.

"Seek out those who can instruct you. And do what you can to help others in need." I added.

I never saw the man again.

Only two days passed when I heard of another. A millers' agent. Wealthy, I was told. He had been passing through on his way to the coast and had suffered strong pains around his heart. He had put up at a local hostelry, and hearing of the "miracle" sent his servant to me.

"I am not a doctor," I protested to the hapless man who hung around our gateway. "There is one who practices near the Porta Nova. He is the man you need to see."

"He has already seen my master," he said, "but he has done nothing and the pain persists. Please, will you come? My master is a wealthy man and he can pay." But then he realized looking around that money may not have moved me.

"In the name of Jesus the Christ, will you come?" he pleaded.

I gathered my herb bag and accompanied him. Although the distance was not far, he walked so quickly that I feared I would need some of my own medicine. As we reached the inn, the landlord was just exiting.

"You come too late," he said. "He is dead, or near to be."

However, I have never believed in lost causes until I have seen them for myself. I pushed past the man. "Where is he?" I said.

A crone directed me up the stairs. The place was filthy and I wondered why a wealthy man would stay in such a place until I remembered that the people were suspicious of strangers and even more superstitious of sickness—as they had right to be. Besides there was nowhere else.

The merchant was lying on the floor, doubled up in agony. It seemed that he had been trying to get up to call for help when the pain had increased suddenly. Now it seemed that he was barely conscious. I reached into my bag and proceeded to ...

But I forget myself. Such knowledge is for a few only, for those who know how to use it.

The man survived, and like the farmer, came a few days later to thank me personally. He handed me a purse full of coins.

I waived them away: "Give them to the poor," I said, and then I gave him the same advice I had given to the farmer:

"Remember that you have been spared. Imagine that you have been born once again, and think of the choices you now can make. The Christian God is One with you. Go into the world and preach the wonders of our lord, and above all, read! Read the scriptures, day and night: not just the prescribed gospels, but search out others. There are many, but you have been denied them. You have been given a second chance. Go and spread the word! Use what you have learned. Seek out the high places now and think, and when you are ready, come back to me."

He was to join me later. Not just him but others: women as well as men. As my reputation grew, many were to come to listen, to learn.

As you will see.

*   *   *   *

Much to my surprise after Elpidius' description of him as a mild mannered man, Instantius proved to be like a breath of fresh air: fragrant with new insights, vital, enthusiastic, more outspoken than I had expected. I wished that he and I had met before. But, despite his office, and his conviction, it was clear he was no leader. He was young, and like myself, had come from a wealthy family. This I knew, but it was irrelevant in the present context. Salvianus I warmed to immediately, though it was clear to me that his life was not to be long; though now, I cannot say why this struck me at the time.

I showed them the Codex, and left them to their privacy.

*   *   *   *

Later, over a light supper: leek soup and good fresh goat's cheese from our herds, we discussed what we had been given.

"Elpidius knew you before," said Instantius to me, "he has told us of your great standing in Rome ..."

"Ah, but we ought not to boast of what we once were," I said, gently. "Times have changed, and I no longer seek the riches of power, for they have proved faithless."

"Ah, yes, your wife ..." said Salvianus, but he had the discretion to leave the rest unsaid.

"My friends, we have in our possession something that the Bishops of the Roman church would prefer we did not. Oh yes, I know that in name you belong to that fraternity, but by being here alone, you have proved that you are not of this persuasion ... or do you come to arrest me?"

Both looked uncomfortable.

"I jest! Of course, I jest. My friends forgive me. But if we are to wage against these men, we will need to be armed with the truth. Tell me what you think about what you have read."

There followed a discussion such as I have never experienced in my life.

*"As I see it, this is not an issue of what is true and what is not. This is about power,"
Salvianus said, and Instantius nodded. "The Church in Rome have decided what we
are to learn—and in our case what we are to disseminate ... we may hold other
thoughts in private, but we are not to deviate from what we have been told we may
reveal to others. The Council in Nicea—50 years ago now—took certain writings and
collected them, but many others were cast aside, considered ... shall we say "inappro-
priate" ... but these were only those which disagreed with what kept the balance of
power in Roman hands. This book alone ..." he held up the Codex with reverent
hands, "which has been rejected as heretical ...? But how can that be? We have, to put
it simply ..."*

*"Simplicity is far from the aim of these so-called Christians!" put in Instantius, and I
had to agree. "Yes, because these teachings, these rejected ones, can put truth into the
hands of all men ..."*

*"And women," I added. Amantia had just joined our discussion as I had invited her
to.*

*"Yes, why not," Salvianus continued. "Our lord was accompanied by women, through
his ministry and until the end ..."*

*"Mary Magdalene may have been the first to see Jesus after he came back to life!"
Instantius interrupted. "That would make her the first apostle, not Peter. And where
does it mention her, except in menial and less than flattering terms?"*

*"Let me finish for you, Salvianus, if I may," I said. While I was in agreement, I was
becoming impatient with the trajectory our discussion was taking. "As I see it, one of
the first things we have learned is this: we can learn who we are, where we have been
cast out, what we have become, where we are bound, what we have become purified of
(if we allow ourselves), and what life and resurrection are all about. The answers to
all these questions are not only within our grasp, but within our power, in this life to
know, by examining ourselves and our relationship to God. The Church, as it insists it
is today, will tell us that the answers to all of these things will come through reading
the scriptures—that is, those currently available to us—and later seeking redemption
through its deacons, priests, and bishops. They have cut us off completely from personal*

communion with God, as though we are not worthy, or capable, of framing the questions with reverence and personal insight, and certainly not deserving in our present state of sinfulness, of receiving the answers ..."

I looked around for interjections but there were none:

"This book tells us to drink from Christ's mouth. Those who can do this in openness will: 'become as I am'. Of course the Bishops will not allow us to think this way! If we can do this we will become as Jesus is: 'I myself shall become you, and the things that are hidden will become revealed to you'."

"No need for intermediaries," added Salvianus. "Do you think that the people are ready for that?"

"Perhaps not," I answered, "but at least the choice is there! And what do they call that 'choice'? 'Heresy!'" Again, I looked at the two of them. There was no reaction but I sensed that both had become uncomfortable.

"Does that word fill us with fear? If it does not, it should!" Look at the words of Irenaus on the subject of the Gnostics. What does he say 'Every day each one of them generates something new ... according to his ability; for no-one is deemed perfect, if he does not develop some mighty fiction.' Fiction, my friends! Interpretation and personal revelation is deemed fiction. And such thinking percolates through the statutes of the Roman church today. Anyone who considers interpretation according to his or her own beliefs is accused as a Gnostic, or Pelagian, or a Manichee, and therefore a Heretic: a threat to the power of the Roman hierarchy. Yet 'Hairesis'—a word from the Greeks, from whom we as Romans have borrowed much—means nothing more than 'Choice'. We, as Christians, have been denied choice! Does anyone have the right to deny us that?"

I stopped, wondering if I had gone too far. These were, after all, Bishops, my guests, regardless of their thinking and their reasons for being here. I was but a layman. But again, I met with no interjection. And so I continued, emboldened now:

"Look at what we have been told: that Jesus died on the 23rd day of March and that he came back to life, bodily, on the 25th day. Yet these days coincide directly with the death and resurrection of the pagan god, Attis, and the Equinox. A coincidence? That at Pentecost, the followers of Jesus were reported as speaking in tongues, when in Greek

temples, the Pagan goddesses were also said to have spoken according to each person in his own language, at the same time of the year. That Jesus and his followers were said to have taken a ritual meal in which they partook of bread and wine and that this today, symbolically, is an essential part of the Eucharist service. It is not spoken, though many know it, that an inscription to the soldiers' god Mithras reads: 'He who will not eat of my body and drink of my blood, so that he will be made one with me and me with him, the same shall not know salvation' *but that in the Gospel of John we read Jesus' words:* 'Except that you eat the flesh of the Son of man and drink his blood, you shall have no life in you. Whoever eats my flesh and drinks my blood will have eternal life; and I will raise him up at the last day.' *Does this not sound familiar to the simplest soldier of the Empire, who reveres a shrine to Mithras? How easy to switch allegiance because the Emperor commands it? There are more: The scriptures say that Jesus was crucified between two thieves. One went to heaven and the other to hell. Yet in the mysteries of Mithras, a common image showed him between two torchbearers, one on either side. One held a torch pointed upwards, the other downwards, and this symbolized ascent to heaven and the other descent to hell."*

"I have read also, though I gave little thought to it," said Instantius, "that in the Taurobolium, *the initiate stood beneath a platform where a bull was slaughtered and the blood flowed down covering him. Afterwards, he was considered to have become 'born again'. But the poor people could only, after immense expenditure on their part, afford a sheep, and so they were said to have been washed in the 'blood of the lamb'. This practice was absorbed by the Christians who interpreted in a symbol."*

"Mithras and his cult have always held a special fondness in the heart of the Roman soldiers," added Salvianus, "and both the followers of Mithras and Christians too celebrate a ritual called the Missa, *involving bread, and both have seven sacraments. I have known it, but it is the first time I have spoken it aloud. It is easy to see how Constantius the Emperor could have persuaded the followers of the soldier's god."*

All paused for a moment to consider the weight of what had been uttered.

Amantia remained silent, as was her custom. But I knew she was listening.

"Perhaps it is time to talk of Hydatius, the Bishop of Augusta Emerita, which is one of the reasons we have come," said Instantius.

CHAPTER IX

▼

I awoke refreshed, perhaps more than I had done in many a year. Having shared some of my concerns—no, I am too mild in my speech—some of my outrage with these men consecrated and supposedly devoted to Jesus' words, I knew that my mission—as such I was beginning to see it—would not be alone. If these men had their doubts, there would be others too: men and women who wished to take up Christ's message but too intimidated to challenge the mighty power of the decisions of the Roman church.

Despite the youth of the day, I found both were up before me. Salvianus was outside the gate, seemingly in communion with the wolfhound. Instantius was in discussion with Amantia and both became quiet when they saw me. My daughter made her retreat to the kitchens.

"You slept well, I trust?" I asked.

"Indeed," said Instantius, "there is a peace in your house, Priscillian, that I do not often encounter. Ah, here comes Salvianus ...

"Good morning," the elder bishop bid us. "The day is fresh, and the company so far has been enchanting." Cerberus accompanied him and settled himself comfortably at his feet. Had I been another man, I might have felt betrayed.

Amantia appeared with a tray of food to break our fast.

"Please, daughter, stay. Our talk includes you as well," I said, as she made to withdraw.

"This bishop, Hydatius, of Emerita," I said, continuing on where the night's discussion had left off, "he is powerful and wordly, I have heard."

"Both, and less than spiritual," said Instantius. "He wields the Sacred Scriptures like a club over the people of Emerita, and there is no platform for those who would speak against him. It is not as we would wish for one of our cloth."

"Perhaps I may prevail upon you to speak more of him," I asked.

And as we ate, the story which concerned them both began to unfold.

"You may recall," Salvianus began, "that in 306, after the persecutions of the Christians instigated by the butcher Diocletian ended, nineteen bishops attended the council of Elviria. All of the five provinces were represented including one bishop from Galicia ... whose name escapes me at the present moment."

"It is of no matter," I said, "please, continue."

"Thank you. Their main concern was paganism. The bishops declared that no member of the church who worshipped an idol could be admitted to communion, even at the end of his life. A number of those assembled disagreed with this, but most agreed that this was a difficult issue since all Roman civil functions had, to that point, been concerned with religious life. A concern of theirs was whether or not Christians should be allowed to marry pagans, Jews, or heretics."

"Only a few years later, the council of Arles excommunicated a Christian woman who had married a pagan," put in Instantius.

"Yes, but at the time there were three problems which concerned them most of all and those concerned the wealthy members of the church. Anyone, for example, who permitted his clothes or ornaments to be used in pagan celebrations or games was to be excommunicated from the church. The council advised all wealthy Christians to have pagan idols removed from their households; but the power of the old religion was so strong that they allowed the owner of slaves to continue to have these idols in their

houses, if their removal might arouse his slaves to violence. He was instructed, however, not to do or say anything which might indicate an approval of such idolatry."

I considered our small kitchen shrine, but refrained from comment.

"Two of the canons which were issued as a result of this Synod were concerned with the conduct of Christians at cemeteries. The bishops forbade women to spend the night there with their dead because, they said, the pretext of prayer was used for crimes, secretly committed."

"Crimes against the church?"

"Just so. They were also forbidden the use of lighted candles during the day at the tombs of the deceased for they said that the spirits of the dead were not to be disturbed."

"The placing of candles in this way were also vestiges of pagan practices," Salvianus reminded me.

"Forgive me, brothers," I said, "but what has this to do with Bishop Hydatius? Paganism at that time was still the official religion."

Salvianus looked puzzled for a time, as though gathering his former thoughts together.

"Yes, yes. At that time, as, in actuality we see today, many of the clergy showed too keen an inclination to engage in commerce—bishops no less than priests and deacons. They decreed that clerics who were married before their ordination were to live with their wives as they would with their sisters, under pain of deposition. Although, not surprisingly, opinion on this was divided."

"Ah yes, I am beginning to see. Which, no doubt, brings us to the good bishop under discussion?"

"Indeed," Instantius said. "Many now agree with Bishop Siricius, who is likely to become the next Pope, that the church has become too lax in turning a blind eye to clergy who have begotten children—and we are not just talking about the occasional bastard—but legitimate offspring of their due and lawful wives, the defence of which, they appeal to scripture. Siricius claims that all clergy in major orders must be conti-

nent from the day of their ordination, that they may be pure for the offering of the mass. And it not just, as has been, enough to refrain from sexual intercourse on the day they are to perform the Eucharist."

"Conjugal acts are unsuitable for one who officiates in the role of Bishop," Salvianus said with conviction.

"Hydatius not only cohabitates with his wife, but has secretly produced, an infant, or two, or three if you listen to the gossip, and it is rife. The people of Emerita are scandalized. And it is more serious than that. A number of the clergy have withdrawn from communion with Hydatius. Charges have been handed in to both our churches, and those making the charges say they will not resume communion unless he is cleared of the charge."

"Which seems unlikely?" I said.

Nothing was forthcoming. It was a question from a former rhetorician. But I was compelled to ask the next, and nervous in the asking:

"Why then do you come to me?"

"Is it not obvious?" asked Instantius, his frustration barely suppressed. "Especially now that I see this Gospel of yours. This man is feathering his nest as a powerful force of the church, meanwhile continuing to behave as though he had no respect for the holy vows he has taken, nor the people he has taken them for. If we are to be a beacon for our flocks, surely we must lead by example. Not only do we come to you for advice—as Elpidius suggests we should—but also to ask you to consider replacing Hydatius in his office."

My friends, I have to say that I was more astonished at his words than even I was at reading Agape's secret book.

"But I am a layman, Instantius! It is not for me to assume such a position."

"All of us were laymen before our ordination, Priscillian!" the elder of the two admonished me. "No-one is born bishop. And that notwithstanding, knowing of your reputation as a good man—one who lives by Christian principles …" I was about to speak but Salvianus waived me down … "with persuasive power: a person with position but

living in relative humility, and especially now that we come to meet you and speak with you in person … We do ask you to consider our petition," Salvianus held my astonished gaze with rigid certainty. In another life, I might have been flattered. Now, I felt, upwards of all else, afraid.

I glanced at Amantia who was biting at her nails. I perceived the slightest shake of her head.

For one of the few times in my life, I did not know what to say.

✳   ✳   ✳   ✳

Amantia left us then. Perhaps she had the same sense of foreboding that I felt. The fire had burned down to red hot embers; even Cerberus had found the heat too torpid, and disturbing himself from in front of it had padded like a dead thing into the kitchen in search of morsels. The atmosphere seemed equally unmoving, glowing with potential like the fire; waiting only for me to put on another log—or to speak.

Finally, I said:

"Naturally, I shall consider, seriously and in private, what you have asked of me. This Work that I have been given: we have no reason to believe that it is not the final words of Our Lord, or certainly, some of the most final and perhaps most important, and very little of it is available for Christians to know. I feel that I have been given both a great gift and a great burden receiving these words, and they have given me much to dwell on.
I paused. They were waiting for more than this.

"In the meantime, I would ask you to do this: go to Symposius of Astorga. He knows Bishop Hydatius, and I think does not think well of him. Go then to Bishop Hyginus of Corduba. He is orthodox in his approaches but does not care to hear the name of Jesus trifled with. They are men of your orders, and good men. Have speech with them, and then send me word." I stood up, wishing more than I have ever done in my life to isolate myself from men and their world.

Instantius and Salvianus exchanged meaningful looks. It was obvious to them that no further speech would move me to action until they had done as they said.

"We will do as you suggest," Instantius said finally and with reluctance. "And then we will go to Emerita to see Hydatius and speak with him ourselves."

"That may not be a wise move, my friends. I doubt you will be the first to try, and he has powerful 'friends'. Have care." I warned.

"Be that as it may," said Instantius, "it cannot continue as it is." And both rose to take their leave.

As I bid them farewell,—sadly, for in many ways for I had enjoyed our discourse, at least before it involved me—Amantia appeared with travel packages for them both. She knew me well.

"May God bid you good speed, and a sympathetic reception," she said.

And then they were gone.

✳   ✳   ✳   ✳

We have, or at least we had, a small property in the mountains, not far from the mines near the Iron Bridge. When I was a boy, my father would take me hunting there, and he would tell me of his own boyhood, and as he grew to manhood, how his own father had taught him of the old gods. It is surrounded by pastures, and although cold at almost any time of the year, it is the place where I most feel at peace. As the days slipped by, and I realized that I could not think while surrounded by daily doings, I decided that I would go there for a few days to reflect on the visits of the month past, of the charge that had just been laid upon me, and most specifically, of the message in the secret gospel, which I took with me. I had meant to go alone, and after leaving a message for my daughter telling her not to worry, slipped out at sunrise. I made ready my horse: my beautiful silver grey stallion in whom I had perhaps taken too much pride for no-one could ride him but me.

I suppose I shouldn't have been surprised that I was accompanied by my shadow.

"Very well, Cerberus, you may come. In truth I will likely become glad of the company. But you must promise me that you will not say too much."

*   *   *   *

The air was keen in the mountains. There was snow still upon the peaks and I knew from experience that the blossoms in the valleys would be gone, and leaves green and verdant would replace them before I returned, and long before the snow melted. I saw few upon my travels. No more than a shepherd or two who looked upon my hound with concern. It was a comfort to see the old stone house again. I need not tell you that it was damp, and the fire needed much persuasion, and a prayer or two to the old gods, before it was to light, but once the wood began to burn, the place with its old stone walls became such a home that I wondered why I had chosen to live in the city and laughed to see myself as such a ready hermit. I had brought a few provisions—dry stuff for the most part, and set about preparing myself a meal. I knew I would not want for drink as the spring which chattered beside the house was more than willing to donate a little water for a weary traveler. Weary in more than bones.

I fought off an immediate need for sleep. Cerberus was off chasing rabbits (many were there for his entertainment) but although I had slept but little the night before, or any night since the bishops' departure, I immediately pulled the book out of my saddle pack and began to read once again.

The Words were even more refreshing than the water had been, or sleep could ever be. I knew that I was not alone.

*   *   *   *

I will not trouble you too much with what I considered over those five days. By the time you read this, perhaps you will have had time to consider such questions for yourself. Most of all, I considered the ideas both the codex and the bishops had presented me with: what is man if not a body and a spirit? If God is all good and all powerful, then why does evil exist in the world? What is the hold of sexual pleasure over us that we produce more of our kind, only to see them suffer the same misfortunes? What of the role of women: are they not entitled to participate in the life of the Spirit in the same way as men? Should we partake of animal flesh in our daily meals, and should we allow wine to make us forget who and what we are? What is Heaven and Hell if it is not to be found every day and in the world around us? Who and What died on the cross for our shortcomings, and what are we to make of such a sacrifice? And finally, and the question which tormented me most: where is this place of redemption which Jesus promised: where is this Light that I might seek it out?

I knew it was not in the established Roman church, nor was it in the words of the Jews, whose God frightened me with his lack of kindness; nor in those of the pagans, though they had more to offer than I had formerly considered, even when it was the religion I professed. What, then did nature have to teach me about my Being? The church was noticeably silent on this, but did not Jesus advise us to consider the lilies of the field …? Here in my mountain solitude I felt far more holy than when I entered a church—heretic thoughts! Oh yes, Priscillian. They will take your words and corrupt them with their fear. There is a reason they are afraid of the solitary places where they are humbled in the face of true power. For what you are thinking, you will be called "Manichee", and they will see no difference. How should I overcome this blindness the religion of my dear Cecilia inflicts upon me? And what about the love between a man and a woman?

I looked to the crystal sky. Too many questions, my dear wife. And why are you not able to send me answers! If you are in heaven now, surely you must know the truth. Help your poor husband know which way to turn.

A rustle in the underbrush, a galloping monster from the abyss, a sniffling snout, and a rabbit at my feet.
I laughed. "Thank you, my best friend, you are truly a pagan! But now I am Priscillian. And this time I will not take your gifts! Enjoy it and be glad you are not human."

And I went inside to prepare for myself my beans and carrots.

✻   ✻   ✻   ✻

As I told you, all of this was two years ago. Elpidius came back to me and told me that before she had left for the holy lands, Agape had gathered together a following, mostly women, to whom she promised to write. The miller's agent sought me again as I had enjoined him to. Gradually they came to me, my 'followers', (I blush to use those words even now that they number in the thousands and are, like me willing to die for their faith). We met first of all in my mountain retreat; later in the homes of others in the hilltops and outside of city walls. We rejoiced in each others' company. Ate sacred meals. Danced in bare feet upon the hilltops for the sheer joy of being alive and in the

Truth. I did not question that it was right, and even now, that I am to die for it, I do not wish it had not been so, for it has brought joy, and even love back to me. I am alive, and no-one can take that life from me. That, now, is my power.

But there is much more in the telling, and I hope that you will read on, for the dawn is not yet. And Priscillian of Avila is still living to tell the tale.

PART II

"Every day, men are straying away from the church,
and going back to God"

*   *   *   *

Lenny Bruce

CHAPTER   10

▼

So, that's that, **thought Miranda.** Not only have I worried myself silly about Kieran and his so-called disappearance over the last few days, but I am, willingly or as a slave, carrying his manuscript closer and closer towards Compostela, while he's holed up, God knows where? And why don't I say, "Screw You" and ditch it?

That of course was the question, because she didn't, and she wouldn't: and even though she had only read a small part of the new pages, she felt it was some-how—What? A privilege to be carrying them?

"That's ridiculous!" she said, arguing with herself. "If anyone is being used, you are. And why? Because he had nice eyes? Because he seemed to be carrying some sort of burden? Because I find lame dogs worthy of my love and attention? Because now **he's** sitting comfy in some bloody hotel lounge with his bloody Greek dictionary, while **I** am transporting his book to ... who knows where? If he thinks I am taking this lot to Santiago he has another think coming!" Yet despite her bravado, Miranda did want to know what would happen next. And she did want to know why Kieran had not joined them in Puente la Reina as he had said he would. And anyway: she hated mysteries.

But, he was cute in a sort of ...

No, don't go there! You've just freed yourself of someone else's burdens. You're here to think of your own ...

She missed Felix. She wouldn't have admitted this to anyone else. He was damned annoying, but his lightness of spirit had kept her going and now that he was not with her, she sensed it gone. Kieran had been her spiritual conscience; but Felix had kept her grounded, and laughing at herself and what they were doing, and now that he was gone, her walk seemed, somehow, heavy; heavier than before.

On the other side of the bridge she located the second refugio. The hospitalero and one other were busy cleaning and didn't look too well on the idea of an early pilgrim. However, when she explained that she only wanted to look at the *Libro de Peregrinos,* they left her to it. There was no sign of Kieran–she had really hoped that the mystery would end there, but now that she had the envelope didn't really expect it.

There was, however, one D. Guzmann, Valencia. There was something written after it, but Miranda couldn't decipher it. It looked like it had been written in haste.

Maybe he can give me some answer? she thought, as she hoisted up her heavy pack and walked on–alone for the first time in over a week.

There were many pilgrims on the route now. Some were alone, looking like they walked and talked with God only; some were in groups of people all of whom shared the same jokes, or the same language. Either way, she felt she didn't belong. She couldn't find her place at all. And then what occurred to her was that that had never been the point: "Belonging". She had expected to do this alone, but now she was bothered that she **was** alone, and she didn't know if she should make some attempt to accept that (much more difficult than it may seem), or, if she should try harder to overcome her base nature and try to fit in with a group.

She realized that it would only take a few words: "May I join you?", in any language, and everything would change. We often don't stop to think of how a few words, an inconvenient or difficult, or even embarrassing discourse, or disclosure, can change our direction entirely. A small chance taken. Existentially, and that was her specialty after all, just one person who is receptive to you at that moment, can change your life forever, if you follow up. Invite you to possibilities you might never have considered. Simple? Yes? Frightening? Even more so. The answer: Yes or No, can change a life. Miranda knew this, and she wasn't ready for it. Better, security in obscurity.

Today, she had only the past week to consider, for she walked with no-one now and she was more or less happy that way.

Or was she?

In actuality, Miranda preferred that no-one asked the question.

She walked to Estrella: The Star of the Camino. It should have been beautiful. It was not. To begin with, once she woke in Puente, she realized that everyone else had gone and she cursed herself once again for a late riser. It seemed without someone prodding her in her ribs at some God-awful early hour, she could not get out early enough. None of the Europeans seemed to have this problem. Was this a jet lag thing? Surely not after all this time. But the other thing on this day's walking was that she somehow had missed the path. The lorry drivers here didn't seem to care whether she was a pilgrim or not since she, presumably, wasn't even supposed to be there on that major highway: Pilgrims were hidden each according to his or her own way, but nothing to do with the necessary routes of commerce: they followed the arrows she had somehow missed that day. Perhaps it was meek formation, but at least it kept them off the main roads, which after all, had probably been the original path. It often meant extensive detours from the most direct way. But pilgrims, by and large were purists: they followed where the arrows and their guidebooks told them to go, regardless of short cuts. At one point, realizing that she had strayed a long way from the Camino, and feeling bereft, she had stuck her thumb out. Car after car had passed as it she didn't exist. Miranda saw this as a punishment for her weakness, and that didn't help boost her spirits when she arrived in Estrella (sounds very pretty, she said to her guidebook): now, where's the *refugio*, and showers, and hopefully oblivion before I consider tomorrow.

For some time, Miranda had been writing random thoughts in her diary. Almost all pilgrims did this: for most it was a travelogue—only of interest afterwards to the one who had written it. Miranda realized that early on, and because of this had written little. Tonight however, on finally reaching Estrella—her first stretch alone since she had met up with Kieran in Canfranc, today, she wrote in self pity—something she hadn't felt for many days:

The backs of my legs hurt. They've put me in front of the showers, on the floor, because there's no room. There are tribes of Brazilians in the kitchen tonight, and no-way to enter in. Perhaps if I spoke their language ...? But no. What I have seen of them says that they would admit me, language or no. So who's to blame? Me obviously. I have a mattress on the floor by the toilets. I complained at first. Like a guest in a luxury hotel. And where did it get me? It's me; it's me! I can't blame anyone else. What is it about us which builds up layers of defensiveness like skins on an onion? Is this just a Canadian thing: we're so used to enduring the cold for so long? I don't know. Maybe I will never know. Maybe I am a fool for just being here?

And that night, Miranda went to sleep, climbed over by other pilgrims bound for the toilets, and she didn't see her place there. In fact, she looked for a way out. She forgot the manuscript in her backpack. She forgot her former companions. She forgot her reasons—tenuous as they may have been—for coming so far. In short, she tried to find reasons for going home. And tried even harder, not to.

This was what haunted her as she began to dream, and even her dreams left her no peace.

The next day took her past a slaughterhouse. Though no vegetarian, it left her feeling uncomfortable. She found herself walking alongside a good-looking man from Madrid. His name, she gathered, was Jose, but there was little conversation, and he walked faster than she, and soon he was well ahead. And a good thing, she told herself. I have no time for impure thoughts. At the *Monasterio de Irache,* she took a walk around the cloisters, and as she exited found a pilgrim landmark: the *Fuente del Vino*: a fountain, and wine, from a spigot. Like the others she filled her bottle with the cheap *vino*, but somehow, looking around, it was the cats she noticed more. She opened and left them her lunchtime can of tuna. After that there were oak woods, and a tunnel. She remembered a hymn from when she had been a teen. It was the words of John Bunyan:

> *"He who would true valor see,*
> *Let him come hither,*
> *One thing will constant be,*
> *Come wind or weather.*
> *There's no discouragement*
> *Shall make him once relent.*

> *His first avowed intent …*
> *To be a Pilgrim.*"

She sang it aloud to re-enforce herself in the recesses of the tunnel; an unplaceable smell of honey assaulted her nostrils, and she felt an immediate strength return to her:

She was not alone, after all.

She was connected across the ages to all those who had crossed this path before her.

She had to remember this moment.

But still she had traveled very few kilometers before the need for solitude and introspection claimed her, against her wishes, once again.

In Villafranca la Mayor, only a few kilometers on her way, the promise of coffee and respite made her consider whether or not she wanted to go further that day.

"Here," a small gospel of St. John was thrust under her nose, "what do you take in your coffee?"

And so she met Francis.

He didn't seem to need to know where she had come from that she needed this time. It was enough that he did. He showed her to a small room on the second floor of the private *refugio*. There were two single beds, both made up with sheets and eiderdowns. It seemed like heaven sent. Francis left her to it. "We eat at 7:00," he said. "I hope you will feel like joining us."

At first, Miranda tried to sleep. But she resisted it. Finally, she sat propped up by pillows, and read the Gospel she had been given. It opened up a lot of questions, especially in light of the pages of Kieran's translations that she carried with her.

"I am not here for deep theology," she thought, fighting off the questions, and eventually her feelings of *malaise* overtook her.

It was about 5:30 when Francis' voice woke her: "Miranda, I have a roommate for you!"

In honesty, it was the last thing she wanted. She fought the intrusion. But she suddenly found the room overwhelmed with such a presence that she awoke from her hazy dreams. Later she recalled of this first meeting, that it felt like the sun had just come out from behind the clouds. But she was too half asleep to notice it at the time.

"Hi," she said lamely. "I'm Miranda."

The newcomer had a mop of dark wild hair, and striking turquoise eyes. She threw back the covers on the neatly made bed and emptied her sleeping bag onto it in a disheveled pile. "I can't wait for a good bath," she said throwing the pillow on the floor. "Have you seen it? Not too many of those on this path, I think." And off she went.

Fifteen minutes later, she returned: "Miranda! They have hairspray!" and so the conversation began, not to stop for another 5 weeks.

"Sorry, I'm Alexandra. I should have introduced myself." Miranda tried to place the source.

"From …?

"Germany. But they say I speak English with a French accent." Alexandra continued to turf things out of her backpack. One thing which landed on her sleeping bag was a large bottle of *Gio* perfume.

"Hey! That's my perfume," said Miranda, and produced an identical bottle.

"Ah," said Alexandra sagely, "so we are pilgrims second, but we are women first!"

On much lesser things have friendships been forged.

*   *   *   *

Late that night, after an excellent dinner, she found herself alone with Francis. They were sitting outside admiring the softness and quiet of the warm summer night. Neither was able to sleep:

"I read your book today, and underlined it," she started. "One thing spoke to me. All my life I have been looking for a place to belong, but I have never found my way in the Gospels. They left too many questions open: too many contradictions. I've found more of myself in Buddhism, or Taoism. The life of Gandhi has always made more sense to me than the life of Jesus. But today I read that there were "many mansions" in the Lord's house. Where does that leave people who live a good life but are not Christians?"

"Christ accepts all those who come to him," Francis said, simply. She had noticed that after dinner he had withdrawn with a select few who seemed to have taken some kind of discussion—communion—with him. His response didn't really answer her question and she said so:

"This Gospel says 'No-one comes to the Father but by me'. But surely that is discriminatory? What about the many Moslems, Buddhists, Jews, Atheists even, who live a good life. Are they to be barred from God's presence?" It didn't make sense.

"But I am not a member of a different religion or a different race, said Francis, matter-of-factly. "To accept their religion means being a part of their culture, from birth; how can I do this? This is my creed, and Jesus is my Savior. It is only Jesus that I have known personally, so how can I answer your questions? It is a matter of faith."

He began to tell her that he had once been an important man in the world of commerce, and she could believe him. He had that look. He was tall, 40's, with a crest of dark graying hair, and the chiseled jaw of a Scandinavian, or a Dutchman, or German. It had taken the death of his wife, too early, and too tragically, to make him challenge his faith. Somehow, it had led him here, though he admitted he had never walked the Camino himself.

"Someday," he had said.

His personal revelations made her admit to an earlier experience of her own:

"When I was in my teens," she said, "I joined a girl's religious group. I was given a verse to memorize. It was Revelations 3 verse 20: 'If you stand at the door and knock, I will hear you …' or something like that. I am still waiting." and then she paused.

"What would you do if you were me?"

"I would get down on my knees," Francis said, and he sounded as if this was the definitive answer. "Just remember, the handle is on the inside."

"Maybe I'll try that, "said Miranda, before she joined all the others in sleep.

*   *   *   *

The next day, after breakfast, she and Alexandra were on their way. They walked to one village where there was a fountain and Miranda thought she had never tasted better water. There was a *refugio* also, but Alexandra wanted to see beyond the next corner, and despite her weariness, Miranda went along with her new friend's enthusiasm.

Alexandra, it transpired, had walked from Le Puy in France, and had had many adventures before an injury to her knee had sent her back to Germany:

"The whole time I was away, all I could think about was getting back," she said. "It's not fully healed but … I can manage." To prove it, she showed Miranda a way of getting down hills by crouching—kind of walking into the pain.

"It works!" Alexandra said. "Try it!"

And Miranda did, feeling self-conscious, though afterwards she never had problems with her joints as many others did.

They reached Torres del Rio. Francis had told them of a new *refugio* there. It was not in their guidebook, and certainly, with the number of pilgrims increasing, it was clear that there needed to be more places for them to spend a night, but this one proved disappointing.

"All we need is somewhere to have a shower," Alexandra pleaded with the *hospitalero* who held firm. It was to no avail. They were sent to the church *portico*.

As it turned out, this as the first opportunity Miranda had to see pilgrim ingenuity and *camaraderie* at work. A communal meal was gathered. Someone had the good idea of blocking the drain of the *fuente* with stones, and everyone helped everyone else to have at least a ritual bathe, and even more, a shampooing of hair. There was an attitude of Pagan-ness about it, and the feeling transcribed into an evening of perhaps the kind of looseness that the Mediaeval pilgrims might have enjoyed.

Later, there was a feast that she would never forget, in which everyone participated. Communal wine flowed. Candles were lit. Some pilgrims paired off with others, and several places outside of the church doors were seen to be less shared than cohabited. Then she remembered a pilgrim adage: *Go a pilgrim and leave a whore.* She couldn't help but surprises a twinge of envy.

Alex had a twinkle in her eye no-one could have ignored.

"Hmm?" said Miranda.

"Ignacio … from Buenos Aires," she said, but she wouldn't comment further.

*   *   *   *

The next day, Miranda had a distinct hangover. From her sleeping bag, she watched an intriguing interchange between Alexandra and one of the members of the Brazilian group whom she had assumed were connected to some kind of religious fraternity. But as she was beginning to understand, appearances could be deceptive on the *Camino*. Or maybe not? As she hoisted her backpack, the troublesome strap broke, but as the day went on she learned to compensate by holding on to the broken strap extra carefully, and, she was assured, there would be someone who could fix it at the next village. And there was.

Its name was Viana. By the time they got there at midday there was already a queue mustered in front of the refuge. Beyond that was Logroño, but no-one in their group seemed eager to get there that night, and later she found out why. The *refugio* in Viana was less than de-luxe, but it had a kitchen, and a good view over what they had passed, and what was to come. Someone had left macaroni and tomatoes, and cheese and yogurt, and Alex set about making a feast for all of them.

"You should make a cookbook," Miranda said: "100 things to do with spaghetti."

"One Hundred and One," she winked.

That night she got little sleep. Not only were there mosquitoes, but one man beside her spent the night sighing and talking to himself. When she gently tried to awake him he turned and murmured:

"*¡Pues, estamos en el Camino!*" and there was no arguing with that.

The next day, Miranda went first to the Post Office and sent her camera home. That at least was one small weight off her back, though she didn't think of leaving off Kieran's manuscript. That she saved herself for Logroño.

With her m*ocilla* fixed, and a lighter frame of heart (I'll see you in Logroño, said Alexandra who always walked slightly faster), she walked on.

It was only a short walk, but along the way she passed at least one young *impresario*. He had several rows of home-made jewelry:

"*Señora.,* buy this and I can buy the books for the school."

She bought an ankle bracelet which she lost almost immediately, but at least felt that she had contributed somewhat to the Spanish education system (more likely *chicle*, said Alex later, but never mind.)

She had hoped that Logroño might have given her more news of Kieran, but it was not to be so. Not only that, but the refugio was full. There was a notice, at least, from her German friend: *Have gone on to Navarette: see you there.* Miranda paused to have a look at the cathedral (closed), and then a tapa and brandy at a bar close by called Picasso's. There she stopped and considered her guidebook: *will I only be able to see these cathedrals by reading about them* she mused? So many churches had been closed to them. ('It wasn't like this in France', Alexandra had told her, with regret.) The music in the bar was a welcome diversion: Ricky Martín singing "Living in New York City". It took her home, but not for long. She realized she had left it too long to walk on to Navarette. How much for a taxi, she asked. Too much. She took the bus.

Now this was the first time that Miranda had "cheated", and the guilt she felt was much more than she had expected. After all, it was only a few kilometers. She was a bit peeved that Alexandra had gone on, but then she had to chastise herself for so easily feeling she had some sort of claim on the German women's friendship. Alexandra had, after all, been walking for weeks. By the time she reached Villafranca, she had walked the same distance as they had yet to walk to Santiago. No wonder the extra distance was nothing to Alex, yet an additional, unexpected burden to Miranda. But remembering the morning before and her feelings of bereftness, she didn't want to go back to being alone now.

There was no one else on the bus, so she asked the driver what to expect:

"Five Star," he said.

It wasn't. It was what she had come to expect. Luckily, Alex had saved her a bunk, but was no-where in sight.

Instead were the usual Frenchwomen with their *Coche de Appoyo* (some already well-fed and snoring), and the ubiquitous Brazilians in the kitchen. The *hospitalero*, it seemed, was an expert in foot massage, but Miranda was too shy to enquire. The Brazilians were cooking things with great garlicky smells, and again, Miranda felt very out of things. She went to have a solitary coffee on the terrace in front and was writing a few somewhat negative comments in her diary, when suddenly Alexandra put her head around the corner:

"Miranda! We have Pacharan! She said, brandishing a chiseled bottle, and, with it proceeding her, barged her way into the kitchen.

"Come, let's drink." she said to no-one in particular, and suddenly Miranda began to experience what a difference being on the inside meant.

"No-one will escape me," Alex said, pouring portions for everyone in the kitchens.

And gradually as the liquor was consumed, the feast grew, like loaves and fishes, to encompass all. Many songs were sung, and later the Brazilians danced her to her bed.

The French ladies were still snoring. But by this time, Miranda couldn't have cared less.

CHAPTER 11

▼

And so the days passed. Hot days, for the most part. They climbed the hill called *Mataburros*. Former pilgrims had dreaded this stretch of the Camino in days long past, for as the name suggested, it had been hard on their pack animals, and many had found themselves on foot, as she was, carrying their possessions unintentionally. The hill, as it turned out, was less of an obstacle than she had been told to expect. Cairns of stone had been placed over the years on both sides of the path by pilgrims; there were literally hundreds of them, and Miranda could see Alexandra, and others: *'Spread out like pearls on a necklace,'* she mused. It looked like a garden with piles of rocks instead of flowers, and she found the whole thing so enchanting that she was at the top before she realized it.

Alexandra had gathered a group of on-lookers. She had brought a home made kite with her and was attempting to launch it "I can do it!" she cried, like a child, and her joy as it sailed into the air was infectious. Miranda watched, and taking her notebook out of her pocket, she wrote:

Alex's Kite

On the brow of a hill in the north part of Spain,
Not a cloud in the sky, and no mention of rain,
She stops on the way and examines the breeze:
"I can do it!" she says, "I can launch it with ease!"

A rush of the wind, and a pull on the rope,
A kite in the air, on a journey of hope.

Alex is struggling with forces up high
As she wrestles to harness her bird in the sky.

With a pull on the strings and a flick of the wrists
As the wind joins the fun, Alexandra persists.
Then she cries out with joy, in her childish delight,
At the spinnaker silk, which is Alex's kite.

It was a simple tribute to determination, and Miranda felt a little silly at its childish rhyme scheme, but Alexandra was delighted.

"Here, you next," she said, handing over the rope bar. It was tricky at first, but as Miranda got the hang of it she began to do daring loops and drops. More daring than she realized, because on one too-confident pass, the kite hit the ground with a thud and Miranda landed flat on her back.

"Youch! I think that's enough of that," she said laughing although she had hit the ground with an unexpected thump and the back of her head was stinging. "The wind went out of my sails!" She got up carefully.

Walking into Najara, they passed a man on a corner who gave them each an apple. "*Bienvenidos Peregrinas,*" he said, with a flourish. "Good people here. Look for the poem."

Shortly afterwards they passed verses written on a wall in Spanish and German:

Polvo, barro, sol y lluvia
es el camino de Santiago
millares de pelegrinos
y mas de un millar de años.

Peregrino, quien te llama?
Que fuerza oculta te atrae?
Ni el camino de las estrellas
ni las grandes catedrales.

No es la bravura Navarra
ni el vino de los Riojanas
ni los mariscos Gallegos
ni los campos Castellanos.

Peregrino, quien te llama
Que fuerza oculta te atrae?
Ni las gentes del camino
ni los costumbres rurales.

Ni es la historia y la cultura
ni el gallo de la Calzada
ni el palacio de Guadí
ni el castillo Ponferrada.

Todo lo veo al pasar
y es un gozo verlo todo
mas la voz que a mi me llama
lo siento mucho mas hondo.

La fuerza que a mi empuja
la fuerza que a mi me atrae
no se explica ni yo
sólo el de arriba lo sabe.
Eugenio Gariibay
Amigos Camino Santiago (Najara)

"It's beautiful!" Miranda said. "I understand some of it too."

Alex was studying the German translation alongside it:

"Dust, mud, sun and rain, is the Way of Saint James; thousands of pilgrims and more than a thousand years. Pilgrim, who calls you? What dark force brings you here? It's not the Way of the Stars, nor the grand cathedrals. Neither is it the courage of Navarra, or the wine of the people of La Rioja. It's not the seafood of Galicia; it's not the countryside of Castilla. Pilgrim, who calls you? What mysterious force attracts you? It is not the people of the way or their rural customs. Nor is it their history and culture. It isn't the cockerel of la Calzada, Gaudi's palace, or the castle in Ponferrada. Everything you see in passing is a joy; and the voice which calls me, makes me feel much deeper. The force which pulls me, attracts me, I cannot explain it. Only he above knows why.

"Something like that. It's better in the original. I'm no poet," she said gravely, and then laughed.

"That's beautiful … That's it, too, isn't it?" Miranda commented, "That's why no-one ever asks: 'Why you? Why do you put yourself through all of this with blisters, and tendonitis, and strained muscles, and sunburn day after day." No-body can explain why; I certainly can't. It's not a religious thing, or even a spiritual thing although I feel that growing every day. If I wanted simply to see the scenery, taste the wine, eat the seafood, I could have booked a package tour, stayed in the Paradors."

Alex said: "And you would have entirely missed the feeling of connection to the Camino we all feel. Take my shell, for example. I feel a closeness to it, a real love for it, and when I see it in cathedrals, or churches, or even on the road signs, I feel: 'That's mine; that's my symbol.'"

"You know that book I am reading—the manuscript? Well when I was first walking with Kieran in the Pyrenees—I told you about Kieran and Felix, didn't I?"

Alex nodded.

"Well, Kieran claims that St. James isn't buried in the cathedral anyway, and that it is a bishop called Priscillian whom the Romans executed for heresy. It's a good story. Do you think if that were widely known that people would stop walking the Camino?"

"That would be a terrible shame, and no, I don't. I'll bet if you asked almost anyone walking or bicycling they would say that it doesn't matter if St. James is there or Mickey Mouse; it wouldn't have stopped them from coming. There are as many reasons for going on this so-called pilgrimage as there are pilgrims. It is as the poem says: some mysterious force brought you here, and me, and everyone. If you just wanted to walk or bike 800 kms, or even more for those who come from France as I did, you could go anywhere couldn't you?"

Miranda was thinking so hard about this that she didn't look where she was going and slid and fell on some loose gravel. When she examined her knee she found she had left a good chunk of it on the ground. Alex immediately poured the last of their water over it.

"That's going to need looking at soon or it'll get infected. Never mind, not far now."

*   *   *   *

The outskirts of Najara were industrial, and many of the factors seemed to have been abandoned, but the center of the town was not unattractive. As they walked into the *refugio* they were immediately struck by a sense of coming home. The decoration had a certain femininity to it, whereas everywhere else they had stayed had been Spartan and utilitarian.

"Hi! I'm Evelyn, here let me help you with that," she took Alexandra's pack, and then noticing Miranda's weepy knee, went in search of the anaesthetic. "There isn't a lot of room left," she said, "just a couple of top bunks upstairs."

Looking around, Miranda saw fruit and almonds on the tables, posters of Galicia on the walls.

"I thought this had a woman's touch," she commented.

Evelyn smiled: "Why not? The pilgrimage should be a joy, not totally a hardship. There's some soup in the kitchen. Help yourselves. Just throw in some more water and herbs and add some more pasta for the next arrivals."

Miranda and Alex climbed up to the loft. It was very cramped. All pilgrim refuges lack space especially when boots and backpacks take up the floorspace, but this one bordered on the claustrophobic. Alex looked around for the Brazilians. She was disappointed.

"I don't understand them," she said, and Miranda intuited that some arrangement had been made unknown to her which they had not kept. Alex looked suddenly sad.
"Come on, let's go out, "she said.

Miranda's guidebook said not to miss the *Cueva de Santa Maria* and it turned out that this cave was a passageway of the church proper. There were many caves in Najara, but this one it seemed had a special story attached to it. They went to investigate. The official guidebook told of the legend: Miranda began to read as they walked:

"It says here that in the year 1004, a young king named Garcia spotted a partridge while out hunting and sent a falcon to bring it down. Both birds disappeared into a cave and the king went in after them. What he found was a statue of the Virgin Mary and Child and at her feet was a vase of lilies which perfumed the air. Beside them were the two birds, wholly at peace with one another. The king was so surprised and overcome at this sight that he knelt down to pray. He saw this as a sign of victory and protection in the imminent campaign of reconquest of Spain and … Alex, this is starting to sound too familiar …"

"Never mind. Keep going, and what?"

"O.K. The next year, the king entered triumphantly into Calahorra, having won it back for the Christians. He decided to build a church in Najara with the cave at its heart and he took the vase of lilies as the symbol of the order of knights he planned to create. He promised to sing the Hail Mary every Saturday …"

"Why Saturday?"

"I don't know; it doesn't say … and chose this site for his burial place."

The statue looked almost dwarfed by its cave surroundings. Mary's face seemed gentle, even a little puzzled, and on her lap was Jesus not as a baby, but as a grown child of perhaps nine or ten. There was a vase of lilies beside them.

"It's peaceful," said Alex, and bent down to kiss the Virgin's feet. Miranda was somehow surprised.

They wandered around the church separately. It was impressive with its Gothic columns and gilt *retablo*. Miranda found a beautiful statue of Christ holding a lamb. She gazed at the face for a long time.

"*Get down on your knees,*" Francis had said.

She tried it. Bending her damaged knee was painful, but the cold stone took some of the pain away.

Nothing happened. Ridiculously, Miranda felt betrayed.

Afterwards they were outside in the cloisters, laying down on the grass. Miranda told Alex what Francis had said. "I tried, Alex, I really tried. I was ready to accept Jesus' message; hell, anybody's message! I want to believe—in something. I am sure there are truths beyond what we see and accept in the modern world today. I'm envious of anyone who has faith. Why can't that come to me? I have been looking for that key since I was in my teens, but even when I think I have found it, nothing changes ..." To her surprise, Miranda was almost in tears.

"That's your problem," said Alex, "always problems with keys! Didn't you tell me that?"

Miranda began to laugh. "Well put! You know me too well after only a couple of days! Come on, enough sanctity for one day. Let's go have a beer!"

*   *   *   *

But later, it was Alex who was restless. "I think I want to sleep by the river," she said.

"And then I wouldn't get a wink worrying about you."

They were back at the *refugio*. Plastic bags were rustling and lights were going out.

"There are too many people here, "Alex said. "Come—let's go on." She cocked her head at Miranda.

"Go where? Alex. It's almost 11 ... we don't even have a flashlight!"

"It's only six kilometers to the next town. There's a moon ... Let's go!"

They bumped their packs past the crowded bunks on the way out.

"*Donde vais?*" said one man whose boots Alex had fallen over.

"We're going to walk under a pilgrim moon and seek whatever adventures may come," said Miranda romantically, and a little giddily.

"*Locas!*" he said and put out the lights.

"You know," said Miranda as they began walking. "He's right. We **are** crazy."

"Yes, but better crazy than normal. Normal is no adventure. Come on, you'll be in your sleeping bag by 1:30."

As they began to walk outside the town and in the velvet darkness, Miranda suddenly said:

"Wait a minute, Alex ... I've just thought of something ... The doors of the refuge won't be open, will they? They'll all be fast asleep!"

Alex kept walking, unperturbed: "I only said 'sleeping bag'. I didn't promise 'refuge'."

Miranda cursed herself for a gullible idiot.

As it turned out, the six kilometers went by as though they were only one. They laughed, and sang songs in German and English, and told ghost stories like two children on a camping trip. And by the time they arrived in Azofra, neither really cared to sleep at all, so where they ended up was immaterial.

As chance would have it, the door to the *refugio* was unlocked and ajar. And despite the usual pilgrim paraphernalia, not a soul was inside.

Two girls came by. They were dressed as witches.

"Wait a minute. Did we miss something, Miranda? When I woke up this morning ..."

"Yesterday morning ..."

"... Either way, it wasn't Halloween!"

Three boys came by in costume.

"Oye, peregrinas. Vamos a la fiesta de disfraces. Ven!"

Alex curled up with laughter. "It's a fancy dress party! No-one is going to get any sleep tonight. Did you bring your dancing shoes?"

Miranda looked at her friend as if she had gone quite mad.

"Come on, leave your pack. We're going to a *Fiesta.*"

*   *   *   *

Miranda woke early the next morning on a small ledge just inside the refugio. Alex was on the floor beside her. No-one was stirring though the sun had long been up. The door was still open. *"That was quite a dream,"* she thought, before she drifted contentedly back to sleep.

CHAPTER 12

▼

Nobody moved much the next day. Actually, no one who had come to the *refugio* the day before, had moved at all. A few pilgrims came by as the morning went on, and unknowing of the goings-on of the night continued without realizing that the somewhat dazed pilgrims they saw gathered around the breakfast table with their bottles of wine had not moved for hours. It was a secret spirit and a common remembrance (or oblivion) which bound them together.

It was probably Maria's wine that did it. Maria was the *hospitalera*, and being the purveyor of homemade Rioja wine, was a natural Santa Maria for weary pilgrims, especially those still hung over from the night before; thus, she naturally brought extra bottles at any request. In the aforementioned entourage must be included one Canadian woman and one German, the former of which had seriously swollen feet on the morning in question. Anyway, the weather was read to be uncertain, and the hour too late to contemplate anything constructive. The company was good. They were an ill-assorted, but happily compliant chosen few. One of them had an infected knee. One couldn't clearly remember a six kilometer walk in the darkness, or what happened after. She also couldn't quite remember which language she spoke.

Each chose to enjoy this unexpected *dia libre* as he or she appreciated it. Miranda spent it in reading—Alex, in furthering her understanding of the opposite sex which involved seeking out bell towers, as will be revealed, but not in depth.

Since the day allowed for, or perhaps begged for is more accurate, more walking, they both felt they should stir themselves. But the weather forbade it, Miranda took the opportunity to peruse the refugio's small library. She came across a book. Perhaps she would not want to disclose the name of the author, but then it will be found later, if you care to look. As she read, she became more and more incensed:

"Listen to this man, Alex. Can you believe it? He thinks that somehow he is experiencing the walk of the Camino, but what does he say as he gets closer to Santiago:

'I did not check the distance, because I knew at the beginning I was going to cheat.' Then he goes on to tell about a *refugio* he arrived at; he says: *'I expected sympathy in having walked for so long in the rain.'* The waiter, apparently ignored him. Then, hang on, let me skip forward a little … he's in Galicia and … here it is: he got to a refuge or a hotel, I am not sure and the waiter said: *'You are lazy,"* and he shook his head. *'Lazy?'* says this writer, *'You don't know the half of it.'* … lots of name droppings and he gets to Santiago de Compostela: he's in front of the Cathedral, and what does he say? *'There were tourists everywhere, including pilgrims, still carrying their staves and rucksacks around the Cathedral as if it were a marketplace.'* Then he goes on to Finisterre, and he find: *'Pilgrims, just as tanned and pleased with themselves as the pilgrims I had seen in Leon, when I started my journey'.* Listen to this! Not one of us would tell his story."

"He hadn't the faintest idea of what he was talking about." said one listener. "No. Because he took the easy way. That's sad," said another.

Alex wanted to see the bell of the church. Earlier she had cornered a conversation with the Minister: "Why are all the churches closed?" she asked. "It wasn't this way in France." Either way, it seemed that although she hadn't received an answer to her satisfaction, she had managed to get the church opened. Miranda followed while Alex went above to wait for the five o'clock bells, with someone who had taken her fancy. There always seemed to be one or two. It must have been those iridescent eyes.

Miranda had loved to sing since she was in her teens. Now given the perfect opportunity and with no-one else around, she stood at the back of the church,

with its old oak pews in the choir and its fold-down seats and at first very tentatively and nervously, she sang the only thing that came to mind:

"Adeste Fideles, laite triumphantes ... "
The acoustics were prefect and the sound was so beautiful that other songs came
tripping over themselves:

"Amazing grace ... "
"And did those feet ... "
"Kyrie eleison ... "
"In excelsis deo ... "

Miranda totally forgot where she was, until she suddenly looked up and there was
Alex, watching her:

"You know," she said to Miranda, "apparently there was a priest a few years ago
who was standing exactly where you are. A stone fell out of the roof and fell upon
his head ..."

"And?" Miranda said.

"Well ... and ... but keep singing ... it's nice."

∗   ∗   ∗   ∗

Later, in the pilgrim diary, Miranda came across something which to this day she
says has changed her way of thinking. It said:

*'At last, we are only creatures of time ... dust ... when I die, I will donate my useful
organs and the rest of me may be cremated—ashes scattered over the Camino, so that
no-one may weep over me, but my essence may be taken, in this way and with the
rains, on the boots of my fellow travelers, once more to Santiago de Compostela.'*

"Yes," said Miranda, quietly and to herself alone, "That is just as I would wish it."

*   *   *   *

The next morning there were thunderstorms early. The angry clouds swirled around the *refugio* and looked deliberately threatening. A few drowned souls came in with hooded ponchos dripping and the incumbents made large mugs of hot chocolate laced with brandy brought the night before by Claus, from Heidelberg, who had walked out of his door a few months back and was now on his way back to Germany. The other pilgrims, regardless of where they had entered the Camino, treated him as a god.

The day alternately cleared and worsened, and Alex and Miranda sat in the doorway with boots and packs ready to leave, or not to leave. In the end, thunderous clouds still kept them indoors. After a while when a few groups had passed through, and none had returned in half an hour, Miranda said:

"Right, listen. If we're going to do this, now is the time."

Alex looked doubtful still. The sky was the color of a recent injury:

"It's still swirling round. I'm not so sure …"

But it was obvious to both of them that if they were to move, the time was now. The rain had more or less stopped, and there had been a steady flow-through of pilgrims for most of the morning.

"Right. *Nos vamos* …" said Alex, and as she put one foot out of the door a left over thunderclap echoed with a great explosion.

"Dear Santiago," said Miranda, to the retreating sound of the thunder, "I would love to make your acquaintance. But please, not today."

For a while, the weather seemed to favor their decision, and then without warning, the sky simply opened and the only source of shelter was a ten-inch ledge from a hayrick. That didn't even keep them dry, and nothing could help their terror, as Thor sent every weapon in his arsenal aimed directly at them:

"Come on … Let's sing," said Miranda, in a terrified whisper.

"Sing what?" said Alex. "I suppose I didn't tell you my feelings about thunder-storms, did I?"

"Come on ... I ... love ... to ... go ... a ... wandering, along ... the ... mountain ...

And her voice was joined with the German descant, first just as tentatively, and then growing louder and louder, until the thunder would have been challenged to overcome them, and until finally the two women were so doubled up with hysteria and abject terror that their tenuous overhang of straw and protection could no longer protect them and both were thoroughly drenched, and felt more alive than perhaps they ever had in their lives.

*   *   *   *

They went back to Azofra.

Alex cuddled up in her sleeping bag as the storm blew itself into oblivion. Had Miranda a teddy bear to hand, she would have stuffed it in with her, but since she didn't she bid Alex to sleep and dream of tranquil passages and good-looking pilgrims..

Miranda knew she wouldn't sleep. Instead she got out Kieran's manuscript, and read.

*   *   *   *

To Our Noble Bishop, Hydatius, Bishop of Augusta Emerita, by the Grace of God, from his Brother in Christ, Hyginus, Bishop of Cordúba, Most Cordial Greetings and May the Grace of God continue to be with you:

I write to my dearest Brother of a visit I received today from two of our calling: Bishops Instantius of Salamanca and Salvianus of Braga. It has filled me with such forebodings that I cannot explain why it should be so. Both are concerned with certain—shall we say, rumors, of certain—deviations—in your diocese, and both of whom mentioned to me the name of one Priscillian of Lugo. This Priscillian, now that I rack my memory, is the same man who has in times past been well-known within circles of

Rome for his erudition, and his place in the Senate: It would seem, that after some period of quietude has now re-entered the public forum as a speaker and proselytizer of our Faith, though I believe him formerly to be of Pagan stock. What has led him to this position, I cannot say as the two were noticeably reticent to speak of it. As that may be, I think that you should be aware that what they say may be of its nature dangerous. Their words reminded me of none less than the proclaimed heresy of the Manichees, of which we have been forewarned.

Perhaps this information is of little notice to you, but, were I in your position, I would be well concerned. It would seem that this Priscillian is in danger of gathering some not insubstantial following in his native Galicia. I was able to gather that this man— not it must be said as one of our Cloth—has received into his being some word which he claims to be the lost words of Our Lord Christ, and that he has received these directly from the East: from one Marcus of Memphis, (with whom you may be cognizant) and via him, transported to our shores through a woman named Agape, and another, whose name is weakly known in the Capital, by the name of Elpidius. It would seem that this lost "scripture"—if that it may be—has certain messages regarding the behavior of the ordained, the holding of the Sabbath as a fast day, and certain other things pertaining to the rite of Baptism, and, although it was barely mentioned, the role of women in our church.

I treated these two bishops as I must: with courtesy and consideration, but I think them dangerous, as I have said. It seemed to me that they were of a mind to visit you in times not long to come. Perhaps in preparation, you might have questions for them more suited than I, who was unprepared.
Again, in most Humility,
Your Servant, Hyginus

*   *   *   *

To our Noble Brother in Christ, Ithacius, Bishop of Ossunoba, in the Province of Lusitania; May the Grace of God, etc.,

My Friend, it has been too long since we were able to sit and talk of such matters as I must write, in comfort. I am sending here a letter I received some time ago by our Brother Bishop, Hyginus, in Cordúba. Its contents will explain to you an occurrence which took place in my church today of which I have certain regrets, but harbor no conscience as to the outcome.

The two bishops mentioned, one Instantius, born wealthy and thereby elected to the Sacred Position we hold, and his companion, Salvianus of Braga, (whom you know) and who ought to have known better, which placed themselves in Our audience today. They accused Us of certain improprieties of which I will spare you the details, and even suggested that if We were not able to act as a guiding force for Our people, then they had the temerity of suggesting someone else who could do as well, or better. The name is of no consequence.

I need not tell you what my populace here in Emerita Augusta, long held as a repository of mature sensitivity and knowledge, had to say at such an imposition!

But the two refused to leave with good grace.

In the end I had no choice but to elect the bodyguards to eject them from the Cathedral.
It is to be regretted that one of them, Salvanius I am led to believe, was somewhat injured in the ensuing scuffle.

As I know you, dear Brother, and as you, I know, hold certain truths of our office to be Inviolable, I am sure I can count upon your support should any of this take greater precedence than it deserves.

I hope to see and speak with you as soon as the roads allow.
Hydatius.

*   *   *   *   **

"He threw us out, Priscillian, not just with his words, but with actions, and the scars on my noble companion bear witness to such barbarous actions!"

I too was scandalized, but somehow what I heard did not surprise me. The world, now, was full of such injustices. I looked around instead, as I thought of what was to come.

The apples were falling from the trees, and the scent of winter was just to be perceived upon the chilled air. It was likely the last time we would dine in the courtyard. Our fare had changed, and we had exchanged our pheasants for the vegetable produce of our gardens. There was unfermented juice, but no wine. No-one seemed to mind, except perhaps my servants in the kitchen, who mumbled and who had difficulty understanding why our animals were now to be husbanded and milked, but not slaughtered. I knew that they went into the taverns to enjoy the flesh they were accustomed to, that is when they could afford it, which was not often. I had made no attempt to convert them though they were loyal, but curious. Herakles tried to follow the ways of his master, but did not always succeed. I knew this but tried to pretend that I did not. Even as it was, they followed the old ways for the most part as though the Romans had never come. Feasts meant pork and lamb when it was available. We had only a few feasts. So I let them have their enjoyment where they might. It was a personal choice, perhaps with little to support it, especially to the unlettered.

In the meantime, Instantius fumed, and was quite clearly was incensed at such behavior from a fellow bishop, and was only quietened by a tisane of camomile from Herakles, with whom he had become—in stages—quite comfortable. Salvianus said nothing. His shock at such treatment was too great. But it was clear that great injury had been done in more than just pride.

I stopped to consider what had been presented to me that afternoon:

"Oh my friends, my most faithful friends," I said at last, and I forbade to say to them now, too late, 'Did I not warn you?'. "I am deeply sorry that you did receive such a reception. But from what I have learned, from what you, as others since, have counseled me, it could have been no other. You came to offer me his place. Surely, he would have seen it in no other fashion—your being there?"

Galla brought salves from my pharmacopia to bring healing to Salvianus, but it was obvious that his spirit and beliefs had suffered more than just physical injury. And anyway, most of the wounds were not to be seen by now.

"And where, then, do we go from this …? I asked, though I believed them to have no answer. The question was more directed at myself.

Instantius said: "We have heard that the matter has been taken up by Ithacius of Ossonuba—a distant outpost, yes, but since he is one of the few in power there, a threat to be taken seriously. This is only the beginning, Priscillian, mark my words. Though we, now, have many followers … and not just in Galicia …"

"That is what they fear ... We shall see," I said. But in my words I noticed a doubt I had not previously considered, or perhaps not as seriously as I should have.

✳   ✳   ✳   ✳

It was only to be expected that a Synod would be decreed and it was. In Saragossa, almost two years later.

I wasn't there. Since I was not, then, in holy orders I need not be. And anyway, I had not been summoned. Neither was Instantius, nor Salvianus. Neither as it turned out, was Hyginus of Cordúba, as his health forbade such a long journey, or maybe his misgivings warned him of the climate he would have to expect. However, my neighbor, Symposius of Astorga, attended, and it is his report I give here, and it is how he came to me:

"There were only twelve Bishops: from the regions of the Aquitaine there were Phoebadius of Agen, Delpinius of Burdigala, also Audentius of Toledo, or was he the Audentius of Marcella, I forget; I, Symposius, as we have come to note, Photinus, Hydatius of Emerita, and Ithacius of Ossonuba: there were others. All had traveled far. But that there were so few in attendance seemed to claim that the issues were of little importance on the whole."

Just so, I thought. However, that Delphinius was present was a warning to me, as he and I were known to each other; I had spent my younger years in his province and had gained somewhat of a following, even then, and, not to his liking. But who explains his younger years and the paths which he took then? Phoebadius was a hard-liner known to me by his insistence on orthodoxy with regard to Arianism. Though we had followers in the Aquitaine, I knew that we were not welcome there.

"They discussed many things with which I have feelings for and feelings against," Symposius, told me. "First, Priscillian, they discussed the role of women and whether or not they had the right to attend bible readings with men to whom they bore no relation, and whether they should remain silent in church, as our blessed St. Paul decreed. They also discussed fasting—as I know you and yours do—in between the days of Christmas, from the 17th of December to the 6th of January. Later they discussed the Eucharist: they esteemed especially dangerous those who took the sacrament but took them away with them".

"I don't understand the problem here," said Salvianus, who was present at our discussion. He seemed somehow old to me now, though I had never thought him so before.

"Well, look at it this way, if you do not immediately consume the bread and wine in the presence, then maybe you do not accept them …? It is the practice of the followers of Mani. Furthermore, they censured those who go into mountain retreats: 'latibula cubiculorum ac montium', *and, although I am at a loss to explain it, they said that anyone walking without sandals or shoes was to be deemed outside of the church …"*

Salvianus and Instantius exchanged confused glances here. Did that mean excommunication, or outside of church control? This hung wordless between them.

"They see Pagan ghosts in every farmer's field! What else, Brother, pray? Your information is more valuable than either I or anyone in your hearing can say here." I wished in many ways I could have been present to dispute the absurdity of these dictates. What had they to do with the scriptures of Jesus?

As if reading my thoughts, Symposius said: "You know, my friends, but I was there but a day only—for me it was quite enough—and only that because I had been called by them on some so-called importance. I hoped to discuss matters of faith, not gossip like little girls."

"But please continue. There must have been some agenda," said Salvianus.

"Indeed. I will try to explain why they met, though their reasons make little sense in the name of our Lord who proselytized only tolerance … where was I? … ah yes, they were clearly concerned about clergy who withdrew to become monks, and also, oh, yes, they were very specific about women who were unmarried taking the veil before the age of 40 …"

"Virgins, you mean," said I.

"Well … yes … I suppose so." answered Symposius who had entered the clerical world very early.

"They were also very particular about anyone who claimed the name "teacher" when unauthorized to do so."

Several glances were exchanged.

"And what was the end result of this meeting of the powerful?" said Instantius, a little cynically: a little too carelessly.

"Well, that was the strangest thing, and only something I learned of as I was about to withdraw. Apparently, at the end of the Synod, they received a message from Damasus, our Vicar of Rome. It said that no decisions were to be definitively declared by this gathering of bishops against anyone who was not in attendance.... so," he looked around ... "none of you could be held guilty of any of the charges unless you were there to defend yourselves. It was most unexpected, but I was glad to hear it, as before the first day was through I was thoroughly sickened by their pomposity."

This will not be the end of the matter, I thought ominously. Ithacius of Ossonuba does not like to be slighted, and he has long arms.

CHAPTER XIII

▼

Yet, despite my fears, those arms appeared to touch us at not at all.

We continued to gather in our conventicles, in the mountains and outside the city walls, in the places of wildness, or at least privacy. And we gather more and more to us every day. Did not St. John say: "The Truth shall set you free"? We continued to elect our leaders on an everyday basis: as the suggestions—and we considered all—arose: women as well as men, and equally so. We continued to search the gospels and other apocryphal sources for truth. We continued to fast on the Lord's Day, and other important times in the Christian calendar; for by doing so we freed ourselves of the world and it of us. We removed our shoes for communion, even as had the Egyptian monks before us. We ate neither flesh nor did we drink wine. We sought our pleasures in the joys of Nature. We welcomed new members into our flocks with ritual baptism: complete emergence in the cold and pagan springs of the north: naked if they wished it; partially clothed if they did not. It seemed to me that any form of ritual must needs change with the time, the place, the disposition of those present, and so we held no hard-and-fast rules. If the Spirit came to us whole, clean, prepared for change, we welcomed it into the true fold it had once—by listening in soundless corridors, to dry rivers—left. We had few mysteries, although some parts of the truth were accepted and absorbed completely by some who came to us, but, by a few of us only. The others, we let alone to study and join us later, or not.

We knew that. Not because we were in any way selective, but because deep truths sometimes may not be understood by all, as our Lord Jesus knew. And perhaps, nor should they be, or what are leaders for? For those "who had ears to hear" the messages *we imparted were indeed profound and mysterious, but the core was simple:* **you are not supposed to be here.** *The world was created by a lesser, vain god, who believed himself to be the creator of Everything. The soul was dragged into the body by curiosity, and being held enslaved and fascinated by what it found was unable to escape. (Did the True God even succumb to this? It is a question I allow myself only while waiting for death: I leave this to later, perhaps more open and enlightened ages to consider.) The goal of the spirit is Release, by purification, by removal from the so-called "pleasures of the flesh".*

Possible for all. No! Of course not. I think in times to come, people will read of the beliefs of those who follow me and hold dear and say: "This makes no sense. How could someone who preaches celibacy possibly have had so many converts?" Or at least I hope that that will be so. Celibacy is not our natural requisite. It and, or, the lack of it creates the most spiritual and necessary questions, and so ...? For without these questions, what I have created makes no sense. Those who are within our understanding, perhaps understand. Those who are not, please, I ask you ... read on.

Just as, in the established church, members of the clergy are being called upon to practice continence, we were likewise to impress this upon those who seriously elected to spread our word of Liberation that sexual continence was to be decided as a personal issue and in familial context. It is not easy to do as Jesus decreed: to give up everything. (And did he even follow this? Again posterity may discourse upon i.) For, the powers of evil know and use to their advantage the power of the pleasures of the flesh—for that it was decreed—and for this reason they have made them pleasurable, enjoyable, and to be sought without conscience. A few moments of inexpressible ecstasy can lead, and often does lead, to the beginnings of new life: as the human species—as is the case of lesser creatures—is often drawn together in the highest times of bodily fertility. And new life is what these powers demand: more grist for the mill of earthly deception.

Am I wrong? Then if so, why do we desire so much to conquer the body of the other? (Make no mistake—women can do this as well as men). And if so, at other times, why do we crave so much for escape in our moments of personal piety, in the bases of our passions and yearnings? Why, if life on earth is so perfect, so fulfilling, would we look to God at all? Surely, if our life here is so desirable it must be Perfect, without evil, without pain, without loss, without Conflict? Without Oppression. Without War?

Yet the God of our Learning relieves these terrors not at all.

Life, can be Joy. But it is in times of sweet and momentous of moments. Short. Those times when we realize our unlimited possibilities. It is not All. We find it in sexual yearning. If we are fortunate, we find it in prayer. Even that does not last, unless we are blind. (And this is what society feeds upon. It makes all of us equal.)

What does the Bible tells us? That it was a woman who brought truth first into this pristine world? No, it neglects this. That we do not read: It begins with Eve: set up by the Archons to perform the first betrayal of her sex. This has given rise to sects which have in their own courts of law, found women as dangerous and thus to be reduced and un-empowered in every way possible. What else does it neglect? That Adam's first wife, Lilith rejected him because he sought to impose himself upon her, when she already knew that in some ways she was superior and wanted equality? She claimed she would not lie beneath him. Unbeknownst to perpetuity? No. And Yes. Are we permitted to know this? No, she dared to challenge him. Whence have gone the goddesses, now? And why would the gods deny us the tree of knowledge? That they are a plurality is plain enough in the Book of Genesis. Wasn't that our Right? It was only after we established our equality that they threw us out of Eden. How dare we ...?
But we have never entirely forgotten it.

No. Our longing for God the Ineffable—"It" without gender, without parts, is our longing to return to who we were as equal spirits, partners in our completion, in the Fullness, before we were dragged—as children are to sweets and pretty lights—into this incarnation once again.

Gnostic? I? Am I a knower? Perhaps. I know not, and for that do not call myself Gnostic, or Manichee, Mandaean, or Pelagian. I have denied before all affiliation, despite the trials they have put me to. But perhaps also, I have reduced all other reasons to dust by the Force of Logic. And that I have learned within this Roman establishment within which I have grown, and which now forces the Limited Way upon its people. We have been told that the god of the Christians exists and He is Three. We have been taught that the god of the Jews is vindictive (and in all honesty it is hard to see him otherwise). Beyond this: we have been told that God is all powerful, all knowing.

Yet, there are hideous realities in our world which defy even God's Omnipresence. We are but fractions, particles in the wind: blown hither and thither by the world's caprices. And why? Because the god we revere in the books they have permitted us is not the true God. Because he is only the creator—satisfied in himself that what he has given us in our fleshly incarnation is Enough, and for these crumbs we must be pre-

pared to sacrifice mind, body, soul, spirit—and Hope, and believe that there is no-one above him whom—they say—knows us better than we know ourselves. The angel, Samael—the Blind One. He leaves us only the dry cast-offs of so-called faith in obedience. The beliefs that others insist we follow. According to their rules.

I deny this, and they kill me for it. Though they have other excuses.

Why does the true God allow this? This is the Mystery. I do not know. Any more than I know why, perhaps, His true son (as we are all) had to die simply because Jesus had an insight into this, and was foolish enough to try to put it into words that ordinary people could understand. And they killed him—as they do me—for what? For an instigator; a troublemaker; one who went against the established Law? Is this familiar to those "who have ears to hear"? Who was responsible?

Many have washed their hands. Christ was crucified and only those who committed crimes against the Romans suffered this terrible fate, though stoning could hardly be a better end. Yet, the Romans, now, after 300 years, have told us that this is all there is: that it was the Jews themselves responsible for our lord's death; and what they tell us we must now believe, or be hunted down in one of their purges against their so-called heresies: One God and so? One Emperor, Constantine, who decreed it thus—on his deathbed and after many atrocities, may I say. And they will kill me for it. And they reduce it to numbers! Four points of the compass—four gospels!

Even Pythagoras knew better.

I am no philosopher. Nor do I claim logic or mathematics as my basis for truth. I am too simple a man for that. I was reared in the Old Ways. Perhaps only Music takes us close to God. I do not know for sure, but I have been told, that a Chinese Sage of old said that Truth was the generation of All Things, but that it was diminished when it was put into Words. I do not know it. But I believe it. Even as I write I feel thus limited. My remaining hours are few. I may say as I wish now. They will be coming soon …

And so to return to our so-called insistence upon celibacy, for much has been made of it. We recognize the love of man for woman, and of she for him. We know of the pleasurable burden such love bestows. And so I suggested, yes, and taught, the old way of avoiding earthly conception—and yes again, I admit that much of such teachings came from me personally. I had learned this from boyhood. Perhaps it is an irony that

*Nature has provided us with such a means. But there are, and have always been known, ways to gain carnal knowledge of another—the mystery: the **beauty** in that; the sustenance—without the inevitability of creating a new earthly incarnation— another life to serve his masters as his parents have served. One to cry out at birth in despair, as his mother and father have cried. More young soldiers for the Emperor's sacrificial mill. That much is earthly life regardless to the manner born. **We can avoid it!***

I have been accused of providing means of aborting life. I, who would not harm so inferior a life as an insect—do I not practice vegetarianism? Where life exists, I do not condemn it. No, in this, my friends, there is a difference, and it may be for ages to come to consider this subtlety. Yet we—that is those who follow my ministry—have always allowed those who do not feel a calling to teach to continue their lives as their earthly desires dictate it. And feel no need for penance. And so we ask it: be in one thousand years hence—it is too much to ask of all, after all, for all to eschew the bodily love of the other. Some are called to this; some are not. Perhaps it depends on life and tide. I too, have known the love of a woman, and of women before I met my beloved Cecilia, who gave me my daughter, who is more to me than I can say.

Nay, I say, and Nay! But we can join our spirits together in love. And in protection. These simple peasant ways are known to you. If they are not (which I doubt) seek out the Old Ones in your community. Christ said to leave your loved ones—it is much to ask for most of us. Perhaps this is the only way to achieve liberation from the body? Can we know each other before we are condemned to join our flesh in procreation? Yes! But my warning is this: do not forget the Lord who allowed you this, but still allowed you to praise the Lord that would forbid it. This, in truth, is Love, is Perfect Love …

Would I have followed this before I gained the truth? I cannot tell you. It is the most difficult of questions that you could put before a man, or a woman. But for those who have gained the truth, I do not forbid them that love, only I ask that they consider that they at least endeavor not to bring forth another soul from its perfect sojourn in Heaven.

And yes, I have suggested the means not to make it so. In that they may execute me in all good conscience.

For this counsel, and other—false things,—they have condemned me to death.

*   *   *   *

The news came to me slowly. It was Elpidius who made me prick up my ears. Agape had long since left for the East.

"They will come to speak with you soon. Instantius and Salvianus, and even Hyginus of Cordúba who once expressed his doubts. The See of Avila has fallen vacant. You are the one they have chosen to fill this vacancy."

"No," I said. "I have already told them that I and what I and those who follow me hold true do not want to be part of the established church. How can I change that if not from without?"

"Nonetheless, these are consecrated bishops; yet, they follow you. They believe it must be changed from within. They will be here within a few days to persuade you to take this position. I, as you may know, am with you in whatever you decide, I suppose. Perhaps this is part of the burden God has given me, or you." he concluded, but without the conviction I needed.

"But," he finished gravely, "there are dangers." It was nothing more than I expected.

Perhaps it is necessary for all men to have doubts at times like these. Doubts which tell them to abstain from involvement; doubts which tell them to go home to their wives and children, and listen no more. Or, to the male of the species, doubts which urge them to take advantage of the opportunity of their inherent propensity to fight. I didn't know which to listen to at this stage. Our movement had grown. Yes. Our message was important. Yes. Our opposition was powerful. Yes. But why was it powerful? Because it had a voice from the Inside? Bishop Priscillian? I? In a short time, I had established a following perhaps as great as theirs in the establishment and through Choice, not Persuasion, or Law, or that which was and likely always would have been. Maybe this was the opportunity I sought to bring the Message to more and more people. Foolish is the one who does not listen to the inside; he who does not know that sometimes "lies" have greater influence than Truth, does not know the voice of politics. But was this where I started? Was this how our movement had become? Grown?

I knew, I had to be careful. I had experienced power before. I knew its seductivity. Remember, I had been Senator. I had the gift of Rhetoric. I had the name and face of Fame.

Still I listened to Elpidius. I had started with him and he had returned to me, sacrificing his own individual voice.

"The people ask for you, Priscillian. They have heard of your following in Galicia and Lusitania, and important parts of sub-Baetica. They await someone to lead them forwards into truth. You have been elected for a Holy Purpose, man! Who are you to decide against that?"

As for me, I did not know how to respond. I made a mistake, perhaps, as many a maverick has done; I let myself be co-opted into the other side. And so I became the Bishop of Avila. There was pomp and ceremony from those I admired, in front of those who, most likely didn't not know who I was, but hated or distrusted the "other side". The feeling, I am reluctant and sad to say, was as heady as it had been when I had been created Senator. But like those days, it was not long to last.

I was not long to enjoy my new address.

But somehow I think that the future will remember me as this: Priscillian, Bishop of Avila. Even if the official records will reject and erase it.

*   *   *   *

Forgive me: I insert myself into Priscillian's narrative here, though my name is probably lost to you and you will find it in few other places, if at all. It is of little mind to me. You may have met me before, but I am of little consequence. It is only love of his daughter which keeps me close to this narrative, which I keep close to my heart, from which, I am glad I can still greet you.

I am tired and can write little beyond this, though I will try. I write because here is one thing that you will need to know: The details of my Master's imprisonment.

They will tell you that he came willingly to having been held. It was not so. As you have seen, Priscillian was superior in the arts of persuasion, but it meant nothing to these men for whom their Rule was Law. Then, through force of their own power—

and that meant preferment with whomever was Emperor—though please do not mention who suggested this—they cared little but to achieve their vengefulness.

Another thing that they will deny is torture. I need not tell you that this is not so, and that others who have courageously endured as I have, will say the same or less.
I would give you names: Latronianus, our blessed and beautiful poet; Euchrotia, who having loved our master in the only way that was open to them, gave her life for what he, and subsequently she, chose as preferable to life without him ... no, no. Here I will give no more. My eyes fill with grief at the remembrances and I can say no more ...
Let Priscillian finish his tale.

*   *   *   *

Bishop Symposius, of neighboring Astorga, had ridden through the night to bring me the news. The rain whipped the dead leaves around the domus *into a fury, which caught one's face and stung like a leather whip. Herakles came to take the Bishop's horse, and rather than awaken the household further and bring more attention to Astorga's sudden arrival, I went into the kitchen myself and brought out grapes and cheese, and the remaining soup from our supper earlier. The fire was still burning, embers white hot.*

"Come, let me take your cloak. Bring yourself closer to the fire. What news is so urgent that you come like the Furies out of the night. You'll catch your death, man."

"It could not wait. I learned today that Hydatius has sent a report to Milan, to Ambrosius—a good man, but one too far away from what we speak; he knows little of you except what your enemies tell him. Hydatius has enlisted the good Ambrosius' support. He has thereby gained a rescript from Gratian the Emperor, who, as you know has been for some time on shaky ground in view of his enlistment of men from the Alans in his army: those men were heretofore considered the enemy of Rome, and many still fear them."

"Yes, and ... So?"

"He has spoken of ... forgive me ... 'Harassment by Pseudo-Bishops and Manichees' by which he means ..."

"Yes, I know of whom he speaks."

"But perhaps you do not recognize the severity of the Emperor's demands, Priscillian!" Symposius admonished me. "This rescript decrees that all heretics must leave their homes, and their churches! You, Instantius, Salvianus, even Hyginus of Cordúba now that he has sympathies with you—all of you must make yourselves scarce. Hydatius believes himself now to be in such a strong position that he has sent a letter around all of the churches formally, **formally** indicting Hyginus. If he can do that to the one who originally appeared to be sympathetic to him,—you know it was Hyginus who originally wrote to Hydatius?" I nodded; it was old news now. Hyginus had been so scandalized at the Bishop of Augusta Emerita and his treatment of Instantius, and especially Salvianus, who still suffered from his injuries that Hyginus had insisted he and I meet. The result was now his affiliation with us, although he did not join us as such.

"Priscillian. I beg of you … Just think then of what he thinks he can do to you. You must leave here and go into hiding."

"And then what? What of my followers, Symposius? What of my church? What of our beliefs? What of our work? I am no heretic. There have been no charges. The Council of Saragossa was a bear without teeth."

"Then I do not know what to suggest to you. I am safe because they do not know of my involvement with you, though I think that some do suspect it. That is why I came here under cover of darkness. You could be being watched."

"Then heaven help them if Herakles finds them first!" Even in this urgent moment, the idea was amusing. "I will contact Instantius and Salvianus. We will go to Rome."

Symposius stepped back. Even the faint light from the oil lamps illuminated the incredulity on his face.

"Are you mad?"

"No, my friend. I think not. Only cornered by a black weasel in a Bishop's miter, and I like not the smell. We will go to Rome and we will go to Milan to Ambrosius, to plead our case directly: saner, less calculating minds will see that we pose no threat."

"Then may the True God be with you on your journey. But I tell you, I fear for you all."

CHAPTER XIV

▼

"So," said **Instantius,** *rubbing his hands together as much with glee as cold, "when do we leave?"*

I had to smile at his youth and devotion.

"Wait a minute, Brother," I said, "have you stopped to consider the perilous position we are in? They will be looking for us. You, at least have the opportunity to hide for the time being. It is me they want."

"Us," said Salvianus. It was true: he had aged since I saw him last. The pressure of our position, the insight into our sudden exposure had not been lost on him. Yet, as he continued, I knew he was not only my staunchest ally, but my dearest friend:

"Yes, us! Priscillian, do not turn your face to me in that way. I am just as implicated in this rescript as are you, or our friend Instantius here. Do you think I would retire to the mountains and leave my flock, just when their understanding, their faith, their trust in all of us is imperiled? If you think that you have underestimated me. Look not at just this old and injured frame. My spirit is intact and ready for a fight!"

I doubt I have ever loved another spirit more.

"Very well then. We are three. But we will need to plan our itinerary with care, and on the way we shall consider our defense with even more. I suggest we go by the Aquitaine first. I have friends there. And we have followers."

"We are not loved in the Aquitaine," Instantius said with more reservation than his earlier enthusiasm had shown. But he was right. Bishop Delphinas of Burdigala was no friend of mine, and by implication, of my friends neither.

"No, we are not loved, but we are welcomed in certain parts. While we are here in Hispania, we will go with God, as long as we disguise ourselves and our intentions. Those who know us will let us pass. Once we arrive on the other side of the pass at the Pyrenees, we will go straight to Elusa. My old tutor, Delphidias, will welcome us into his household. He is a pagan, but he is not unacquainted with our movement. His wife, I have been told, is a Christian, and if she loves her husband, then she too is of open mind. From there we will plan our strategies …

I waited for some sign from them. There was none.

"maybe make some new converts too …?"

"We have followed you this far, my friend Bishop," said Salvianus, "our faith is with you and the true God. As my young colleague asks, when do we start?"

∗   ∗   ∗   ∗

If only my household had been as easy to persuade! First, there was Herakles, who wanted to accompany us. I tried gentle persuasion, but it was not to make any differ-ence. He said nothing, of course, but he made preparations for the journey which included His horse (mine actually, but who argues with a giant?), His provisions, His knife.

"No, Herakles, no! We are to travel in secret. How does one hide a giant! You will draw attention to us and that I cannot allow. I need you here." In the end, logic won out over love.

Then there was Amantia:

"You have not taught me to hide behind my sex," she said. "I can fight as well as any man."
And it was true, despite my gentle wife's tutoring, and my daughter's current domestic position, she was, at heart a fighter. That she had no skill with a blade deterred her

not at all. But in her naïveté she thought that force of arms may be all we needed to persist. In the end I gave her the same logical reasoning as I had given my giant.

She retreated to the kitchens—though not without noisy protestations: there was much banging of pot lids—and prepared to load us up with so many possible provisions that I thought my horse would collapse under the weight!

Finally, when the morning came for us to ride out—we three, only—I found my traces dogged.

"No! Cerberus! Not this time! Go home!"

In the end I was forced to take him by his studded collar and lead him back to the kitchens.

"Feed this mutt! Do not let him out of the doors for a fortnight."

But I could hear his howls for many leagues, and even after, they carried themselves on the winds beyond Asturias.

Our trip was uneventful. We wore simple clothing and we were seen as Roman merchants, and the coins in our purses saw us through many a checkpoint. We passed through the snow-clad peaks of the Pyrenees without incident, and while our lodgings were sometimes friendless and flea-ridden we suffered no more threat to our journey than sick stomachs, saddlesores, and itchy welts.

Now, I thought, as we passed by Roncesvalles, for the beauty of the lands where I first found myself a man. And the man who challenged me to think beyond the boundaries of the scriptures, the illogicality of the god's caprices, and the Will of the Roman Emperors.

I did not expect to be so captivated by what I saw.

*   *   *   *

I am Euchrotia. I have followed my lord into the gates of death. I have been told that I am blessed with the Muses who influence the words of the willing. And so, I write to you of what came to me, and hope that you who read my words will heed them and remember them in the times of religious openness which must needs follow, for this is story which must be told. His, more than mine. He came unexpected, unwanted, denied, and later embraced in whatever limited way such intimacy was allowed us. I do not regret it, despite the emotional pain, and later the physical torture my Love brought my way. Now that I am alone, and awaiting the sword of my captors, the latter was but little. I regret nothing.

I must start with a day when spring came early, for there was snow still on the ground in the higher parts of our estates.

I was less annoyed with the intrusion than I was with the state of the rider's horse. He had come from the passes. His mount was covered in froth. He bore a message for my husband.

I was not, at first apprised of why it had to come with such urgency.

Later, he told me.

"But why? We have a good estate now that you are retired. They know you are Pagan, but they leave you alone. They know the power of your words, so now that you are silent, they do not bother us. Why now do you welcome such a party, knowing that they are pursued? No, I will not have it, and that is final!"

We had married late in his life. Attius Tiris Delphidius, my liege lord and soulmate was old now. But he had been a force to be reckoned with when he held court at the colleges of Burdigala. I had been overtaken by his tenderness and yes, a little over-awed by his reputation. I was still young, but not uneducated. He had wooed, and worn me down with his tenderness and sincerity. Later he had the same success with my father—God bless his departed soul.

My father had already been careworn at the caprices of my sister,(she had married a poet—not of my father's choosing—and they had traveled far from us to Galicia, where she had been born; she was seldom mentioned); in the end, he only wanted a good marriage for her younger sibling. I was perhaps too headstrong, as my dear mother had been. He feared a further bad marriage. We had no brothers. Now Delphidius and I oversaw our flocks and our fields with the tranquility, which comes from retirement from political outspokenness. We were at peace now. We had raised our daughter, Procula—our only child, blossoming more with every springtime—as a

Christian: I had lost two others in infancy. She was the pearl in our nest. Our life was simple but good. And now he was to invite a noted and sought after heretic into our hearth?

No, it would not do, and I would fight with every particle of my influence and intellect against it!

As always, he had worn me down, and in the same way he had wooed me:

"Beloved wife, this man has no crimes against the Romans; his only fault is that he challenges the restricted beliefs of their orthodox church, (he did not say "your": he knew of my misgivings). Have I not done likewise? At first openly, and now, as only you know, still, in private. He was my best student. How can you ask me to turn him away in his time of crisis? Where is your womanly heart?"

I knew I was beaten before I began:

"Very well, then. Out of love and respect … but not liking for I like it not."

"Perhaps you would not be my lady wife if you did not question it. But believe me, Priscillian is good. And he needs our help."

That day I went to the market, and I ordered triple of our weekly fare. The town was small and young, organized after the cardinal points of the compass. I was known there, though not all had respect for me. Delphidius was known as a pagan, and most of the inhabitants were of the Roman faith. On my return, I gave instructions for many of my favorite animals to be slaughtered. And I brought up most of our last years' vintage. I might not like it, but I will not be accused as a miserly host. Bring on our unwanted guests! They will find Euchrotia of Elusa serves a goodly table!

✳   ✳   ✳   ✳

I had only a few days to wait. They came shortly after the New Year celebrations, or, shortly after we had mourned the death of our Lord Jesus, and celebrated His resurrection. My husband as was his custom, saw in this period in is own way, yet he celebrated it too.

I was on the terrace when I saw them approach from the west. I had been in my herb gardens. My fingers were covered in dirt. My garments saw the imprint of a gardener's hands.

I sent my servants out to greet them. But seeing them hesitate, then I went myself. Though I cast off my aprons.

Delphidius had kept himself to his bed that morning. He would not tell what ailed him but I had sent a tisane of herbs. I was known in the district for such knowledge. He had many such attacks lately.

They were three horsemen: a chestnut, a white, and a bay. None attended them. As persons of rank and respect I had not expected them to be unaccompanied. I approached the white.

"Bishop Priscillian. We have been expecting you. Please, my groom will tend to your horses. You are welcome here."

A man, clearly sick and sore, dismounted. "I thank you for your welcome lady. But I am not the Bishop you greet." He motioned to the rider of the bay.

He looked as disheveled as the rest, yet as he dismounted and pulled back his riding hood, all I saw was the intensity of his blue eyes. They were like lapis lazuli and held as much ancient knowledge. In the end I forced myself to concentrate on the entirety of the rider. Riders, that is.

"My dear lady, you cannot know the joy your words can bring to such weary and heartsick travelers as we."

What can I tell you?

That I fell in love? I believe not in such instant things. But his smile pierced me even then, and I knew that despite my misgivings, my lord's words had been true. Here was one who deserved not to be persecuted, and my feelings were nothing other than 'feed this man, and give him respite, for he carries the weight of worlds upon his shoulders.'

Well, little other.

I may have colored. "Please, come this way … all of you". I remembered my manners. I am the daughter of noblemen, after all.

I motioned to my servants to tend to their horses, and then asked them to follow me.

We had not known when exactly to expect them. There was soup on the boil, and bread in the ovens. I gave orders to be ready to produce both. And strong wine for the weather was yet still cold.

I showed my guests to their rooms. They were well-appointed in the Roman style, but not luxurious. I reminded myself that these were un-invited guests after all. I indicated the way to the tepidarium. I assumed they would know what procedure to follow. There were soft towels. I was still … well … somewhat taken aback by my own responses. Still, I had fulfilled my appointed role as hostess. I withdrew with the grace that breeding gives.

"When you have bathed and are settled, we will be ready for you to eat with us. I shall speak to my husband about your arrival; but I must warn you, his health is not good these days, and I do not want him to be overly disturbed by your arrival."

I am sure I sounded more direct and protective than I intended. Even then, I asked myself: 'Do you want to keep these visitors to yourself?'

I made a speedy exit rather than consider this question.

In the hypocaust, I adjusted my dress, and checked my face in our expensive bronzed mirror.
I went into the kitchens myself to add more meat to the soup.

The servants had alerted my husband to the new arrivals to our house before I had chance to myself. He was delighted. All traces of paleness left his eyes. I was glad to see that.

"Help me to dress, Woman! I have an old and distinguished friend to greet. And open our kitchens for I find my old appetite again."

I was to be laid low, despite, no, because of my preparations. I could have hated him then. Instead, I chastised myself later, as only women can.

They came to dine as changed men and for the first time I had chance to evaluate each:

The one called Instantius was younger than I. I learned that his father had been bishop before him and that the son had followed his calling after his father's wishes. That did not mean, however, that he lacked conviction. Far from it. He was the first to speak of their journey and of its mission. Yet I was not the one addressed:

"Most noble Delphidius. It is great honor to be seated here at your table," he turned to me then, "and I thank your dear lady for her hospitality. We have been sent in exile from our own dioceses—as you know—for speaking against the established church. Yet, those who follow us have sought for an alternative to the restrictions of the Church they have been told to observe. For you to receive us, thus, is a blessing, and we honor it and thank you ... and your lady wife, of course."

I smiled, as a gracious hostess should do.

The elder was quieter. He commented on the salad greens. He liked my oil and sweet vinegar dressing seasoned with garlic and early herbs from my garden. He smiled at me. I saw an inner pain, though I knew not what or why. It had been a long journey.

Of Priscillian ... well I shied away from his glance. And perhaps he noticed this. Perhaps he saw it as hostility. As the course ended he said:

"I know that, despite old friendship, neither of you are entirely comfortable with us being here, and please know we will not burden you long. At this point we are weary travelers, in bone and in spirit. Would that we had not had to undertake such a journey. Yet our beliefs have made it necessarily so. We must travel into the Lion's jaw— at least, our foes have made our beloved Emperor into a lion by feeding him rotten meat. Now we must defend ourselves or lose every thing we have fought for, every innocent soul we have touched with truth. For myself, I cannot thank you enough for your hospitality. Delphidius, I salute you ..."

As he raised his glass to my husband, he turned his gaze to me. Forgive me ... I thought I would melt.

"and Lady Eucrotia too, for this cannot have been an easy decision for her to make ... to welcome those persecuted into your hearth and home ..."

I noticed at this time that the other two bishops, Sylvianus and Instantius, exchanged quizzical glances amongst themselves, and then towards their leader whose glass was raised. I saw the briefest of nods, and then the glasses were drained.

What was that all about? I asked myself. But then I called for the second course. And the suet pudding which followed.

*   ✳   ✳   ✳   ✴*

"They are vegetarians." It was not an admonishment, but how, in my shame, could I not have seen it as such. "And they abstain from wine." I pushed hot tears back from my eyes.

"Why did you not tell me!" I said angrily. "Why did they not! They ate what I put on their dishes. They said nothing!" I was too deep in self-pity, embarrassment, and remorse to listen to any answer, but still Delphidius spoke.

"I? I had forgotten. Because it was unexpected, their arrival today ... and my state of health, well this morning was not good. They, because they are gentle born."

He took my tearful face in his tender hands. He tipped it up to his.

"Weep not my lady. They are well born Romans. You and your serving maids will not make such a mistake in the future. You were not to know. Later, you will search your garden for its freshest produce; you will pick with your own hands your most healthful herbs. Tomorrow, you will send Procula and Philip to fish in the river for the spring trout. They will love you for it then."

But then, I hated him. And Priscillian even more.

The next day—though orders given—it was I who took to my bed. And hoped for them to leave.

CHAPTER XV

▼

Procula came to my room with flowers in her hands. *They were a competing confusion of spring shades: purple, pink, the brightest yellow, blue and vermilion, each fighting to take precedence. Their delicate scent pervaded the room. I had opened the shutters now, and the morning sunlight streamed through onto the marble floor.*

"Why thank you darling! What a lovely thought ..."

"Oh no, mother," she interrupted, "I did not pick them. They are from the tall bishop, the one with the amazing eyes."

Obviously, these eyes had not been lost on my thirteen year old daughter either.

I felt myself color, but before I could say anything, Procula continued ...

"He told me about his daughter, Galla. He says she is about the same age as me. He said that he hoped that you were feeling better and that he prayed that they would make you smile again. And look! They did! Will you get up now? Philip is going to help me to train the new mare today. You can come and watch me. Please ...?"

Philip was one of the many stray dogs who sat at my hearth from time to time—at Delphidius' feet actually. As in old times, he had students still. He taught them of the Greek philosophers, the Roman stoics; he taught them to compose poetry, to write and speak with accuracy and fluency. 'Rhetoric' he said, 'should only be resorted to once truthful persuasion has ceased to be an option'. For such they loved him. Philip had been with us for over a month now. His father, Senator Ampellius, maintained an estate near Burdigala, when he was not in the Capital. He had been one of my husband's first students and so he now sent the son. I had met Ampellius once, when I first came to Elusa as Delphidius' new bride. He had a large and well-appointed domus *in the town. I found him condescending and opinionated: a rigid man with rigid ideas. I was surprised that he had been a student of my husband who was anything but closed-minded. Certainly, he had paid little heed to me. Of the son, I knew very little really. In fact, I had had almost nothing to do with him. He had followed Delphidius like a puppy when he first arrived, and in fact he was little more than a pup: seventeen or eighteen at the most. However, he had proved an asset to my husband in that he had taken on much of the management of the estate, and that, at least I was grateful for. He seemed to have a given talent for things to do with numbers. It was not one of my strengths. I cannot say that I felt love for him, but that didn't matter. He and Procula had seemed to set up a friendship, and they shared the same love of horses. When her father bought her the new mare, Philip—who lived up to his name—offered to help her school it. The boy seemed inoffensive enough to me and I was glad that Procula had company nearer to her own age. I had been too preoccupied with the running of my household, and not least of my husband's declining health to pay him much mind.*

I arranged the flowers—as much as such a profusion can be said to be 'arranged', then dressed, and I have to admit that I did so with extra care, selecting a tunic of olive green wool to wear over a soft brown skirt. To this I added a belt of calf leather with embossed bronze disks. I wore supple sandals, which showed my trim ankles in good light. I told myself I was acting foolishly. Yet I stopped to consider my reflection in the mirror as I passed through to the terrace. Celtic blonde hair bordering on auburn, tied back with a silken cord, though very little could be done to keep it tidy; a skin too tawny for me to be mistaken for a city matron; some lines in the corners of those green eyes now. A little more weight around my waist than I cared to acknowledge. But I smiled at what I saw and was not entirely displeased.

I stepped out into the morning sunlight. What met my eyes was one of the strangest sights I think I have ever seen. Two of my guests were seated in the shade with beakers in their hands. Of the third, well, I can only say that he was racing up and down, dodging this way and that, robes flying! Our gracious bishop was running, circling, and doubling back, chasing Parmenides, our black sheepdog—yes, and even barking at him! I doubled up with laughter.

"What the devil are you doing!" I spluttered out between giggles.

"I'm helping him to perfect his technique," Priscillian answered. "I have just done explaining to him that if he is going to be a sheepdog, he should strive to be the best. He's a good pupil. Look ..." and he tore off away again around the rose trees.

"Enough, enough ... you are making my cheeks ache!"

He gave up the chase, and Parmy at once fell in the dirt exhausted, his face on his paws, and his tongue lolling out. He looked a fool.

"Now look what you have done. Is this your usual exercise in the morning?"

He grinned. "I am glad to see that you have color in your cheeks. I thought to hear that you had expired in the night."

"No, I have more resilience ... Thank you for the flowers;" I added shyly "they are very lovely."

Priscillian scanned my face, as if about to say something. But he did not. I turned away abruptly. I thought he would hear the beating of my heart.

I knew I would have to keep my thoughts in check. I felt as though they were written on my forehead. I must not let Delphidius see. He knows me too well.

My husband, alas, had once again taken to his bed, and I feared that the excitement had proved too much for him.

I moved to the shaded side of the courtyard, to where the other two men were seated. Both made to rise at my arrival. One very stiffly.

"No, no, please. Don't get up. Have you broken your fast? I hope that the servants have seen to your needs? I must apologize that I did not do so myself, but ..."

"We are only happy to see you are looking well again, Lady Eucrotia," the one called Salvianus said. "Indeed we have been well taken care of, probably better than we deserve," he glanced at Priscillian and I gathered that something may have been said

between them concerning their consumption of the first night's dinner. I hoped that nothing further would be said about it, and, thankfully, it was not.

Priscillian had recovered both his breath and his episcopal dignity.

"We have many plans to make before we depart for Rome. In particular, we will need to compose a defense in which we will answer these "charges" against us. This we shall present first to the Bishop of Rome and ask him to plead our case with Gratian, our Emperor. So I wonder, could I trouble you for vellum and a writing instrument?" he asked.

"Of course. My husband will have plenty." In a few moments, I was back with both.

"Shall I ask the servants to set up a table for you here in the courtyard?"

"That would be kind, lady. Thank you. Perhaps here in the shade?"

And with that done, I left them to themselves.

*   *   *   *

Later that day, as the sun was descending, I fulfilled my promise to Procula and went to see how the horse training was progressing. Priscillian had beaten me to it.

He was seated on the stone bench besides the stables. Parmy was with him. It was a favorite spot of mine. Here I had sat when my daughter toddled over on her chubby legs and pulled Beauty's tail. Beauty was my horse, and lived up to her name: towering, far too big a mount for a woman, but she and I had been inseparable ever since Delphidius had given her to me as a wedding gift. My husband had raised our little girl high and placed her on Beauty's back. Procula had squealed with delight, grabbing onto Beauty's mane and pulling perhaps a little too hard. Kicking her little legs as she jogged her body up and down. My mare had a sense of occasion, thankfully, and as Delphidius led her around the pista, it was clear that our daughter would be a lifelong lover of horses.

Today she stood in the center of the sand with the lunge rope. A whip hung idly at her side. She had no need of it. She cooed and chucked to the dappled grey, which circled in slow but perfect form with her Arabian head and tail held high.

"They make a fair couple," said Priscillian, pointing with his chin.

"Oh yes. She is proud of her new horse. I think that she will bond with this mare as she has with every horse since her first pony."

"No doubt," came the response, "but that wasn't exactly what I meant.

Philip had wandered into the center. I hadn't noticed him at first. He reached down and picked up the whip. Standing behind Procula, he took her hand and still holding it, gave a little flick of the whip. The mare began to canter.

I laughed, but somehow uneasily. "It doesn't seem five minutes ago when she was still a little tot. Now she's my big grownup daughter. A big girl now."

"Forgive me my lady, but I don't think you have looked at her that closely lately. Your little girl is a young woman, and it does not seem to me that she is objecting to the touch of a young man's hand."

It was so obvious! Was I a blind fool that I had to hear it from a total stranger to our family. I turned to him almost in anger.

"Forgive me. I had no right to say such things," he stood up. "I must get back to my writing."

The two in the center of the sand had not seen me. I was embarrassed for my naïveté. I crept away like a cat in the night.

✳   ✳   ✳   ✳

A week went by and then another passed. The weather now was in full spring. The bishops had received a message that Damasus, the Pope, was not in Rome and would not be until June, and therefore they were forced to postpone their journey. It seemed obvious that Priscillian was eager to set out; yet he also seemed just as content to remain with us. Little by little, I began to see his attentions to me as something more than mere courtesy to the wife of one's host. Sometimes when he looked at me, I saw almost pain in his eyes. I wondered if he saw the same reflected in mine. If the others saw it, they did not seem to remark upon it. After all, when two people fall in love, they think the whole world must be aware of that silent and burning energy. Yet often, if it is revealed, it is a surprise to all. I hoped that that was the case.

Delphidius was up and down. Some days he seemed almost his old self. Other days the return of the old pains laid him very low. They were increasing in strength. I feared for him.

One morning, early, after a particularly bad night, he asked to see Priscillian. They had been with us almost a month. Later the bishop looked drained. He asked after certain herbs, wild ones, and the stamen of certain flowers. He said that this would quell the pain. He gave me their scientific names, but I knew them only by others: the names the countryfolk called them. Gradually, we were able to identify the ones he needed. I said I would tell him where to find them, but my directions—clear enough to me, but with mystifying landmarks to a stranger—produced very little more than wild mint which immediately went in the lunchtime soup.

Perhaps you could show me?" he asked tentatively.

I blushed, I am sure I blushed. I had avoided being alone with him at any time. Luckily Procula and Philip were just then passing deep in conversation, their heads bowed. They carried a pole of fish.

"Darling? You know where the ice cave is, the little one, not the big one. The little pathway, past the stream, where the bluebells are at this time of the year …?"

Procula looked up as if shaken from some deep dream, something they shared … she looked startled.

"Sorry …? Bluebells?"

"Yes, darling …" I could feel impatience rising, I already had a feel for the outcome of this and I wished, above all, to avoid it: "the plants by the little path: the red ones with the long slim stems, and the seed pods that grow by the ice cave …, you know …" I added, futilely, spreading my palms wide.

Procula was staring at me. She almost looked afraid, cornered, suddenly exposed. I felt like I had stepped into a play.

"Darling …? Could you take Priscillian there so that he can gather some of them for your father?"

"I don't know what you mean," she said sharply. "Can't you see I am doing something else right now."

I was taken aback. She never spoke to me thus, and no, I couldn't see anything of the sort. But she continued walking after Philip, and I was left with Priscillian, alone.

I wished he had not witnessed such rude behavior. I would have to talk with her later.

"Truly, I am sorry to inconvenience you;" he said, "it is just that I believe I can make a special tisane to help Delphidius. He seemed in such pain this morning and …"

"Yes, yes, of course," I said distractedly, gazing after Procula. "Yes," I was brought back to the present moment, "Yes. We will go now. Just give me a minute to change my tunic. It can be damp there at this time of the year."

*   *   *   *

I should have gone for them myself. I need not have sent Priscillian. But hindsight is always the truest thought. The day was beautiful. Warm, and soft. Blackbirds sang their appreciation. And the little bees buzzed in and out of the dozy flowers. It felt as though the woods slumbered. Slants of sunlight filtered in broken patterns and made the green ferns glisten almost white. We walked without speaking for the most part. Priscillian carried shears and a burlap bag. The silence between us spoke more than any words could have done. I felt as though there was a magnetic force between us, in perfect equilibrium: it pulled us together; it kept us apart. I reminded myself that we were searching for herbs and flowers, medicinal help for my poor husband's pain. I told myself that I shouldn't be enjoying this so much. I told myself to be very, very careful with word and deed.

It was as though he had read my thoughts. "I wish our cause was less serious this morning. The day is too joyful to be centered on pain."

I thought to turn the conversation to our mutual skill with plants. He told me that he had learned all he knew from his childhood nurse, one of the meigas *he said. I said the word was unknown to me.*

"It is a Celtic word," he explained. These were the protectors of the tribe. They worked alongside the druids, as their muses, and sometimes their lovers ..."

I bent to pick a wild iris. The word made me uncomfortable, but he didn't seem to notice. He continued:

"They passed the lore down to their daughters, and sometimes young women they adopted. It was a more of a communal society: children were raised by all. I showed a fascination at an early age; I simply liked the smell of most. She noticed it and encouraged me. You?"

"Oh I have very little skill. I was born in an area where herbs and grasses were abundant on the mountain. There was a woman who would gather them and bring them by to our house. One day I talked to her and asked her to tell me what they were for. I was still very young, no more than six or seven. After that, I began to go to her house when she was making a batch of medicines. The grasses were hung up all along the low roof. Like you, I liked the smell. She acted as the village midwife. I assisted her with a breech birth once. The baby died. I was horrified. But I helped her again on other occasions. I was in total awe of her skill, her way of calming people: reassuring them. I never dared tell my father; he was very protective of me. My sister knew, but she was good at keeping secrets. Oh, here we are. Are these the flowers you were talking about?"

And so for the next hour we gathered blooms and blossoms, greens and grasses. We could have been the original children of this earth.

✳   ✳   ✳   ✳

"What will you do when Delpidius passes?"

It was out in the open, then? What we both had left unsaid. We were in the thick of the bluebells now. Gathering their long stems to grace the dinner table.

"I don't know. I just don't know ... I will stay, I suppose. It is our home, Procula's and mine ..." to my annoyance, the tears filled my eyes. Lonely, fearful, born of too much pent up longing, too much guilt.

He dropped his bag; he pulled me into his arms crushing me, my hands, and the bluebells against his chest. I let out a great sob. "Why has this happened to us?" He released me then kissed my hair, taking my tear stained face in his big hands.

*"I think the creator god has sent you to challenge me. I thought my viewpoints were so fixed, so inviolable. I was so wrong. I thought celibacy would be so easy.... yet ... I want you, Euchrotia! I live with an ache in my heart and my loins. I cannot sleep at night for the wanting of you. I would never have dreamed that I could feel so much desire for another, and yet I know that I must overcome it. **We** must, Euchrotia. I will not be called hypocrite, and there are so many people relying on us to be chaste. He touched his finger to my mouth. I kissed it, ever-so-gently letting it pass my lips. He pulled me to him again, and this time I thought he would never let me go. He murmured his love into my hair and I thought I heard him crying.*

Eventually, I pulled myself free. I swept the tears from my cheeks, leaving swathes of dirt.

I tried to recover my composure: "I am glad that this thing is open between us now, Priscillian." I could not look at him now. I dared not. "We both knew it from the start. Let us not now spoil it by breaking our own rules. We can keep this moment forever, but I would not that we had anything that we would have to lie about."

And then he smiled. He bent his head and feathered his lips against mine. "Come, my love," he said. "I have a patient to see."

*   *   *   *

The bluebells were crushed and we left them where they lay. As we walked out of the wood, I noticed an area which had been flattened, and recently. Stalks and blooms were broken and bent, scattered every which way.

"It looks as though we are not the only lovers to pass this way today," observed Priscillian.

And I laughed.

*   *   *   *

Delphidius had had one of his turns. While Priscillian was preparing his medicines, I went to my husband's side. His face was ashen. His eyes colorless. It seemed he had aged ten years since I had seen him early that day. I asked him if he wished me to read to him, as was my custom.

"No wife, not today. I think I prefer to sit with you in silence."

But after a while, he said, quietly. "How do our distinguished company fare? Do they have everything they need? It must be galling for them to have to wait so long to clear themselves. They should never have been accused in this way in the first place. That devil Ithacius! I remember him of old. Never happy unless he is spreading his poison …" He began to cough.

I tipped water to his lips. "My husband, please, do not excite yourself. It matters not what this man does. What is done is done. Now, all I care about is for you to get better."

Priscillian came with his medicaments and tea. When Delphidius first smelt it, he looked at Priscillian and smiled: "Ah yes. I know this. Thank you my old friend." He closed his eyes, still smiling. Soon he was sleeping peacefully, his breathing regular for the first time in many days.

Priscillian left. I stayed. Once my husband opened his eyes and said to me. "A good man, my love. Priscillian is the best of men," and then he slept once again.

*   *   *   *

Later, when I had taken a few moments to check on the household, he sent for me. And Priscillian. He seemed quite lucid; quite strong in mind. He motioned us to come towards him and patted either side of the bed.

"I am ready to take my adventure. The skies await me. Mourn me not. I go in the greatest of peace. I have already seen the face of love, and I know that is what awaits me on the other side …" he took my left hand and he joined it to Priscillian's right. His own, he clasped over both. "Take care of yourselves, and each other. Spread your

love to everyone who crosses your path. Go now with the blessing of your God, and with my love and understanding. You will need to be very strong to face what is to come. Go forward to meet it together, and you will not break," he smiled, and closed his eyes. Then briefly, he opened them again. He looked at Priscillian: "You will remember?" The other nodded. Delphidius pulled our hands to his chest.

It was less than an hour until his passing. He did not regain consciousness. We stayed thus in silence, Priscillian and I. Taking in every last contour of the other's face; until at last, the third hand released its grip.

✳   ✳   ✳   ✳

It is astonishing how fast word travels. Within two days of my husband's departure, more than fifty people came to pay their respects. They came on foot, on horseback, in litters, on donkeys and mules. They were nobles, and farmers, tinkers, and merchants, the poor and the very rich. And all were just as affected at the great man's passing. Between us, Priscillian and I had preserved the body long enough for my husband to receive these, his last visitors.

And then, as he had told to me long before, we burned his body, as the sun was setting, and the moon had yet to rise. And though I tried to cry, the tears would not come. Procula was beside herself with grief and sought solace with Philip, and later alone in her quarters. She did not come to me.

✳   ✳   ✳   ✳

On the day of the full moon, the mourners had left, or were leaving. We remained a much diminished household. A few of our closest tenants remained. I saw Priscillian in close conversation with Marcellus, Delphidius' chief planter. They went off together. Since the night my husband died, I had not been alone with Priscillian and we had shared few words. I don't think I have ever felt more lonely.

To my surprise, however, I found a friend in Instantius: he acted as a go-between, helping me in practical ways to make sure that all the visitors felt their presence was welcomed. I cannot tell you exactly what it was he did; I only know that the passage was made smoother because of it.

Late the next afternoon, the ashes were gathered. Priscillian took the pottery urn and placed it within my husband's household shrine. He bought lamps and surrounded it with light.

"We have a final task to perform for your husband tonight," he said. "Please tell the household and the others who remain that all are welcome. I have the last part of a promise to fulfil." Then he went to his rooms.

∗   ∗   ∗   ∗

A small procession accompanied Delphidius' last journey. We walked the short distance to the grain field. The small green shoots were already well above the ground and the poppies grew all around the circumference. I had expected to see Priscillian and the other two bishops in their episcopal robes, but Salvianus and Instantius were dressed in simple togas, while Priscillian's robe was plainer still: a white linen tunic, unbound at the waist and with no fastenings that I could see. It looked to be made without seams. I had chosen a pale green silk—Delphidius' favorite. It was unadorned. Procula was in blue. The rest, I forget.

Marcellus the farmer was waiting for us. He too was dressed in a very simple white robe. Priscillian took the Urn from me.

"Your husband was the greatest of men; yet he has chosen the simplest of ends. His desire was to return to the earth of the place where he was born. To grow once more in his own fields."

We had formed a line at the edge of the newly burgeoning crops. The sun behind us had scattered its light into strata: aqua blue, apple green, the softest pinks and peaches. The birds ceased their singing. A sliver of orange rose on the horizon ahead. Priscillian and the farmer walked forwards into the field. We remained. Not a word was spoken by anyone. The sliver gradually turned into a fireball. Priscillian handed the urn to Marcellus, and then slipped out of his sandals. Then, to my astonishment, he pulled his robe over his head. He was naked. He took the urn once more and walked forward again. He raised it to the ascending moon. He seemed to be speaking but the words were lost to me; they seemed to be in another language—Greek perhaps—and besides, at that moment a small breeze came up and carried them away. He continued to walk forward, scattering my husband's ashes into his own fields. Covering the life of the green shoots with a layer of gray.

It took me then. The tears I had held back coursed down my cheeks. I felt a weight on my upper chest: a knife embedded; a strangled cry ceased before it began. I thought I would choke.

Priscillian was on his knees. The moon framed him like a halo. I followed him to the ground and one by one, all sank to the earth. Priscillian's voice rose in a song: I knew it not. But the two bishops joined their voices and to my utmost incredulity, so did Marcellus, the farmer, and three others of my household, one, Claudia, a dairymaid from Marcellus' farm, his daughter whom I had known from birth when I had a acted as midwife. Donatus, Marcellus son, a young man but not unlettered thanks to my husband, raised his voice with them.

Then it was over. Salvianus and Instantius began to turn back, and we followed them. I glanced over my shoulder. Marcellus was bringing back the empty urn, but Priscillian, his robe still on the ground where it had fallen, was walking into the moon.

CHAPTER XVI

▼

"Tell me now of your God," *I asked him then.* And he did.

* * * *

The time had come for them to move on. Their business awaited them. Damasus was once again in Rome.
I went with them, and so did Procula.

She had seemed so distraught after her father died. I tried to talk to her, but she seemed closed to me. I was bewildered. Why, now, did she choose to hide her feelings? In the end I sent Priscillian. I know not of the content of their discourse, but he had more success than I. I had not intended to travel, but I could not part myself from what I had so lately found. Priscillian raised no objection. There suddenly seemed so much to do; but Philip assured me that he would take care of the details, and I saw no reason to distrust him. Anyway, his gift for organization seemed so much more than mine, especially then. He said he would speak with the tenants, organize the harvest, manage the sales of the crops and the livestock. I began to understand just how much my husband had relied upon him. I trusted him then. The house, I realized would run without me. I was, however, surprised that Procula elected to come with us. She had just turned fourteen.

"I will make a pilgrimage," she said, "to give homage in the name of my father." And I knew that no words of mine would prevent her.

"It is right," said Priscillian. *"We will make a small procession to the apostles and martyrs of Rome. And with the help of the True God, we shall have our say."*

*   *   *   *

Once again, I must intrude myself into this narrative. I have included Euchrotia's own words and feelings. She wrote these in her diary as she, too, awaited execution. Some, most, I have omitted, out of respect for their love and their privacy. I can at least tell you that her devotion to my lord the bishop knew no restrictions, her love never faltered; but it is time to pick up the words of my Master himself. There is much more of the story to be told, and I am the only one who now has the knowledge now to tell it. My name is Herenias. And I alone am left to tell this tale, for, though it may not be read let alone be understood in my lifetime, it must not be forgotten. It seems that Priscillian's presence on the estate—and his devotions to Delphidius—were known to many, despite his short sojourn there, and the small party of pilgrims grew to encompass many followers, many of them women. He welcomed all. I cannot tell you how they became his followers. His message was not unknown in those parts—as he had told you in his own words. There were many who shared his beliefs, even outside of his native Spain. How they came to us—a few more every day—remains a mystery to me. But by the time they arrived in Rome, they were more than thirty. I was not amongst them—my arrival came later. It was gratifying to him; but it was to prove his undoing.

The three bishops had brought with them Letters of Communion: support from their clergy and their communities. They asked only that Damasus, the Vicar of Rome, should refer their cause to those who had brought accusations against them, and their request for pardons, you will recall now included Hyginus of Corduba, who was implicated along with them. They asked to speak before a council of bishops. Perhaps I have said enough at this time. It is not my story.

*   *   *   *

I, Priscillian, then addressed my most intimate followers:

Our request," I reiterated, *"does not means that we feel obliged to run away from any secular tribunal, if Bishop Hydatius prefers to bring his cause before that. We ask only, and humbly, that in this matter of Faith, our convictions, should be judged by the saints, instead of those of the world:* quia ecclesiastici non debeant ob suam defensionem publica adire judica sed tantum eccleciastica. *Our colleague in Christ has sought an Imperial rescript against us. Yet we seek not to a burden to anybody: "nulli graves". We only petition that, although we stand accused of studying apocrypha, we wish it to be understood and accepted that our constant belief remains: that **all** documents under the names of apostles, prophets, and bishops, if they agree with the canon of scripture and proclaim Christ to be God, should not be condemned. At the Council of Saragossa, not one of us was censured, none of us was heard, nor put on trial. 'It was agreed, by your Holiness,' I continued to read, 'that no bishop was to be lawfully deposed on the grounds that previously, as a layman, he deserved condemnation.*

"*We come in peace: to see the Senior and Most First of all Bishops—to the glory of the Apostolic See—who alone can speak with Petrine authority.*

"*Our request is merely for a proper hearing, either by the summoning of Hydatius and Ithacius to Rome to substantiate their charges, or by your Holiness remitting the case to the Spanish bishops. Surely, by such a spiritual court, the bishops need not fear that, if they fail to prove their accusations, they will still not have recourse to a secular court. We ourselves, should we be acquitted, are very ready to forgive their sin against us.*'

"*So, what do you think?*" I asked my episcopal companions. "*Will this be enough?*"

"*Well,*" said Instantius, "*it is clearly implied that the imperial decree of exile against us was improper when our case has not been formerly heard by a Synod.*"

"*This is so,*" added Salvianus. "*The procedure you seek is in accord with that with that requested by the Roman synod of the year 378, in the Year of Our Lord, asking the same emperor to relieve Damasus the Pope himself of liability to prosecution in the Courts. You carefully use your words to frame most carefully request that theological disputes be settled in the hands of official episcopal gatherings. Such has Rome always found congenial.*"

Yet we were unable to submit our petition to a personal interview. We were to be rebuffed.

And adding to this setback, our dear Salvianus shortly thereafter succumbed to his illnesses—and in my opinion the malicious treatment he received at the hands of Hydatius' thugs thus hastened his death.

I was left bereft. He had been a noble friend, a good bishop, and a stalwart companion.

Euchrotia was beside herself in grief.

It was too much, and in too short a period, and even my love in her attempts could not assuage my sorrow, nor I, hers.

Instead we went to Milan. We hoped that Bishop Ambrosius would speak on our behalf. Yet although he was no friend to Augustine—whose diatribe against the Manichees was gaining notice—he too refused to see us.

We went then to the palace. It was not as I had wished.

Macedonius, the Imperial quaestor, *perhaps the second most powerful man in the Roman Empire was known to be antagonistic to Ambrosius. We were given to understand that he might be amenable and sympathetic to our request. Yet he was unaccountably, and ominously slow to reply.*

"Money", I said, to no-one in particular. "He wants money."

"Then we shall give it to him," said Euchrotia. "A suitable sweetener will succeed where words have failed. No Priscillian, do not glance at me in that fashion! Have you forgotten that as the widow of Delphidius' estate I now am a wealthy woman in my own right. It is the Roman law. I have credit in Rome, in Delphidius' name. Whatever he wants, let us give it to him. Yes, my dear love," (any other pretence had long left us) she said more softly, "I know this is not your way. But cease to be a bishop for a moment, and become a citizen of Rome. It is the only way to oil the wheels of influence. You know this as well as I."

I was surprised at her practicality, yet I recognized the truth in her words. I was grateful for her generosity. I had good credit of my own, but perhaps not enough to satisfy Macedonius' greed, (my domicile was further away, and my name all but forgotten) nor the urgent need of the Emperor, who had wars to pay for. Gratian was not then popular: his personal bodyguard was chosen from amongst the Alans, former enemies of Rome. It had not gone unnoticed.

Macedonius—who had once refused to give an interview to Ambrosius, much to the latter's fury, agreed to meet with us.

*   *   *   *

"We are successful!" I brandished the parchment in triumph, "It says here, quite clearly that we are free to leave. We may return to our respective dioceses in Spain." I sat down. I could scarcely believe it. Euchrotia was at my side now. She rested her hand on my shoulder. Instantius could barely contain his excitement. It was more than we had sought and more than we had expected, despite out convictions.

"It is true! Though yet I can scarcely believe our good fortune. The proconsul of Lusitania has summoned Ithacius to answer charges before him in a formal trial. These charges will presumably include calumny, for which heavy penalties will be imposed. I have heard even today that Ithacius has fled to Trier; no-one knows where Hydatius is, but he had kept himself scarce these last weeks.—Ithacius will be disappointed for the Emperor is absent. He may gain the ear of the ear of the Vicarius of the Spanish provinces, to whom he is answerable. But he, I have learned today is a friend of Macedonius, the very quaestor who has helped us in this matter. He can be relied upon to please his powerful patron, with access to the emperor. But we, my dear friends, we can go home!"

I should have held on to my excitement. Of course, no good news is incorruptible. As it turned out, although a guard of soldiers had been assigned to conduct Ithacius to Spain, he evaded them, and found refuge at the home of the bishop of Trier, one Britto, with whom I was unacquainted. He found Britto more than a willing ear, and with him Ithacius found a refuge. To make plots anew. But I knew nothing of this at the time.

We accompanied Euchrotia and Procula who returned to Elusa, where the harvest had been gathered and little had changed. Philip agreed to remain. Our parting was hard, and I will not write of it. But we had honored the vows between us.

I returned to Galicia. But it was not to be for long.

*   *   *   *

On a hot and a thunderous day which hung in the air but did not visit, both Elpidius and a letter came to me. Elpidius was not unaccompanied. He rode with a young man called Herenias, a recent convert, and a decent soul.

"The news is not good. It comes from Gaul. It seems that Magnus Maximus has been successful in leading a revolt in Britain. He is of Spanish origin. Not, it would seem a practicing Christian, but all who need a following, after Constantine, are Christians these days. We may not assume he is sympathetic to us. From what I have come to understand, his army met Gratian's in Paris. Gratian was abandoned by his own forces and had to flee in disguise. But even this was not successful. He was captured by a trick at the Rhine crossing. He had been promised safety by swearing a solemn oath on the Gospels. What that oath was we may never know, nor whether he broke it or not. For he has been murdered by Maximus' own cavalry commander. All of the provinces are gradually falling under Maximus' control. He is a butcher, this man! There is revolution in Milan. But by all accounts, we have a new Emperor, Priscillian. I shudder to think of what may well follow. Macedonius is in trouble and has sought asylum in a church. But the story is that he was a pagan and was refused admittance, perhaps by Ambrosius himself. I know not. We owe allegiance to a dangerous man, Priscillian. And were I you, I would beware."

Subsequent inquiries were to confirm the truth of Elpidius' words. Maximus claimed to be an orthodox Christian. It was clear enough that he would have no ear for what he and his henchmen would consider "heresy". I learned that Ithacius—who must have considered this coup a divine intervention in his support—had lost no time in presenting grave criminal charges against me and my followers. Britto, the Bishop of Trier, had presented the case, and no doubt animosity towards Gratian had fuelled the fire. No doubt the promise of money and lands had too, for the new Emperor must have been hard put to pay back his expenses for the uprising.

What transpired was that the case was referred to a Synod at Burdigala.

It could not be argued that I had not chosen this. A meeting of my peers was what I had requested. Now this I had. But I had enemies in the Aquitaine, as I have told you. I knew I would look for no friendly faces. Delphinias' hand was clear enough in this selection, and it was not intended to protect us. Letters, I learned, had been issued to the praetorian prefect, and to the vicar of the Spanish provinces, who could not this time hide behind Macedonius who had by that time "disappeared". We were to present ourselves at Burdigala, and this time there was nothing in the order which allowed us to decide otherwise.

The letter which came to me on that dark day was from Euchrotia:

"My Dear Priscillian," she wrote, "There are difficulties here which I cannot handle alone. They concern violations of trust that I cannot share to you except in person. Forgive me, but I need your help.
May God be with you,
Your loving,
Euchrotia.

It was on the hottest day in August that Elpidius and I set out. Herenias accompanied us. Instantius had remained in the Aquitaine, though I learned he had not spent much time at Euchrotia's estate. He had written to me, but his letters were short. Almost condensed. I thought at the time he had been exhausted from all that had accompanied our journeys. This time, I took Galla with me for I had not the heart to refuse her, though the wolfhound and Herakles stayed behind, just as reluctantly as before. My silver horse was ill of an unknown cause. I rode the bay. I asked that Herakles do what he could. I had taught him some of my skill.

I knew not then when, or if, I would see my home again.

*   *   *   *

I did not need Euchrotia to tell me of the urgency of her message, for it was quite clear that Procula was pregnant, and some months on, though she was pale, and seemed rather to have lost weight than gained it. I knew I did not have to ask who the father was. Philip came to me the first day. He spoke of his love for Procula. But there was no conviction in his words. Worse still, I saw greed in his eyes.

Euchrotia and I were alone that night, and for once I took a small glass of wine to accompany her. Perhaps I should have felt guilt, but compared to the other temptations in my mind, it was but a little shortcoming.

"There are monies missing. I may not be that knowledgeable in this, but going through the accounts with Marcellus—who is literate and distrusts Philip—at least he told me he has come to distrust him—it is clear that our accounts are not as healthy as they should be. Procula all but avoids him, despite his claim to love her. And she is not well, Priscillian. I have seen many pregnancies and I have seen all cause early distress, but her sickness goes on and on. She will not tell me how far along she is; she may not even know. I have sheltered her too much despite her lifelong exposure to the animals of our pastures. It is not right, this pregnancy, I feel it. All is not well with this. And I know not how to rid ourselves of Philip. Or even if I should. I know not how to confront him. He doesn't even show remorse. I cannot abide his arrogance. He has used my widowhood as an excuse to take command here, and I ..."
I took her in my arms then.

"You must not blame yourself. It is too late for such self-torture. You have been through much, and you must not chastise yourself for your trust, for at the time it seemed well placed. The question is, what do you want now? Will you approve of this marriage?"

"No! I do not approve of it. Neither do I feel that Procula wants it. But there is to be a child, Priscillian. What of that?"

"That remains months away. What then do you wish of Philip? Do you want me to ask him to leave?"

She looked at me then and I saw the subjection in her eyes. Now that I knew, her message to me had been well founded: she couldn't deal with this on her own.

"First, please, talk to Procula."

∗   ∗   ∗   ∗

The daughter sobbed in my arms as her mother had.

"He told me he loved me, Priscillian," she said. "He said it was natural between a man and a woman, and only he had considered me so. I was my mother's child; my father's little girl. I knew things of my own body—that I was growing and had a woman's desires, but ... My mother was so concerned with my father, and then you arrived ... when he ..."

"Forced you …?"

"No. No. Well not exactly, no. I just didn't know. He just said it was a kiss. A different kind of kiss. That I would like it. That only he could see how grown up I was. I did like it …"

"The day of the bluebell wood?"

"You remember? You said nothing to my mother?"

I shook my head.

"That was the first. There were others after. On the day after my father died, and then again before we left, and when we returned. He said he was so overjoyed to see me. Mother was so overcome with grief, especially the day you left … Oh!" and she began to cry uncontrollably, like a little girl, though by Roman law she was of an age to marry.

"And Philip, now? Does he still claim to love you? He wants to marry you? Has he asked you?"

"That is it … no! He just assumes because I bear a child, his child, that that is what will happen. All of the gentleness towards me that he showed me is gone. He thinks that now he can take my father's place … Oh … I feel so sick! "She rocked to and fro. I held her head as she vomited on the mosaics. She groaned in self-pity. "I hate this baby. I HATE it." She beat her little fists against her stomach.

I went to Phillip then.

"I suppose because you know how to fuck a woman you consider yourself a man! You were welcomed here, as a son. Is this how you repay those who sought to give a home to you? And what of these reports of missing funds. Hmm? What have you to say for yourself, Boy?"

He rounded on me then. I had not expected such from him.

"And who are you? A fugitive! A heretic! A seducer! An adulterer! Do you think no-one has seen the way you look at Euchrotia? My father is a Senator. You have nothing to threaten me with … Bishop." The last words were hurled at me in contempt, though there was fear in his eyes.

"Get away from here! Take your self and your things and do not return. We have no need for you. You raped that child and now you think to gain the reward of riches, just because your puny seed has taken home in Procula's womb. You disgust me! Go now, or I will not take heed of my cloth …"

He hesitated. He clearly had more to say but without the guts or the convictions to say it.

"Go! Or I will reduce your pretty face to such a pulp that no woman will ever look upon you again but to flee in terror!"

We did not see him again, though his presence was implied by its absence, and I was to live in regret of ever hearing his name.

CHAPTER 17

▼

Miranda was beginning to see her life as a blur, between what she read, and what she was experiencing. She was lost in the past. She had no time or energy to reflect on her own reasons for pilgrimage. She felt secondary to the narrative she had read:_ an unfinished tale. She walked still as one called, yet she began once again to think of Kieran, in between her reflections of Priscillian and Euchrotia and the fate that clearly awaited them. Where was he and how could he leave such a story in her lap? She had to know what was to happen next, yet every refugio, every guestbook left her more and more annoyed at the author of the story she now felt so caught up in. Needless to say, there was no sign of him, and no more of the manuscript. *'Where is he? How can he have burdened me with this? Is there to be no end to this narrative?'*

Why should I care? She left it unanswered.

She shared some of the story with Alex, but to her surprise, her companion showed no interest. In fact, she sounded openly hostile.

"It is only a **story**, Miranda! You are writing your own book! Look around you; look **inside** you. What do you see, what does it make you feel? No, I will not read it. And I advise you to put it aside. Leave it behind, if need be."

They were approaching Burgos, the first city of any size they had encountered thus far.

Perhaps, there?

Alex had regained her walking strength. All pain in her knees was gone—the tendonitis having completely healed. She walked on ahead, perhaps to distance herself from Miranda and her retellings. More and more Alex found other companions: Peter and Josje, from Belgium and the Basque regions respectively, who had struck up a friendship in Vezelay, and had remained inseparable ever since. Michelle, who had walked out of her house in Lausanne, (we are made from the same wood, Alex said), and Ferdinand who had walked with her since St. Jean-Pied-de-Port. Miranda once again saw herself as an outsider, and she knew she had placed herself there.

There was no more longing for Brazilians. Alex took her experiences as they presented themselves to her.

Miranda knew she had to get back to the real reasons why she was there.

But Kieran's story was so real.

And then, in Belorado, she met Felix again. She was travelsore that morning. They had slept that night in the *Polideportivo*, on the floor. The ache in her knees and calves was slowing her down. So were the misgivings in her heart.

She saw him getting off the bus. The others were well ahead.

"Hey!" he said, literally sweeping her off her feet, backpack and all. "Don't tell anyone about the bus … but I couldn't quite keep the pilgrim in me quiet. Besides, Pamplona was crazy, man. Talk about a death wish!"

"So, did you run with the bulls?"

"Me? I ran behind them. Safest place. I never saw so many falling-down drunks in my life! I like a bit more serenity in my life. But I'll never admit it! To anyone else, I have scarves soaked red with bovine blood, mixed with my own, blue, of course. I can, of course, rely on you not to give me away?"

"Of course," Miranda giggled, "what are friends for? I'm only too glad to see you alive! I could use a good laugh, to tell you the truth."

"So, how's it been? … Wait a sec …"

At the church, just before the descent up the hill, there was a *coche de appoyo* with three French ladies, filling water bottles and jettisoning their packs into the boot.

"Limp," said Felix.

"Pardon me?"

"Watch and learn," he said and he approached the white station wagon with a gait like Long John Silver.

"Excusez me. *Parlez vous Anglais?*" he said, with a pained look on his face. Miranda watched in fascination.

"My *compañero* and I have problems with the …" and he pointed to his knees, "*voulez vous* take our …" with this he unloaded his backpack … "*a la prochaine* refugio?"

He smiled that smile, the Felix Grin, guaranteed to melt the hardest Gallic heart.

"*Alors, bien sûr,*" was the response with an understanding smile, and it was no sooner done, than Miranda, in response to Felix' wink, was unloading hers too.

The white car sped off along the main road. The French ladies began the climb up the hill, also unburdened and in sharp formation, and Felix, turning to Miranda, said:

"See? Pilgrimage doesn't have to be an entirely unpleasant experience."

"You," said Miranda, laughing despite her embarrassment, "are incorrigible!"

"Yes, but you love me for it. And so do they. They think it is in the name of bonding EU relations. God knows, the French don't do much of it. Everyone wins."

Ask Miranda now and she will tell you that the walk that day, that stretch of the Camino was the best of all, despite the beauty of Galicia. She felt free. At first there was heather in the *Montes de Oca*, then oak trees. Climbing, always climbing. After a while they came upon a plaque. Miranda, whose Spanish had improved considerably, partly due to Alex, translated:

"1936: Rest in Peace" she said: "'*No ha muerto su semilla.*' It is memorial to the fallen of the Civil War. I think it means: "Your seed hasn't died." That is so sad. What a horrible time that must have been for Spain: brothers against brothers."

Both left the sprigs of heather which they had fastened to their *mochilas* and continued on. The forest growth began to change. Pine trees took over in profusion. They were deep; yet often, small paths, sometimes larger logging paths, led away from the Camino.

"You know, if I didn't feel that my way is marked for me, I would be tempted to follow those paths to see where they lead," observed Miranda.

Felix, for once, said nothing.

After a while, as the Camino led them down, and then steeply up, they came upon an open space. In the middle there was a small stone, and paths led to the points of the compass. They sat and ate a shared lunch.

"You know, you could go in any direction from here. It is a temptation away from the Camino," Miranda remarked.

"Which way would you choose?"

She was surprised at the question. "Well, that depends where each goes, doesn't it?"

"Perhaps." for once, Felix was serious. "But what if you don't know? What if there is only One Way. And that, once you have chosen it, become THE Way."

They sat in silence for a while.

"Yes," she said eventually, "and I have already chosen it. Now none of the others exist."

"That's about it, isn't it? That's life."

There was nothing to add to that. They continued on the main path.

*   *   *   *

The Monastery at San Juan de Ortega was overgrown, with nettles, as the name suggests, but also with history, and mould and rot. Yet the devotion of one man had kept it alive. His name was Jose Maria. He was the priest there, and he was known not only for his determination in securing donations for the restoration work, but for his garlic soup.

The refugio was dirty. The mattresses were lumpy and old. The pillows were musty, and the blankets better avoided. Still, it was a hot night. The pilgrims set out their sleeping bags and went out into the courtyard and the cold fountain to wash their hair, and their underwear. Alex was waiting. Miranda made the introductions and Felix wormed his way into their little group with little effort. Their numbers were growing. They seemed like a family now, with every family's loving concern and differences.

That evening, garlic soup being off the menu until October, they passed around jars of olives, red peppers, *garbanzos* and tuna, and some stale cheese contributed by Felix.

Jose Maria took Mass then showed them a carving which, every fall equinox, showed in reflected light the story of the nativity.

"Who knows why they are going?" he asked in Spanish.

Barely one quarter of those assembled put up their hands.

"And who is Spanish?" he took a glance at the pilgrims, you, you … He got to Miranda. "Not you," he said, taking in her blonde hair.

Then he took them into what remained of the cloisters. A huge wooden beam lay prostrate: "Tap it," he said. One of them did. "See! No termites!" came the triumphant cry. "But for how long?"

A sign regarding the expectations of donations made Josje, the Basque angry: "The Roman Catholic Church has investments in millions," he said, "yet still this priest must plead for money!" His disgust left the others in no doubt that nothing would come from him, he forgetting that not a penny had been spent for his night's hospitality.

Alex was disappointed there was no wind. She had been itching to show off her kite to Philippe from Paris, whom she had met that day. "He is avoiding me," she said to Miranda, and went to bed early.

The next morning, Jose Maria made milky coffee and asked again for donations, but it seemed there was little forthcoming. The church and its cloister was left to molder more. Miranda bought a pin in the gift shop, yet still couldn't shake the feeling of being a freeloader. Felix, to her surprise, gave a 1000 pesetas note.

"Good coffee," he said, "Why not?"

Uphill, the party was met with a perfect wind, and Alex once again launched her kite, though the object of her lust had gone. Miranda expressed a craving for bacon and eggs, and was astonished at the next village to get her wish, washed down with a local beer, though it was only 10:30 in the morning. Along the way, they passed the French ladies under poplar trees, enjoying a lunch spread across a picnic table. Felix tipped his straw hat, trimmed with his Pamplona bandana. Then it was up, and up.

The view over Burgos was deceptive. It seemed so close. They stopped for water, and cigarettes.

"I don't want to go into the city," Michelle said. And the thought was echoed by all of them. And they smoked another cigarette. Miranda abstained.

As it was they had plenty of time to prepare themselves. Instead of leading straight down, the Camino seemed to be leading them directly south, away from the city they had seen below so clearly. They left the path and began to walk on tarmac and all felt the heat rise through the soles of their boots. Alex complained of blisters. Felix just complained. The sun cream was passed around, and nearer to the next village, Miranda and Alex, who were then walking alone, were nearly swept off the road by a man in a yellow Renault, who, presumably not considering himself to have done enough damage to pilgrim spirit, came back and flashed his middle finger at them. Both returned the salute. In the next bar they were overcharged for cider, and a dog barked furiously and snapped at Miranda's heels.

On over the overpass, the builders whistled at the women, past the military installation.

"What was that all about," moaned Alex. "We look awful!" On to the main 'strip': the car dealerships, the furniture stores, and the shopping centers.

"Give me your sunglasses," Miranda said to Felix. "And your earplugs too. I can't stand this." The transport trucks passed them by with not so much as the minutest reduction in speed. Except for the odd horn-blowing, they were invisible.

They stopped for ice creams. Maria Blanca, the proprietor offered sympathy. They were sitting in the dust by the bus stop.

"Come on. My treat," said Felix and they all piled on, with only a sliver of guilt. They had to stand, but no-one cared.

"This is not the Camino," said Miranda patently, but with only a trace of remorse.

They got off the bus in the center of the town, by the gateway, near the river. It was altogether charming, but no-one had sightseeing on their mind. They followed the yellow arrows to the refugio. It was somewhat out of town: several wooden huts, but recently built, with showers, and a sports complex just across the road. It was clean, though almost full. The pilgrims spread themselves and their packs in whatever corner they could find vacant.

Later that evening, after they had aired their swollen feet and had a siesta, they were more of a mood to explore. The city proved enchanting, but expensive. The cathedral was the first stop, but Miranda found it oppressive: it was one of those church buildings where the choir stalls intruded on the whole perspective. Instead she went in search of a swimsuit. But she was not to use it.

She met up with Felix.

"Do you remember that pilgrim in Jaca? The one you told me about? The one you saw Kieran with? The German?"

Miranda had to rack her brains. She had met many Germans. "No, I can't say that I do. Describe him."

Felix tried, but it still didn't jog any memories.

"Sorry. Why? What about him?"

"He's here. I saw him in the bar outside."

"Let's go see," she said.

But the German, whoever he was, had gone.

"Why? What was so special about him. I don't understand," she said.

"Didn't you tell me you saw him with Kieran? Before he disappeared?"

Again, Miranda had to cast her mind back more than three weeks. A lot had happened since then.

"Heavy set? Very intensive eyes? Bushy beard?"

"That's the one."

"He's Spanish. From Valencia. His name is …?" But try as she might, Miranda couldn't recall it. Not even on the tip of her tongue. "Felix—we've got to find him!" she said. But where to start?

They gave the refugio a good looking-over. It was almost 11 o' clock. The last in the showers were taking to their beds. (Miranda had avoided the showers since it meant walking through the men's changing area, and she wasn't at all happy about that. Even now.)

They scanned the guest register for a name which might sound familiar.

"I'm certain he wasn't German. I'm sure it was a Spanish name. I remember it reminded me of someone from history, but I can't remember who. Damn!" Miranda said.

Then the lights went out and there was nothing to be done but to turn in.

The next day they had nothing more to show for their search and there was no choice but to continue on. Miranda, Felix and Alex walked on together. Alex had the sniffles and was brandishing a bottle of Belladona she had picked up at a nearby pharmacy. "Homeopathy, "she said, "is the only way to go."

But her pace slowed down, and Miranda for once surged ahead. She had found that swinging her arms from side to side rather than back to front increased her pace: so did humming Souza's marches, remembered from her childhood. Her father had been German, but he had had a vast collection of them. She conducted an imaginary military band as she walked, and the miles sped by.

They met in Tartajos. It wasn't far. Alex, when she arrived had bags under her eyes.

"Sometimes," she said, "it is a mistake to take on other's problems. They are too heavy. Everyone must find their own way. I need to rest today."

Clearly something had passed which had saddened her; she did not seem herself. But Miranda did not ask. Pilgrims were allowed their inner searchings, and even Alex was subject to her moods.

They stayed that night in new company, and it was to prove rejuvenating. Miranda thought she might see Kieran's companion, but it was not to be.

There were nine at supper: Alex, Miranda, Felix, Peter, Josje, a gypsy named Ricardo from Galicia, Catherine from Australia and her boyfriend Kevin from Cork, and the host, Jose Luis, who had seen many pilgrims come and go, yet his hospitality was still fresh. Michelle and Ferdinand had disappeared. It was often so that others went on ahead, not to be seen again. Josje gave grace in Basque.

After supper was concluded and the dishes washed (Miranda noticed that the women did this, but made no comment), Jose Luis opened a bottle of brandy to be shared by all:

"**Listen** to the Camino;" he said," don't hurry." Gradually, all began to open up:

"I have grown a new skin," said Ricardo. "When I left Galicia, I had a job, and a girlfriend, a car, many things. I went to Rome. I left from there. Different things are important to me now." He wore amulets around his neck. He stopped talking as if he had said enough. He had a silence hidden in his handsome face that few would ever uncover and it was clear that he knew this now.

Felix, much to Miranda's surprise, took up the thread:

"I may not be much of a pilgrim—I take shortcuts when I can ..." he looked at Miranda, but she said nothing, "... but in spirit, I am glad to be in this group tonight. You have all humbled me with your friendship and your words of encouragement. I hope the Good Lord gives me enough courage from here to finish this path. I have reasons of my own for being here, and so have others who are not of this company tonight ... there are many of us, walking at our own pace; thinking of our own dreams, dwelling in our own pain. Let's raise a toast to them."

"*Verdad*," said Jose Luis, and more brandy was poured.

"Any old excuse," said Felix to Miranda, with a wink. She scowled at him.

"And you, Catherine? You've come farther than all of us. Why are you here?" It was Kevin who spoke. Miranda had assumed he was her boyfriend but maybe not.

"My father died last year. It was always his wish to do this walk. I started out doing it for him, but now I can see I do it for myself. I'm not religious ..." there were heads nodding all around, "but I am beginning to see that there is purpose in life, even if our choices seem sometimes limited."

"I once described myself to a faculty colleague as an 'Existential Determinist'," added Miranda. "She laughed at me: she thought I was simple-minded. 'There's no such thing', she said to me, 'you believe one thing, or you believe another', but she was wrong. Now I think that we have limited choices, but as those choices are presented to us, we choose one or the other. Once that choice is made it opens up others, and closes those which are left behind. It's not 'Fate'. Nothing like it." Then she fell silent.

As the others continued to discuss her point, Miranda took the remainder of the *morcilla* outside to share with the dog with the long nose she had seen hanging around. He was clearly hungry, and abandoned, yet he was willing to take the risk to accept what this stranger was offering.

"You know what I mean, don't you?" she said as she avoided her fingers being consumed along with the meat.

CHAPTER 18

▼

They walked on, the next day. Alex's spirits seemed better but she was tormented still with the sniffles: a weight upon her chest, and it slowed her down, the homeopathy not yet having taken effect. Miranda was well ahead, in excellent health, still conducting her imaginary band. But her energy was only what drove her forward. After the last night's interchanges—and the events leading up to them—she had much to think about.

They met Catherine and Kevin again in Hornillos. They had wanted to break their hike early. Still they all continued: there was nowhere to stay. The temperature reached well beyond what anyone had expected. The atmosphere thickened, and Miranda's mood took on a distinct change. They were on the *Meseta* now. Miranda wanted above all to rid herself of her pack, and her thoughts. It became claustrophobic and tense. There was no sun, and the gathering clouds felt like they would stifle them. Miranda pulled out her inadequate poncho, once again, in readiness.

Then, it began to rain, gently at first, yet all agreed—although virtually unheard of at these latitudes at this time of year—it was needed to break the tension. Miranda was prepared this time, but—her spirit felt saturated: smothered. They were on the plateau in the middle of a thunderstorm once again, and there was no shelter this time. Not so much as a diminutive hayrick.

There are several stages of the Camino: she had read this. The first is Birth: from the Pyrenees to Pamplona. Then from there until Burgos is Life: a reawakening of the sensibilities. A New Beginning. But it is false: there is more to come. After this is Death: for those who dare look themselves in the face. The *Meseta*, from Burgos to Leon, is a place where even true pilgrims (whatever that may mean) lose their way. Many get no further than this. Miranda considered this nonsense, but now that many thoughts had been cleared from her mind (she believed), they came back to haunt her dreams, and her waking, walking thoughts. Other people, not even remotely connected with her personal journey, came to mind: Jonathan, her career, her parents. And later Kieran once again.

Outside of the Refugio of Los Angeles, she met up with a kitten; it came to her, soaked through as she was. Mewing in fear and loneliness. She placed it inside her poncho and gingerly—why was she afraid to enter? She went towards the refugio. There was no other respite in sight. Not so much as a tree of any size. It should have brought her joy at the sight, but, somehow, it did not.

"I don't feel we are welcome here," she said to the little life snuggled against the warmth of her breast.

The hospice was small and claustrophobic. There was a *cupola* painted with New Age motifs. It should have felt comforting. Instead it seemed somehow threatening. She cursed herself for her instincts but they were strong. 'We are not welcome here,' she thought again, but the promise of shelter won out. She asked for food and milk for the kitten:

"No animals are allowed inside!" It wasn't gently said. She wondered who indeed was welcome. The girl in the tank top coming downstairs snatched the kitten from her embrace and put it outside, in the wind and the rain. Miranda sat, looking at the pilgrims assembled there who made no move. There was no conversation, no joy. The place seemed static and rule bound. People sat in their places and looked as though they thought of where to go next, but made no move: it was a place where hardy souls give up, or become absorbed. Abandon their spirit and their dreams. Even the very atmosphere felt rigid. There were stars painted on the ceiling and goddess-like motifs. Candles and incense. But the feeling she got was anything but easy, or spiritual. She wished that Alex were here, and wondered what had held her up. Felix at least would have given the place a sense of humor, but he was behind them walking with the Australian and the Irishman with whom he was developing a friendship.

She went outside. The surroundings had a place of power all to themselves, and maybe on another day, in another weather, she might have felt differently. But she could not. The kitten was sheltering in a corner, trying desperately to find a place out of the wind and the rain. She felt a kinship with it. She found a cardboard box and emptying it made a makeshift shelter. A German man, who seemingly was the owner of this strange place put his head out of the window: "Yours?" he said.

"Does it matter?" replied Miranda she could not hide her animosity now. "She is small, and hungry; cold and frightened. No-one else seems to care."

He put his head back inside. The conversation as closed. Miranda could do whatever she pleased.

'I will stay here until Alex comes,' she thought. 'I will be a kitten too. I don't want to go inside again where there is no welcome for us.' And she cuddled it close to her. The tiny creature began to purr.

Her friend arrived soon after. With Ricardo, the gypsy from Galicia. They both looked at Miranda with astonishment.

"What are you doing outside?" said Alex. "It's nasty out here."

"Because there's no welcome for either of us," she said, and to prove her point, she pulled the kitten from inside her poncho.

"Alex, all I can think of is 'get me out of here!' Do what you want, but I will not stay here tonight. I'm going on, Alex. I am tired and wet, but I will not stay. I can't tell you why."

It was then that Alex showed her true friendship.

"O.K." she said, "We started together; we will finish together. I am as tired as you are, and the rain isn't likely to stop. But we'll go on today. O.K? But," she added it gently, "you know you can't take the kitten."

Miranda knew that it was not because of the kitten that she felt so vulnerable. That was just how her insecurities had manifested themselves. But she couldn't leave it so easily. She made a bed for it inside the box. She left it her ration of ham. She kissed it and bid it farewell. And even then, she wondered what part of her she had invested in this tiny and fragile animal, who seemed to have no home.

They continued. The rain stopped. But Miranda's fears did not.

She knew that in leaving Ricardo, Alex had made a supreme sacrifice for her. But it was a few days before she had the chance to investigate it. For the time, they were together still as comrades in arms. She loved Alex for this, but still she thought: 'When will it become obvious, our parting of the ways?"

She knew it was to be soon.

The road into Hontanas is flat: that is to say the approach is flat, but Hontanas is below the road. Perhaps you have to walk the path to appreciate it. The rain had stopped and a rainbow was before them. A cross appeared on their path. Gradually it increased in size until it was fixed to a spire, and then a building. It is a strange mirage to approach a town. Had it not been that their pilgrim Guides had warned them of this apparition, they might have felt the same awe that countless generations of pilgrims must have felt. Even then, it looked like a Miracle.

But, miracles said and done, they saw it only as a welcome shower, a bed for the night, and a hot meal, although, there were other warnings too, which shall be explained.

*   *   *   *

Outside it was stone. Inside it was stone and oak, recently refurbished. The place was spotless: someone had taken great care to welcome them. Only donations were asked for. The overall effect of the place was rustic and charming. The bunks were well spaced, and there was an area with a desk, beside a south-facing window. The showers were clean and the water was hot. In short, it was pilgrim paradise. The only thing lacking was a kitchen, so the pilgrims went in search of a restaurant. Despite the warnings, they settled on Alberto's. The guides warned single pilgrims—single women that is—to beware. There had been numerous 'complaints', but the nature of the complaints was not specific: anyway, there was no-where else in town, not then anyway. Alberto stocked a good table. All *caveats* were set aside.

There first was garlic soup, and all who had missed it in San Juan de Ortega wondered if it could have possibly have been better. Then there was a lamb main course (no chance to be a vegetarian on the Camino—be warned!). This was followed by an orange dessert, and copious wine. Alberto had a party trick which likely he still performs today. He would take a carafe of wine and pour it down his nose and, not missing a drop, consume it. Whether this was without also succumbing to its influence is a case in point, for there were suggestions of attempted seductions of gullible female pilgrims, but his clientele seemed not to listen for such hearsay. Miranda had the chance to glance at the kitchen and had to note that the conditions were less than most would consider 'sanitary', but later had to admit it was one of the best meals she had ever had in her life. Felix, just toasted everything and everyone, and his opinion cannot be considered reliable.

Suffice it to say, at some ungodly hour of the morning, one Australian, one Canadian, and one German woman, all university educated, were seen to walk the (admittedly short) distance down the road to the refugio linking arms and singing arias from Tosca. Felix was beyond walking and how he got back, no-one the next day could say. Though at 10:00 in the morning, long after he should have been thrown out, he was still snoring in his backpack, but happily, it must be said.

And so they continued, this happy family of strangers. Catherine walked fast and it was all that the others could do to keep up with her. They passed a man with a flock of sheep, all black. "*Un abrazo por Santiago,*" he called after them. They passed a strange, abandoned convent, with an intricate archway, still intact, though the rest was slowly decomposing. An imposing castle beckoned from the top of a hill, but none took up the invitation. A surprisingly cold wind came up, and Miranda stopped at a local bar for an early brandy and a coffee; some tortilla for breakfast. The locals looked at her as though they had never seen a pilgrim before, and she downed all too quickly rather than be an object of their intrusive stares, or their incomprehensible comments. She was wearing shorts, walking shorts admittedly, but short enough to show off her good legs. She had clearly created a breach of conduct. Women didn't go into these places of domino-playing men. These men had been effectively separated from women since their courting days. Since they were "*noviasgos*": perspective suitors. Women belonged in the kitchen with their offspring. Women kept themselves decently covered. Women didn't indulge in alcohol, especially at such an hour. It was only 11 o'clock. The men with their *anis*, were of course, exempt.

Once back on the path, straight now and bordering the road, there were no other pilgrims in sight. Miranda walked the next few kilometers *sola* and despite the warmth the brandy had brought to her head and her stomach, she thought dark thoughts. The path of death was having an impact.

For the first time in weeks, her feet hurt. So did her heart. She got to a stone bridge and beside it was an ancient building. It was a refugio maintained by Knights of Malta: a real "*hospital*". It was still early and she hadn't walked far, but she decided to go in for water. Once she entered, she knew she had to stay.

It was small, and resembled a chapel rather than the hospices she had grown accustomed to. All around the altar there was a semi-circle of chairs, all trimmed with regalia. It hinted of absent souls. There were many pilgrim shells. Red crosses in the Templar shape. There was no-one in sight.

'*I wish I had brought the kitten here,*' she mused. '*I wish Alex were here. She would have loved this.*' But the wine had seemed to have done what the Belladonna had not. Or perhaps it was the combination? Alex had gone on ahead.

'*I wish I was not so fragile right now.*'

There were no more than sixteen places. One of them only was claimed. Beside the sleeping area was a modern—or so it seemed—carved stone statue of St. James. A candle burned beneath it.

Miranda felt a feeling of peace creep over her.

A monk entered. He brought her a glass of cold water upon seeing her face, and her flushed cheeks. Somehow he intuited her pain. "Sleep now," he said to her, gesturing towards the bunks.

And she did.

When she awoke it was to cooking smells. The other occupant was seated at a small table, writing in his diary. No-one else had elected to stay: it was only a few kilometers to the next town. He introduced himself first in French, but then seeing her look of bewilderment, switched to clear English. His name was Julian, and he was from Brittany.

Two monks joined them for dinner. It was set up in front of the altar at the eastern end of the building. It seemed they were the only full-time residents. Both spoke English well, but at times, Julian had to translate a point. He spoke five languages, he said, including Esperanto. But very little translation was needed as the meal was eaten in virtual silence.

It was simple, ageless, like the building and the dress of the monks themselves: Miranda felt her appetite return and she tucked into potatoes and rice, olives and sardines washed down by a carafe of wine although one, from Sicily, kept one carafe beside his plate: "This is for me," he said. "Imported especially". Had he been any other man he would have said it with a wink.

Tucked up later in her sleeping bag, Miranda lay on her side, looking at the face of the statue of St. James, illuminated now by the candle: the only light.

'I will remember this," she thought, as she dozed into dreamless sleep.

*   *   *   *

On to Boabdilla, and hot once more. She wondered where Alex was, and Felix, and Catherine ...? She felt she had lost her pilgrim identity without them and was eager to catch up. All had stayed in the next town, Ytero, over the bridge. They had written for her in the pilgrim's guestbook. 'Not nice,' Alex had penned: 'Wherever you are, it's better than this. See you at the next. Besos. A.'

On top of the hill, a white car was parked. The owner, by name Jesus, said he would take her to the *refugio* at Boabdilla. It was new, he told her, but welcomed pilgrims like herself. It was only 1000 pesetas. He had built it for weary pilgrims etc., etc. Or at least that was the message she got. She had discovered her Spanish was not nearly enough without Alex' translations. She first thought him a bit of an ambulance chaser, but the seven kilometers remaining sped by, and she was glad of the assistance, though felt guilty at the foot-mileage lost to St. James.

All but one of their party were there: The Belgian, the Basque, Alex, Catherine and Kevin. Ricardo alone was missing.

"Perhaps he was captured by the angels in Los Angeles?" said Alex.

"More likely eaten by the owner and his girlfriend," Miranda countered.

Alex looked at her in good-humored reproach: "Now, now. You know what the English say: '*If you can't say anything nice, then don't say anything at all*'".

"Hmmm," Miranda said. But she knew in some ways her friend might be right. Maybe it was just her. She let it pass.

They walked into Fromista and its Romanesque church, and its columns, topped once by obscene carvings, now in a museum in Palencia, the capitol of the Province.

"My guidebook says it was to remind worshippers that they left the Devil outside," said Alex.

"So why were these inside," asked Miranda.

No-one seemed to know.

There was no-where to make supper so they went in search of a cheap *menu,* but were disappointed at the tourist prices, and shared a plate of *patatas fritas* instead.

"Good for the soul," said Miranda, dolloping a proffered bottle of ketchup.

"And the purse," added Alex. "Mine is getting a but thin."

The Camino joined the main road again. There were signs saying "*Camino de Santiago*", but they were intended for the car-pilgrims. Not for them.

"We are a tourist attraction," Alex offered. And Miranda could think of no objection.

*   *   *   *

Carrion de los Condes found them in search of an alternative. The refugio was full, even though they arrived early. Miranda, who had somehow got separated from Alex, went in search of the Convent she had been told offered beds for 1000 pesetas, but even there, there was no sign of Alex. Where could she have gone? She found her later, waiting by the crowded refugio. "I went to the Monastery," she said, almost in tears. "They wanted 9000 pesetas!" For the first time in a long while, Miranda saw her friend close to defeat. "I have no clean clothes," Alex said, as if in explanation, and it seemed like she had reached some sort of personal crisis.

"I've found us somewhere; come with me," she said, and she took Alex's backpack across her shoulder, in addition to her own, though thanks to Kieran's manuscript, hers was far the heavier. For once, she felt like she was the mother, Alex the child.

*   *   *   *

At the nunnery she brandished her pilgrim passport and Alex's own. Her German friend had sunk to a waiting bench. Miranda signed in for both of them. But then, turning with the key to a twin room, she saw two big tears coursing down her friend's face. This capitulation brought out some long lost motherly instinct in her.

Bed, and a good hot meal was clearly the best place. Perhaps for them both, though Miranda suddenly saw her new role in a new light.

Once in their room, Alex collapsed on the bed, and pulled the clean sheets over her head.

"I'm wet," she sobbed, "Even my pillow is wet!"

"I'm going to make you a solid meal!" Miranda said, her hand on the door handle. "In Aragon I had *Migas*: it means breadcrumbs. Enough of this miso soup— you need proper food!"

But the door refused to open.

"Looks like we're locked in," she said, giggles rising to her mouth.

"Good!" said Alex from under the covers, "I don't care!"

But with brute force, Miranda was triumphant and returned half an hour later with a platter of, rather burned, shredded bread, and couple of crispy friend eggs.

Alex was fast asleep. Miranda ate her feast herself, and was rather glad she didn't have to admit her lack of Spanish culinary skills to anyone else.

*   *   *   *

"I'm over the mountain," Alex said the next morning. "But let's stay another day."

Downstairs, Miranda found a copy of Paulo Coelho's The Pilgrimage. She spent the day reading.

It was not her pilgrimage, but no pilgrim shares another's pain. She found it astonishingly Masculine, yet some part of her could relate. Coelho had not stayed in any of the pilgrim hospices: he found his own—he and his spirit guide. He encountered his own Black Dog.

"Where will mine turn be to wrestle with this creature?" thought Miranda as she placed the finished book back on the shelf?

CHAPTER 19

▼

Alex had met up with Josje and Peter, the gay couple, or at least it was obvious to everyone except Alex herself. "They have the best legs on the Camino," she said. They walked much faster than Miranda, and Alex, for her own reasons, kept up the pace. Felix had vanished, and Catherine and Kevin were up ahead. They had left early.

Miranda was feeling sorry for herself. The road, though easy now, in brilliant summer sunshine, and not too hot for walking, lagged behind. She felt ill-used.

Seeing her companions disappear over the horizon, she stopped.

"I don't want to continue!" she said to herself, as she drank her liquid yogurt. "I Hate this walking!"

At the next refugio, only a few kilometers—her companions were signed in but nowhere in sight—she went in search of lunch. At a small cramped bar she found Ricardo, the gypsy she had first encountered in Tardajos. He was writing intensively in his diary and she at first held back. At some point he looked up. The denizens of the bar were watching a nature program: a lion copulating in some Savannah. They seemed fascinated, for although the bar was thick with smoke, there was no conversation.

"Are you a lion?" Miranda asked, and then realized the implications.

"No, I'm a snake," he said, he winked, and went back to his writing.

Miranda slunk away.

By the time she got back to the refugio, Alex's bunk was bereft of her things. She had left, without so much as a note.

Miranda decided, despite herself, to follow them. Along the way she met Margaret and Ian from South Carolina. It was obvious—that southerly drawl.

"Ah, yes," Margaret said: "but I don't have an accent where I come from."

At the next refugio—a private one with full baths—Alex appeared.

"Where did you go?" she said.

Miranda had no answer, but still felt betrayed.

That night she joined the three of them, and Ricardo, who arrived later. She drank too much wine.

Afterwards—or was it during—she talked with Alex about the time to separate. It seemed obvious. The time she had dreaded had come.

A distance was definitely there.

"You are still talking about Kieran," Alex had said, "it is interfering with your Work."

The next day, Alex went on. "If we meet again, then, we meet." Then she was gone.

*   *   *   *

Miranda walked on, alone. The others were God knows where, and why should **she** care? She had started alone. She would finish alone if need be. But it was a sad realization, and it slowed her down. She missed the arrows and got lost. She tried not to cry, but the tears were close. She felt like an outcast. Even Felix had disappeared once again and was probably on the bus to Santiago by now.

"I'm far too sensitive," she said to herself in self-recrimination.

She walked more than 30 kilometers that day, but to this day remembers very little of what she passed except hollyhocks and gathering their seeds, for some future garden.

Sahagun was ugly on the outskirts. She saw it well before entering, and it seemed grey like her mood. But the refugio was a five-star deal. It had once been a church: in fact the church part was still there though seemed to be occupied by a conference group, and was separated from the pilgrim dormitory. There seemed little connection between the two.. Miranda chose a bunk bordering the glassed-in partition area at the end. The backpack bordering hers looked like something belonging to someone she had once known. Perhaps in another life. It had been a long walk that day.

"Miranda!" beamed a familiar face, followed by a hug. "Now I am sure that God wants us to explore together. I have been missing you all day."

"Peter and Josje?" she said.

"Them? They've gone," was the response. "They're gay, didn't you know?" as if it was an explanation.

But Miranda was too overjoyed to care.

From there they could look down—God-Like—on the proceedings. There were curtains, but easily pulled apart by curious hands and eyes. At one point they found themselves listening to Mozart; on the proceedings far below them in the church. The water in the showers was hotter than any they had so far encountered. It came in pulses, but it was only because of the overworked boilers. There were sixty four bunks, but only two burners.

Communal washing was thrown into communal washing machines, and sorted later. For once, the pilgrims felt like human beings again. Even the cyclists shared their wine in return for some of Alex's inevitable miso soup. Ricardo the gypsy shared their space and Miranda noticed it was she he winked at. "What makes him so attractive?" she thought.

In the night, someone was shouting, maybe in their sleep. And the next morning she noticed a small, lacy, black bra on top of her sleeping bag as she was packing up. Ricardo's doing? she asked herself. But there was no answer to that, although Alex seemed a bit miffed.

They went to visit the famous church of Santa Lucia, under renovation at that time. Miranda bought Alex a comb as a souvenir of their time together. It seemed obvious now, that need for separation. She had expected it, but wanted it on her own terms. Selfish? Perhaps. It didn't matter. She had to think of why she had come in the first place: now seemed like that time. "I'm going to stay for tonight," she said. "I need a bit of time before I go into Leon."

"Maybe you're right," was all Alex had to say. They exchanged e-mail addresses, and then the German was off. Miranda felt strangely free.

*   *   *   *

That night, having managed to explain to the *Hospitalero* (who was from France but spoke perfect English), that she needed to think a bit more, (normally this necessitated a visit to the doctor, blisters, that sort of thing, but she was in luck this time: an understanding ear,) she went in search of a good dinner. Something fitting to celebrate her new found independence. She wandered the streets for a while, looking at restaurant prices, and finally decided to splurge. The meal was excellent, the wine well appointed, the waiter captivating and polite. There wasn't a pilgrim in sight. Miranda, who had even applied make up and perfume that night, in addition to sweet smelling clothes, felt like a woman again. Well, almost.

On her way "home" she decided to stop for a brandy, to watch the passers by. To look at normal people in normal shoes. At the first bar she passed, she saw someone familiar.

It was the same pilgrim she had seen on the first day. The one who had been seen talking to Kieran. The same one that the two women had said they had seen Kieran with—God, it felt like years ago! He was alone. On the table was a bottle of wine, half finished and the remains of a meal. A notebook, scribbled in. And a book. A photocopied book. And another which he was eagerly searching through, a pencil in his hand.

She stopped for a minute. What was she supposed to do at this point? Go up and challenge him? Where did you hide my friend? My friend whose book I still carry? Who are you anyway? Why haven't I seen you up to now? And anyway ... **where is Kieran?**

Instead she sank into a corner chair and watched him. No doubt about it. He was working on something, and seemingly oblivious to anyone around him. What would he have to fear anyway? she thought. What the hell is he doing with Kieran's book?

She bided her time, but then seeing him ask the waiter for something, she knew she either had to follow him to who knows where ... and what for? or confront him there and then. Or be a good compliant citizen/unknown pilgrim and leave the whole thing alone.

The last option was not in her nature. She downed her brandy for courage and then she got up and walked in his direction, standing between him and the artificial light.

Once there, she realized that she didn't know what to say, or how to say it ... in any language. It was too late: she was exposed by her own hand.

"*Perdone*," she said timidly and then realized that the direct approach as her only option, "but what are *usted* doing with *el libro de Kieran*?" She pointed to the manuscript using her hands in a questioning pose. She felt afraid. But it was too late to back down now. She wished that Felix were here.

He looked up at her in surprise. He made a gesture to cover the manuscript. She after all, had had half an hour to peruse him whereas he had no idea of her threatening existence.

"*Este libro? Por que? Tu haces?*" She said again.

He picked up all his books and documents and glowered at her. "*No es asunto tuya!*" he said. And slapping a 1000 pesetas note on the now empty table, he beat a hasty retreat.

Miranda was left dumbfounded.

"What the hell was that all about?" she thought. But her better nature fought down the instinct to follow him.

Back at the refugio, she asked the French *hospitalero*, who was writing up the day's proceedings:

"What does 'no-es ass-un-to-too-ja' mean?" she asked

It means 'It's none of your business!" he said, and went back to his work.

PART III

*If a man could mount to Heaven and survey the universe,
his admirations of its beauties would be much diminished
unless he had someone to share in his pleasure*

*   *   *   *

Cicero

CHAPTER 20

▼

She thought she might see him at breakfast, but scouring the town added nothing to her search. There was no point looking at hotel registers: she didn't remember his name anyway. And what would it have lead her to if she had? She could hardly have reported him to the Guardia Civil for expropriating a photocopied book—especially a book which wasn't supposed to have existed—from a man she had met almost a month before, whose name she didn't even know! She couldn't even report him for infringement of copyright!

Miranda took the train to Leon. A two day hike, or one for Catherine the Marathon walker. Had there been no train, perhaps events would have turned out differently. But there was—at 12:20, in twenty minutes time. She felt a little guilty, but it didn't matter. She had to share her research findings with Someone! She knew if she could find a way to stay overnight in Leon, she would have a chance of meeting up with Alex, who, despite her disregard of "Miranda's book" might at least have been a willing ear. And maybe the others. "Even a hotel will do," she thought.

Sitting nose pressed to the train window for signs of Blackbeard or her companions, Miranda felt as though she had been wrenched out of security. The Camino flew by, flat and poplar-fringed here, overlooked by monstrous blue skies which dwarfed everything including the train. This movement was too fast and Miranda felt dizzy at the thought as she saw pilgrims in their ones, pairs, and groups slip into a visual Doppler Effect as the train sped by them and not one looked up from the way ahead.

Why should they? The Camino was a world in itself: a microcosm where the trials, tribulations, and triumphs were all almost all internal. Walking long distances provided its own agenda. There were no runner's highs, no dramatic climaxes. The Camino was all: ever following the sun during the day, and under the Milky Way at night. Miranda thought about her first two days walking and how vulnerable she had been, how tightly wrapped; how many self-doubts had troubled her. Now she saw the weeks in between as gradually unfolding herself, taking off un-needed swaddling clothes a little every day until now she felt free to start every day with only one goal in mind: to reach her chosen refugio, and to stay with her friends She had also allowed others to come close and had become less suspicious of other's motives. When did I become that way, she wondered as the train passed a congregation of pilgrims, none of them "hers".

She thought about the little group she had become a part of—a family with a common purpose: Felix the joker, Alex who perhaps was the heart. She thought about Catherine and Kevin and how Kevin seemed to bask in her Australian sunshine, just happy to be wherever she was. A few weeks ago, he had no idea she even existed, and now it was obvious to everyone that they were smitten with each other. Then there were Peter and Josje. The two gays came from very different backgrounds. Josje's family was rich and supportive, and nominally Catholic; but he had known that somehow he was different from quite young, and so had his mother, although through his father's eyes it had taken much longer, and even now was not completely accepted. Peter, on the other hand, came from traditional working class parents who knew nothing of his sexual preferences and as far as Peter was concerned, they never would. He knew what it would be like to see his father's anger and denial, his mother's sense of guilt. And so it was Josje who was more openly homosexual. With Peter it was much harder to tell. He had told Miranda while they were walking together one day that he was considering marrying, perhaps even having children in order to maintain the fiction his family believed. He said he had no illusions of staying with Josje after the Pilgrimage was over and that he thought that maybe following a traditional family future— the one his parents were waiting for him to follow—might eventually make him change. Miranda had inner reservations that this was not a fair thing to do either to another person, or to himself, but she kept them to herself. She adored them both and thought them well suited. It's a pity the world is not more accepting, she thought.

Ricardo she found dangerously attractive with his long black gypsy hair and handsome face. However, his attraction was much more than just looks. There was that exoticness; that enticing aspect that he could not have turned off even had he tried: knowing that he belonged to an ancient race of people who had always been somehow on the outside, continuing their own ways, telling their own stories. Alex was clearly taken with Ricardo and Miranda wondered what hidden insecurity in her friend would allow her to try to get so close to his flame. Alex radiated a light of her own, but Miranda couldn't help but think that inside she was perhaps rather lonely. Certainly she did seem to seek out male company whenever she could. Ricardo was her latest quest.

After almost a month's walking she had found that she had managed to push concerns about Kieran's whereabouts almost to the background. Where Kieran had initially pre-occupied her thoughts, now it was Priscillian who seemed the more real. Or were they one and the same? Walking with Kieran had the more dreamlike quality. Now, having set out to capture Blackbeard, Miranda realized that she had to focus once more on Kieran and it came as a complete surprise to her that she found herself missing him. She had gotten used to Alex seeking out male company. It had not occurred to her that perhaps she needed some of her own. Yes, she had only walked with him for one day, but by the end of the day she had felt that they were a team, albeit a team joined by Felix, and she recalled the disappointment she had projected as annoyance when she realized that they were not to walk on together out of Jaca.

In fact, what struck her was that Kieran as a person, rather than as a missing person, had never really left her at all. The thought annoyed her.

Leon, too soon, her family all behind her now, Miranda set out to find the refugio and was tempted by the idea of a hotel. She passed many, and at one, the Hotel la Reina, which looked nice, and cheap, she thought to go in and inquire. A private room and bath was certainly a temptation; she would have loved to spend some time alone, thinking about her latest insight. Instead she kept walking into the town. She didn't exactly know when the others would turn up, and she didn't want to miss them. But she wrote the name and the telephone number in her pilgrim book, just in case the refugio was full.

The refugio, a convent, was a good distance from the station and her pack had never felt heavier. In addition to her own misgivings, she also had Priscillian, and

Euchrotia, and their inevitable fate to consider. She knew that since her companions wouldn't have yet arrived, she might have to wait another night, and that, generally, was all but impossible. Felix, out of no-where, came to mind: "Limp!" he had said at the Montes de Oca.

Miranda limped.

The nuns agreed that she was in no shape to continue further, and once she explained that all she needed was the chance to rest up, and the support of her friends, "… since the Pyrenees," she whined, convincingly, they said she could stay if she would agree to help out tomorrow morning with the cleaning. Naturally, Miranda agreed.

As it turned out, she need not have been so penitent.

"Jesus! Felix!"

"Yes, I agree there are certain similarities," said the occupant of the upper bunk. "How the hell are you? And, may I add, where have you been? It's time you got here. Charm has its limitations you know. I've already peeled the potatoes and cleaned the loos."

She thought she would tear his neck off with her hug!

"You have no **idea** how glad I am to **see** you!" she said. And then, to her chagrin, she burst into tears.

"Hey! Hey! I know I am irresistible, but …?"

On seeing Miranda break down, Felix had a sudden, and largely uncharacteristic feeling of conscience:

"You're right. I haven't been the best of pilgrim companions. Come on … the cheapest Pilgrim *Menu* in town is on me. Drop your stuff and let's go."

After, Miranda explained in answer to his questions that the others were behind, and anyway she had had reason to go ahead from Sahagun. She told him about her encounter of the night before, and she filled him in of the missing details.

"You are sure? It was Blackbeard? With Kieran's book? Hmmm. This new development may need a bit of Felix's grey matter after all. *'It's none of your business*? That's what he said?"

Miranda nodded over her *patatas a la pobre* and egg.

"He got up and fairly **ran**, Felix! Why would someone do that it they had nothing to hide?"

Felix made no comment but drained his *copa* of Rioja and asked for another bottle, hoping a bit belatedly that the restaurant accepted credit cards (*there's always the washing up—and I'm used to that,* he consoled himself.)

"How much did Kieran tell you?" he said, once the next bottle was uncorked.

"About what?" Miranda said, she too was beginning to feel the heady combination of adrenaline and wine.

"About himself?"

"Well …? You know, not much really. It was one day … He spoke most of the time but it was all history, and conjecture … about himself … nothing," she replied with surprising discomfiture. After all, she had begun to feel, in the intervening weeks, that she knew him well.

"Nothing, then, about his past …? Or his state of health?"

"State of health? No. Why? Felix, what are you getting at?"

Felix paused:

"Miranda. Kieran has leukaemia."

It was a stone. A heavy rock dropped on her brain cells in a moment of unguardedness and mental exhaustion. It wiped out everything she had conjectured, everything she had built up—almost in self-protectiveness as well as fascination, over the last four weeks."

"Jesus!" was all she could say.

Felix poured more wine for both of them. There was nothing to say for the moment.

Finally, Miranda recovered, if just for the time being.

"How do you know this?" said, in a very quiet voice.

"Do you remember I told you I had been with Kieran at Lourdes?"

It was a long time ago, but, yes, yes, she had to admit, eventually. Yes, I do remember that.

"Well, we went there, but not by chance. You see, Kieran and I were at Uni together, in Bristol. I was a Psychology student—don't laugh, I got an Honors, though still don't know how—Kieran was in Theology and we met in a 3rd year psychology class: Freud or Jung, I think. I still can't tell much of a difference. Anyway, after he went to the seminary in Dublin and I got a real job, we stayed in touch. First by mail, and in the last year or so by e-mail. Our letters were more about girlfriends—mine that is, and the lack of, nor need of, in his (he claimed)—but they brought a lot of closeness between us. After a while as is inevitable as people move on, we lost touch. Then I found the woman of my dreams. I became engaged to Jessy, and he got more and more ready to take his Holy Orders, though, had he asked me, I would have said that I didn't think he was ready. On the other hand, he probably would have said the same to me about marriage."

Miranda remained silent, but took another sip of wine, and for the first time in many years, craved a cigarette.

Felix stopped talking for a few minutes. He seemed truly disturbed by the topic of conversation, so Miranda pushed her remaining *patatas* around her plate.

In the end, he continued: "Anyway, our correspondence got shorter and fewer and farther between. You know how it is. Then one day, after a long interval, he wrote to me: two things had happened to him, he said. One was that he had been sent a manuscript from Rome. He said he couldn't tell me much about it as he wasn't even supposed to have it, but that it had caused him tremendous doubts about his faith in the New Testament gospels. The other, he said, concerned his health. He was considering going to Lourdes. Would I be willing to accept a visitor in Bristol—along the way to his Pilgrimage, he said? I wrote back, 'Yes. I could really use a friend right now.'"

"Jessy broke off the engagement?"

A choked silence. But only a short one: one which had passed the state of shock.

"Jessy was killed in a car accident, Miranda. Drunk driver. On the way to her Hen Night. She and two of her bridesmaids."

"Oh, Jesus!" Miranda said. She shut her eyes tight. She wanted to hug him, but knew it would decrease rather than increase their closeness at that point.

It took a while before he spoke again: "Kieran came and stayed for almost 6 weeks before we set out for France. We didn't talk much. Men don't. In a way we had both lost our heart's desire: the magic carpet had been swept out from under us both and in all honesty, the last place I wanted to go was Lourdes. I didn't believe in God. I didn't believe in anything. But I had been to Lourdes once before, and I had been moved by the faith of others. In the end, I guess, we convinced each other to go."

Miranda didn't know what to say: 'What was it you both hoped to find?' was uppermost in her mind. But she knew there was no point asking it. In moments of hopelessness, reasons don't come to us for the actions we take.

"Anyway, we took the Chunnel, and then we bused and hitch-hiked south. We finally walked the last part from Toulouse, and found that walking opened up a lot in each of us that we hadn't been able to share before. Lourdes was almost an anti-climax. I think both of us had progressed in different directions, and you know how it is: after a while there seemed to be not so much to say. So afterwards, we parted company. I intended to go back to England, or maybe join the Camino in Burgos—I mentioned both. Kieran had his book to translate. I felt, well, in the way by that time."

"Then, we both met you in Jaca. For some reason I thought that you two had actually met in Lourdes. I understand now."

"But then, in Jaca, he went off, and you didn't understand that. I couldn't betray his confidence now, could I? You were virtually strangers, though, I hoped, for his sake, that there was something more. You seemed, I don't know, maybe suited …? I've come across as a bit of a lightweight, I know. But with my world swept away, Miranda, I didn't know how to be serious anymore. I've been looking for something too. Answers to my questions. Trouble is, I haven't had the courage to ask the real questions. I don't even know what they are. So I've made my own answers. All short term."

Miranda looked around them. Normal people were out and about: students, tourists, couples, families with children. She, as a so-called 'Pilgrim', felt particularly unworldly and separate at that point, especially in light of all that had happened in the last twenty four hours.

"Where do you think he is? Kieran, I mean?"

"Who knows? Probably gone back to Ireland. He had his 'off days'"

"And his manuscript?"

"Why has someone else got it? Jeez, Miranda. I wish I could answer that question. It makes no more sense to me than it does to you. Maybe it's just one more of life's mysteries that we have to accept, and walk on—literally in our case. I'm too close to Compostela to back out now."

"You know I've got his book? Kieran's?"

"Book? What book? I thought you said that Blackbeard had it."

"Kieran was—is, I hope—writing a book about a bishop who lived in the 4th century. He gave me part of it in Jaca. Do you remember he left me something with his note?"

"In your pack. Yes, I do. Why would he have done that …?"

"I don't know. At the time I felt like his mule, but there was something sent to me in Puente la Reina too. I've been carrying it all this way, hoping to meet up with him again."

"You still have it?" He left off asking why she hadn't mentioned it before.

"Yes, of course." Miranda felt a bit hurt at the suggestion. "It's good too. It's called <u>Pilgrimage to Heresy</u>, but I still don't know how it ends."

"Maybe that's the metaphor," said Felix. "None of us knows how "it" ends. I'd like to read it though."

And over the next day, while they were waiting for the others to catch up, and some semblance of the missing "Ominous Pilgrim" as Felix now called him, that is exactly what he did do.

"Man, we've gotta locate this guy!" he said. "And we've got to find Kieran!"

*   *   *   *

Then the family was one again: in dribbles and drabbles. Hot dusty pilgrims re-grouped in the convent refuge in Leon: first Catherine and Kevin, then Alex, then Ricardo, later followed Peter and Josje. All were astonished to see her there, yet after she had brought them up to date with the latest news–"Blackbeard" as the group began to call him, and who got more and more satanic with every re-telling—Kieran's illness, and finally Miranda felt compelled to tell about the photocopied manuscript. All agreed that she had done the right thing in "cheating Santiago" the few extra miles by train.

"So what do we do know?" asked Alex, and the plural pronoun was not lost on Miranda who suppressed a smile. "We haven't seen him at any of the refugios since we began so he's unlikely to turn up at this one, and you two aren't going to get another extension. It's hit the road or the Hilton tomorrow."

"Maybe we could try that," Catherine suggested, "Split up and check out the smaller hotels?"

"Thanks guys, but I don't know what his name is, and even though he's pretty distinctive looking, we can't exactly do an "Identikit" picture, can we?" Miranda looked from one face to another.

No artists in the group revealed their secret identity.

"Well, that's it, then, stay tonight, hit the town and hope to see him somewhere (*and ask him ... what?* Miranda thought secretly, but at least they had two Spanish speakers now). If not, on to Santiago tomorrow, and trust to luck. The Camino gets pretty sparse from here and there's no hotel between here and Ponferrada that I know of."

It turned out there were quite a few hotels in varying sizes: this was "Santiago Country", but no-one fitting Blackbeard's description could be found. They had given up checking the books at the refugios since it was obvious that he wasn't staying in any of them, at least since Puente la Reina.

"He could have a tent?" Felix put in, and all looked at him in antagonized despair; the variables were bad enough as they were.

But Blackbeard made no appearance, with or without camping gear, and they continued on their way the next day, leaving as their internal clocks dictated: Miranda and Felix making up the rear, as it was when they started.

In Puente de Orbigo, Felix found an Internet café, and looking up hotels in the vicinity of the Monastery of San Juan de la Piedra, where Kieran had said he was going, gradually ticked each one off the list. Lastly he tried the monastery itself, cursing himself for not doing it first.

"Kieran O'Donovan? What date was it you said?"

Felix repeated it. It was almost six weeks prior.

"Yes," the receptionist came back after a while; Felix's stash of small change was diminishing by the minute. "He stayed here for ... let me see ... three nights, or was it four? No, three nights."

"Do you have any idea where he was going? Did he say he was going to rejoin the Camino? To take a taxi down to Puente la Reina?"

"I'm sorry, *Señor* ... what did you say your name was again?" Felix told him. "We are not in the habit of inquiring after our guests' plans after, or even during, their stay with us. Most people stay in a monastery because they guard their privacy ..." Felix could hear the barely veiled recriminations in the thin voice, "and what they do or don't do is none of our business." *Nor mine either*, thought Felix ... *I get it.*

"Yes, yes, of course, I understand, but do you happen to remember a big man with him, strongly built, black beard, very beady eyes ..." *(should have left out the last bit ...)*

"I'm sorry *Señor*, I really cannot help you further, now if you'll excuse me ...?"

Felix felt the icicles form on the telephone receiver.

"Thank you, yes," he said.

"No luck?" It was obvious by his face, but Miranda was still hoping.

"No luck, and I've got frostbite too."

"Never mind, you tried. Thank you for trying," said Miranda and she reached up and gave him a little kiss. "Onward and upward ..."

$$*\qquad*\qquad*\qquad*$$

The refugio at Astorga was full, which, judging from the scowls of the Dutch *hospitalero* was no bad thing. One by one, the pilgrims trouped around Gaudi's Bishop's Palace and all agreed that it should have been an oxymoron, although the architecture itself was original and stunningly beautiful. The cathedral was closed for renovation work.

"I am a Pilgrim on the *Jacobsweg*, and I have only seen one cathedral: Burgos," Alex said. "Are they trying to tell us something?"

At the next village they regrouped at a fly-blown café, but at the next refugio Alex, Catherine, and Kevin wanted to go on, Peter and Josje wanted to sightsee a nearby "*pintoresco*" village, Ricardo had disappeared again (he always did, but he always turned up again, which Miranda put down to gypsy instincts) and Miranda felt that this might be the reason why Alex wanted to continue on. It wasn't far, but the day was hot, and the present refuge promised washing machines (which subsequently didn't work anyway, as it turned out). So the little group split up once again, agreeing to meet in the St. James Confraternity *hostal* in Rabanal del Camino.

∗   ∗   ∗   ∗

Santa Catalina de Somoza, and the Bar Peregrino. They were more than two thirds along the Camino. The pilgrim refuge had a barn beside it and hung on lines all around were T-shirts, shorts, and assorted underwear, hanging jauntily in the summer wind. "Signs of Happy Pilgrims!" said Felix, cradling his cold beer. Miranda asked for a glass of wine, but once it appeared it was tiny. "*Mas grande!*" she yelled to the bartender who grinning, brought her a water glass and filled it to the brim.

The refugio itself had enormous windows, though all were closed and the place smelled of sweat. Towels were hung all around. A lollopy puppy came and plonked himself beside Miranda's pack. His smell blended with the other scents, or perhaps that was what brought him in the first place. Miranda opened the windows. Felix lay on the top bunk with his arms behind his head: "Like it here," he said, and then dropped into a sound sleep. Miranda smiled: they had walked a long way that day. She went in search of the promised washing machine but found an "Out of Order" sign, but that was O.K. She was used to washing out her smalls in the fountain by now. Anything else would have been too perfect. If it had done nothing else—and it had done much, she reflected—the Camino had taught her to be happy with the little gifts that Life presented. She showered (cold), and then following Felix's example, prostrated herself on top of her sleeping bag, and joined Felix in his dreams.

"You snore!" he said, as later they went back to the bar and had chicken soup and chips. Felix was in a chatty mood:

"Through the Gates of Death, across the Plains of Penitence, now free to enjoy our new state. I feel like a new man!"

"Felix," said Miranda, "You took the **bus** from …?"

"Palencia, actually. I just missed you guys in Fromista, but I was fascinated with the book by the altar. About the missing obscene carvings? Well, it said they were in the provincial capital, so I took a detour to see the museum there, but it was "closed for alterations". I got into Leon the day before you did, and since I didn't see your name or Alex's, well, I decided to use the Felix charm to stay and wait. I **can** count and multiply, you know. Ah, yes, but the doubts of never seeing **you** again … seeing all those pilgrims along the roads and knowing I was not a part of it … that was the real torture!"

"Fool!" she said laughing at him and his ever-ready quips. But she had to admit it: she wouldn't have wanted to miss the *Meseta*. Like Ricardo, she was "growing a new skin".

It didn't have to stretch as far as it used to, either. Her waist was easily defined. She had developed a new posture in having her shoulders forever forced back by the weight of her pack. Her skin was glowing with color, and her hair was bleached wheat with the sun, like so many of the fields she had passed through. She felt "Born Again" too, and it felt good.

Felix brought the subject back to Kieran.

"Do you think we will see him again?" Felix had sent e-mail from Puente de Orbigo, but they hadn't had the opportunity to check if there was a response.

"I … I don't know …? He's **your** friend. What do **you** think?"

"Well, let's look at our options, Watson. Either he is dead …"

"J—E—S—U—S, Felix!!!" said Miranda, in horror.

"You asked. May I continue?"

"Yes, but stop being such a drama queen!"

"Sorry. Either he's ... or he is back in Ireland writing his novel...."

"That's more like it," said Miranda.

"... or ... he's a couple of days behind us, or else he's ahead."

"How could he be ahead? We've even spent a few extra days at refugios ..."

"Yes, but it depends how far he took that taxi ... or, some pilgrims feel OK about the occasional bus ride ...?"

"Like you—Hah! Call yourself a pilgrim!"

"I do actually ... some start in Burgos, some in Leon: some people even walk from Triacastela, that's only 100 kilometers from Santiago. But they still get their *Compostela*, signed and stamped and ready to hang on their dining room walls."

"Part-time pilgrims," said Miranda in contempt.

"Maybe not, Miranda. Maybe that's all the time they can spare. You've fallen prey to pilgrim snobbery. Lots of people walk out of their doorways in France, or Germany, or even further afield. Much further than either of us. It's not a contest, you know."

She felt chastened. She remembered Claus from Germany, who was on his way back when she and Alex had met him in Azofra, during the thunderstorm. She had the good grace to look contrite.

"Sorry," she said.

Felix made an Arabic gesture of forgiveness and ordered some more tortilla. "I could get used to this," and produced a bottle of Tabasco she had never seen him wield before.

"What will you do when you get back?" she asked later.

"Me? Don't know really. Look for another job; find some poor unfortunate woman who is willing to take on a wounded man …"

"Oh Felix … you really don't **realize** what you have to offer! First, you make me laugh. That's a tremendous gift you know: GSOH? Second, you never really push your judgments on me, even when you are right … sometimes," she said before he could comment. "**And** you have the ability to make everyone feel special—men as well as women. You fit in. Your company makes me feel special, and I am more than honored to share it." She kissed his nose, which had a peppery taste; the beer had made him lose his coordination.

"Aw, shucks!" he said.

*   *   *   *

The next day they walked the few kilometers to the next refugio, called "*El Ganso*": the Drake. The Camino was filled with references to geese—The Montes de Oca, for example. Someone in San Juan de Ortega had told her that the Spanish children's game—La Oca—had deep pilgrim significance.

It was a straight track, and the scenery was glorious. It was a perfect day for walking: not too hot. Along the way they passed a picture in the gravel of a man with a semi-circle over his head, made entirely out of stones. "*El Indalo*," a passing pilgrim told her as she and Felix admired it and added a few stones of their own, showing a staff and a water gourd. "*Buen Camino!*" he said, as he walked away.

The "Cowboy Bar" at El Ganso was a famous stop on the Camino, but it was packed with motor tourists, admiring its wall art. But instead of pausing there, they turned left into an adjacent bar.

Alex was there, with Ricardo, and Peter and Josje. There was another man in pebble glasses who, to Miranda, looked vaguely familiar. He was reading, and nurturing a glass of red wine.

"Hey!" said Felix, settling right in, and seeing Alex with a proper English pint mug went up to the bar and ordered a round.

They fell to discussing the relative merits of the past night's refugio. Alex had stayed in El Ganso.

"These two good looking boys just walked up before you," she said.

And then, it happened. Inevitable as it was, no-one was prepared for it. The day had been too good, and the meeting up was too fortuitous.

A man came out of the bar. He was a big man, bushy beard which almost covered his whole face; he looked through them and sat down at a neighboring table.

Miranda and Felix exchanged excited glances. "Him?" Felix seemed to say.

"That's him!" Miranda could barely whisper, and all around her heard it. "That's 'Blackbeard'!!!"

"Are you sure?" Alex said. "What are we going to …?"

But before she could finish, another man walked out brandishing two pints like the others'. He began to place both carefully on the table where the bearded man was sitting.

He almost dropped them when he saw the new arrivals.

"Miranda! Felix!" he said, looking at both of them incredulously. "I was beginning to think I would never see either of you again!"

It was Kieran.

CHAPTER 21

▼

Kieran made the introductions. Everyone else was too dumbfounded to respond.

"This is Dominic," he said.

"Hi," said Dominic, good-naturedly, and in a familiar accented English. "Great to meet you guys," and he hoisted his pint in salute.

"Wait a minute …? Wait a minute! You speak **English**?" It was Miranda who finally broke the silence.

"Well, I guess so, though a few Brits wouldn't exactly call it that."

"But …?" Miranda was stupefied, and couldn't say any more. She looked first at Felix, then at Kieran.

"Dom's from Los Angeles," Kieran said. "Well near it. Valencia, California."

Felix spluttered into his pint. Then he started to laugh, really chuckle. Then it turned into a belly laugh, and Miranda—and the others—looked at him in total exasperation.

"What's so **Bloody Funny**?" she said.

"Valencia … **California**!" Felix couldn't contain himself by now. "Don't you remember? Jaca? You thought it was Valencia … **Spain**!" He was laughing so hard that gobs of spit were adorning his beer.

"JESUS! Felix?" Miranda said. That only made it worse.

"We thought you were **Spanish**!" Felix spluttered out, and started to laugh again. He was really doubled over by now. Froth flying in all directions.

Miranda was furious with him.

"O.K.," she said, "That's **enough**! I don't get the freaking joke!" She looked at Kieran and back to Felix, and then to Dominic, who was supping his beer quite peacefully. "You mean you **know** each other?" Felix tried to shake his head, but that had no effect on his mirth, out of control by now.

Kieran carried on: "I met Dom in Jaca, you know, the day you and I walked together? We got talking. We've got a lot in common. He's studying to be a priest too, but, it's a bit different; so I went with him to San Juan de la Pena. You didn't look up to much walking that day, neither of you. Anyway … it's a long story. Hey …" he glanced around, "Isn't anyone glad to see me?"

＊   ＊   ＊   ＊

It was a short walk from there to Rabanal. Miranda collared Kieran. The others, ahead a bit, knew they would have to wait for their explanations.

"Look, I know we only walked a day but you …" she searched for the words, "you **burdened** me with your book, Kieran. We, **I**, thought you were dead! And then when Felix told me about …" She didn't know how to say it now. "When he told me you were … ill …"

"He told you about the cancer?"

"Well, yes … but not until Leon. I thought … we thought … And then I saw Dominic with your manuscript … and, well …" She left off where words failed.

"Did you get the rest …?"

"Of your book? In Puente? Yes, but … that's not the point Kieran!"

"I asked Dom to find you and give it to you. I didn't think you would mind. Miranda, I had to trust someone with it. We seemed to get along well. After San Juan de la Pena, I wasn't sure even if I … I couldn't load it on poor Felix. He's got enough to deal with. Dom had the translation to do. His Latin is better than mine. In San Juan de la Pena, I came face to face with mortality. I thought that I could continue to write the book, but I didn't know if I would be able to finish translating the manuscript. And that's what's important. People have to know that there is more to the New Testament than centuries of clergy rule would have them believe. Did you know that the Vatican has never made an official comment on the Nag Hammadi Gospels? Not one. There are still only a few people in the world who know that Jesus had a message for the man in the street, and another for the ones who could penetrate to the core of his teachings. No-one needs a church and all the saints and angels, to talk to God! It's a very personal thing, but more than that: we've been lied to, Miranda. Seventeen hundred years of lies—church control—which are totally accepted and unquestioned by most of the Christians on this planet, Protestants as well as Catholics, who don't even know **why** they are Christians, or what the Master, Jesus, had to reveal to them! Dom knew. He's training to be a Gnostic priest."

"But I saw you in Jaca, together. It looked like you were arguing. You were shouting at each other and he was rapping his fingers against your book …"

"Ah, yes. The "Last Supper", actually the first between Dom and me. You should have joined us. The conversation was fascinating. Anyway, what he was saying to me was: 'You've **got** to bring this to the world's attention.' But then I got to San Juan, and I felt so weak. It was a long way up. I wasn't sure I could carry on. I was afraid the message would be lost. Dom studied Classics at Irvine. He was the only one I knew who could do this translation. The only one I could trust. That's why I gave him the photocopies. I had to take the opportunity. Why …? Oh, no, I get it! You thought he was a Vatican spy and that he had somehow disposed of me …!" He began to laugh, and sounded a bit too much like Felix.

"Well, what else could I have thought! You disappeared! Then in Jaca, your book—you were speaking in Spanish!"

"Well, how else am I going to master this language in this life? He's fluent. His dad is from Mexico. I've got pretty good. Anyway, I asked Dom to give it to you personally."

"Well, he didn't. And until Sahagun I didn't even know who he was. Though Felix thought he had seen him in Burgos. Kieran, I've been worried sick about you!"

Kieran, thinking, began to see it from her point of view. "Well, yes, I can see ..."

Kieran looked closely at Miranda and remembered many of the things he had put out of his mind since they had parted. He had really enjoyed the day's walk and the easy familiarity between them. "I didn't want to give up your company, even then," he thought. There was something about her that had attracted him. Much more than looks. She had an inner beauty that intrigued him, something lost and waiting to be found, but there were many pretty, lost girls who had crossed his path. Miranda had somehow been looking for something he recognized intuitively or why else would he have opened up? Why else would he have entrusted her with the book, his book, so important and so precious an insight? Yet he knew he had little to offer her. Those thoughts came back to him, and truth to tell he found them somehow ... embarrassing, even now. It was long since he had thought of himself as a man with a man's desires. He found himself with little more to say.

They walked a bit further. Finally, Miranda couldn't contain her curiosity anymore.

"Felix found out that you stayed at the Monastery in San Juan de La Pena, but that you only stayed there for three days. So where did you go after that? We checked every refugio, for miles and miles. Then we gave up. You were supposed to meet us at Puente."

"Yeah, sorry about that. But I wasn't up to it, and I didn't realize there were two, and I thought that Dom would have told you, and told you about our plans, his and mine. After I left San Juan, I got lost on the Camino coming down. I have to admit that my courage failed me a bit at that point, and then I fell and hurt my knee, scraped it, actually quite badly. I couldn't stop the bleeding for ages. I started thinking about Ireland then, going back and doing the chemo, but I didn't want to give up so soon. I knew it wasn't going to be easy going but I wanted to continue as far as I could. Then I stopped for lunch at Los Serros, and the waiter told me that there was a woman in the village who occasionally put up pilgrims, so I went to see her. And, well, it was quiet: a place to think, and write. It was cheap, and Beatriz well, kind of mothered me. I needed that, I guess. So I stayed. I worked out when I thought you and Felix would be in Santiago—Dom had his itinerary well planned out in advance, and we had agreed either to meet there, or maybe in Leon if I was feeling up to the walk. I planned to take the train. But I got restless, and thought 'why not go on, in stages', so I walked as far as Ruesta, and stayed there for a couple of nights. But the walking was hard going."

"We didn't stay there," said Miranda, "it was full of kids."

"It was when I was there too, but you can find a quiet spot if you trespass a bit. The church is amazing, falling down bit by bit, but fascinating. I got the key, even though they told me it was on my own head—so to speak, Templar symbols all over the place. To make a long story short, I got the bus back to Pamplona—that was after San Fermín …"

"Felix went back for the running of the bulls. Ask him sometime—it's the quintessential "cock and bull" story!"

"I'll bet, more bull than cock though. He's all talk. Anyway, after I got rested up a bit I got the train to Leon and met up with Dom there, and well, you know the rest."

"Did you stay at the convent in Leon?"

"No, we didn't. Dom had booked into a cheapy *hostal* called Hotel La Reina. We got the bus to Astorga. Cheating, I know, but in my state of health, I shouldn't really be here at all!" It sounded apologetic.

Miranda had a sudden sense of *dejá vu*.

"So that's how Dominic got ahead of us! I was wondering."

"He's stayed in *hostals* mostly. He didn't want anyone or anything to disturb his thinking. It's a big decision to make you know, becoming a priest. People look at you funny, then change the subject! But since I met up with him again, well, I persuaded him that it might actually help, being around other seekers, listening to their stories. I told him: 'You don't **have** to share yours'."

They had got to a crossroads in the Camino. Three men, heavily hooded, were surrounding another, a middle-aged man in thick glasses. It looked, to Miranda's still suspicious eyes—having focused so much recently on conspiracy theories—well, suspicious.

"Are you O.K.?" she asked, tentatively. The other three looked like some form of Spanish Ku Klux Clan. She had gotten used to thinking in terms of conspiracies.

"Beekeepers," he said. "They've been showing me how they do it. Here, have some," he handed them a piece of the comb with sticky fingers. "Sorry, I'm Stephen. I would have introduced myself before, but you all seemed a bit pre-occupied. From Cardiff."

Miranda and Kieran took a break from their personal enclosure. Then with Stephen, still nibbling on his honeycomb, they walked the last few kilometers up the wooded track to Rabanal. He was, he said, a physician.

"But, there's more to me than meets the eye."

Miranda experienced a few more moments of *deja vu: "*You're the **Templar** man! I remember **you**. You told me about the Templars in …?" But she didn't remember.

"Eunate?"

"Near Puente la Reina?" He nodded. "Yes, that was it! Miranda," she said by way of introduction, "and this is Kieran. He's back from the dead."

Stephen didn't bat an eyelid.

"We **all** die on the Camino." he said, with total seriousness and conviction. "Then we spontaneously resurrect. If, that is, we've been listening and looking carefully enough."

*   *   *   *

There was an orderly gathering of pilgrims at Rabanal. Most fairly quiet. Amongst them was a black-bearded pilgrim with an enormous backpack, who had settled himself in the shade of the church portico, beside the hollyhocks, and was writing with great intent, a dictionary beside him. It was still early, about two, and all were sharing lunch. The doors didn't open until four o' clock. A few—especially those who had got up at six, and had already walked twenty kilometers or more that day—were complaining noisily about the late opening. An even more limited few had gone on—the next refuge was remote, and by all accounts very sparse in terms of pilgrim necessities, even for those who had gotten used to it. But Miranda was glad to see that none of "her" pilgrims had made that decision, though Alex told her that Peter and Josje had gone to another private refugio, around the corner. The Confraternity refugio was well-known for its hospitality and its library of Camino-related books (and its strictly enforced eleven o'clock curfew), and there was an ancient church across from it. Miranda's guidebook—still occasionally consulted—told them the time for evening mass, and that they could expect Gregorian Chant.

"Let's go to the bar," said Alex and all trooped behind her.

*   *   *   *

Seven o' clock found the friends settled, showered, and perhaps more together than they had been in weeks. Everyone went to mass. There were only four monks. They sat facing each other before the altar. But their combined voices, singing God's praises in perfect harmony, affected every single soul gathered in the ancient stones. Incense and candles added to the atmosphere, and, each one felt like a pilgrim of old—somehow trapped in a Twentieth century journey, yet connected to all journeys of hope and all the other searchings that had preceded them. The sound of the monks' voices, swirled back on itself, rising then falling, then ever ascending to greater and greater harmony: simple, primitive, and persuasive: it seemed somehow almost pagan, outside of space and time; the words, lost to all, yet familiar to all. It missed no-one in that assembled congregation of the hopeful and the weary. It spoke to something much deeper in their souls.

Miranda, never one to be at all religious, a skeptic who had sought for truth in reason, found the spiritual strength she needed, that night. At some point in the singing, and unaccountably, she began to cry—tears of happiness such as she had never known before. *Thank you; thank you,* she said in her heart, as she let them flow. She gripped the fingers of both hands together in a cradle shape, and held them tight. It was her way of prayer. *Thank you. This is why I came.*

*   *   *   *

After the others had left, she remained seated. And then, when she felt ready to leave, she looked behind her. Alex, alone, remained. They exchanged smiles, Miranda still in tears.

"I am happy for you," Alexandra said.

*   *   *   *

In the adjoining bar—also a hotel, they met up with Dominic, who had abandoned his dictionary for a brandy, and Kieran. Alex took it upon herself to explain Miranda's smile of peace. Miranda herself was still, shaking, from the experience.

"You now know the light of God. I am happy for you," Dominic echoed Miranda. "It is the light of Love for all who open their hearts to the beauty of the infinite Mystery. That mystery is just beginning."

But they still only just made it back for eleven o' clock curfew.

*   *   *   *

Cold light of day saw them evicted by eight. Miranda barely had time for her coffee before the American *hospitalero* herded them out into the stark light, and even Felix' charm was to no avail.

They were walking on an overgrown track, not the main Camino which seemed to have been absorbed by the main road, which though lightly trafficked, was asphalt. It was raining, but only very slightly. Mist, more than anything. They passed group after group of crocus, somehow surviving the harsh climate which was the *Maragatería*: the High Moor of Leon.

As the sun rose higher, and the mist cleared, the view over the surrounding countryside, though harsh and unforgiving as it was, was unforgettable. It stretched in every direction, with few habitations in sight, and those that remained were largely derelict. This was not a place to bring up a family. It was a place to retreat to; to retreat inside oneself. They reached the abandoned village of Foncebadon. Miranda felt an annoying call of nature, and brandishing what she had left of her toilet roll, went in search of a private spot. She found it beside a crumbling wall. Sheep were herded on the other side. Despite her quiet approach, they ran from her and herded together on the other end of the enclosure, looking back with collective panic. As she finished, she found herself face to face with a snarling sheepdog. It blocked her path out. She suddenly remembered Paulo Coelho. The only way back to safety was to snarl back. She did, and the sheepdog, whining in distress, made a swift retreat. "Well, if it's that easy ..." she said to herself.

In the village a church was being restored, though it looked as if the work was progressing slowly. She asked a worker about it. A new refugio, she learned. A new life for an old abandoned village, and she cursed her lack of Spanish, and not for the first time. She wanted to know more.

It is an old tradition, at the oldest symbol on the Camino, to leave a stone behind. She had seen many piled in cairns at wayside passages, especially on hills, and beside fountains along the way. In recent years, that tradition had evolved into pilgrims leaving behind something of their past, and the resulting heap of alarm clocks, traffic tickets, and other things which presumably had some personal significance for those who had passed, only leant some silly unreality to the *Cruz de Hierro*. The pile of stones under them was impressive, however. So much so that it was impossible to tell how high the actual pole, topped with a small iron cross, really was. She had read that it was old, very old. It had been a sanctuary of Mercury, and before that the winged god, Hermes. It probably even dated from before the Roman occupation of these hills. They had exploited these mountains for iron. Miranda had brought a small quartz stone she had found just outside Rabanal. She found Felix tying a small bunch of heather onto the gate of a somewhat graffitied stone chapel (locked) which stood nearby. It was called the Chapel of Santiago. Dominic appeared with a large stone, an almost perfect sphere, which he reverently placed on top of the accumulated detritus at the base of the *Cruz*. He made no comment when he came up to Felix and Miranda. Just nodded.

"Dominic?" Felix sounded unusually shy. "I lost my fiancé in a road accident, six months ago. Kieran said you are going to be a priest soon. Would you mind saying a prayer for her?"

"I'll ask for a mass for her, from my Bishop, when I get back. What is her name?" He wrote "Jessica" in the back of a small green paperback book.

When Miranda and Kieran left, they saw him walking off alone. He had a morning prayer to say, he said, and Felix knew that Jessy would undoubtedly be a part of it.

Despite the time of year, and the heat they had become accustomed to, the mist swirled around them as they climbed higher. Miranda was walking ahead of Dominic. Felix was a little behind. Kieran was slightly ahead of all of them. She came upon Alex, and a pair of very, very longhorned cattle. Alex was immobile.

"I don't like the look of these," she said. Alex was a city girl.

"Just walk through like they don't exist," said Miranda, talking her hand. She had, after all, stared down Coelho's black dog at Foncebadon.

Then they came to Manjarin. The refuge of the "last Templars".

The first thing they heard was the strains of country music. Then the tolling of a single bell as they approached closer.

"What do you think, Alex," said Miranda, "do you think we are still in Kansas?"

CHAPTER 22

▼

"These are the Last Templars", Kieran said, "At least, that's what they style themselves. Come on, I'll you introduce to Tomas, he's the Capo de Templars!"

They were at the *Refugio de Manjarín*, mid-way between Astorga and Ponferrada, just before the fog had descended on the bleak mountainside, and the refugio was totally unlike anything else they had encountered on the Camino so far. It was remote, tiny and ramshackle, surrounded by curious signs and symbols. Tomas, a middle-aged short man, who looked anything but Miranda's idea of what a Knight Templar should look like, was in a small office-like structure beside the main room where the pilgrims were congregated on benches beneath an enormous tapestry, all looking a little bit uncomfortable. The office was lined in books, all in Spanish. Some looked very old. All were bearing the signs of dilapidation in this climate. The Maragatería was an exposed wasteland and experienced heavy snow in the wintertime which cut it completely off from road traffic. Tomas was talking with Dominic and Stephen. Miranda heard the word "Tau" and what she thought must mean Sacred Geometry. (The Tau is an ancient cross form, Kieran told her: much, much older than the Roman cross.) They were looking at a book and Tomas was tracing a pattern across a map of Spain. His finger seemed to connect Santiago, and Andalucia ("*El Cruz de Caravaca*:" Kieran told her, looking over Dominic's shoulder, "very interesting goings on between Knights and Moors there"), and another line seemed to intersect towards the Pyrenees in the direction of Lourdes, but Miranda couldn't follow the conversation, Kieran couldn't quite translate it, and she was still too shy of Dominic to ask. Instead, she found Felix, who had walked after her ("what cows?"), and who was standing beside the fireplace which was burning brightly, despite the month. A small tortoiseshell cat was sitting contentedly on Catherine's lap beside it, and there were a few *chubasqueras*—wind breakers—scorching their hoods, hung up too close. It was downright chilly outside. They were many meters above sea level.

"Have you seen the accommodations?" Felix asked Miranda,

"No, why?"

"Better not to turn on the light," was all he had to say.

Tomas was explaining something to Kieran about Mary Magdalene, but again, Miranda cursed her lack of Spanish. Lunch was being prepared. Alex and another woman were in the kitchen area, deconstructing chicken carcasses. Kevin was peeling a mound of carrots, and Miranda, feeling a bit left out of both activities—the sublime and the mundane—found a knife and began to do the same with the potatoes which she struggled with, being used to potato peelers. Everyone else just sat around looking a bit bemused. There was little conversation, and what there was, was hushed.

Done, the stew was left to itself to simmer on the open stove. The fog lifted, and the sun came out though faintly through the clouds, and an unexpected kite-flying wind had come up. Alex couldn't contain herself and left like the Pied Piper with a train of pilgrims in tow. Stephen, of the glasses, had joined them and seemed to be fast becoming a member of the family. They all went outside to play.

The vistas from the top of the mountains were almost overpowering in their remoteness; they stretched in every direction and there was not a cottage or farm to be seen; but closer to hand, all were forced to take a better look at the "facilities". Swathes of toilet paper littered the ground as far as the eye could reach. Eventually, past an odd hut-like structure, the group found an open field which seemed less polluted. Alex, having unfurled her bird, began to run up and down, which was more difficult than it might at first seem, since the down part, went down several thousand feet.

All waited for their turn to try their hand, including Stephen, who, surprisingly, turned out more masterful than the master, Alexandra, whose attempts to prove her prowess almost took her down the mountain. Felix fell and hurt his knee and decided that he was better at other Olympic feats, though he didn't elaborate.

But inevitably, given the limited room to maneuver, the kite fell, and the strands of thin cords, raveled themselves into a labyrinth, and they suddenly noticed that there was more toilet paper on the ground than anyone had realized. They set to untying the strings, which had knitted themselves into intricate physics-defying puzzles. Still, no-one gave up. They were all seasoned Pilgrims by that time. Obstacles were nothing to them now.

"Lunch" was served closer to a British Teatime. There were twenty assembled (most had gone on) but even then, the table, such as it was, was no-where near big enough.

"*No pasa nada,*" said Tomas, clearly used to this, and he and his helpers—two of them—appeared, both Knights Templars, Miranda was told. Between them, they set to solving the problem. One called Ramon looked perhaps South American but since he never spoke, no-one could tell. Between them, they proceeded to brandish screwdrivers, and before you could say "Santiago", the door was off its hinges, and placed horizontally, on top of the original, turned into a banqueting table.

Stephen, the physician, at first looked a bit squeamish. But taking a plastic knife and fork out of what appeared to be an arsenal of plastic cutlery, tucked in with greedy relish, as did they all, though Miranda left some of the chicken on her plate. ("If you don't want that …?" said Stephen, expropriating her remains with a plastic fork.)

"I did some of my intern work as a volunteer in Bolivia," he told Miranda, who was seated between him and Kieran. "There you had to chase your turkey and catch him first! They weren't always eager to be caught. And they say turkeys are stupid!"

Dominic was across the table. He informed them that Tomas and his refugio had been under threat of closure for years. "Health regulations," he said. "They even cut off his electricity by the sound of things. It was in all the local papers. But he's still here. You gotta admire the man," and he helped himself to a portion befitting his size. No-one objected.

Afterwards, the women coaxed the men into doing the washing up, and then most of them went outside to experience the views alone, or in twos. No-one wanted to check out the sleeping place—which was up a small ladder—for themselves, at least not until they were too tired to care.

Kieran and Miranda walked along the tiny road. It was bordered by low drystone walls. After a few hundred yards they came upon one which had been written upon: "*Jodido, pero contento!*" it said in white letters. A recent date was added.

"What does that mean?" Alex asked Kieran, who was about to climb higher. He came back down to investigate.

"Fucked, but happy!" he translated. "Kind of sums up the whole thing, doesn't it?"

Someone up on a promontory was singing. It was Felix: "*It's such a perfect day,*" he sang, to the mountains, "*... and it keeps me hanging on.*"

Kieran and Miranda passed a gateway, then climbed over it. There were horses, flicking each other with their tails under a scrubby tree; a big black pig was at the bottom of the field. There were two fat calves, seemingly minding their own concerns, and when Miranda turned around to watch Kieran clamber ungainly over the gate, two small black cats were watching them closely, one washing his paw over his face.

They sat together without speaking, looking over a landscape that, but for the walls, hadn't changed in hundreds of years. Kieran began to laugh, very gently.

"What are you laughing at?" Miranda said, just as gently.

"Nothing. Just laughing," he said.

She wasn't at all surprised when he reached over and took her hand.

*   *   *   *

When they returned to the refugio, more had gathered. Alex couldn't find her sleeping bag, and only located it after moving the behinds of several latecomers, the offending pilgrim a Frenchman in dreadlocks who had fallen asleep on top of it. Alex managed to extract it without waking him. Another was the doppelganger of Sean Connery, but he walked on after coffee.

It began to get dark. Kevin, Kieran, and Miranda went privately in search of their respective areas outside. The Milky Way was clearly in evidence. *I'm walking under it*, Miranda thought.

"Miranda!" They are doing the Benediction! Come!" Alex had sought her out.

"I'm so glad you were there," Miranda said to Kieran, a few days later. 'I couldn't have begun to describe it.'

The numbers had shrunk back to twenty or so, though not all were the originals. Of Miranda's group, all had remained, with the exception of Stephen, who had sought her out. He explained that he was going to carry on that night to the next refugio. "I'll meet up with you in Ponferrada, hopefully," he said. Then the evening swallowed him.

The Knights had changed clothes. Tomas was wearing a red T-shirt. On the back was the Templar cross; Ramon had on a padded jacked despite the heat inside, similarly emblazoned. The pilgrims sat around the benches. The other wore the same as Tomas, though it looked like it could use a wash.

They turned first to the west: a short homily was spoken by Tomas (he's thanking God for bringing us to this place; this is going to be a Pilgrim blessing, said Dominic). Miranda heard the words "San Miguel". Then the three turned to the east: "San Rafael...." and more she didn't understand. This was followed to the other points of the compass: "San Gabriel", afterwards "San Uriel" whom Miranda had never heard of. All the pilgrims afterwards said that they had felt bound together, by some invisible silk cord. There was something in that bizarre night that legitimated their wonder, their sense of having been somehow "chosen" for this journey. Maybe it was hokey, but yet, it was somehow Real. And it gave them another waystage, to journey on from.

Late that night, as the others were beginning to make tentative steps up the ladder, a last pilgrim joined them. He was dark skinned, slight, and had angular cheekbones, though his Gallic good looks were hidden by a growth of beard. His eyes, when anyone had a chance to see them, for he kept to himself, were the most vivid blue. Alex couldn't keep from looking at him, even after he slept. He had a regular pack, very small, nothing much in it, well traveled. He sat by the fire in silence. And stared into it. He looked at no-one, though all looked at him, furtively. Though none of them could explain it afterwards, all felt as though he had been somehow ... expected.

"That's André," said one of the Americans quietly. "He has cycled on an ancient bike from Jerusalem. He's taken a vow of silence. He carries a notebook, and if he thinks the question is worthy, he'll write you a brief answer. That's what I've been told, anyway. He doesn't need anything."

The others nodded. It wanted no explanation.

Before the pilgrims woke up the next morning, he had gone without ever saying a word to anyone. No-one ever saw him again, though reports of sightings became legendary. "I took a photo of him and his bike in Logrono," said one, a cycle pilgrim with a brand-new top-of-the-line machine, "but when I got the pictures developed, that one didn't turn out."

"*Es un angel*," Tomas said.

✳   ✳   ✳   ✳

Afterwards, Miranda and Kieran went out to watch the ascent of the moon. They didn't talk of what they had experienced. In honesty, they didn't know, really, what to make of it, and still felt a little embarrassed by it. Beside the little hut, by the bell, at the entrance to the refugio, they heard snoring. In front of it, a large shaggy dog looked up at them and sniffed as they passed from the refugio out into the clear night. It settled its head back down without so much as a whimper. They were free to pass.

"I think we can sleep safely tonight," he laughed. "We are in a cloud of protection: no wolves, and no devils." And to her enormous surprise, though not, it must be admitted, her dislike, he took her face in his hands, and gave her a soft kiss. She found herself returning it tentatively, then backed away. "I didn't expect that," she said. "I didn't think you would," he replied. "I didn't expect it either."

The two slept on top of their respective sleeping bags that night, alongside André, but in front of the diminishing fire, as the others dreamed in the loft above. And the morning found them holding each other's hands.

*   *   *   *

The walk down from Manjarín surpassed even the walk up in beauty, and Miranda felt that somehow she was seeing it through new eyes. Below them, the clouds gave the illusion of distant sea coasts though they were still many days from Galicia, and at the brow of one hill, someone had written W O W in stones at the side of the road. "Perhaps it was God," said Miranda. She and Kieran were bringing up the rear. Even Felix had gone out early. They passed through a small village nestling along the hillside where tractors and overburdened donkeys waited side by side outside the only bar.

They continued.

"Will you tell me … about … the leukaemia?" she finally got up the courage to ask Kieran, who was looking noticeably tired. "When did you find out?"

"I went in for a routine medical. They did a blood test. Then they did another. I'd been feeling fine—well, a few headaches, bruises which seemed to come from no-where, but nothing that had been a problem. Oddly, when they told me I sort of began to … I don't know really … fit into it. It was one thing after another. I went for more and more tests and I began to feel like the hospital was a second home. It takes you over, you know. Knowing that something has invaded your body. Anyway, they were all very reassuring: Chemo … that would fix me up. But I just didn't want to accept it at that time. That's when I talked to Felix and told him I was thinking of coming on this pilgrimage. Actually, no, I don't think I had really even thought it through that far. I wanted to go to Lourdes. Felix had been before and the way he described it, well, I just figured that it was something I wanted to see. I am Irish, after all!"

"Yes, he told me he had been there before. I just couldn't figure it at the time; you know how he is."

"There's a lot more to Felix than meets the eye. He was devastated by Jessy's death, Miranda. Lots of people talk about "soulmates", but they were. They bounced happiness off of each other. I only met her once, and that was before I went to the Seminary, but even then, even before they became an "item", it was obvious: you can tell with some people. There's a force field between them, they kind of create it …"

"Chemistry," Miranda said.

"Yes, and think about what that means: compounds, inseparable from the time they come together. You can't help but wonder whether some kind of knowing intelligence designed it, organized it. But then afterwards, when something like this happens, you wonder 'What for?' All that energy just dissipated. There was nothing left for Felix but despair. We had kind of got out of touch, but when I called him, and he told me, I felt that there had to be a reason for the contact, just then. I had read the manuscript by then, though I hadn't started to translate it, and anyway, I had also been reading a lot of other apocryphal material …"

"What does that mean, anyway? 'Apocryphal?' I read it in your book, the secret gospel?"

"Well, that's exactly what it does mean, or what it came to mean, but more really. 'Gospel' means 'Good News'. In the 3rd century there was a bishop named Irenaus. His diocese was in the region of Leon, in France. You have to understand the times really. Lots of people think that Christianity was one religion with one book: The New Testament. But in fact, there were many other books, written by many other Christians—Irenaus even mentioned one called The Gospel of Judas, but other than that it's disappeared. There was one by Thomas, another by Mary Magdalene, another by Peter. The Apocrypha were those books which hadn't been included in the New Testament. Later it became illegal to read them and many were thought to have been destroyed. But it was Paul who really turned things on their head because he sought to open up Christianity beyond the area we think of the Holy Land. Jesus wasn't a Christian, Miranda, neither were any of his disciples. People tend to forget that. They were Jews, practicing

Judaism, perhaps as an Essene. Many think that Jesus was trying to break away, or already had done. Trying to bring the Jewish religion back to some orthodoxy, that is, of the way it had been. All religions go through metamorphoses: look at Buddhism … and Islam: changed completely in many ways from that revealed to Mohammad in the Qu'ran."

"I'm ashamed to say it, but I don't know much about Islam, said Miranda.

"Well, look at the infighting that following Mohammed brought to his followers only a few years after his death: look at the Shiites and Sunnis; how they are seen to want to destroy each other. Over what? Points of principle, written in the Haddiths, added much later …? Anyway, that's why Jesus overturned the tables of the moneylenders at the temple. He was disgusted with the way his religion was going. And you also have to remember that his land was occupied by the Romans. Many people simply wanted the Romans out, so there were many political influences. The Siccari, for example, were a militant faction. They always carried a dagger with them—that's what the name meant. Judas may have been one of these Siccari, and there were others of the disciples who may have had the same political leanings. Today we might call them 'Freedom Fighters'."

"Or terrorists. Not much has changed, has it?"

"Indeed no, especially not in parts of the world with what they look upon as an occupying force. You know what they say: 'The winners write the history books'. Where was I?"

Kieran had slowed down a lot.

"The 3rd century bishop…."

"Yes, well, Irenaus hated those who were adding more and more gospels and wanted to bring some sort of order to Christianity. It was still outlawed by the Romans in his day, and there were some terrible atrocities against those who practiced their faith openly. Many flocked to be martyred. Irenaus decided that the only way was to "standardize"—to use a pretty modern term—Christianity was to decide what was to be followed and what was to be discarded: he believed that the number Four had special significance: four points of the compass, four winds …"

"Four loves. It was in your book"

"Ah yes: Eros—sexual love; Storge—affection; Filia—friendship, and Agape—charity. So Irenaus suggested that the four gospels should follow this pattern. The four he chose, the familiar ones today of Matthew, Mark, Luke, and John, were the ones he favored. The first three are called the Synoptic Gospels, and although they differ with one another slightly, they agree on most of the major points of Jesus' life, and they tell it in stories. When you read Jesus saying: "Those with ears to hear, let them hear," he is talking about his secret teachings, known only to a few. Only John is different. It even starts in a different way, but later it appears to agree in principle with the others—though many people now think that a lot was added later."

"John, I remember as one of Jesus' disciples, but Matthew, Mark, and Luke …?"

"Were not. Or at least not Luke, nor Mark. Mark was the probably the first to have been written, or maybe collected. Even John was written long after Jesus' death. We don't really know who the authors of these gospels were. Matthew wrote what we follow as the Nativity Story, but no matter how we might want it, there's little historical evidence of Jesus' birth, or Herod's atrocities, or the flight into Egypt. Jerusalem was totally destroyed by the Romans in 66 AD, in response to an uprising by the militants—and probably they were Siccari—who had taken hold of the city. The Jews were completely dispersed. Many were sent to what is today the area we call Iraq. The others, well, that's what they mean by the Diaspora. But by and large, they were Jews, not 'Christians'."

"So when you talk about the other 'apocryphal' gospels, were they written by Peter, and Thomas, and Mary?"

"They may very well have been, or else they were written some time afterwards, by the Gnostics, the 'Knowers': those who had a special insight, and who were severely criticized by Irenaus, and Tertullian, who was a contemporary living in North Africa. Eventually, they were outlawed, especially after the Council of Nicea, in 325; by then the gospels as you know them were codified by the bishops. That is when the Doctrine of the Trinity was also formalized. That was after the hideous killings of Christians by the Emperor Diocletian—when the Christians were 'thrown to the lions'—and after Constantine supposedly converted to

Christianity after the battle of Milvain Bridge, though it took another 50 odd years before Christianity became the official religion. It suited Constantine to unite the Empire under One God—with himself as One Emperor. The Roman Empire was vast, remember. If you like he 'consolidated' all of it in himself. Even took the ancient *Chi Ro* symbol, the Sacred Name of Christ, and changed it into the cross."

"I've never figured out how the symbol of Jesus' crucifixion has become such an important part of Christianity. It's like worshipping the gallows your father died on."

"Precisely. Blame Constantine for that. Plus, many of the practices of his legions, most of whom followed Mithras (no women did, for instance) were very similar to those followed by the Christians. What better way to command their unswerving obedience and loyalty and placate large numbers of your citizens at the same time. Same practices, different name—Mithraism started in Persia, where the Zoroastrians were …"

"Zoroastrians—that's Zarathustra, isn't it?" Miranda had loved Nietzsche's book; it was one of her favorites. But she had always thought of Nietzsche as a Godless man, despite his special insights into the nature of man.

"Yeah, I'll get to that … But there had to be controls …"

"Hence the priests and the bishops?"

"Hence the priests and the bishops. That's what Priscillian was rebelling against—control, and the prohibition of choice. I don't think he wanted to 'join' their establishment. I think he felt if he were to influence the people, he had little choice. If you like he was forced into it. He knew his beliefs were outside of the organization of the Church. But he was a proud man, with a proud man's desires. He had been a Senator, remember, though he counseled his followers: "Do not think on what I have been". I think he was a Gnostic, and as such had far more in common with the older religions such as Zoroastrianism and Manichaeism which came from Persia and recognized both a dark and a light force which controlled our destiny. And a Superior Man who could rise above the conflict. Like Nietzsche. It was the Nazis that got that wrong …"

"Thanks to his sister, Elizabeth—she was an anti-Semite and twisted Nietzsche's writings in The Will to Power. Poor man was dying of syphilis by then."

Kieran suddenly stopped. He looked winded. "Let's sit down a minute. I'm beat."

They were on the flat now, walking along a young river, the path dappled with sunlight. It would have been a perfect place to pause, Miranda thought, but for her concern for Kieran, and what was clearly the remains of a recent forest fire. The smell of carbon still hung in the air.

"Are you alright?" she asked.

"Yeah, fine. It gets me every now and again. But I hate to give into it. As long as I take it in stages, I'll last 'til Ponferrada. Then, we'll see."

CHAPTER 23

▼

Just outside Ponferrada, at the first bar, they met up with the others, all, that is, but Catherine and Kevin, and Ricardo, who had gone on ahead.

Felix called for a beer for Kieran, but the latter said, "No, just water, please and a coffee," he added, looking over at Dominic who as writing at a side table with three empty cups in front of him. He was working with his dictionary. Kieran's reappearance didn't seem to have altered their arrangement. He looked up as they approached, nodded in greeting, and then went back to his work.

"There's diligence for you," said Felix, who seemed, despite the hour, to be mildly drunk, but it was obvious he was developing a respect for "Blackbeard" as were they all. He didn't say much, but Dominic's presence was powerful. Miranda thought how odd it was that a little bit of knowledge could change a person's perspective completely.

Stephen was waiting hopefully for them by the castle, which was closed for a public holiday. The refugio wasn't closed but it as already full and no-one wanted—or in some cases could afford to—splurge on a hotel, though Miranda tried to convince Kieran. "I'll stay with you. The others will wait."

But in the end, they all walked on, past the bus station, past the hideous slag heaps (Ponferrada had been an industrial city for centuries, Stephen told them), and finally out into the open, and, given the remoteness of the past two days walking, surprisingly domesticated landscape. There were market gardens, and small farms, but most of all, there were vineyards and industry of another kind. The grape harvest was fast approaching.

Kieran needed several rest stops. This time Felix and Dominic walked with them, but very little was said. At the outskirts of Cacabelos, Catherine, Kevin, and Alex had come to intercept them.

"We've saved places for you," Catherine said. "And, guess what? We've got jobs! They need people for the harvest. It only pays 5,000 pesetas per day, but the hospitalero has taken a shine to Alex, and says we can stay as long as we want. What'ya think?" Ricardo, it turned out, had gone on, and they weren't to see him again until Santiago, when, looking very ordinary, he had bought them a round at the bar he was working at.

Alex didn't seem to care.

On the final stretch into Cacabelos, passing the famous restaurant Prada el Tope (free wine for pilgrims there later, said Felix), Miranda got into conversation with Dominic.

"Had a Harley once," he said, to her surprise. "Typical Hell's Angel! But I met a guy in a bar in Arizona. He told me he had read a book called The Gnostic Gospels by Elaine Pagels. Someone had left it behind, with a tip for the waitress who had tossed the book into the garbage. She probably didn't think much of the tip … anyway … he fished it out, and read it, and later, he gave it to me. Lots of underlines in pencil and notes in the margins. Lots of exclamation marks! Anyway, I got reading, and man, did it open my eyes!

"Anyway, to make a long story short, I sold the bike, and I went to Utah, (don't ask me why; I was still a bit mixed up then), and I found that there was a Gnostic church there. I went to a service. The priest was this cool soft-spoken guy who seemed to know everything. He was a psychologist. Taught at the University. What he said made so much sense to me. I asked him afterwards what I should do if I was thinking of becoming a priest. I thought he'd laugh at me—you know, I didn't even finish High School—but he didn't. He took me completely seriously. I said my sister lived in L.A. and that was where I was thinking of heading next—you can imagine, I didn't exactly fit in in Salt Lake—so he gave me the name of the bishop there, wrote me a note, and a couple of weeks later I was on the Greyhound. I didn't even look at bikes anymore. The Bishop, Reverend Hoeller, is a really approachable guy, even though he has written lots of books and stuff. I kept coming back. Got a job at a gas station, got a room at a hotel, (my sister had just kicked her boyfriend out and wasn't feeling too sociable), and I bought another of Elaine Pagel's books; eventually I began to feel like, you know, this makes sense to me. The first thing Bishop Hoeller said to me was: 'God is supposed to be All Good, and All Knowing, and All Powerful'. I said, yeah, and.... so? Then he said: 'So why is there so much evil in the world? If God is all these things, then he should be able to stop it.' He left me thinking. So I started to read, and I began to see that it only made sense if there were two gods: one all powerful etc., but another who had control over human beings. Of course, at the beginning, I thought of the devil, and so on. But I read everything he gave me. I did the late shift at the gas station, and even in the early mornings: there wasn't a lot to do. What I read said that we were all parts of God's essence, but that, by some mistake, (I'll tell you the whole thing later if you're interested), we had become fascinated by an earthly existence, got drawn into it, and that once the creator god got hold of us, well, it would take a supreme act of recognition to break out of that. I began to see that ... well, that could happen in one life, if we could be open to the Real Message of God. That seemed to be the message of the Resurrection: it can happen to us—in our lifetime. So, as I said, I kept reading, and then I decided I did definitely want to be a priest. But I was a long way from it. First, I went to night school and got my Diploma, then I got into university in L.A. and began to study classics. I didn't really need to, but I found that the more I learned the more I wanted to know, and I couldn't believe how good I was at it! I did Latin and Greek, and all kinds of other stuff too. In some ways, I'll always be a redneck, but I bet I am the first Hell's Angels Gnostic!"

Miranda was fascinated, They were walking along what looked, in many ways, like a cowboy town. It all seemed to fit with his story.

"So, what do you have to do now ... to become a priest, I mean?"

"Reverend Hoeller told me that many people think about becoming priests, but many also do so for the wrong reasons. There's no glory in it you know, no salary either! He said it was an 'Inner Formation Process' and not to expect it to happen overnight. He said that when I thought I was ready, I should ask to be baptized. After that came what he called a Chrism. I'd never heard of that before, but he said it was a kind of confirmation, and then I could become a full member of the laity—that is the regular followers who were serious about their new beliefs. There are five 'minor orders' to go through. Once you've completed them successfully, you can go on to 'major orders', but you have to be recommended by the Bishop to do that. That's pretty well where I am right now."

"So, do you become a priest after that? I don't really understand," Miranda said. She was feeling a bit uncomfortable about asking anyway. She wasn't used to being surrounded by priests, ordained or not.

"No, I'm already serving a probationary period as sub-deacon, next, if I'm any good at it, I will become a deacon of the Iglesia Gnostica. It takes about seven years. I'm ready. There's nothing else I really want."

"And this Pilgrimage?"

"Well, you know, dedicated Gnostics are few and far between. As I told you, there's no salary or anything like that. All the priests are voluntary and most have other jobs. I've been teaching a bit: literacy and stuff. You need to have a complete devotion to God—a Vocation: that means a 'calling'. Some people simply want to help others, but maybe they would be better off doing work as psychologists, or in social work. It's certainly no way to gain 'respect' from anyone else: most people don't know the difference between Gnostic and Agnostic and often you have to explain it. In fact, at the beginning, you try to avoid it. It's not an impossible dream, but not an easy one. Anyway, I think the rewards are very satisfying. Anyway, that's what I've seen so far from those who have gotten any distance along the road."

Kieran just walked along beside them, listening intently.

"The Camino is a good metaphor for the path to Holy Orders," he put in. "I went through a similar process, but towards the end I felt that the dream I had was just an illusion—based on lies, and unreasonable expectations. It wasn't just because I had found out I was sick. The doubts started long before that. I also found it discriminatory at the end. Can't women serve God as well as men? Do they always just have to be in a subsidiary role?"

"So women can become Gnostic priests?"

Kieran nodded.

"And gays and lesbians," Dom said. "Why not? The true God is in us all, speaks to us all. Maybe they even have a better understanding. I honestly think that we will become better human beings once we realize that there are more than two sexes. Gays and Lesbians have a special service in L.A., if they want to attend it. The issues are the same, but the perspective is different."

Miranda had the feeling that Kieran had heard all of this before. She asked him later: "In Jaca," he said. "It seems like another lifetime now."

$$*\qquad*\qquad*\qquad*$$

The refugio wasn't just one building but several. They were old houses unused by the municipality. Each had a kitchen area, and upstairs there were four bunks in some rooms, six to eight in some. Catherine and Alex had strategically placed one of their scanty possessions on each, (including Alex's perfume—Miranda took that bed). Between them, they occupied a whole household, except for Stephen, who had found a bunk in the house next door. When Miranda went to sign in and offer their pilgrim passports she noticed a sign on the wall:

Prayer of the Pilgrims

Lord, you who recalled your servant Abraham out of the Town of Ur in Chaldea, and who watched over him during his wanderings, you who guided him and the Jewish people through the desert, we also query you to watch your present servants, who for the Love of Your Name, make this Pilgrimage to Santiago de Compostela.

Be for us,
a companion on the journey,
our guide at the intersections, the strength during fatigue,
our fortress in danger,
the resource on our itinerary,
a shadow in the heat,
the light in our darkness,
our consolation during dejection,
and the power of our intention,
so that we, under your guidance
safely and unhurt, may reach the end

of our journey, and strengthened with gratitude and power,
secure in your love, and filled with happiness,
may join our Home.

Dominic was beside her as she read: "You see, it fits all faiths," he said. (and all genders, was left unsaid, but Miranda thought of it anyway.)

*   *   *   *

That night, the group gathered together: Miranda and Kieran, Catherine and Kevin, Stephen, Alex, Felix, Dominic, and the late arrivals, Peter and Josje. They ate rice and salad, eggs, *morcilla*, and bread, all washed down with local Cacabelos wine from the last grape harvest (next year, pilgrims will be drinking our wine! said Alex). Josje said grace in Basque, Alex in German, Dominic in Spanish, and Kieran in Gaelic. Felix was hungry: "Good food, good meat. Good God, let's eat!" he added and all fell in. Stories ricocheted off the walls, drowned in exhausted laughter. Peter to everyone's surprise produced a recorder and began to play skillfully. Miranda sang early English folksongs, learned as a child, and the evening finished up with Felix' shaggy dog stories which made everyone groan.

By midnight, all were in bed, except two newly found lovers, holding hands and talking softly upon the steps.

*   *   *   *

The next morning, the grape pickers were gathered at the town plaza by 7:00 where they waited for a truck to take them to their new jobs. Dominic stayed in bed, dreaming perhaps in Greek, but Miranda and Kieran went along to keep them company and take a group photo. Afterwards, they went back to bed, and a room meant for six, but now holding only two.

*   *   *   *

Over the next couple of days, they settled into a familiar routine: familiar in its most literal sense. During the day the "Breadwinners", as Felix called them, went to work in the fields. At night they tucked into dinner prepared by Miranda, Kieran, and Dominic (and occasionally Stephen who proved better at washing up: he was very thorough).

By day three, the workers diminished in numbers and some went on, at least Peter and Josje did: "I will not be a slave!" Josje had said dramatically. Felix decided that it was not for him, but, volunteering his services to the *Hospitalero* (who was alone, overburdened, and delighted) found work with bucket and broom.

"Should have been born a woman!" he said, avoiding Miranda's feigned knock-out punch.

During the day, while they waited for the others to come 'home', Miranda exhausted the sparse library, and sat in the sun with her Spanish dictionary, and Dom's pilgrim guide (in Spanish). It was much better than hers. Dominic carried on with his translation, and once completed, colluded with Kieran to check on its accuracy. Kieran himself got to working on the final chapters of his book. Stephen traveled around the town, making friends with the locals, and generally enjoying himself. "Time for me to move on tomorrow," he said. "I'd like to spend a day in Villafranca del Bierzo. Might even book into the Parador for a night or two. I think I've earned it." And the next day, off he went.

"We'll probably meet again," he said.

By day four, the remaining field workers were beginning to get itchy feet. Their fingers were sore. Their shoulders were burned. They had made a little money, and the Camino and their real purpose beckoned. They were less than 200 kilometers from Santiago now.

Miranda looked over Kieran's shoulder as he was writing. "Can I see now?" she asked.

*   *   *   *

To my Brother in Christ, Ithacius, from Hydatius of Emerita:
I am in Burdigala. My passage from Trier was safe and secure. In fact, I find myself
in a certain luxury. It is something of an improvement over the dungeons Gratian
invited me to! But I do not have to tell you that Delphinas has received me well.
We have them in our net! Come soon.

*   *   *   *

The Synod approached. Supporters and followers came to Euchrotia's estate, amongst them an old friend of Delphidias, Lacrotianus the Poet, formerly by all accounts, a pagan, perhaps a druid, but a recent convert. He rode on a mule.

"They are blind, greedy, and above all, vengeful. They will not let you escape if they can prevent it. You need as many who support you as can. We must come with you to Burdigala."

Instantius sent word. He too had been summoned. He would find friendly places for all to stay, he said. But they must beware: rumors were rife in the city. In particular, one which would not go away was that Priscillian had impregnated Procula. Priscillian knew who to blame.

But in truth, he was more concerned for Procula's health. Every day she grew thinner and more weak. She had occasional heavy bleeding, and Euchrotia insisted that she rest. Between them, she and Priscillian made her meals of iron rich vegetables, and when she was unable to digest these, simple broths. Nothing seemed to work.

"She will lose this child, Priscillian," Euchrotia said, "and maybe that is no bad thing." But she was saddened for her daughter's obvious distress, and feared for her life.

For once, Priscillian had nothing supportive to offer her.

The summons came, as all expected it would. Instantius himself brought the bad news.

"It is time, Brother," he said. "We all are implicated. They would resurrect Salvianus from his grave were they able. It is time to make preparations to leave."

The next day, Procula miscarried. The child, a boy, appeared to have been dead for a long time. She was, to Priscillian's reckoning, near five months gone. Despite her professed hatred for her baby, she wept uncontrollably, and no-one could comfort her.

"May God curse Phillip!" was all Euchrotia could say.

Priscillian didn't respond. Perhaps it was he alone who knew whom god had cursed, and any who had followed him.

The next day, Donatus dug a grave, and Priscillian, weeping for the injustices of the world where the child had been given life, said a prayer to send its soul back to where it belonged.

*   ✳   ✳   ✳   ✳*

Galla remained with Procula, who was bleeding still. Her life was feared, yet no-one else could stay with her. Claudia, Marcellus' adopted daughter, who had embraced the faith, moved into the house. She had developed some skill under Euchrotia's tutelage though she was not much older than Procula, or Galla who stayed to help where she could. Priscillian had forbidden her to accompany him. The house was a place of pain, and fear, and it has to be added, in the face of overwhelming odds, not a lot of hope for those who remained, and those who now journeyed. Herenius chose to remain also: "I will take care of them," he said. Although he had traveled with Elpidius, who but a layman, insisted on making up Priscillian's party, Herenius was neither implicated, nor, was he called. Priscillian's following was too vast now to identify everyone. Though information traveled fast and it was hard to know who to trust.

"Herenius is not Phillip," said Euchrotia. "I like his eyes, he is Gallego I think, like … and his sincerity is obvious. He will not betray me."

Priscillian remonstrated with Euchrotia. 'I go where you go', she said, and even her concern for her daughter would not dissuade her, though it was clear that her very soul was rendered asunder.

*"You are **not** called!" Priscillian said. "I will not permit it! Your place is here."*

"I go with you. We are one now," Euchrotia said.

*   ✳   ✳   ✳   ✳*

A black mare, a bay gelding, a surprisingly compliant mule, and several others arrived unannounced in Burdigala. Unannounced, but not unnoticed.

"See," hissed Phillip to his friends at the eastern gate. "She comes, and she even leaves her pregnant daughter behind. What sort of mother is she? She is a harlot. Priscillian's whore!"

"The daughter is not pregnant anymore," a companion said with a smirk. "News travels fast. He did it, then he destroyed it! They are godless men, and the mother is the worst of all!"

CHAPTER XXIV

▼

GAUL, 384 CE

News travels fast indeed. *In Burdigala, they were met with open arms by many. But Priscillian's supporters knew in their hearts, theirs was not the majority view, not, at least, in Aquitania.*

Ithacius (behind whom Hydatius stood physically and metaphorically) had listed his charges, and they were damning indeed. He said that Priscillian, Instantius, and Hyginus, who had also been summoned, even though he had never actually openly challenged the established beliefs, were charged with holding a heretical doctrine of the Trinity and studying heretical apocrypha (all of which were true with the proven exception of the latter—according to the established, now, Church of Rome). He said that the so-called bishop, Priscillian, was a Manichee in disguise, which, he claimed explained Priscillian's overt, "Supposedly," he said smirking, addressing the assembled bishops, propagation of the celibate ideal. He also claimed to have it on good authority—though he declined to name his sources—that Priscillian had indulged in sexual orgies, had participated in peasant rites of pseudo-magic, and that he had consecrated a sacrament by proclaiming the sun and the moon, naked. He met secretly with women, Ithacius said, and said the mass without footwear. He did not go so far as to say that Priscillian had engaged in magic, only that he had been a party to some age-old ritual in the countryside. And finally he supported his charges, to his satisfaction anyway, by claiming that Priscillian wore an amulet inscribed with the names of God in Hebrew, Latin and Greek, and which bore the symbol of a lion. The latter *was certainly true, and Priscillian took no trouble to remove it during the hearings. Finally, Ithacius claimed that Priscillian had compromised with popular beliefs about magic and superstition all under the supposed* aegis *of a bishop's cloth, though he stopped short of actually accusing Priscillian of dabbling in the "black arts". The implication was enough, for his carefully gathered audience.*

On the first day, all of these and more were hurled at Priscillian, who, wearing his Bishop's vestments, did not flinch. But he held his peace until his time should come.

"All of these point to a flagrant disregard of the teachings of the Church of Rome," Ithacius summed up. "Priscillian stands charged by this Episcopal court, as chosen by our Bishop of Rome, and sanctioned by our Emperor, Maximus, of grave moral enormities based on a radical Gnostic dualism."

*Others were brought forward to add their diatribes, though no witnesses to these alleged actual events was brought to give testimony. And in every case, nothing new was added, except "evidence" from a "protected source", that the Priscillianists used an apocryphal book called the "*Memoria Apostolorum*" which contained supposed revelations about the rulers of wetness and fire, clearly Manichean in nature, and clearly damning.*

Priscillian stood as charged.

He was forced to remain silent. He was not yet to answer his accusers.

The implied charges of magic were indeed dangerous. The early-formed church held all forms of magic in abhorrence. Its message was to abstain from all contact with evil powers, and the logic which questioned the premises of this conclusion were hard to challenge as the church held the premises to be inviolable. "Magic", by implication, was as they decreed. Evil, by its very contact with the Devil.

Instantius was called first:

"We have been accused as though we were Manichees, following Manichean practices. I can assure this distinguished gathering that that is not so. We regard the Manichees with the same abhorrence as you. The Manichees are associated with a dual nature of God, with black magic and moral enormity, for which I agree they should be punished by the sword. I, personally, have never suggested such doctrines to my flock."

Instantius' words were to prove fatal for his master, but he didn't seem to see it then.

"Yet, you are ordained Bishop, wearing the same cloth as did your father, a man we hold in great respect." Ithacius paused. Several murmurings were heard from the assembled. "The language used by your leader and 'master', the accused and accursed Priscillian, is remarkably akin to that used by the false prophet Mani, who claimed a universal gospel valid for both east and west. Not only the books of the Hebrews, which we respect, but also those of other Eastern teachers are claimed to be inspiration in the advancing religious experience of the human race. For did not Mani claim—as do the Priscillianists—that wisdom and deeds have been brought from time to time by God's messengers, and other names, which we do not accept are mentioned, including the heathen of the Indus and their ilk?" Instantius was not permitted to answer. "Jesus," Ithacius continued, "the false Mani claims, is but one of the prophets. Indeed, pagan gods, such as Hermes of Egypt, and even Plato of Greece are thought to be equal to our Lord Jesus, who was the substance and Son of God! It seems to us that you, as a member of this heretical and unfortunate group of so-called Christians, are guilty of combining alchemical principles with the Liturgy of the Sacred Mass! The Devil urges men to evil by instructing them to 'lift up the stone to enquire what is under it'. And what lies under?" he looked around at the gathering, "The serpent! How can such a highly placed and educated man such as yourself be so easily led astray by such false teachings?"

The assembled Bishops concurred: "Instantius comes from a good family," one said. "His father was a faithful servant of our Holy Church in Rome, even in difficult times he followed the teachings of the Gospel, to the letter. His son has been seduced by false words. If he is guilty, it is only because he is weak and followed a corrupt man, with evil and dangerous ideas, not even his own."

The Bishops concluded, after deliberation.

"You have been blinded, our colleague in Christ. Bewitched by this evil man who stands beside you and says nothing in your defense. But we cannot allow you to return to your diocese as wickedness flows in your blood like the poison of a deadly nightshade flower. You will go to the Scilly Isles, far from the coasts of Britain, and there, perhaps, in that desolate and remote place, you will search for God in His Purity once again."

Hyginus of Corduba was called. He was asked very little, and said even less. His sentence was as Instantius': exile.

"Take a copy of the True Gospels with you," Hydatius hissed in parting, as the two were led away. "It will bring you illumination in your Godless hearts. Perhaps, after you have served through your purgatory, you will beg to be accepted back into our fold again."

The two were whisked away, with never a chance to speak with Priscillian, who anyway, held his shaking, sobbing head in his hands.

The Synod was adjourned, and Priscillian, under house arrest, was led back to his host's domus. *All knew the implicit danger for any who had agreed to shelter him, but Urbicus had insisted. He and his daughter, Urbica, had done nothing to antagonize the Bishops nor the citizens of Burdigala, he protested; he only offered shelter, as a good Christian should. "Did not the Good Samaritan offer such charity?" he said in his defense.*

Euchrotia awaited him. He was shaking, not in fear, but in anger. "They are corrupt, stupid, greedy men, who care nothing for the truth! Even Jesus would have told them the same." But he would not discuss the day's proceedings; instead, he took to his bed without supper, and read the night through.

The next morning, Euchrotia approached him: "They are not of your understanding, but do not let them make you lose your composure. Tell them the truth."

Instantius' seeming duplicity haunted him still.

"Unlike some, I have never had any intention of doing otherwise," he answered her, and when they came to accompany him, from his look, they did not dare to constrain him: "I am a man of the cloth, charged with sacred deviations of which I intend, today, to prove myself innocent. Touch me and I will report you all to your Supreme Commander." His escort knew that he meant the Emperor, and they left him to walk by himself, quicker than they, as it turned out.

The assembly hall in the Bishop's Palace was packed. Many were there who had no right to be. Priscillian recognized some faces he knew of old, some friendly, most not. One of them was Ampellius, whom he later learned was Phillip's father. Ampellius nodded in obvious insincerity as Priscillian passed by. They had been students together, sharing the same teacher, Delphidius. Ampellius had been suspected, and proven subsequently—though it had not been Priscillian who had informed against him—to be a cheat. Even on this day, the day he was to emerge victorious, or exit in captivity, Priscillian had not made the connection between father and son. Euchrotia was to apprise him of that that evening. It explained much.

He did not give his accusers the chance to reiterate their charges.

"My fellow Bishops," he began, giving none the chance to challenge his assertion. "I stand before you accused of Manichaeism, for which you have the right from Rome to judge me, and of the scarcely veiled implication, of practicing magic, for which you do not. That being so, I will not answer any of the calumny which was brought before my fellow bishops yesterday, though they have been treated shamefully."

He looked around him: Yes, his foes had gathered, like hungry lions they sought to capture and tear apart the cornered gazelle. They thought he was beaten. Even in that they were fooled. For he knew himself as a lion, far less starved than they.

Phoebadius of Agen, he noted, Delpinius of Burdigala, Audentius of Marcella, Photinus, Hydatius of Emerita, and Ithacius of Ossonuba who looked as though sleep had not been kind:

The latter sought to interrupt, but Priscillian waived him down.

"You have said, and done, enough, I think," he said, and continued in his defense:

"I have been accused of teaching a sharp duality between God and the world, and the devil, yet to do otherwise would have gone against the expressed teachings of this assembly, and of our Mother Church. If evil exists, and it has been assumed so in this very room, must it not originate in either God or Satan? Since no-one here believes that it originates in God, then, by implication, it must be otherwise. I have said no other. I have proclaimed that celibacy is the life to be sought by those who follow a sincere calling. Other Synods, most notably that of Elviria, sought to enforce such a ruling, long ago. Yes, I have taught my hearers not to allow the body's desires to weigh down the soul. I have stated, and restate here, that the downward pull of worldly good contaminates the spirit, and our holy war is against persecution and demonic powers. Yes, I practice vegetarianism, and voluntary poverty, such as I can. Is this to also be a

source of judgment for any of you? Jesus certainly did not proscribe such dietary habits. This is a personal decision, and those who are my followers may do so if they wish. I have also expressed my conviction that those who have the means to do so should give what they can spare to the poor. Again, search the gospels as you wish, you will not find Our Lord disagrees with such practices. I have also expressed a personal belief that slavery is to be abolished, and that Christ preached no distinction between men and women. This too, you may not disagree with, regardless of the present policies of the church. Christ had many followers, women as well as men. The Lady Magdalene was but one of them. Christ our Lord, by his supreme act of sacrifice, abolished our slavery and obligation to the old words of the Jewish Testament: by him mankind was saved of a curse upon the species. All things, my friends, are in God, and God is in man. Any distinction between God and Christ is like that between mind and speech. It is in Jesus' incarnation on earth that God is known." he looked around him. Not a word was spoken. Hydatius seemed to have shrunken into Ithacius' shadow. Someone murmured something that sounded like "Trinity", but no-one spoke their thoughts aloud.

He continued: "I have said that the laity have essential obligations to God; that the righteous—whether called to the priesthood, or not—are engaged in a continuous spiritual war against the evil powers. We are, in the realm of the creatures of the earth, but are a seeming elite called to share in a mystery which God has predestinated. Some of our brethren and sisters have laid down their lives in the arena for their faith, and to them is gratitude due from every church.

"Our goal as Christians is to daily renew the inner soul, to study the gospels day and night to find our earthly salvation, to know the eternal precepts, while there is still yet time. In St. Paul's words: 'We must apprehend that for which we have been apprehended'. Ultimately, that apprehending requires an end to all compromises with the world, of the flesh, avaricious acts, envious quarrels, of worldly goods, of the drive to power—these we must strive to renounce so as to make our hearts pure for the sweet and simple words of God, our Father. Is friendship with the world enmity with God? Yes, I believe it is. For the world and its unkindness lies in the hands of Satan who originated in a lie and mankind have fallen to become the sons of perdition.

"Yet we retain our free will, do we not? We must never ascribe responsibility for our acts and our sins to the devil, nor his accomplices. Man is a mixture of Divine and earthly elements. It is our burden, to rise above that, in this life. That is redemption. That alone is the message of the Resurrection. It is possible through the sacrament of Baptism and belief in the redeeming sacrifice of our Lord Jesus. I have never taught

any other than that which you, in your own churches, have preached. The Divine Pity offers refuge: a harbor in the storm of earthly torment. We seek it in acts, faith, prayer. The believer is called to make a temple to God within himself, and this I have striven to do, and teach to those who follow me. But the way is not easy. We are not followers of Christ by word only. There is a downward drag of the soul which can only be countered by the determined and confident will of the spirit.

"Though made by God, the body is 'figura mundi': *our bodily appetites are not made by the devil, but still, we are weak and the devil exploits this weakness in us.*

"I realize that my words are capable of producing the response of true faith in some, but they are sure to scandalize others." He looked directly towards the assembled bishops. "It is right to affirm that Adam and Eve, our earthly ancestors, were given powers of reproduction. But it is my conviction that there has been a gradual progress from them through to the gospels of Jesus, just as we now perceive God to be Love. Higher things are now expected of us. Just as God created Heaven and Earth in six days, and rested on the seventh, we too are called to enter the Sabbath rest of the people of God. Again, I call upon you to read, as I, and those who follow me have. All the words of Christ, not just those judiciously selected for our consumption."

There was an audible intake of breath at these words, but still no-one spoke, not even Ithacius, who seemed to have been struck dumb and was staring at his feet.

"Renunciation of the world is the highest and truly the most Christian way, but it does not mean the loss of hope for those who want to belong to the church, but still retain their homes, to marry and bring up their children, if they wish. That is a matter of personal choice. I have not sought to impose otherwise. My message is not to induce despair in ordinary Christians with family obligations that they may be unable, nor wish to sever.
It is not a calling to all: though it is one to emulate, if we can. What is more, Jesus' words to the rich young ruler shows that hell is not unconditionally the destiny of all rich men. But almsgiving and a rich inner life are what set us on the road to salvation. Little by little we may attain to those things which are highest in the sight of God. It is for us to take the soul back to where it belongs, not to call it forth to this realm of sorrow, but to rise above the earthly cycle of reproduction.

"Bible study, as I have said, by daylight and by candlelight, is the way to apprehend the higher truth to which we are called. The scriptures invite readers to stretch their

*minds. There are many hard sayings and parables which, in prayer, may become accessible to the humblest. When Jesus says: "Those who have ears to hear, let them hear," he is asking us to **think**. To us, learning, all learning, is to understand the way of Deus Christus: God's Holy Name. Say to Him: 'I am the Lord's servant. I am held as Your witness.'*

"And what therefore is sin? Sin is man divided against himself. These are our short-comings as fallible creatures of dust and clay. All created beings under the sun are 'viteriorum divisa': we are divided life. Christ, however, is the symbol, the very principle of unity. He is One in all things, and desires us to be One in Him. This is the Imme-diacy of Christ, His Grace in us all. I have no more to say to you, gentlemen. If these truths needed to be presented to you in my 'defense', then I have done so, and then I rest my words here."

Around him in the general assembly heads were nodding: soft mutterings showed some amazement. The Bishops themselves were stunned into silence. Priscillian took them all in, and then to everyone's astonishment, he stepped down from the platform from which he had given his address, and without another word, and neither a look left nor right, walked out into the sunlight. No-one, neither priest, nor citizen, nor soldier, made any move to intercept him.

*   *   *   *

Euchrotia waited before the door of Urbicus' house.

"They are dry canals! Limited greedy men with limited greedy minds. I should have told them what I really wanted to say! That their hunger for domination over the free-dom of men, and their jealous attitude towards the possibility of learning truth from an unusual source ...

Here, uncharacteristically, words failed him. He let out a long held in breath.

*"I should have told them that the Holy Spirit is both male and female equally, but that in the realm of the Spirit, there is no distinction: the realm of sexual differentia-tion is left behind. We are all One in Christ. I should have told them that such detachment from all that is narrow and limited is the only way to approach God's mercy. I should **not** have been brought to this. I should have told them that it was the **immediate** grace of God that saves, not some mediated channel through the normal*

and officiated authorities of the church. It is the gift of charismatic prophecy which God has given to us. It is that which is our freedom. The Spirit is not confined to the episcopate and the deacons on whom they lay their hands in ordination; it is to be found in all those who aspire to holiness and to an understanding of the deeper meaning of the Scriptures. I should have told them."

"And they would have damned you for it."

"They will damn me anyway, Euchrotia! I could see it in their eyes. They are weak before such as Ithacius. Even his crony Hydatius hides behind his robe. Make no mistake, my love. They will exile me, and attempt to humiliate me as they did to Instantius and poor Hyginus, who has done nothing against them. I will not return to this travesty of so-called Ecclesiastical justice. I will go the Emperor to plead my case. I will not reappear before them"

"Oh God!" was all Euchrotia could say, for she knew him in this mood, and knew that no words, hers or others would dissuade him.

$$\ast \qquad \ast \qquad \ast \qquad \ast$$

The next day, seeing her continued distress, he sought to reason with her: "I will lay my case directly before Maximus at Trier," he said. "We stayed away from the Synod at Saragossa, and when we went to Milan, we managed to negotiate remarkable favor. Perhaps we can do it again."

Maximus is not Gratian, thought Euchrotia. His political situation is entirely a different thing.

But she went to pack her few things, hers, and Priscillian's.

"Promise me one thing," she pleaded, "Let us go by way of Elusa."

"Of course, my dear love," he said gently. He knew there was no point in forbidding her to accompany him. The sight of her devotion moved him to softer mood, and taking her upturned and pleading face in his hands as he was accustomed, kissed her firmly. "And then again, we will return to it, and peace and prosperity soon enough. We shall sit in your herb gardens and drink mint tea before long. But I will be no more their 'Bishop'. From now on, I will lead my own followers in my own way."

CHAPTER XXV

▼

It is no surprise to Priscillian that he and his entourage were less than welcome at Trier. *Maximus had matters to settle, wars to pay for, and informers to pay off. To the new Emperor, here was a tiresome complication that the bishops at the Synod of Burdigala had failed to settle for themselves. It meant little to him. Now his ante-rooms at the palace were filled with bishops and clergy and laymen all demanding audience in one way or another, and he had little time and less interest in dealing with them. To him it was a Church matter, settled by Church leaders, and for that reason, he had let Ithacius and Hydatius proceed. He cared nothing of the outcome.*

He already had sufficient problems as it was. He had to rule Supreme and that meant deciding whether to be conciliatory, or punishing to those high officials who had followed the ousted Gratian. This was his first preoccupation. The clerical matter was well down in his list of priorities. What is more, he wanted to settle matters in the outer provinces, west from Britain and Gaul, and in that he had so far failed. He had no money. His treasury was lower than anyone else knew. At least all but a few. These lesser men were powerful in their own right for they held the purse-strings of the Empire, (and he resented them and their constant bad tidings) and in that, they were to play a leading role as to the fate of the bishop, and his followers, many of whom held vast estates in Gaul and Spain. 'The Priscillianists have vast estates', they whispered in his ready ear. Perhaps Priscillian could be a Godsend after all? He mused.

But he also needed the support of the Pope, though he wished with all his heart that he did not.

He called Siricius who had been newly elected Bishop of Rome (Damasus had died) from Rome to Trier. Siricius sent Ambrosius.

What the Emperor discovered made him angry beyond measure. Siricius looked upon himself as Maximus' equal, and in this he had the full support of Ambrosius, who himself was a force to be reckoned within the church. Many felt that he, Ambrosius, should have been elected in Damasus' stead, not Siricius who was old. Ambrose, to the Emperor's fury, openly challenged Maximus to his face, calling him "usurper". He directly challenged the new Emperor's legitimacy to the Purple, and he had turned and left forthwith. Furthermore, and to Maximus' dismay, on Ambrosius' return to Milan, he sent word to this effect to Siricius, and the Pope was delighted in his ally, even though they had had cause to differ in the past. And by the time Ambrosius returned to Trier, as Siricius had dispatched him, neither the Pope nor the Emperor had publicly conceded the other's right to reign. It presented a stalemate. Yet the latter found an unexpected ally in Augustine.

Augustine had been a Manichee, but now embraced the official doctrine of Rome. In fact, his diatribes against the Manichees were listened to in many quarters, perhaps because he was thought to be a man who knew much. He was now powerful and a voice to be heard in ecclesiastical circles, challenging Ambrosius' own. Ambrosius had little time for this "upstart" as he called him. But it made little difference to the new Pope, who had his own ascendancy to consider.

Maximus in his defense claimed that Gratian had brought about his own downfall. He said that it was the previous emperor's policy of favoring the Alans, and the Germanic soldiers, former foes, which had brought this about, long before he, Maximus, had sought to challenge him in battle. Furthermore, he claimed in his justification, it was not after all by his command that Gratian had been killed—even though he had made no move to remove or censure the officer implicated.

There still remained an atmosphere of high tension between the Orthodox and the Pagans. Rome was a newly created Christian state. Maximus was no fool. He knew that only by taking an unchallengeable stand on the nature of the orthodox teachings could he gain the gain the support of the church, though personally, he cared little for them. In short, he knew that any weakness towards heresy, schism, or paganism would result in his own downfall.

Unfortunately, Priscillian was not to know this. We may judge him as naïve in hind-sight, but his nature was to trust in the Truth, and he knew he wielded it. It was not his fault that the ways of the world outfought and subsequently overpowered him, and had a more immediate message. Power, money, management of the Empire's resources: that was the kingpin in this time's chessboard. Those of you who read this many years hence, may see one day, perhaps, a similar imbalance of God and Power in your own world.

Or perhaps you will have recognized that the only true Power is God's Love. We are but shadows in the dust compared to Him, and our hubris is our constant downfall.

In this volatile atmosphere, it was tantamount to impossible to expect the new Emperor to be a willing ear of a renegade and headstrong Spanish bishop, especially as he was considered heretical in both Rome and Milan. What is more, it is hardly sur-prising that Maximus would reject what had been decreed by his predecessor. Any favor Priscillian might have secured in the past was due to moneys which had changed hands between the Priscillianists and Macedonius—and Macedonius had long since fled back to Spain. Macedonius, it becomes clear to me now, had little interest in Truth.

Priscillian had no allies in Trier, or Rome, or Milan, and sadly, he was still oblivious to this.

My name is Herenius, and perhaps you will remember me from before in this narra-tive. I had not expected to be so visible, but perhaps you will forgive me. I have a story to tell.

I had come, perhaps you will recall, with Elpidius, and while the latter was in Burdi-gala with Priscillian and Euchrotia and the others (even though as a layman he had not been called), I remained at Euchrotia's estate. With Procula, and Claudia who was to prove a most skilled healer, and her father, Marcellus—and Galla, Priscillian's daughter. Perhaps you will permit me now to take up the story in my own words, for although I had no key role to play, I saw much that needs to be reported, both in Elusa, and later, after our journey to Trier. Before and after. Galla's story, and mine. But that came later.

Claudia, as I have said, not only gained the confidence of Procula, but also managed to help her to recover, day by day, slowly, for she had been sorely wounded by the events which had overtaken us all. I gained the friendship of Donatus, Marcellus the farmer's son.

And gradually, I gained the friendship and trust of Priscillian's daughter.

Daily, I audited the accounts of the estate, and they showed many discrepancies, as Marcellus thought they would. It was clear that someone had been lining his pockets, justified, perhaps he thought, by his own guilt. Maybe he knew that he would never be the master of the estate, and had sought to compensate himself in other ways, especially as Procula, as her pregnancy advanced, had steadily rejected his company. Whichever the case, there was less in the treasury than perhaps even Euchrotia or Marcellus expected. In fact, in monetary terms, there was almost nothing.

I confided this to Marcellus and Procula.

"He has rendered the estate virtually bankrupt," I said. There was no way to soften the blow.

"We have the land, and the stock, or did he mortgage that also?" Marcellus asked.

"No, luckily, he was not that clever. He sought to make a quick exit. I think that he assumed that with his marriage to Procula—and he was clearly confident that that would be so, to avoid her shame—he would become the master of the purse, and that no-one would be able to challenge him. If it suited him, he would re-introduce some of the money he had stolen, to save the estate, and if not.... well, even now there is no proof, but that it is circumstantial."

"There is enough to keep the household intact, I hope?" said Galla, who knew a good deal about such matters, having handled Priscillian's since her mother's death.

"Yes, yes, you may rest assured," I said.

Though I was far from sure of this myself.

"But just in case, just in case," I said, at Galla's look, "perhaps Marcellus we should sell off some of the lambs and kids. After all, we may milk their dams, and the household no longer has any need for their meat. We will change our production into cheese making, and the grape harvest this year should prove a good one for we have had fortunate weather."

I did not say: 'Though we will not be drinking any of the result.' It was still a hardship for me to give up wine!

"And then?" Galla asked.

"And then we wait for Priscillian and the Mistress to come home. They will, you know. These "Bishops" have no legs upon which to stand, or they would have done something to prevent Priscillian's travel by now. In fact, I'll wager, they are licking their wounds in Burdigala by now and wishing they had kept silent!"

But I was to be proved wrong, and in later days, I was to reproach myself for giving Galla false hopes.

She was to prove my heart's desire. Thought I have never spoken of it to her nor to any man before this time.

✳   ✳   ✳   ✳

Priscillian was followed to Trier by his major accusers: Ithacius and Hydatius. They were accompanied by Martín of Tours, who had been at the Synod but kept his council, and who did not seem to either oppose or support them. Maximus, it is certain, would have looked upon their presence as loyal support for he wined and dined them, in a luxury to which they (some) had become accustomed. Martín, he saw immediately, was a different kettle of fish to the other two, as he made it clear that he did not necessarily agree with his host, even though he accepted Maximus' table and offer of hospitality. Maximus' pride was such as then that he gave it little thought. Bishops were Bishops. He, first and foremost, was a soldier. In secret he followed Mithras: the soldier's god.

Ithacius had the advantage, however, since he had made many friends while in exile there under Gratian's rescript and which he had evaded. In particular, he called, as his friend, the Bishop, Britto, with whom he had sought sanctuary. He also intuited from the Emperor's conversation that ecclesiastical considerations were secondary. He cared little about Maximus' personal convictions. Ithacius was no led sheep—as he considered his henchman, Hydatius—he knew that since Priscillian had submitted himself to the secular arm (Oh fool! That he hands himself to me on a silver plate), and that his former implied charges of magic would be considered in a secular court.

He knew that Maximus wielded bloodier arms than the combined might of the bishops could ever hope to. Metaphorically, he rubbed his hands together in anticipation.

He had even more Priscillianists in his web now, and he would not let them go.

But not all the bishops agreed with him. In fact many had doubts of their own. Was it right, they asked, that a bishop who had been charged primarily with heresy should be judged by a secular court? The former Pope, Damasus himself, had invoked the ecclesiastic right to rid him of the charges of homicide, no less! Bishops and Emperors had good reason to stay clear of the other's territory: Bishops because they believed that those whom God had called should not be in litigation before worldly judges (and much of this was to protect themselves from otherwise blatantly secular charges); Emperors because they did not care to take upon themselves arbitration in ecclesiastical matters pertaining only to the bishops and to God. They knew where their jurisdiction ended, and did not care to cross it. Even Valentinian the First, had he not declared: "It is not for me to judge between Bishops"?

The Bishops themselves, felt only capable of judging matters of correct doctrine and discipline. So in Trier, Ithacius did not find himself so wholeheartedly supported as he had expected.

Ambrosius—who had not heretofore been friendly to the Priscillianists, and Martin of Tours, who had been at Burdigala, and who had held his council, both felt that Priscillian and his followers were, yes, heretics, but as such, should not have been forced by circumstance to present themselves to the Praetorian Prefect. Neither even did they consider whether the implied charge of Ithacius, that of magic, was either inside or outside a lay court of law. Most of the bishops conceded that Priscillian was a Bishop, had been ordained a Bishop, had been summoned to Burdigala as a Bishop, and hence such a charge would have been an implausible assertion. Capital punishment, which was the end result of the condemnation of those brought forth and found guilty of such a charge (of practicing magic, that is), simply was unacceptable to them, even if in agreement with a civil Code of Justice.

So, to make a long defense short, it was not to Ithacius' advantage to bring such charges with him. There were many more bishops who thought it wrong in principle for him to be the accuser of a colleague in Christ in a capital court. Ithacius (and Hydatius, who could no longer be seen to speak for himself), found himself ostracized, much to his surprise.

The trial itself took place in September 386. Others will dispute this, but I, Herenius, remember it all too well, and sorrow accompanies the memory. In the fields, the peasants were bringing in their harvest, tasting their first young wine, glorifying their crops to God and praising His name, offering them in sacrifice (what else is a 'Harvest Festival' but an ancient rite?), and thanking Him for bringing yet another year to fruition. And their lives to enjoy His bounty.

Some, in secret, made offerings to older gods, for the same reasons.

In Treveris, there was little to celebrate for Priscillian and those who had followed him thus far.

First of all, you must know, that in a charge of employing witchcraft, severe torture could, and would, be used. Sorcery was associated with the charge of high treason and no distinction was to be made as to the nature of the "magic" performed: black or white. Torture, I reiterate, was standard policy in Rome, and no thought was given to those who may have been innocent of such a charge. They were to be torn apart by the rack, or lacerated by hooks, and only their "confession" was heard, not their cries of innocence. Under such duress, is it not certain that many men—and women—will "confess" to crimes they have not committed, or which they do not consider crimes at all, and from which, either way, they will emerge with mangled bodies, and tortured souls if they do not die from their wounds.

I don't know if I can continue …

Priscillian, Euchrotia, Elpidius, Latronianus, that most gentle of poets, Felicissimus, Armenius, the two clergy … no, I cannot!

But I must! Priscillian confessed to "crimes" of "interest in magical studies; nocturnal gatherings with women; praying naked, saying the Holy Mass with unshod feet …"

Oh dear God! How could he have done otherwise! How could they? And all so innocent, to the glory of God, and with ultimate, absolute love, and faith, and devotion. All those misguided, misconceived, self-serving charges were true! And none were worthy of such terrible censure!

Of lesser charges, by being guilty by association, were the others brought to the rack. I narrowly missed the same myself, for at the end I was present. All "confessed". How, in God's Holy Name could they have done other?

∗   ∗   ∗   ∗

The case was brought before Erodius. I will waste no time nor emotion on what transpired, for you, must, by now, know it already, for there can be no other conclusion to this narrative ... and you have known it from the beginning. I thank you for staying with me, your lives can only but be enriched by what you have learned.

Erodius found Priscillian, and all those charged with him, guilty of sorcery, and Manichaeism was but a secondary charge. Even in a law of 381, Theodosius, the then Bishop of Rome, had proclaimed civil charges against the Manichees, depriving them of their property, prohibiting them their assemblies; and against certain sects in Asia Minor, more severe penalties were enacted. All those who knew of their existence were empowered—and expected to be monetarily enriched—to report such sects to be censured and bought to "justice". The death penalty had been enacted for all: crucifixion, for most were not Roman citizens, and only those who were could choose the sword. All properties were confiscated by the state. No doubt, Ithacius (that evil man) would have influenced the decision against the Priscillianists with his lies: that the Scriptures (especially those he cited of St. Paul, whom many may cry was a misogynist, but much has been added. He was not so at the beginning) proscribed against the voice of women—hence, as Priscillian did not discriminate between his followers, he was condemned. Those damning charges, impossible to escape: that Priscillian had gotten Procula with child and subsequently assisted at her abortion; and moral pollution which colluded with the substantive charge of witchcraft, which was, and had always been a capital charge. They dictated the terms of the syllogisms, my brothers, and none could argue against them. May God look kindly on he who sought to proselytize such a bankrupt form of logic. For I cannot!

Our Master, and the others, were executed with Imperial permission, on these charges, but the taint of Manichean heresy made it all that the easier to substantiate.

I have said I would protect their privacy. Perhaps I am wrong in allowing you this glimpse of their intimacy. But, I must. I must.

Her diary has come to me, and I brought it to her daughter, as Euchrotia had wished. She gave me permission, on the day they were lead away, to read it. My intrusion must be interpreted and excused, or not, by those who read it now, wherever, and whenever you are. It says little about God, but much about faith and obedience, and yes, even more about human frailty. Even more about Ultimate Love.

Euchrotia, and Priscillian, forgive me.

*   *   *   *

I had journeyed with my lord thus far and my woman's heart would fail at this point were I not compelled by the truth to report to you thus.

We had waited in the Emperor's ante-rooms for so long, day after barren day, Priscillian and I, and the others; finally, we were six. Others waited upon the outcome, both women and men. As the days passed, and Maximus' closest advisors passed us by with nary a glance, we began to realize that no-one would come to offer witness on our behalf, though we had heard of Ambrosius' presence, and that of Martín, who had been at Burdigala, and who had known my husband. No word came. Even he, my hopeful lord, must have acknowledged this, and the silent distress this caused him knew no bounds. Eventually, we dispersed, and waited for the official summons, though Priscillian, my dear and optimistic love (may God spare him torment at this time!) thought that all would be aright in the end.

We had taken rooms in the city. They did not guard us then. Surprisingly, no-one had come for us. In fact, we felt so invisible that I, at least, suggested that we simply disappear into the night. "We are no longer invisible," he said. "They will find us, and if we go, then our cause will be the less. Something good must come out of this. I believe not in martyrs, our deaths would only perpetuate our cause. It will not come to that."

I felt a goose pass over my grave.

"But we shall have our say!" he continued. But I did not by then believe in justice, in hope, nor prayer, nor, forgive me for saying it, in God. I only believed in the bonds of Love.

That night I made him supper, he and I. The others had the good grace to leave us alone. We said as we believed then. What more could they bring against us after all, I thought.

After we had eaten, I went to him then. I knelt at his feet, and I put my hands on his shoulders. "Will we meet again?" I asked. His answer told me that his hope had been but for his followers. "I doubt they will let me go. They know I will not stop.

"I was with you before I saw your face," he said in answer, "before I was born in this or any other life. My wife will forgive us for she is We: souls can be separated you know? All of those who love with such intensity are truly One in God." He lifted me up so that we looked into each other's eyes, as we had done the night that Delphidius died. As if to read my mind, Priscillian said: "Perhaps we are a Quaternity, or more: you, Delphidius, Cecilia, me? Who is to know in what fractions the Great Soul divides itself?

"Come, my love, come into my arms, this one last opportunity that the time offers us. I will not break our vows but I will be with you tonight."

He unfastened his robe. He lifted my tunic over my head. And he led me to his bed: a simple trundle in a simple, unadorned room. "All I need is your beauty tonight," he said, as we continued our undressings, and his lips found my breasts and my most secret parts.

We did not break our vows, but I will tell you, that night, I knew my lord, and he knew me.

*   *   *   *

They came for us with the morning. We were taken, not to the Emperor, who, it was claimed, was too busy to see us. But directly to trial: to Maximus' henchman, Erodius, whom, I had learned to my distress, had little time to spare in the subtleties of argument. Ithacius and Hydatius were key witnesses. Then, they took me from him, and I was not to see him again.

May God have mercy upon our souls. Our only crime is Love.

CHAPTER 26

▼

The workers returned that night to no supper. And no sign of the usual chief cook. Miranda was in the shared room, seated on her lower bunk, her head necessarily low, for it would have been anyway. She was crying. Her breath came in long, agonized sobs, and she saw no distance in the vast intermediate centuries which separated her from the lovers and her own love of Love.

Kieran sat across from her. He did not touch her; he knew better.

"No! I will not accept it. It can't have ended this way. Kieran, it's **your** story! Change the ending, please!" she continued crying hopelessly, for she knew his answer already. The end had been explicit at the very beginning.

"I can't Miranda. It's their history. I'm only the conduit, and even I don't know the real ending. It may not have been as I have portrayed it …"

"But it was! It was! How could you have ever written it so if they had not sought to tell their story to you!"

"That's my point, Miranda. They did. And I did. I can't change the ending, not even for you."

But Miranda kept crying.

Kieran went downstairs and suggested pizza.

"Where's Miranda? It's our last night here. She can't just butt out like that!" Catherine exclaimed; her hands were blistered and her arms were scratched, and she wanted a celebration of moving on.

"Leave her alone," Kieran said; "she has 1700 years of injustice to deal with, and I'm sorry to say it, but when she emerges from that, she'll have more."

Dominic stayed silent. He already knew the end of the story.

*   *   *   *

Kieran left early the next morning. He felt a conspicuous energy, and he wanted to explore it on his own. It was seven kilometers to the next refugio, Villafranca del Bierzo.

"There is a church there," he told Miranda before he set out, "Romanesque, dedicated to Santiago. The pilgrims of old knew it well. Villafranca isn't like the other towns. It is where those, who could not, for whatever reason, continue on to Santiago, were able to pass under the *Portico del Perdon*, a special door, and receive the same forgiveness for their sins that they would have done had they gone all the way to Compostela. I will make a decision today," said, and although he would not say what that decision was, Miranda thought she already knew.

Instead, she walked with Dominic. On the outskirts, they reached a church: La Virgin de las Angustias. The outside was Baroque, but looked somewhat unprepossessing. She had grown to love the simpler ones. She would have walked on but for the name.

"*Angustias?*" she asked him.

"It means 'Our Lady of Sorrows'," he translated.

"Well, we seem to have more than our fair share of those right now. I will go in."

Even then, she felt little connection. The joy which had seized her at Rabanal had not made a second appearance, and she began to doubt her reaction. But there was a small statue: a young Jesus, playfully beside St. Anthony of Padua. She had begun to recognize these statues now, and looked for them. They were comforting to her: some semblance of continuity. Her favorite was San Roqué, walking along blissfully unaware of his injuries, accompanied always by a small dog which danced in his shadow. He was clearly a pilgrim. "He's like the Fool in the Tarot pack," she had said to Alex somewhere along the Way. "He doesn't really know where he's going, he's about to step off a precipice, and he doesn't even care! He's so sure his is the right Path. I wish I could be like that!"

Outside, Dominic had his green paperback in his hands.

"Tell me about the Gnostics," she said. "What is it that you believe in that makes your faith so different?"

"It's more than faith," he said, "it's divine revelation. But I'll tell you if you like."

As they walked on, he said:

"You'll tell me if you're bored?"

"How could I be bored! It has inspired you, it had clearly influenced Kieran, and anyway, I've learned a little from Priscillian. Tell me, please," and they settled into a slow rhythm, their packs long forgotten by now.

"First of all, 'Gnostic' means 'one who knows'. The Gnostics were those who claimed more than just simply a belief in Christ, but an immediate revelation. They considered themselves, if you like, 'true witnesses', and they were persecuted for it. Gnosis is not knowledge in the way we think today: we tend to associate knowledge with 'book learning' and the intellect. Gnosis, instead, is a personal religious experience. I believe you may even recently have had such an experience yourself?"

Miranda responded with a hands wide gesture which said 'I don't know'. "I've never had any cause to consider myself receptive to such things," she said. "But do go on."

"I'll start with a question," he said. "Do you believe that the world is perfect?"

"The world? You mean the mess we are making of things? No!"

"The Gnostics hold that the world is imperfect because it was created in a flawed way."

"How can that be? I thought that God was supposed to be perfect and so how could God create an imperfect thing?"

"Good thinking. Keep that in mind. The Buddhists say that life is full of suffering, that there is a cause for the suffering …"

"And the way out of the suffering is to choose the Eightfold Noble Path. I learned that in Graduate school. What does that have to do with Christianity?"

"I'm getting to that part. Many religions blame the 'First Sin'—of Eve, and Adam, for bringing the imperfections of the world into being. They say that Eve's tempting Adam with the Apple of Knowledge brought about the 'fall' of creation. After that failing, humans had to take what came to them because they had brought it on their own heads. But Gnostics say that this is not the way it was at all. Instead they blame the Creator. Sounds like blasphemy, huh? The Gnostics agreed with the Platonist view of the world as an imperfect copy; they said we should look instead to the forms of knowledge which existed elsewhere and that we could only ever have a small idea of what was truly true. It was intuitive, but fleeting.

"Yes, I've got too much knowledge of Plato, probably … I've never really thought of this in connection with Christianity though, it was 400 years before Christ!"

"So was Hinduism, and Buddhism, which I bet you've also studied …" She nodded. "Their view is that the Doctrine of Karma explains how the chain of imperfection and suffering works, but, it doesn't tell us why a system such as this, with its endless reincarnations—before we 'get it right'—should exist in the first place."

"True. Back to Square One?"

"Back to Square One!"

"Hmm. Stalemate?"

"No! Once you can get over the little voice inside you which says 'God'll get you for this' anytime you question orthodoxy, the Gnostic view makes remarkably good sense. There is more than one god ... Yes, I can see that voice speaking to you right at this very minute!"

"But Dominic, that's ... that's ... blasphemous!"

"That's your religious instruction teacher at school talking. That's all of the priests and ministers you have heard. But think of it this way," he stopped and looked around at the clear skies they walked under. "Not much chance of being struck by lightning ... no? Shall I continue?"

"Please."

"You see in the Gnostic view, there is One True God, the God of the Christians, the Moslems, (The Sufis, in particular, had very similar views), and the Jews (you find it in the Kabbalah), as you and I would think of Him: ultimate, transcendent, all knowing, all powerful, merciful, but he has never created anything like this world, that is, in the way that we would normally understand the word 'create'. Instead he sort of "thought" the substance of everything. The Gnostics use the word 'emanate', and I agree it is a hard concept to understand—you have to go well outside the intellect to get a handle on it at all. But think with your heart. The concept of God as Love is Universal. He brought forth everything which pre-existed within himself: the visible and the invisible. You could say that everything is made of the substance of God, that everything we are, plants are, rocks and frogs are, galaxies, and whole universes Are, came from inside God, and are a part of Him still. It doesn't mean that each of these is a god—that is Pantheism. It means that God is God, there is no other, and we are all God as his essence is us. Are you still with me?"

"Only thanks to a degree in Philosophy which had some pretty amazing profs in Eastern Studies! Why would God do that though? Do you mean that maybe he was lonely?"

"You know, I've never thought of it that way. Perhaps Love means little without the beloved. And if the universe was created as a Supreme act of Love, that could make a good deal of sense. Maybe God wanted to 'Know' more, to Love more, and the only way to do that was to somehow, I don't know … 'spill over'? I'll ask Bishop Hoeller about that when I get back.

"The basic Gnostic belief is that there are immediate beings which exist in between God and ourselves.…"

"Angels?"

"Well, if you like to think of it that way, but it's really a bit more complicated … even angels are only 'messengers', Miranda. They, together with God, make up what is called the *Pleroma*: that's a hard word to translate but the closest I can get to it is 'fullness'."

"I've heard that before, I think Kieran mentioned it in his book somewhere."

"One of these beings, called in the Gnostic myth, Aeons, was called Sophia.…"

"Wisdom."

"The very same. She is very important to the Gnostic view. She was a questing and a questioning being, and wanted to know more, and in the course of her wanderings she emanated something from herself, with the best of intentions, but it was a flawed being which emerged. That being became the creator of the Earth, and he created it in the image of his own flaw, because he didn't know any better. He is often called the Demi-Urge, or 'Half-Maker', and as he created, so he created cohorts: the reverse of the Aeons—the Archons, and they between them became the rulers of the universe."

"Whoa! I don't think too many people are going to find that palatable."

"No, I agree, back to your Religious Studies teacher again, but bear with me. You see human beings, our body and spirits, still have the divine spark in them: they are God, well, 'bits' of him, if you like …"

"I get you, millions wouldn't."

"You see the difficulty for Gnostics? 'Damned' before we start.…"

"Like Priscillian: his judges made the rules, and they'd already decided what was what and so there was no way he could excuse himself of their charges," Miranda said.

"Yes, as I said: human nature represents the duality in the world. In part we are the spirits of the True God, yet we are also of the creator, Samael, or the 'Blind One', because he insisted that he was God and there could not be another above him. We, ourselves, are thus kept in ignorance of our true nature, and our destiny as children of Love and Light. Anything which causes us to be attached to worldly things, keeps us as slaves. If we do not become aware of that while we are still alive, and seek to break free of our bodily prison, on our deaths, we will be hurled back again, only to repeat the cycle once more."

"Like the Karmic regression. So, just a thought experiment: does that mean that anyone can become aware of this, and by doing that they can avoid being … sent back, as you said?"

"That's the sad question, I think. Some of us want to and find it natural and seek out like-minds; some of us would, if we only knew how to question what we have been told, but we are too obedient to The Rules; and some of us just don't care: life provides our little luxuries, and we don't want to be taken out of our 'comfort zone'."

"Like the ones in Plato's cave."

"Exactly. And what did they do to the one who ventured out of their world of shadows and brought back news of the sun outside?"

"They killed him. Yes, I see the problem."

"I thought you would." They were passing a bar. Truck drivers were enjoying their anis and coffee. Mostly in silence. It was 11:00.

"Let's stop for a bit. I'm afraid we might be catching Kieran up."

Miranda looked at him. What had been said between the two of them, that Kieran had not confided in her?

Dominic ordered a '*sombra*', Miranda a *cafe Americano*, and indulged in a brandy which proved far too large.

"Tell me more," she said, as they ate their breakfast *magdalenas,* and her words reminded her of that first day's walk, with Kieran, so long ago in the Pyrenees.

"Well, it's a sad story really. Because human beings are caught in a predicament: they know they have bodily appetites, they know they crave to feather their nests with 'stuff'—ever watched a kid at the checkout counter when Mom says no? Why does a newborn baby cry? We are conditioned early to forget out true origins by asking for, and getting 'more'. Yet, many of us, most perhaps, if we let ourselves go there—if we can get beyond the Soaps—know that we are **more** than that, and we want to know what. So maybe, we go to a shrink where we are taught to follow an individual path, or maybe we get religion, and we are told what we should believe, but what we are told still keeps us away from the understanding of our True Origins: as one with the very Substance of the True God. Messengers have come to help us, but men have corrupted their message beyond recognition and so as to gain advantage for themselves ..."

Miranda nodded.

"Gnostics don't look for salvation from 'sin'—and did you know that the idea of 'Original Sin' only dated from St. Augustine who was contemporary with Priscillian? No. I thought not. Most people don't. Certainly Jesus never said a word about it. To Gnostics the only 'sin' is ignorance. (As it is for the Hindus and the Buddhists). For Christian Gnostics, the only way to dispel that is through understanding that it is Jesus' **life**, not his death which has importance.

"Gnostic 'ethics' are pretty difficult to explain, but I'll try: Gnosticism, like Buddhism, encourages 'non-attachment' to the world; 'non-conformity' to the 'rules'. Don't misunderstand me, I can see the word 'Anarchy' written all over your face! Rules are necessary for societies; they are how we live in order and peace with one another. But they are not relevant to our salvation.

"You know, Confucius, when asked about death, replied: 'why do you ask me about death, when you don't even know how to live', or something like that. That's a quintessentially Gnostic answer. Sometimes when people become religious in one way or another, they are so caught up in the idea of 'Heaven', that they forget that death is no guarantee! And neither is going to church and mumbling the responses. As I have already told you, and certainly as Priscillian believed, it is what we do and realize while alive which leads us to our own 'resurrection', **in this life!**

"Come on, if you finish that brandy, I'll have to carry you to Villafranca, and Kieran ought to be there by now!"

*   *   *   *

Kieran **was** there, sitting dejectedly on the wall outside the front entrance of the Church of Santiago. The refugio stood alongside and pilgrims were already lining up to go inside at 12:00.

"The door is open, but the *Portico* is closed," he said dramatically. "Dom, can you help?"

"I was afraid of that. Kieran, I'm not ordained … I don't think …"

"That's O.K. I need some help, and I'm sure you are the one to give it. Will you …?"

Miranda couldn't make head nor tail out of this, but she took Kieran's place on the wall.

"Give me a few minutes," Dominic said, and he went inside to pray.

*   *   *   *

Miranda wandered inside. The church was all but empty. It was Spartan, except for a side chapel on the right which was more ornate, and which looked like a later addition. It didn't fit, somehow.

She took a seat at the back. From where she was, she could see a wooden statue of Santiago to the right of the altar. It was flanked by vases of plastic roses. He wore the familiar pilgrim garb: shelled hat, belted dark robe, and he carried a staff topped with a gourd, for water. There was something about this one which Miranda especially took a shine to: it was not static. He seemed to be on the move, eager to get to the next rest stop, determined to be in Compostela by nightfall. They all knew this feeling, even in moments of abject despair, and total weariness.

Dominic approached the front of the church, directly to the left of the altar, some distance from where Miranda was seated. He was wearing a simple ecclesiastical shawl around his shoulders, and he carried his green book. He stood, and waited. Kieran, walking down the aisle looked to neither side. He placed himself in front of Dominic. Miranda, without thinking, sank to her knees. Some words were exchanged between Kieran and Dominic, and then Kieran did the same.

Miranda was seized with a sense of panic, and at the same time, one of severe embarrassment. "I should have waited outside," she thought, "Maybe I should go now?"

But she remained where she was: for one thing she didn't want to create a disturbance ('in the air', came to her), for another, she wanted to remain close to Kieran, and to see what Dominic would do.

She was too far away to hear much. She heard the words 'and hail Sophia: filled with Light, Christ is with thee" ... and later ... "We know thee, Holy Spirit, thou giver of Life and Goodness ... remaining on earth to guide and care for us ..." She could not make out the words which followed, though she strained to hear ..., and then the word 'shortcomings'. She saw Dominic place his hands on Kieran's head, and saw Dom throw back his head: his eyes were closed. He was still talking, but the words were lost inside the images in her mind.

And then it happened. In her imagination, Miranda felt those hands upon her own head. She felt a sensation which afterwards she could only describe as "Cream, thick dairy cream, golden in color, pouring very slowly down my scalp, over my ears, onto my shoulders," and as she had done in Rabanal, she began to shake. She noticed her hands were in the same 'saucer' shape of reception they had been during the Gregorian Chant.

As she looked up, she saw Dominic move to leave, and as he brushed passed her, he smiled that knowing, and such unexpected smile of his which changed him from unapproachable to almost saintly.

Kieran remained on his knees. His shoulders were shaking uncontrollably. Miranda was afraid for him; she wanted to go to him. Surely something had gone very wrong? He looked to be crying.

And then he stood up, and turned around. He looked towards where she was sitting, but didn't seem to see her. Certainly he was sobbing, but the shaking of his shoulders was laughter. Totally, uncontrolled, laughing, Joy. The tears were streaming down his face ... He all but staggered to the nearest pew, and although Miranda could only see his back, she knew he continued to laugh, in utter release.

Quietly, she rose, and crept out of the church. Dominic was seated on the bench she had formerly relinquished.

"Better now?" he said.

And like Kieran, she burst into tears. She too had gotten down on her knees: I *did it Francis! She said to herself, within her own joy: I did it!*

CHAPTER 27

▼

It was as Catherine had wished it, that celebratory supper, but only some were moving in the same direction.

They were seated around three tables, squished together, on the terrace at the back of the refugio: *Ave Fenix*. The mythical bird which rose from the ashes of its own destruction. Oil lamps in beer bottles provided the only lighting.

Kieran and Dominic were announcing travel plans, but not westward.

"I have decided that I am going back to Dublin. I'll get the early bus tomorrow."

"I'll go with him as far as Madrid, and then I'll join you in a day or two, in Tria-castela." Dom added.

"I want to come with you," Miranda said, who though denying it now had part expected it.

But to her dismay, she didn't seem to be part of Kieran's travel plans.

"Miranda, you came for a reason. Maybe now you know that reason. Dom and I already knew, though our reasons are different. I'm going back to do two things: one, I have a friend in Ireland who has good publishing connections. Dom has suggested that I include the translated 'gospel' as an epilogue to the book. He thinks that publishers are more likely to accept it that way, and that it will reach a larger number of people ..."

Miranda wanted to interrupt, but couldn't quite come up with the words.

"... then I'm going to the hospital and I'm going to find out what I have to do get the chemo. It could take a while, I know that. But I'm going to get myself on the list."

Seeing her stricken face, he turned to Miranda and said: "I'm not so bad, you know. My spirit is stronger than ever; it's only the walking that has done me in. But I feel that I've done what I set out to do. You guys need to go on. Who knows what adventures await you over the next—what 150 kilometers or so? Dom'll catch you up—when he wants to he can walk even faster than Catherine! Anyway, if God wants me to, I'll be in Santiago when you get your Compostelas, and we'll all go out to celebrate. Don't look so sad—Felix is going on with you."

Miranda didn't know what to say.

"Hey! You've got my address, and my e-mail. I'm not going to disappear—from any of you."

This did not comfort her at all.

"I'll never see you again!" she hadn't meant it to sound so dramatic.

"Yes you will. And you'll be a different person by then."

"I don't want to be a different person!" she said, and to her embarrassment, she began to cry, and rather than inflict it on the group, she fled inside and buried her head in her sleeping bag.

Dominic said, rather inappropriately: "None of us wants to be a different person. That's why it's so necessary and so painful."

Felix just ordered another bottle of wine.

"*Dos*," said Alex, and not much was spoken after that.

*   *   *   *   **

The next morning, early, three pilgrims took a taxi to the bus stop. Two got on. One remained. Holding her hands up to Kieran's on the window as he settled into his window seat, she mouthed: 'I love you', as the bus moved out.

*   *   *   *

It was thirty kilometers from Villafranca to O Cebreiro, just inside Galicia. All up. No-one even thought to stop along the way. Felix wangled a deal:

"Jesus Jato here has a van. He says he'll take your packs on up for …" he looked at the owner of the refugio, a be-whiskered man who had seen it all … "500 pesetas a piece. I have agreed to go with him and to take them all to the refugio and make sure there are places for all of you. No really!" he said to the groans that accompanied this announcement. "Seriously, Jesus says it's a difficult climb, and that lots of pilgrims start from there. There are hotels, but they are all pretty pricey. This way, well, when you get there, I'll make sure they have laid out the red carpet. I'll even put the kettle on."

They were seven now: Felix, Miranda, Alex, Catherine and Kevin, and Stephen, who was refreshed by the facilities of the Parador ("not like it sounds", he said, "but a good buffet breakfast") and Laura, Stephen's pretty daughter, who had joined him in Ponferrada, but who had the typical first days' blisters they all remembered.

Laura said she thought she might go with them in the van: "I only ever promised my dad I'd walk in Galicia," she explained, with a lovely lilting South Wales accent. The others were less judgmental in her case. But as always, the Felix charm, and cockeyed logic, won out.

The remaining pilgrims walked in pairs, and ones. All seemed to be not only wrapped in their own thoughts, but perhaps preparing themselves for the last leg: Galicia, and Compostela.

Supposedly, there was a pilgrim trail which took them off the main roads and up into the hills which led out of Villafranca. But Miranda followed the yellow arrows, and once on the main highway, thronged with vast, fast moving behemoths, she realized she hadn't found it. She was walking alone: Catherine and Kevin had set out immediately after Kieran and the others had left for the bus stop, Stephen had disappeared; even Alex who, thought Miranda, might have intuited her need for company, was no-where to be seen.

As she walked, she walked with sorrows, and the trucks, which sped by and nearly tossed her off the road, did little to lessen her despair. She tried not to think about Kieran. But by the time she reached Vega de Valcarce, where the route finally and thankfully branched off onto a country road, she had reached the bottom of her pit. She stopped into a truck stop for breakfast, but found she had no more than an appetite for salted almonds out of a dispenser, and a bitter coffee which she let grow cold. In Ruitelan, she bought a *bocadillo*, and water, and met two Swiss ladies who said they were going to stay at a new hostel in the village. The hospitaleros were former pilgrims, Spanish, why didn't she break her stay? But Ruitelan was less than twenty kilometers from her starting point that morning. She had lost one pilgrim, two actually, and she wasn't going to take the chance of losing any more, even though they had deserted her in her hour of need.

A white van pulled up beside her. "Hey, *Peregrina guapa*, wanna lift?" said Felix leaning over from the passenger seat. Laura waved from the back.

"No thanks. Some of us have to pretend to be real pilgrims, even if others don't," she said.

"*O Cebreiro está mucho mas arriba*, "said the driver, but Miranda ignored him, and the van sped away, with her pack in it, and her pilgrim spirit.

"I couldn't feel much more burdened than this," she thought, and tried with little success not to do it spitefully.

Yet somehow, as the path became more remote, and the climb ever steeper, she began to abandon her own self-loathings. She didn't even think of Kieran (that much) but instead began to focus on her own experience in the church. What was it she had felt? Freedom. Forgiveness even: a sense that some much greater power than she, not only was watching her, walking beside her, but keeping her safe. And eventually, watching the squirrels chase each other around the dense trees bordering the dense ascending path, she heard a small voice say: "You have never been more welcome. You have never been more sure that what you are doing is right. Where you are going is right. What will happen to you is yours." It certainly wasn't her voice, for hers had just told her the opposite.

She began to measure her steps. Not forcing herself to climb with rhythmic breathing, as she had done at other times, but stopping long before she got tired. Observing closely the birds around her—she rarely noticed birds. Stopping to marvel at each hidden flower, and here in the undergrowth, protected from the overbearing sun, they grew in profusion: tiny yellow and perfect heads which would have long wilted starved of moisture on the *Meseta*.

And then she stepped out into sunlight, and a slippery, slurried path. The cows had clearly just preceded her into the remote hilltop village, but wherever they were, they were nowhere to be seen or heard. In fact there wasn't a soul. It was just noon.

A fat Siamese cross came to her and rubbed against her legs. She bent down to croon to it: "Hey there, pussykins, you lonely?" She scratched it behind its ears, forgetting she was allergic to Siamese dander, and spent the next hour trying not to rub her fingers at her inflamed and itchy eyes and neck, largely unsuccessfully.

The only other souls on that seemingly endless deserted path, were a shepherd with no sheep, riding a fat mare, and accompanied by a lanky golden foal nudging his dam's side at top speed. The shepherd said something incomprehensible, and she remembered to say *'Buenas Dias'* only just as he rounded the next corner.

The arrows disappeared. There was only the track remaining with nothing but briar and burnt cropped grass stretching for miles on either side, with little shade for pilgrims or beasts. Though she could see the track stretch on in front of her, she was surprised to see that the shepherd, horse, and baby had disappeared and she wondered how that could be possible in this vast openness. At one point, she divested herself of her daypack and lay flat on her back in the wiry, springy scrub, and tried to see portents in the clouds. But since they were few and all looked like divided hearts, she took a long draught of her water and continued on her way.

Not since the Pyrenees had the Camino been so bereft of animal life: human or otherwise, not even on the Meseta. She lost track of time and distance and began to enter into the kind of trance one sometimes experiences between waking and sleeping. At one point she thought she would walk into a herd of goats, but they turned out to be misshapen rocks, seeking each others' company out of the solitude of the bare land that stretched on either side, seemingly hurled there by some mischievous Highland Gamesman. After a while, she found it hard to concentrate on where the land ended and where the sky began. It all seemed some incredible vastness in which she seemed so miniscule. She wondered if everything else had been a dream: that only this walk, on this path was the direction of life: alone, as she had been at the beginning. If she had felt lonely then, it was nothing to what she felt now.

And then, Cebreiro. She had imagined it around every hillside, but the hills just stretched on and on. Only a transmitter tower, even higher above, reminded her of human presence. There was a *palloza* at the entrance: one of those ancient round thatched crowned dwellings which dated back to the Castros of the Celts, in pre-Roman times. This one was a herding place for sheep, but it was deserted. She wanted to lie down in it and sleep. She resisted the pull of the refugio. She didn't want to join the others, not yet. She didn't think she could stand their laughter. Something to her had died, and they couldn't be expected to understand her pain.

As she hung around the periphery of the village, Stephen appeared. He was taking photographs with an enormous Nikon. "Hey **Miranda**! They are waiting for you. There's *Caldo Gallego* on the stove, and fresh Galician bread. The refugio is excellent, the corners are swept, and the showers are clean, and I'll be back in a bit. Go and say 'Hello' to my daughter. She's feeling a bit left out of the group." And off he went, screwing on lenses with great anticipation.

"Yeah, right! Go and be the life of the party? That's the very last thing …" But a little voice said: "That's the very thing …" so off she went.

No parador could have done justice to the panorama outside her windows. Everything seemed to go down from there. *If God wanted to create a house on Earth, he/she/it would have built it here,* she thought, and for some reason she turned to the east: "I have come from there," she said, and she returned to the west, where the vista and the Camino stretched before her, a small church appearing in the distance, "and I am going there. Simple. I will not think any more today."

*   *   *   *

The six met for dinner in the inn in front of the refugio. The conversation was subdued, perhaps out of respect for Miranda's silence. They understood more that she thought, but all were too shy to say much. That night, snuggled down in her sleeping bag, which took on more sacredness every time she buried herself in it, she was cold for the first time in ages. She dreamed of snow.

She was walking in it, and it covered her shoes. She carried her pack but it seemed heavier than usual and she decided it was because she carried a tennis racket. She threw it on the snow where it stayed, on the surface, horizontal. 'You ought to mean something to me,' she thought, 'but you weigh too much.' Dominic appeared out of the mist and took her photo. 'Don't forget to give it to Kieran!' he said. But then the camera turned into a high powered rifle, and she woke up.

She thought she could hear pipe music. Felix was on the lower bunk beside her, snoring in peaceful oblivion. She looked around her. Nothing was out of the ordinary, and pilgrim sleep had become ordinary to her. She punched her lumpy pillow and cursed the early hours. "I will not give in to despair," she said, aloud. Felix turned in his sleep and said: "Too few pilgrims; too many big bulls!" And then after a minute or two he was snoring quietly again.

"I love these people," Miranda thought, and then sleep claimed her again, faster than she expected. This time it left her tranquility intact.

*   *   *   *

The morning found something they had rarely experienced. It was a slow connection of spirit perhaps appropriate to the family they had become. Everyone met in the bar for breakfast and made some onward plans. The group had become too intimate, too dependent one upon the other, to leave anything to chance now.

It was a Sunday.

"Right then," said Alex with authority to the assembled. "There is a small church in …" she consulted Dom's guidebook "… *Hospital*. It's only 5 kilometers. That's a bit more than an hour if we walk at our own pace. Sounds friendly. I vote we go out when the spirit moves us—so to speak …" This last was in answer to Felix' unspoken question. "and meet up there. We'll go to Mass. We'll be there a bit before 11:00 and it's not yet nine. Come on, why not? We are on a pilgrimage after all, and so far we haven't shared that with many churches."

Hospital, not surprisingly by its name, was once a very old pilgrim waystage, founded, they learned in the 11th century. It had no refugio now, and had long ceased to be a viable stop on the way. Most pilgrims broke their night in Cebreiro. But the church was still functioning, and by its uneven stones and moss-covered exterior, it was older by far than any they had encountered thus far. It was also tiny. Just before 11:00 in dribs and drabs, the pilgrims began to find their way in. It was almost empty except for three rough-hewn oak benches in front of the altar. Local people joined them and smiles were exchanged, though few words.

"I don't think these people speak Spanish," said Felix, who had walked with Laura who seemed to limp less today.

"It's Gallego," said Dom, "but if you listen closely, you'll understand a word or two of the service."

To the surprise of all, a good half of the congregation—that is to say about eight—wore clogs, and the women were dressed in the same blue dresses: the younger as well as the older ones. The priest addressed them all, pilgrims included, from just in front of the altar, but then to everyone's surprise (the pilgrims that is) he motioned them to stand around him in a circle, in the congregation, not the altar which remained behind him. The local people seemed so friendly that no one doubted that they were to be included. The service proceeded, and after a while, Miranda heard words she had learned in Spanish—not quite the same, but similar. She looked, puzzled at Dominic.

"They are saying the Our Father," he said and joined in Spanish. Those who intuited this joined in their own language. Afterwards, when many of them took the sacrament, the priest looked pleased.

"Thank you for attending," he said in perfect but accented English, as they exited the church and picked up their packs outside the door.

✳   ✳   ✳   ✳

The pilgrims walked on, in a sort of loosely spaced formation, but now they seemed to convene in smaller groups of twos and threes, and it was to stay that way until Los Arcos. Miranda walked with Dominic and Stephen; Catherine and Kevin, and sometimes Alex made up another group of three; Felix walked for the most part with Laura and sometimes they would join the first group making five, but the conversation seemed to stall when that happened.

After Triacastela, which no-one liked, despite the new barracks of a refugio—the locals seemed unfriendly and the prices were set high—Miranda walked with Laura for a while. Felix had slept late. Apart from telling her that she was a History Student at Cardiff University, ("I am fascinated by the 13th century, especially France," she admitted,) Laura said little to Miranda, perhaps realizing that Miranda had other thoughts to process. Laura seemed reticent to share much and her freshness made Miranda feel decidedly 'older'. But as the landscape began to change and become "more Welsh", as she said, she said to Miranda, out of the blue.

"My dad must be in his element."

"How's that?" said Miranda, returning from her reveries.

"Well, this type of countryside. This feeling of ancient history. He did tell you?"

"Pardon me? Tell me what?"

"Well," she said, a bit shyly now. "He's a Bard. A Druid. High Order, I gather, but he doesn't say much about it. Mum finds it a bit weird. So we don't exactly talk about it around the dinner table."

"No, I suppose not," Miranda said.

CHAPTER 28

▼

In Ferreiros, they met up with two familiar faces, and an unfamiliar one who seemed somehow to be joined to them by the hip, by, it must be said, her design, not theirs. Even Josje, never one to keep his feelings to himself, had not been able to say no.

For once, all of the remaining six were within minutes of each other. Alex, who had arrived first, had saved bunks (this, by the way, was becoming harder and harder. There were whole busloads of students turning up day by day). She was the first to give them the news: "Now we are a family re-united," she said, with obvious satisfaction. "I knew it would be like this."

Peter and Josje had never been too far ahead. From Triacastela, they had taken a detour to the Monastery of Samos, and had stayed for overnight, soaking up the monastic—and all male—atmosphere. They had met up with Mary in Sarria, about 20 kilometers from the Monks. Mary was from Las Vegas. She had read Paulo Coelho and decided to "give it a try", as she explained later over dinner— another of Alex's seemingly inexhaustible recipes from left-behind pasta and garlic. "I didn't really understand the book, to tell you the truth, but I thought it might be fun. I've heard Shirley MacClaine walked it too!" Mary told them between huge slurpfuls of spaghetti. There wasn't much left in the bowl for Felix and Laura who joined them later.

"So I started from Cebreiro that's where he found his sword, and boy, has it been hard going! 'Til I met these two guys, anyway." She beamed flirtatiously at the two men, and it was clear that she hadn't figured out their sexual orientation. "Anyway," she carried on, "I guess by the time I get to Santiago, it'll all come clear. I wish I hadn't brought so much stuff though."

So-much-stuff turned out to be a large amount of clothing, including two pairs of designer jeans she couldn't, in this heat, have possibly worn, and which anyone else would have ditched after the first twenty kilometers, plus make-up and other creams and lotions, a battery operated curling iron, mobile phone—"forgot my charger though"—a camera, 3 novels, a bikini—which thankfully no-one ever saw her in—and a veritable drugstore of possible medications. Oh, and a CD player and headphones, and a goodly number of "Alternative" CD's. Miranda realized early that she was going to have a hard time with Mary.

Surprisingly, though, Alex, always happy to make a new friend, and likely believing she would find hidden depths in the American, took an initial shine to her, and for the next day they walked together.

By Portomarín, even she had had enough.

Alex appeared inside the refugio door, looking more exhausted than Miranda had seen her in weeks. She was carrying Mary's pack in addition to her own. Each one slung over a shoulder. Mary had gone to the bar, she explained. She had had "some trouble" with her pack, and Alex in an unguarded moment, had offered to carry it for her for a while. The "while" turned out to be the last 5 kilometers. "I didn't think she'd take me up on it. She's got blisters," she said in explanation. But the others decided a pilgrim was a pilgrim: we all had our loads to carry in the early stages, and maybe Mary had as much, or more, than they said to each other, that is. Though individually, they doubted it.

Mary showed up at curfew, noticeably inebriated, and said, "I hope you've saved a bunk for me?" Alex had, but it was as far away from hers as possible, though Mary, noticing that Alex's upper bunk was unoccupied, moved her things there, and happily snored the night through.

"At least she didn't vomit all over you," was Josje's rather uncharitable remark. He and Peter left very early. They had walked with Mary for two days already.

The group packed early and with extra quietness, but Mary, who should have had the mother of all hangovers, seemed oblivious to her night's revelries (no-one asked), and just as Alex was saying: "Well, perhaps we'll see you at the next refugio?", Mary threw her sleeping bag on top of her pack and said: "I'll be with you in a minute. Just let me get my earphones out. It feels like a Pearl Jam day!" And so, Alex had a walking companion, who, admittedly didn't say much, but at least carried her own pack.

By Palas del Rei, Alex was desperate. "She's suffocating me!" she said, "I know I'm being uncharitable, but...."

"We all have our crosses to bear," Felix said, as he set out with Laura.

Alex hurled metaphorical daggers in their direction.

Miranda thought that maybe by walking with the two of them, she might draw Mary out. But it was not to be. Every attempt at conversation led to Mary saying in a loud voice: "What?" and taking off her earphones. The music still carried on, and audibly. Alex looked at Miranda with a silent voice which could say none other than: "You see what I mean?"

Melide had a famous seafood restaurant. *Pulpo*, supposedly the best in Spain, was on the menu. It wasn't pilgrim-priced, but all of the pilgrim guides, in whatever language they possessed between them, said not to miss it.

"If I have to listen to Mary talking about her boyfriends, her clothes, the concerts she has been to, and the number of times she has got drunk, I will explode!" Miranda said.

"Be thankful she hasn't told you about her abortions," Alex said.

In the end, they did as no pilgrim who has walked nearly 1000 kilometers (or more, said Peter) should have done. They gave her the name of another restaurant.

The pulpo was fresh, the white wine was strong, the conversation was joyful, and not a single person regretted (openly) their decision.

The next time they saw Mary, was at the Pilgrim's Hospice in Santiago … but that will wait.

Melide to Ribadiso, twelve kilometers. Alex, Miranda, Felix, Laura all piled, very guiltily in a taxi. Catherine and Kevin left before sunrise. Stephen had already gone on. In fact they had lost him at Portomarín. "I'm going on to Gonzar," he had told them, and didn't seem to be at all perturbed at leaving his daughter behind to Felix' protection. It was a pilgrim stampede. No-one could face another Maryday.

If there is a pilgrims' parador on the Camino, it is probably Sahagun, but if there is a Heaven Sent refugio, it has to be Ribadiso da Baixo. The river Iso chuckled beside it, just next to the road bridge. The hospice itself was newly constructed out of wood and stone and the kitchens were enormous. Felix went in search of showers ("cold, but who cares?" said Alex returning with a miniscule lightweight towel on her head, before heading out to read beside the river). Felix came back he came accompanied by a familiar face. Well, almost familiar. Dominic had shaved off his beard. He looked quite innocent. All wondered how they could have ever seen him in any other way.

They went to the little bar up the hill. After the hugs and the journey details had all been exchanged, Miranda asked the question which was uppermost in her mind:

"Kieran?" she said.

"Sends his love. I checked my e-mail in Melide. He's on the waiting list—the good news is he's not considered 'Critical', which means he may have to wait awhile. Anyway, he's gotten together with an agent with strong publishing connections in London, and he's very optimistic …"

"About his health?"

"About publication. Sorry, Miranda, I know it's important to you, but I can only say what he wrote to me, you know."

Miranda ordered another glass of Ribeiro. She was quiet after that. She desperately wanted to say: 'Did he say anything about me?' but she wasn't sure if she wanted to know the answer.

*   *   *   *

Arca, only thirty two kilometers to go: 100 places, washing machines, even a supermarket beside the refugio. Everything set to send them on their walk the next day to their journey's end and the place that had been in their hearts from the very beginning. There was not a soul in the place that had not, in some way, regardless of the distance they had traveled, been changed forever. There was a festive atmosphere of anticipation, and many cooks in the spacious kitchens. The meal that night was a communal one. Lots of leftover pasta and even more imagination provided a feast for all. And afterwards, someone produced a guitar from a corner, and began to play it well. Laura proved to have an excellent soprano, and Miranda, whose alto was by no means shabby, joined her in a surprisingly professional sounding descant. All went to bed happily prepared for the next day … and the end of their travels. All except one.

Miranda couldn't sleep. "He should have been here, "she thought guiltily, as she cried into her pillow. "He should have been with me."

*   *   *   *

The final day. A long hard walk in which feelings were mixed. Miranda walked with Stephen.

"This is the land of the Celts," he said. "Well, that's what the tourist shops seem to want to peddle. But how true is it?" Kieran and his Irish heritage came to mind. Miranda said as much. She wanted at least to say his name aloud.

"Oh, it's true all right, though you're right: the image peddled in Galicia and Asturias, and to a lesser extent Cantabria, is more or less an Irish import. In fact, it ought to be the other way around."

Miranda said nothing. She had nothing to say on this subject since she knew little about it. She had the feeling that was about to change.

They were detouring around the airport, or rather the end of the runway, and every so often, a jet would dwarf them. They had only a few kilometers to go. Miranda began to feel that she had left the best of Galicia behind and wished she had talked with Stephen earlier, but she had been too wrapped up in her own thoughts to process much else. Now was the wrong time. "I should be alone," she thought.

"Don't mind me." Stephen said, unaware of Miranda's misgivings. "The Celts … it's kind of a hobby horse of mine."

"I know, Laura told me."

"Laura thinks her dad's a bit peculiar, so does my wife. But they love me so they put up with me.

"Who were these people?" Miranda tried to show some interest,. It helped her to put aside some of the personal thoughts that threatened to dominate this part of the walk. They were only a few kilometers from Compostela. Miranda knew she needed something absorbing to take her mind off the inside, and her fears of completion.

"Well, that's a thorny question and lots of scholars have disagreed over it over the years. In order to find out more, we have to go further into the mists of legend.

"The Irish Book of Leinster makes the extraordinary claim that the ancient peoples of Britain and Ireland were the descendants of some of the lost tribes of Israel! They were, surprisingly, described as fair-haired or red-haired, with light eyes. At least one writer claims that 'Hiberi' means 'Hebrew'.

"Let me tell you a story about a man called Fenius Farsaid, who was the leader of the Scythians—a region to the north east of the Black Sea bordering on the Russian steppes. Several claim that Fenius was the descendant of Noah, via Japeth his son, and that he was active in helping to build the Tower of Babel. The story says that his people—maybe workers and their families—left and wandered to Egypt where they were welcomed by Pharaoh who wanted to learn their language. The son of Fenius, whose name was Niul, (a Celtic name if ever there was one) fell in love with and married Pharaoh's daughter."

"There's always a love story," Miranda said, and tried to keep her attention on Stephen's tale.

"True. Her name was Scota. They had a son named Gaedel Glas. The generations pass, and a great grandson known as Eber Scot was suspected of having plans to take over Egypt and his people were thrown out of Egypt, not surprisingly really. Well, they went back to Scythia where, it is said, they dwelt in their boats in the marshes.

"One day, a holy man, called in the story "a Druid", told them that he had had a vision of a green island to the west which he called Irland. He prophesized: 'Your people will not rest until they reach this land.' So they set off in search of it.

"Once they reached the Danube, some of the Scythians decided to follow it, spreading their peoples upon the European lands as they wandered ever westwards. Unfortunately, since GPS hadn't been invented in those days, the rest went a little off course and ended back in North Africa, likely in the regions of Libya, Tunisia, or Algeria, where they supposedly stayed for seven generations, which begs the question as to whether the Druid, whose name was Caicher, described the topography of Irland to them very well. But I suppose even Druids make mistakes!"

Miranda held her council.

"After a while, someone must have mentioned this curious fact, and they set off once again, first quite possibly to Sicily, which although an island, did not quite measure up either, and from there onto what later became known as "Spain". (Did you know the Romans called the area "Hispania", because it was full of rabbits? 'Land of **Rabbits**', get it?")

Miranda got it, sort of.

"Some of them may have actually gone beyond the "Pillars of Hercules" and entered the area by the River Tagus in Portugal; or perhaps via the already existing Mediterranean ports. The Phoenicians had got there before them, you see, in search of precious metals, and the Scythians may not have been too welcome there. So, from there they gradually worked their way across the Peninsula until they reached the areas of what is now Northern Portugal, Asturias, and Galicia.

The green land they found must have appeared as something which even the most dense amongst them must have recognized resembled the land they had been told to expect.

"Generations pass. The inhabitants of the land become known as Iberians, and many place names begin to appear including the word "Iber" (which probably means "River" but why ruin a good story at this point?). Bored yet?"

"Why is it, when someone is telling me something that is interesting do they always ask if I'm bored? I have a Master's in Philosophy, you know. I want to know. 'Philosophy begins in wonder ...!'."

"Sorry, you know how it is. When you know a lot about something, you always wonder if you're boring people. Alright, I'll continue ...

"To go back somewhat: Two new groups of people emerged in Central Europe around about the late Neolithic period ..."

No matter how Miranda tried, she couldn't keep her attention focused on what Stephen was saying. Every now and then she would hear something like 'Beaker Folk', and 'Urnfeld Culture', some of which reminded her of a paper she had heard at a conference earlier this year. Despite herself, she began to think of the last time she had walked beside someone who had excused himself for lecturing. "I wonder what he is doing now?" she thought as Stephen droned on. *Is he thinking about me? Or now that he is away, back in Ireland, has the Camino become a dream and me with it?* The time they had spent together was so short: too short and too precious to be reality. And yet I am sure that I love him. Miranda felt tears come into her eyes at the thought of her hand pressed to his, the glass of the bus window alone separating them from each other. "Don't be a fool!" she chastised herself. *An ocean separates us. Different lives separate us. Cancer separates us. How can I even begin to think I know him enough to call it love?* Yet the pain in her heart would not go away. "I miss you," she thought.

Stephen was saying something about two groups: Gaelic Celts, who had settled for many hundreds of years in Europe before being pushed west by encroaching tribes, and Iberian Celts whom some scholars claimed had come via the Mediterranean, possible even via Egypt and the north coast of Africa. Miranda silently thanked the presenter of the lecture for the gift of his notes. She had mentioned she was going on the Camino.

"In other words, the Gaelic Celts came later." Miranda tried to bring her mind back to the present. "Were they the group that split off towards the Danube?"

"Everything seems to point to that. But the academic jury, as always, is still out.

"Hang on a minute. Let me get this straight. So the people we call the Celts, may have originated from two different places, even though they started out as one people?"

"Just so, although as you can imagine, there is much dissention amongst the scholars. The Celtic people that entered the Western passes through the Pyrenees appear to have done so as early as 1100 BCE. But that they left a strong impression upon Iberia; especially in the north, there is no doubt.

"However, judging from your look, there are still gaps to be explained. It's a book, really, Miranda, that's needed to explain them, and I'm working on it, bit by bit."

Everyone's writing a book, she thought.

She and Stephen were passing through, well around actually, a valley village called "*Lavacolla*". Her guidebook said that this was the place where pilgrims stopped and washed themselves in preparation for going the last few miles into Santiago.

"Lavacolla, is actually '*lavacola*'. Do you know what that means?" said Stephen.

Her Spanish wasn't quite yet up to the distinction.

"It means this is where you '*wash your arse!*' Anyway, time for a break?"

Miranda agreed. They stopped in at the first bar. It was packed with seemingly clean pilgrims. When she went to the washroom, she fought back a strange feeling. *This is ridiculous,* she thought to herself. Anyway, though she looked for it, there was no bidet. She went back to Stephen, who was grinning. He had ordered beer and tapas, and said no more about the Celts for the time being. Miranda was beginning to realize that Santiago was over the next hill, and in a way, began to wish she had walked alone.

CHAPTER 29

▼

"Right" said Stephen. "Where were we?"

They were walking again, sharply uphill, on a twisting, turning, eucalyptus-lined road, accompanied by many strange faces, walking, and on their worn bicycle tires. The latter passed them, but there seemed a combination of weariness and expectation in them also.

"I '*m not sure I want to do this,*" Miranda thought. "*I'm not ready.*

But Stephen was warming up to his thesis. He didn't ask for permission to continue. In a way, Miranda wished he were not beside her. In another way she was glad of the distraction. Either way, he was clearly her companion for the day. Might as well listen and learn, she thought. Don't really want to go anywhere else. Not today of all days.

"In the present Spanish provinces of Guipuzcoa, Vizcaya, and Navarra, there is no record whatsoever of Celtic dominance. Why? These are the Basque regions, and the Basques have always done things their own way. Some say that the Devil speaks Basque!

"The Celts would have found themselves moving through this area, but it would appear the Basques were sufficiently strong to resist them, or to finally absorb them and completely transform them. Some Celts went no further.

"As is well-known, Basque bears no resemblance to Spanish, or any other language. As they moved westwards, however, the Celts either displaced or dominated the older stocks of people, amongst them would have been the Iberians."

"Their kin who had got there long before them?"

"Precisely! Still farther west and northwest, they found people very much like themselves and they began to blend with them. The Celts wore trousers, whereas the Iberians still wore robes. It's very likely that the Celts brought the domesticated horse with them and it is also just as likely that the Celtiberians adopted the Celtic mode of dress. Easier to ride you see. Another point worth mentioning is that the Celts had no written language, yet the Iberians did, in some cases quite sophisticated. It is this language which has been used to identify the names of the gods inscribed throughout the northwest.

"The Celts came into Iberia with their flocks, families, and wagons. Like the Iberians, they were a pastoral people. In the northern forests there was an abundance of everything they needed for their animals—beech mast and acorns for pigs, and food for their horses, cattle, and goats. On the Meseta, the land proved perfect for the harvesting of crops, and there it was this type of farming which predominated."

"There was certainly a variation between the generally dark haired Iberians (remember they had passed hundreds of years in north Africa) and the taller, blonde or red-headed Celts—we've seen both types on the Camino—but they are quite distinct from the people you see in the south: in Andalucia, for instance: the people there show considerable Moorish influence.

"But ... did these earliest people call themselves Celts? It's an important question. There is some conjecture that they called themselves the 'Iber', and that the land of Iberia, today's Spain, and subsequently Hibernia as the ancient land of Ireland is called, is the Land of Ir, or of Erin. Or the Hebrews!"

Stephen went on. There was no stopping him now anyway: "While he may not have been the first, Herodotus mentions the Keltoi. They are also called this and Galatai by other writers of the period, Greeks and Romans, and later, and it is interesting that the two names are given to essentially the same peoples. They are generally described as having fair or red hair, and blue eyes. But the same description has been attributed to the peoples of Scythia. The Romans modified this to the Celtae and the Galli. But although they were to be found throughout Europe and as far as the Black Sea, the Celts as a people do not seem to have existed. They were instead a great number of tribes who appeared to have acted, for the most part, independently of one another. There was no Celtic Emperor, nor common leader. They had no central administration, no form of government outside of what was determined individually by the tribes. They had no unified army which could be called upon in times of war against a common foe. Perhaps because The European Celts, such as they were, had no common foe. You find this in tribal areas all over the world."

"So, is Kieran 'Celtic'?"

"Maybe, but Felix certainly is. You might be yourself with your blonde hair and green eyes. You find that on the Steppes, even today."

"My father was German," Miranda admitted.

"Even more so. This is where the Germans got their word 'Arian'."

"I think I like that," Miranda said with a sparkle in her eyes. "I've often wondered where I belonged!"

"It's a goodly heritage. Be proud of it!"

It was something Miranda had never considered, her "heritage". In Canada, everyone came from somewhere else. Some kept their traditions, some did not.

"The problem as it appears to me," continued Stephen, who had clearly not noticed that Miranda had lapsed again into silence, "is that we have fallen into a tendency to think of the Celts as a clearly identifiable people, and I hope, at least, I have demonstrated that this was not so. And although the term "Celtic" may mean certain common features in terms of economics, social structure, and religion, even this differs from area to area: it makes them even harder to pin down. Only language seems to be a constant factor and it remains so today, although by this criterion—and this has kept Galicia from being accepted by the Celtic League—the so-called Celtic peoples remaining in Galicia and Asturias, and adopting the Roman tongue, are not Celtic by contemporary definition, because their language is, in its root form, Latin."

Miranda was resigned by now, besides the landscape was looking pretty depressing. There were radio towers and eastern-bloc looking buildings which turned out to be television stations. She was longing for the Pyrenees, and truth to tell, solitude, by this point. She wanted to feel sorry for herself.

Secretly, Miranda was dreading getting to Santiago, but Stephen didn't seem to be the one to open up to emotionally. *Where are you Alex, or Felix, or even Dominic?* she thought.

"What has been suggested is that the inhabitants of the north-west of Spain and Portugal—and it makes good sense to me—began as one and the same people, originating near or east of the Black Sea, as I've said. They left their homeland at some point in Biblical history, and separated near the Danube. There is good evidence which shows that these were of Indo-European stock and in fact originated in Assyria.

"And so, we are free to pick up our tale once again of how the Hibernians got to Hibernia, and what they did when they got there. And that's a good story in the true Irish Style."

Thankfully for Miranda, Stephen did not elaborate. Irish stories were not exactly what she needed right now. She realized that there would have been no way to walk this stretch alone. The trickle of pilgrims Miranda had encountered in the Pyrenees was now a flood. One noisy group overtook them. One of them put something in Miranda's hand. It was a packet of pistachios. "*Buen Camino!*" he said joyfully as they moved on. Within minutes they were out of sight. She realized that she and Stephen had slowed down, perhaps unconsciously. After six weeks of dust, sun, thirst and exhaustion, trauma, and more recently heartache, she had an unreasonable urge to turn around and go back!

"What would life have been like there for the Celt-Iberians?" Miranda wanted a context and above all, she had to stop herself from thinking. Anyway, she had said it before she realized that it would start Stephen off again.

Stephen carried on. If he had the same thoughts as she, it was not apparent.

"One major advantage that the Celts brought with them was that they brought their plough. Although it was of little use on the highlands, it was immeasurably welcomed in the pastoral areas. Up to this point, it was women who planted seed and hoed the cereals for bread and beer (Did you know that *Cerveza—Cervexa* in Gallego—is a Celtic word, by the way; 'Beer' is Saxon?)."

No, Miranda thought, *but it might interest Felix. I'll tell him. It might come up in a Trivial Pursuit quiz one day.*

"So what did they believe in these 'Celt-Iberians'?" She was trying so hard to be polite.

"Their religious beliefs? The truth is in comparison to many other regions, we know very little about Celt-Iberian religious beliefs. For example, it is by no means secure that the Druids were ever in Spain at all, although their presence is clearly attested in Gaul, Wales, and Ireland. While many in Galicia will tell you that there were druids in their land, none of the ancient writers mention their presence in the Peninsula, although there is some conjecture that they might have been known under another name. Certainly, there were priestesses: the *Meigas*, who were the protectors of the tribe, for example...."

"I've heard about the *Meigas*. Priscillian said that his earliest teacher was a *meiga*: one of the Old Ones, he said. Can't remember her name though."

"There were many. After the Romans tried to say who was to believe what, you can imagine, all they did was to drive the old ways underground. The *meigas* were the 'white witches': they knew herbal lore, they assisted in childbirth, and they were often the consorts of the 'druids'. All primitive societies had their Shaman and it was likely that the Celt-Iberians were no exception. Some writers have claimed that Druidism predates the Celts and that the Celts adopted it after their conquest of Britain. Even I don't know. Either way, it would seem that Druidism in Gaul and in Ireland took on a different nature. Caesar (who had a personal vendetta against the Druids and wiped out many) claimed that Druidism originated in Britain independently of the Celts, and that the Gaulish Celts went there to study it. Did you study Sanskrit?"

"A bit, only because I loved the sound of the words. I don't remember much. Why?"

"Well, if you look at so-called Western languages, you'll find loads of Sanskrit words and derivations. Study linguistics next time!"

"Thanks, Comparative Religion was quite enough for me, without comparing languages too. So where, then, speaking of which, does religion fit in?"

"That's tricky, but for you: examine the fusion of the Celtish and Iberian religions as though they were one. It makes intuitive good sense: if similarities existed between them, then coexistence amongst them would have been much easier; there must have been many points of contact, and that seems to have happened, and over time, the two religions seem to have become one and the same, as the inscriptions would indicate."

"What inscriptions?"

"Oh, there are lots! Right throughout the northwest of the Peninsula. These inscriptions abound in the areas in question, most especially around Braga in modern-day Portugal. It is here that many inscriptions have been found on mountain tops and above *fuentes*—fountains, or natural springs. These inscriptions mention gods with unpronounceable names. In some cases there are words written in a native language—more likely Iberian than Celtic as the Celts are not known to have a written language: theirs was an oral tradition. The most notable deity was Endovellicus"

"Sounds Latin to me," Miranda said.

"You are right; all of these names are Roman translations … you've been studying a bit about the Romans lately, right?"

"Yes, how do you know that?"

"Dominic told me."

Miranda was surprised. She hadn't seen any conversations between Stephen and Dominic. But thinking about it, maybe it wasn't so hard to understand after all.

Despite the enormous difference in their ages and outward appearance, they were really quite similar in their outlook, perhaps even in their beliefs.

"You know a bit about the Romans: they weren't too original. They just borrowed as they went along. Easier that way. Keep that in mind.

"Jupiter was especially revered in Lugo. It was a garrison town, remember. "Lug" was a deity who presided over a neighboring mountain. And you know what, although there are almost no traces of Romans worshipping the local gods, several Roman soldiers seem to have written their names on inscriptions to a 'Vagdonae-gus', who was likely a Celt-Iberian god, though of what, we do not know. 'Aegus' signified an older, Celtic god. There must have been many Celt-Iberians in the Roman Legions. And looking at the Celts and the gods they propitiated: there are clear traces of worship of river gods, especially in the north and west.

"Many of the inscriptions have been found over mountain springs. On several there is a picture of what is likely the river god, or goddess. In one case, one appears holding in his left hand a basket of fruit. Water sprites were also thought to have watched over fountains. The people often left wheat stalks and bread at these fountains as an offering. You can imagine, the Romans must have known they were up against a lot when they sought to bring Christianity, especially after the Trinity was established as official doctrine—One God in three persons—to rural areas like these. The Romans were accepted, what else was there to do? But in secret, they, and their God, was ignored by the people who inhabited Galicia. The people had asked their own gods for help in their harvests, producing children and safe childbirth—all of the simple things that simple people want—for centuries. They weren't about to change."

"No wonder they followed Priscillian." Miranda was beginning to see a connection between the present conversation and the accusations against the bishop.

"Ah, yes, Priscillian. Dominic's translation. What's that all about?"

"Actually, it's Kieran's story. He told me about a bishop from the fourth century who is supposed to be buried in the Cathedral in Comspostela. He said that there was very little evidence that St. James had that much to do with Spain, but that this bishop, a Gnostic who was falsely accused of sorcery and subsequently executed, had a vast following in Galicia and that it was far more likely that it was he whose remains were brought back from France and subsequently buried here. Kieran told me that the church has never allowed a proper investigation into the remains in the tomb. Bad for business, I suppose. There really isn't much known about him except a few old documents which are kept in Germany, and a book written a few years ago by an English theology professor. Most of Priscillian's writings seem to have been destroyed. There are a few letters, but other than that, pretty well anything we know about him was taken from the official Vatican story. Not very sympathetic as you can imagine. Apparently, he and his teachings were followed here for well over a century after he was executed. It wasn't until after the Synod of Braga that Priscillianism seemed to disappear. But Kieran thinks that there are still traces of it here in the north." She wanted to say more, talking about Kieran's project made him seem closer, but the memories crowding her were too painful, and so she knew she couldn't continue. Not now, at least.

"Ask Kieran," Miranda finished lamely, and wished that he could.

They had reached the Monte de Gozo. From here they were supposed to be able to see the Cathedral of Santiago.

"Let's stop a bit," Miranda pleaded. She was enlightened, but exhausted.

CHAPTER 30

▼

In the high days of the Pilgrimage, it was a tradition for the first one to reach the top of the Monte de Gozo, to be called the King. Lots of people with that surname, and its variations *del Rey, Köenig, leRoi,* Leroy, probably have pilgrim ancestors without ever knowing it, Stephen told her as they stopped for their *bocadillos* at its summit. It was capped by a rusty cross and a peculiar statue which looked like it was about to strangle it, dwarfed by the marble plinth on which it stood. The whole feeling of the place was 70's Soviet Union.

"You could see the cathedral from here then. *Monte de Gozo* means "Mountain of Joy": *Le Mont de Joie* in French. It was a place of great celebration, and a place to stop and reflect on the journey before the last walk into the city. Often they would stop for the night here. They came in their thousands remember and many from very far away, even farther than us."

"Not a lot to celebrate in this view, alas." Miranda was looking down at what looked like a vast army camp. Rows and rows of uninspired flat-roofed buildings stretched down the hillside in dismal formation. From a distance they looked like portables, Nissen huts. It was the last refugio before Compostela less than 10 kilometers away.

"Looks like a refugee camp, doesn't it? Almost 3000 places. They cut down a whole forest to build it! It was constructed by the *Junta de Galicia* to accommodate the people who came for the Pope's visit, only a few years ago."

"But it contaminates this beautiful hill! They should have shot the architect!"

"Not so bad as that, surely. Come on, let's go take a closer look."

"Must we?"

"Might as well know your enemy. Anyway, there's no avoiding it, is there?"

If there is anything worse than a 3000 place apology for a refugio, it's an empty one. Miranda began to wish someone would blindfold her and lead her through, and out, and on. A few younger pilgrims seemed to be making weak attempts at partying, but even they seemed half-hearted about it. It was mid-day. A few washing lines were strung with T-shirts (coin operated machines); there were a few soulless restaurants, and a few silent, mostly solitary pilgrims outside at iron tables, seated on uncomfortable chairs, writing frantically in their diaries; a few dismal and expensive supermarkets. A few bicycles were propped here and there: heavy padlocks adorned all. The only pilgrim group which seemed to be in any state of abundance were those with their *Coches de Appoyo*. For once, Miranda made no disparaging remarks; she just felt sorry for them. But by and large, she found whatever enthusiasm she could muster for this, this last stage of the Camino, was sucked out of her in an ever-increasing feeling of abject misery. The whole complex was so vast that it was impossible to ignore. There was no doubt that it was a hideous blot on the landscape; somehow it looked like it lacked foundations and would eventually slide down the hill to land in a crumpled dominoed heap at the bottom. *And the sooner the better*, Miranda thought.

"I feel like I am being devoured by concrete and peeling paint. Help! Get me out of here. I haven't felt so alien since we first walked through the outskirts of Burgos. At least there we could take a bus! I am **not** bussing it into Santiago!" Both began to walk a lot faster. Others were doing the same, many of them solitary, looking neither left nor right. Her first view of Dominic, striding past them in the Pyrenees, came back to her.

Once outside of the complex, they reached a corner. There was a stone house with bizarre metal sculptures adorning the garden. Visitors were welcome, the sign said. Stephen decided to go and investigate. "You've probably had enough of my company for one day. Anyway, I think maybe you want to go on alone, think about your own thoughts."

Miranda smiled at him. She suddenly realized that he knew more than he had offered about her own thoughts. He had never tried to give her advice or counsel. Somehow he had intuited her despair, and had knowingly kept her internal troubles at bay with his stories. There was no denying it; Miranda knew she could only do this last stretch alone.

"Thanks for being so understanding, Stephen. And thanks for all the information; it fills in a lot of gaps in the book I'm reading."

"The 'lecture', you mean...."

Miranda made to protest.

"No, it's O.K. I know I can go on a bit ..."

Once more, Miranda had *deja vu*. She was walking along a river, in the Pyrenees. Her clothes were soaked and her heels were blistered. She was wishing that she walked alone.

She had to choke the tears back.

"I'll see you at the Monastery later. We get three days to re-group. Miranda, just think of all that can happen in three days. Tell Laura not to go to Casa Manolo's without me."

"Casa Manolo's?"

"Pilgrim restaurant. Famous. Best bargain in town! Fantastic food."

"You've been here before then?" She was surprised.

"Lots of times," Stephen winked, and disappeared.

*   *   *   *

So, on the final descent, Miranda was alone, as she had started. It took very little time before she was about to be entangled with a busy four-lane *ronda*: the ring road around Santiago de Compostela. Initially, she took a wrong turn. It was disorienting. After weeks of moving unthinkingly west, she had no idea where she was. But retracing her steps she found arrows once again, and had never appreciated their significance more. She began to walk into the outskirts. It came upon her faster than she had expected.

Ask Miranda today, and she'll tell you she remembers little of that part of the walk. It either took no time at all, or it took hours. Either way, she felt herself completely alien to her surroundings: alien in far more than the way one does when one approaches an unknown city. This one had been in her heart for over 800 kilometers, and since long before she had boarded a plane. The yellow paint was her only friend. At one point, outside a small church on the outskirts she stopped. She tried to decide whether to go in, but as she stood there in her indecision, a harried looking woman dressed entirely in black, came out, shut the doors, and actually scowled at her.

It was ten past two.

Her confusion was not merely internal. Around every corner, she expected to see those familiar spires, the ones of her fantasies, pulling her, beckoning her to come close, but they were simply not there, and what is more, she had completely lost her innate sense of direction. She just walked on, a sleepwalker. At one intersection, having gotten used to simply walking in straight lines, she crossed without looking and was almost mown down by a taxicab. She stopped again, and to her consternation, she began to cry.

"Miranda. **Miranda**! Wait!" Hurtling towards her, water bottle in hand and pack bouncing was Alex … and Felix, and Laura, and Peter and Josje.

"I saw you cross over!" Felix said. "What're you trying to do? If you were going to have a death wish the Meseta was the place to do it!"

And she hurtled herself into his arms and simply cried her eyes out.

"Oh, Jesus, Felix. I am so sorry, "she said, once she had recovered her composure, or what she could manage of it. "I never expected this! I thought I had already met my "Black Dog": I didn't expect him to follow me here!"

"Hey, it's O.K. "Alex forced the water bottle into her hands. "We all know that you've been missing Kieran. We just didn't know what to **say**, that's all. Come on, remember Hontanas? Let's sing."

And linking arms with her, and the others, they proceeded down the street singing at the top of their voices: *'La Dona Mobile.'*

After a while, Miranda felt stronger. "It's O.K. Alex, but I have to … you know … do this last bit …"

"By yourself."

"Yeah, don't ask me. I don't know why. I've got to get back the bit I started with."

Alex didn't look too convinced. "You sure?" she said.

"Yes. I'm sure. Thanks, you've picked me up when I needed it most. You guys go on. Save me a bunk."

And then she was alone again, though Felix' glance behind him as he walked away said a great deal, and she was grateful for it.

It is funny thing about the last part of the Camino. Miranda felt instinctively that she must be getting close: the streets became narrower and older, they were flanked with tourist shops, but there was still no sign of the Cathedral she had promised herself so often and so long: that Baroque facade she had etched into her mind. That "almost there" feeling she had been practicing. There were others beside her, behind her, passing her. All with battered backpacks, and all silent. She drifted along with them, offering silent prayers to who knows what or whom.

"Who was Priscillian, and why is he haunting me?" Miranda asked herself. *Was it his message of ultimate love and peace residing in the one God above everything, outside of Evil, corruption, power seeking and war mongering? Is it the terrible injustices which claimed the lives of all of those throughout our fragile history who were faithful in their own way, but who wouldn't accept the words of the priests, nor their abridged version of the Testament? Or is it Priscillian the man and his love for Euchrotia, a love which never could have been? Ended by the sword, yet enduring across the ages through Kieran's words, fiction though they may be. They were too much like us, she thought. We are too much like them. Will our fate be kinder in the end? Do we indeed even have one?* These thoughts occupied so much of her last walking steps that she barely noticed the ancient city as she walked though it.

And then she was alongside what was clearly an ecclesiastical building. Down a few steps, people were entering off a paved area and she simply followed the throng and went inside. The Cathedral was still no-where in sight. It just seemed the right thing to do, and anyway, it was the direction her feet took her, she pretended no control over her body at that point. *It least this will give me chance to get ready*, she thought.

Once inside the church, the smell of incense hit her first. And a sense of stillness, antiquity somehow trapped, yet at home with itself. On her right was a small sanctuary flanked with red candles burning. Behind a grille was a statue she immediately recognized as *Santiago Matamoros*. Although she had seen him periodically along the way, she had never grown to associate him with the pilgrim version she preferred. He had never been her friend.

She did not stop there, as some did. She found herself instead inside a larger building. Much larger. It was plain and powerful. And then, cursing herself for an idiot, she realized this was journey's end. While looking for the Cathedral to reveal itself on the horizon, she had stumbled into it, perhaps as a pilgrim should. It laid out no red carpet. There was no sense of completion. There was no sense of anything at all. Only a numbness which took hold of her body and spirit and paralyzed any preparatory thoughts she thought she might have had.

There was a line of people on the other side, and she joined them, still not quite aware of either herself as a pilgrim or the cathedral as her destination. It dwarfed her. She looked up at gilded angels, massive and, truth to tell, rather tacky ones. She moved with the crowd, still with no sensation of having arrived.

Then she was mounting claustrophobic steps. She was small. The feelings should have been big.

She was behind a busload of tourists, each with a tourist-office issued staff, and gourd, and each looking, truth to tell, a bit embarrassed. No-one gave a blind bit of attention to the "real" pilgrim who followed them: the one with the blank stare on her face, who went where they did, and did what they did. She was an automaton, as they.

At the top of the steps, the woman in front of her "hugged" the Saint, and moved on. Miranda, looking over the statue's shoulder, for the first time, took in the Romanesque simplicity, yet the vastness, from this most prestigious and most sacred of views. She wanted to pause, to take in the enormity: of the church, of its significance, of how far she had come to be here, at this moment. But there were dozens behind her.

"What am I supposed to do? What am I supposed to say? What am I supposed to **feel***?"* She draped her arms around the statue's broad golden shoulders.

"Hi," she said, uncomfortably. "It's me. Miranda. I've come a long way to see you," but despite the potential immensity of that moment, still she felt nothing.

Afterwards, she followed another queue down into the crypt. Some simply acknowledged the silver casket and walked through, some seemed to do even less than that. A couple were on their knees directly by the railing. Their prayerful silence made her feel even more inadequate. Miranda simply stared. She felt not a thing: not for herself, not for Kieran, not for Priscillian, or St. James. Worst of all, all the rehearsals she had held in her head were non-starters. She made a quick beeline for the exit. She wanted to cry in sheer frustration, but couldn't even find the emotion for that. She wondered if she had been wrong to alienate herself, at this the final stage in a journey of friends. But it was too late for that.

Instead she became a backpacked-laden tourist, in worn down boots. Not even a "Pilgrim" for she wouldn't even contemplate herself as that. She visited the small chapels around the statue and crypt, and especially fell in love with one—a Twentieth century statue—she was to later learn—of Santa Susanna, a co-patron of Compostela, in the Chapel of St. John. Susanna stood with her sword, her face resolute. Looking upwards for strength. *If there was ever a feminist saint,* Miranda thought, *this has to be her.* But of Miranda herself and her feelings, there was still no real return. She couldn't deny it. She felt like a fraud.

She did a tour of the stations of the cross, still an automaton, and then made a quick exit, out down the steps, and into the *Praça de Obradoiro.* She crossed over to the other side and finally, forced herself to turn around.

A group of young pilgrims were walking determinedly into the center of the square where, Miranda had noticed as she crossed it, there was a paving stone with a shell. They gathered together in a rugby huddle, and for a few seconds, stayed that way. Then they turned and faced the facade of the cathedral, and for a moment, Miranda felt her spirit soar towards and join them. What she saw made her draw in, almost painfully, so deep a breath that she thought she would never exhale.

The Cathedral of Santiago, its two Baroque towers, the spires of her dreams, reared up in front of her with unapologetic majesty. It was a physical state of Grace, impelling, **imploring** her to recognize what it stood for, what she stood for—all those dusty miles, all those self-doubts, all those tortured dreams, all those hopeless yet tenuous hopes which had never really either taken root, nor died. All those who had come before her, or not made it all. The group in front let out a cheer. Someone threw a hat in the air.

And Miranda sank to her knees and cried and cried.

"I'm home!" she said. "**Oh, thank you dear God, thank you. I'm home!**"

CHAPTER 31

▼

That night, they did three things together. The first, as Stephen had promised her (and paid for all), was dinner at Casa Manolo's, and after all agreed they had stuffed themselves so much, they could barely stagger to the second.

"There's a bar near here that does the Queimada," Felix said. He and Stephen conferred on the direction, and then all followed them up into the town.

"The history of the Queimada isn't exactly known," said Stephen. "But despite the coffee grounds …"

"Coffee grounds?" Alex said.

"It's a later addition, I'll get the recipe for you if you like, later. Anyway, it's an ancient spell, attributed to the *Meigas*, for ridding your home of evil spirits. Ah, here it is … lights out!"

Their waiter brought a large copper tureen and several small glasses. He took a small amount of the liquid and poured it onto what looked like sugar crystals in a ladle, and setting alight to that mixture, gently poured it into the bowl. The liquid immediately took the flame and the room lit up with a bluish glow.

"Shall I?"

No-one, except Felix, who had already grasped the ladle, knew what he was suggesting, but all assented.

As Felix began to stir the flames, Stephen started to speak, quietly at first, but then gathering depth and resonance. Miranda noticed his voice had changed, had begun to take on an ethereal and timeless quality that none of them had ever heard from him before. The atmosphere in the little bar, formerly one of many they had experienced on the Camino, turned into a pagan grove. The pilgrims huddled around him and the dying azur flames. *You could almost hear the wind in the oak leaves*, Alex said afterwards.

Mouchos, coruxas, sapos e bruxas
Demons, transnos e dianhos, espiritus das nevoadas veigas
Corvis, pointagas e meigas, feitizos das mencinherias
Pobres canhotas furadas, fogar dos vermes e alimanhas
Lume das Santas Companhas, mal de ollo, negros meigallos,
cheiro do mortos, tronos e raios.
Oubeo do can, pregon da morte, founcinho do satiro e pe de coello
Pecadora lingua da mala muller casada cun dome vello.
Averno de Satan e Melcebu, lume dos cadavres ardentes
copos mutilados dos inocentes, peidos dos infernañes cus, muxido da mar
embravescida.
Barriga inutil da muller solteria, falar dos gatos que andan a xaneira,
guedella pora a cabra mal parida.
Con este fol levantarei as chamas desde lume que asemella ao do
inferno, e fuxiran as bruxas acabalo das sas escobas, indose bañar na
praia das areas gordas.
Oide, oide os ruxidos que dan as que non poden deixar de queimars
no agoardente, quedando asi purificadas.
E canto ests brebaxe baixe polas nosas gorxas, quedaremos libres
do males da nosa jalma e todo embruamento.
Fozas do ar, terra, mar, y lume, a vos fago esta chamada, si e verdad
que tendes mais poder que a humana xente, eiqui e agora, facede cos
espiritus dos amigos que estan fora, participen con nos desta queimada.

Stephen took over the stirring from Felix, and handed him the translation:

("Now I know what "spellbound" means!" Catherine whispered to Miranda.)

Owls, barn owls, toads and witches.
Evil demons and devils, spirits of the snowy plains.
Crows, salamanders, and sorceresses, the spell of the quack doctors.
Rotten, hole ridden canes, worm holes, and lairs of vermin.
Fire of the soul in torment, the evil eye, black spells, the smell
of the dead, thunder and lightning.
Dog's bark, portents of death; satyr's snout and rabbit's foot.
The sinful tongue of the harridan wife of the old man.
Hell of Satan and Beelzebub, the fire of burning corpses,
the mutilated bodies of the wretched, farts from hellish arses,
the roar of the raging sea.
Barren womb of the single mother, the miaoing of cats in heat,
mangy and filthy hair of the ill begotten goat.
With this ladle I will raise the flames of the hell-like fire,
and the witches will flee on their broomsticks, to bathe on the fat-pebbled beach.
Hear, hear! The howls of those who burn in the aguardiente and thereby
purify themselves.
And when this brew runs down our throats, we will be free of all the sins of the
soul
and of witchcraft.

Forces of air, earth, sea, and fire, I make this call to you: if it be true
that you have more power than man, here and now, make the spirits
of the friends who have departed share this Queimada with us.

Stephen handed the ladle to Miranda. "Now, as you stir it, make a wish.
And make it a good one."

Then they went to Bar Onda, and danced until dawn.

*   *   *   *

There are curfews at all of the refugios. Most are strictly enforced, yet although
they had been told that the rather austere Monastery would be closed at 11:00, at
6:30 in the morning, when a group of nine exhausted but jubilant pilgrims, trying rather unsuccessfully to be quiet, arrived on the doorstep expecting to have to
sleep there, the doors were still open, and all clambered rather guiltily, stifling
giggles, up to their respective beds.

"What happened to Dominic?" Miranda asked Alex, as both collapsed into their sleeping bags on the thin mattresses.

"He just said he had something to do." She said. "Good Night, Sweet Pilgrim."

*   *   *   *

Miranda dreamed of a chapel. It was night and there were no stars. Part of it was in ruins, and there was toilet paper all around. She had a wheelbarrow that seemed to have a hole in it, and some cement which she was having difficulty trying to keep from solidifying. She felt that she was compelled to rebuild it. 'But there aren't enough bricks!' she wailed, but inside of her, she knew if she looked hard and deeply enough, she would find more. There were salamanders under the stones. They stared at her with white hot eyes. Alex appeared at the doorway. 'We can't start the service without you,' she said. 'We're all waiting. They're doing the Benediction. Come!'

'But I can't come in now', Miranda said, 'Look. I've got work to do.'

'Look behind you,' Alex said. 'It was done in the night.' And as Miranda turned, she was outside of Manjarín. It was daybreak. A weak sun rose softly over the eastern hills. She saw Kieran in a simple white robe, waiting at the door. His head was covered. Dominic stood next to him, dressed in a leather jacket with fringes. He smiled at her and turned his back. There was a picture of a black wolf on the back, but as she looked at it, it turned into a Templar Cross above a glowing heart.

'All you ever had to do was dream,' he said, over his shoulder.

*   *   *   *

There was none of the usual pilgrim bustle as she gradually awoke. Though she did hear a familiar whiney voice, and another she recognized as Alex's.

"So, I gave him my walkman to listen to, and my 'Sounds Like the Eighties' CD. But I never saw him again. Men! Just my luck."

Miranda opened her eyes slowly. Mary was squatting on Alex's bunk beside her. Alex had an especially saintly look on her face.

"Dominic came over to see you earlier," Alex said. "But you were in dreamland. He left you a note. It's on top of your backpack."

She rolled over carefully so as not to antagonize the jackhammer in her head. It was a single piece of paper.

Do you remember an inn, Miranda, do you remember an inn?

"He's at the Hostal Suso."

*   *   *   *

Miranda woke softly to a peaceful snoring. She felt a stiffness in her neck, and pulled the single pillow onto his shoulder, gently, so as not to wake him. The shadows in the room were angled now, the sun about to depart. She reflected on the few hours they had spent together in that simple, single, bed.

"I love you," she whispered into his neck, as she too took trails of glistening glory back into the lands of sleep.

*   *   *   *

Both awoke early, though the light had changed, and the swallows were conversing in staccato outside the open window.

"Come on," said Kieran. "I have something to show you."

*   *   *   *

In the center of all, was Santiago. He wore an enigmatic smile. His left hand rested upon his staff, and he is seated. Unique in all the Camino. Miranda couldn't escape the fleeting thought, that he was about to stand, and tip his hat to them. There was no-one to be seen: not pilgrim, not priest, and certainly, not at that hour, tourist.

They scrunched down to his left, propped up by a carved pillar. It was cool there, and she felt that, no matter the time of day, no matter the century even, it would be thus, if inside, one could see him this way. Kieran put his arm around her.

"See. They are laughing! It's the end of the world, and they're laughing, joking with one another as they tune up for the final encore."

They were alone at the entrance to the cathedral, the baroque left behind, the simplicity of the Romanesque inside. What arched above them, still showing traces of its colors, was a stone rainbow: the 24 musicians of the Apocalypse. A halo in stone.

"Did you know," Kieran said very softly, as though his words might distract their attention, "that Miguel de Unamuno wrote: 'Before this Portico, one must pray in one way or another: one cannot make literature.'"

Miranda said nothing, she was trying to focus on each one, individually, through the watery glaze of her eyes. They were, in many ways, irreverent, talking together, ignoring the Conductor, as musicians and choristers do. There was no other way to see them but representatives of herself, themself, themselves. Acknowledging the futility of the world, tuning up for a better one. Recognizing in each of them the music and song that is in us all. Miranda found herself laughing with them. But maybe it was just because she was in love.

"I've never seen such honest humanity in stone. The world is about to end, and somehow, they are **celebrating** it, in music and song … and somehow it's alright! They are saying that even in our darkest hour, we don't know the reality and the beauty of life, eternal life … my God, Kieran. That's what Priscillian said!"

"Jesus, actually, but even he can't claim to have originated it. Come on, I've got someone for you to meet, before we both become statues ourselves. It's cold enough."

They passed into the nave. Kieran—who, unbeknownst to her, had done so the day before, and in the last time he had been here—showed Miranda the self-portrait in stone that is the Cathedral's memorial to the architect of the Portico de Gloria: San Matteo himself.

"They call him the *Santo dos Croques:* the "head banging saint". The story is, if you bang your head against his, you'll receive some of his wisdom!"

Miranda tried it and almost knocked herself out.

"Whoa! I said 'some' of his wisdom. I thought you were a philosopher, not a born-again architect, for Christ's sake. Come on, I want to you to meet someone you already know. And you can't do that with a concussion!"

They walked towards the altar. The scent of incense was even more pungent.

"I hugged the Apostle yesterday," Miranda shared. "I'm ashamed to say he didn't seem to have anything to say to me, but I admit, I didn't have chance to give him much time."

"You'll see," Kieran said, and led her down the narrow stairs to the low-ceilinged crypt.

Unlike yesterday, the air was full of history—forbidden history, she knew before he even made the introduction. They were before the silver casket. The spotlights were not yet on.

"Priscillian, I'd like you to meet Miranda. Miranda, Priscillian." and without further ado, he sank to his knees, not on the cushioned area provided, but on the stones behind them. Miranda did the same.

"It's a long way to visit someone no-one wants to remember," he said.

✳   ✳   ✳   ✳

Afterwards, they went for breakfast. They were seated at a small cafe overlooking the Cathedral. The town was waking up. They planned to go to the Monastery, soon, rouse everyone, and set out to see the town.

They spoke little. Just held each other's hands and watched the swifts darting in and out of the alcoves.

"Did you ever think they were a bit like us? Priscillian and Euchrotia, I mean."

"Think! Kieran, I haven't let myself think since Villafranca. I didn't dare."

"But they are, aren't they? Loving **despite**. Priscillian knew that there were no promises. He made her no promises. He couldn't. His fate was in the hands of others ..."

She tried to interrupt, but he wouldn't let her.

"That's the difference, you see, my fate.... Our fate ... if you'll have me, is in my hands, but yes, also the hands of God. I'm not going to make the same mistake Priscillian did. He made the wrong decision. I almost did the same. I will beat this." He cupped her face and gave her coffee-flavored kisses.

"Miranda. I have to go back to Dublin tomorrow. It's all they would allow me. Will you come with me ...? I know you have your career, and ..."

She jumped into his arms.

"Just try to stop me this time!" she said, and the coffees hurtled to the floor.

*   *   *   *

Later that day, they formed a *cola* at the entrance to the *Museo das Peregrinacións*: Miranda and Kieran, Catherine and Kevin, Felix and Miranda, Peter and Josje, Dominic, and Stephen, Alex, even Mary, who, after the previous night in Alex's company, had become surprisingly quiet. All had agreed to take a "pass" on the "Virtual Camino", just around the corner.

It was housed in a beautiful structure, dating back to the 16th Century. There were surprisingly—though this was still the height of the "season"—few there. It was 1:30 in the afternoon, and they had little time before closing time.

"I'll never get used to this!" Catherine complained. Siestas were not the norm in Oz.

They drifted through the exhibits, largely staying intact as a group, despite the fact that while walking they were almost always a few kilometers apart. Felix, brandishing their sole Official Room Text Information, "In English!", had self-elected to be their guide. Laura hung on every word, and Stephen couldn't seem to keep his smile to himself.

"'Pilgrimage,' it says here, 'is a 'ritual journey, undertaken alone or as part of a group, with the aim of achieving ritual purification, perfection or salvation: a religious experience in which a series of bonds are established, between a place in this world, and a higher sphere; between an individual traveler and a community ..."' Alex was heard to sigh ... "**between,**" Felix continued, sounding like Stephen and with a 'hush' look at Alex, "'a flesh-and-blood-pilgrim and he who is reborn, purified by the consummation of his goal. These bonds are what distinguish pilgrimage from any other types of journey or travel'."

"Sexist!" said Alex and Miranda, simultaneously, and linked pinkies.

"Yada, yada, yada" said Catherine. "How many pages in that book?" She wrenched it out of Felix's hands.

"Apostle's body, the stone boat, no sails, no rudder ... Queen Lupa ... tricks them ... ox cart ... horses covered in shells ... miracles ... buried in Libredón— isn't that miles from here? ... 9th Century ... rediscovery ... Moorish invasions ... Hey, wait a minute, this is worth repeating:

"The author ... who is ... shoot, just says *Junta de Andalucia*: shame, I would have liked to have shaken his hand ..."

"Or hers," chimed in Laura in a rare burst of overt involvement.

"Quite right sorry: anyway, it says, if ..." she surveyed her tour group, "Ladies and Gentlemen you will excuse me? Ninth Century, right?" Everyone nodded. "'This discovery must be viewed within the political and religious context of the time. The belief that St. James had once preached in Spain had arisen towards the end of the Sixth Century and had been propagated widely during the eighth Century, at a time when it was very much in the interests of the emerging Kingdom of Asturias to stress its links with the Apostle....'"

"Bravo!" said Kieran, who then shut up.

"'From this belief to the rediscovery of the Apostle's remains was but a small step, since it was widely thought that the Apostles were buried where they had preached ... bla bla ... Furthermore, it should not be forgotten that Iria Flavia—in Roman times a flourishing commercial center—was by the eighth century one of the most influential sees of the Kingdom of Asturias."

Miranda tried to close her open mouth. "Have you been reading Kieran's book?"

"Book? Miranda, have you never heard of the Internet? Hey, in Sydney this is dinnertime conversation!"

Kieran chuckled, Miranda hurled a look of contempt, and Dominic tried to look interested in a small, rather erotic, stone statue.

"Go on," said Stephen. "What does it say about the cathedral itself?"

"O.K. Gimme a minute ... Yes, here it is. O.K. Troops, your attention please! 'The original tomb was rediscovered in the foundations of the cathedral in 1879, having been lost since the sixteenth Century.'"
Deja vu and Miranda were old friends by now.

Catherine continued talking: "'... two connected apartments ... bla ... various hypotheses have been put forward as regards its original appearance.'"

"Next?" She handed it to Dominic, who still had that inscrutable Dominic smile on his face:

"O.K. Gimme a minute: talks about a stone in El Padron ... *Iria Flavia* ... two kilometers ... Roman altar: Neptune ... rock on which Apostle's body was laid to rest upon ... brought to land...."

"Apostle? Or Priscillian?" Miranda could hold her peace no longer. Dom handed her the book.

But she had gotten the tail end, or perhaps, "tale end":

"It goes on to mention various places in and around Padron where—hey Stephen, you'll like this bit: 'Traditionally hills and mountains have been objects of devotion in Galicia, as is reflected in numerous popular legends'. Then ... it goes on to talk about the importance of the Romans, metal-mining activities, Roman roads ... hang on a minute: *Iria Flavia*. It says that *'Iria Flavia* attained notable importance as a center of maritime trade and as nexus of several land routes. The town's name ... Vespasian ... (How do you get Iria Flavia out of Vespasian?) ("Sounds Greek to me", said Felix.) is testimony to this importance. Archeological remains'—hey, Laura listen to this: your Ph.D. thesis ...? Christian *sarcophagi*, coins between the Republic and the Late Empire ... was James the time of the Republic?"

"No, I don't think so."

"O.K. The plot thickens ... Iria Flavia, importance ... re-affirmed with the estab-lishment of Christianity and its designation as a See ..."

"Bishops," said Kieran.

"Yeah ... 'from the sixth Century onwards'. Hey, didn't it say that was when they started to talk about St. James etc?"

"Yep. After Braga. And about when the Aryans of the Sueves accepted the Catho-lic Church, and when they thought they had finally driven the 'Priscillianist Her-esy' underground. Curiouser and curiouser. Wish I could meet whoever compiled this guide!" Kieran was animated.

"Come on, Kieran, your turn."

"O.K. It says that there may have been a 'Castro'—Celtic, Stephen, am I right?" Stephen nodded, "at the site where the quote 'Sepulchre of St. James', end quote, was discovered. It may have been 'in use between the Roman period and the early middle ages', but by the time of the discovery of the Apostle's tomb it was aban-doned.'"

"So, that proves nothing," said Josje, who was thinking about lunch.

"Yes, but...." Kieran was flicking through the rest of the pages, but it was all about how the Cathedral had grown from a small and protected monastery, through the Middle Ages and its influx of pilgrims to the edifice they had all seen by now. He realized that, academically, he, and Priscillian, didn't have a leg to stand on.

"Read Henry Chadwick," he said lamely, just before the Curator threw them all out.

CHAPTER 32

▼

Miranda had a dilemma to process before nightfall. Not all moral, but mostly. Early that evening, they sought out a travel agent: "They" being almost everyone by now. She had a flight booked to Dublin, via Madrid for 9:50 the next day. She knew that she wanted to spend the night with Kieran, but the others were still quartered at the hospice, and all insisted that they accompany her to the Santiago airport at Lavacolla. Even if it meant two taxis. Stephen didn't apprise any of them of the real name of the airport, and only Dom, who knew, said nothing.

"Oh, Alex!" Miranda said, after a second brilliant dinner at Casa Manolo's, where the owner treated them to *chupitos* of Orujo. "Do you remember that awful afternoon at Los Angeles? When I was snuggling up with the kitten out of the wind? Do you remember what you said to me?"

Alex looked blank. They were at a bar not far from the center of town, near the Market, and the waiter turned out to be the gypsy, Ricardo. He still had that seductive and inscrutable gleam in his eyes, and Alex, despite her plans to walk on to Portugal with Catherine and Kevin, certainly had the old familiar stars in hers. By anyone's definition, the man had sex-appeal and even Miranda, happily contented, couldn't deny it.

"You said: 'We started together, we'll end together.'" Alex nodded, yes I remember that.

"I meant it." Alex could see a plea for help, even if it wasn't explicit.

"O.K." Alex said. "Let's weigh this thing up. You said Kieran has a single room, no?" (She'd told her that. It seemed somehow romantic after all they'd been through.) "You said that there was lots of space in the hostal last night, yes?"

"Well, I think so. There was no-one at breakfast." She had forgotten that she and Kieran had crept out so early, and hadn't actually breakfasted there at all. And honestly, she hadn't paid much notice when they had crept in. But it was September by now.

"O.K. So, if you want … **if** you want, you and Kieran can get a double room, and the rest of us can occupy what's left, and sleep on the floor if may be. 'Small sleeping bags take up little room', Confucius, I think. The owner won't object if we all pay him, will he? From what I gather from my guidebook …"

"Mine too," chimed in Laura.

"… he probably won't mind. Beside all Gallego's are romantics. I'll have a discreet word.…" the look in those turquoise eyes said that the owner wouldn't have a leg to stand on anyway, despite Alex's rather cock-eyed logic.

Well, and so it was. A repetition of Villafranca, a gathering of strangers, a night of stories, and such laughter that no-one who has never joined such as their company could ever appreciate. Alex, who had expected to end her journey as one of a couple said: "There's Portugal left to go, and who knows?" Ricardo had obviously been set aside, or at least, postponed. Catherine and Kevin told the group, for the first time, that this was their "pre-Honeymoon".

"We figured," said Kevin, "somewhere along the way, that there was no point in looking for anyone else, anywhere else. And let's face it, if you can put up with one another on the Camino, well, you've got a pretty good chance for life!"

Stephen ordered more Cava.

"As for me.…" he beamed at the assembled … "well, I am not allowed to say."

Laura blushed, and Felix began one of his jokes. No-one had the heart to tell him they had heard it before … from him, and many times. Besides, as far as Felix's feelings for Laura, they could clearly see the writing on the wall.

Peter and Josje had gone in search of different forms of entertainment. And though no-one dared to mention it, for a break of pilgrim etiquette, Mary, had gone with them.

"Poor Josje!" was the only comment, but perhaps it would be prudent not to mention the commentator. She had once been attracted that way herself. "They do have great legs though," she said.

The next day, it was impossible not to notice the blush on Miranda's cheeks. In a fit of budget consciousness (Alex had cornered a waiter, somewhere), they had learned of an early bus.

At the check-in counter, Kieran gave a small package to Dominic.

"Priscillian?" Miranda asked.

"You can read yours on the plane," he said. And all was hugs and kisses, and e-mail addresses, and tears, and finally, two people alone, waived through the scanning machines, and were gone.

CHAPTER 33

▼

GALICIA 388 CE

They lined the road in their hundreds. *I and, Galla, were too overwhelmed to take in their allegiance, let alone their faith.*

"If Queen Lupa herself were here, she too would fall on her knees," Herenias said in astonishment.

I am Herenius, as you probably have guessed. I never intended to be so visible. We were walking beside the ox-cart and its precious cargo. I felt his strength accompany us. And behind us, a giant of a man on a silver white horse, rode, silently, accompanied now, by an ancient dog, and behind him, the many.

The sun had risen to his full height. Though still winter, it was warm. The sun blessed our passage.

Galla stopped by the roadside. She pulled up a root of flowers. Dwarf Iris. She handed them to me. "These shall be his token", she said, and she smiled at me, the journey's careworn face, no more. Even then, I prayed that smile held just a little in reserve. For me.

Yet, nothing was said, and we journeyed on.

Below the Picro Sacro, *we paused. There were* castros, *and wells. This is a sacred site, many pleaded with us. Leave him here with us, and we will care for him, and honor his name, and uphold his teachings. But still we journeyed on.*

We are taking him home, we said. To Lugo.

At the Ria de Arousa, *we heard the same. The many had turned into the thousand. The giant would leave us and then return and every time he did, more would accompany him. I knew not what to say, and so I said nothing. I, at least have learned that. Galla, never one to share her feelings, stayed close to her father, and as the throng multiplied, I noticed, she moved increasingly close to the big man on the silver horse, who did not share a word with us, but by his very silence, increased the reverence of all.*

Eventually, we stopped for the night. It was not the place I would have chosen as it was ringed around with trees, and I was eager to move on to the mountains.

"No." Galla said. "We will make our nightfall here."

There were many women in our entourage now. They took her away.

I was left with my thoughts. They had been three years growing in silent despair.

*   *   *   *

After Priscillian and their immediate followers had left for Trier, I had stayed behind. Procula had grown in strength from childbirth, but she was never to see adulthood. Two years later, she died.

The causes are beyond my knowledge. Some said a broken heart, but of what? Of parturition of a child which never should have been? Perhaps. After love of the adolescent who fathered it? I doubt it. Procula was of stronger stock. But when the news of her mother's death reached her, when they began to move towards the estate and claim it for theirs, when they harassed her with the same fate? Then perhaps, she lost heart. Perhaps she had her father's poetic soul, but not her mother's Celtic steadfastness. Who is to know?

I, to my shame, to this day, was not there. I followed her mother and my Master to Trier, and stayed there for a while, and for what? What did I hope to accomplish? I was a nothing and a nobody, yet I stayed outside of all implication, for my own safety, and no-one knew who I was, or what my presence may have led to.

Yes, I heard of their torture! Yes, I heard of their censure! I was ashamed to be so outside of what I had grown to believe in. At least I had the good fortune to contact Euchrotia before it was too late.

*"Here!" she said in terror. "It is little, and it is not enough." She thrust a well-thumbed diary in my hand." (I have since learned that women read their own words over and over.) "And here are my Lord's words in his defense. Herenius! He who has been our master; who is given to us: I plead of you, **do not let these words be forgotten**! Perhaps in this Roman domination no-one will heed them, but there will come a time; there will come a time …"*

There was noise down below. The soldiers had come.

"Listen to me! We have no time. Find Instantius and Hyginus: they say they have been exiled to the Tin Isles. Talk with them. Write what you hear from them. Write what you know! And for the love of the True God, the Love of my Love, the only one I can now hold onto: write what you remember! And above all, perhaps, as I am a mother speaking: take care of my daughter, and protect Priscillian's daughter. I have seen by your look that the latter will not prove a hardship for you. But I beg you: treat them as sisters … dear God! They come. Flee, or you will be next."

There are times when I have felt I should have laid my head beside theirs. That my life meant nothing now. But then I have told myself—and this has not been easy—that had I done so, I would not have been able now to honor Euchrotia's charge. Perhaps, in years to come, you will read of Priscillian's words, though I dare not disseminate them now any more than I have done. It has taken a pilgrimage for me to do so—not overland, as many will do after me—but by other ways, sea, horse, carriage the latter with Galla from Elusa—to reclaim the grave of a saint who never could have been, knowing—perhaps later—nothing less, but being called, despite. My pilgrimage has been to the Lion's lair, but this Lion now has other appetites: the pickings become easily found: and finding our Emperor now (Constantius having gone the way of all dictators—may history take note) uninterested in such matters and more than willing to relieve himself of a Martyr's grave, I have brought him back. The new Emperor put up no argument. Just keep it between us, he said. I did not care; we, Galla and I, only wanted him home, and Euchrotia, whom we buried on Marcellus' farm, with the rites he would have chosen. It was then that Galla said she would return to Galicia.

But before, immediately after Priscillian's death, I journeyed wide. Partly, I am shamed to admit, I feared for my safety, but first before traveling, I went to Elusa and sought out Marcellus.

"They may have the Estate," he said, "it is worth nothing, the land only. Of the few flocks left, they are Procula's by law, and she happily gives them to my care. She will remain with me, and with Claudia for we have officially adopted her. She may have no fear. Galla may remain. Oddly, she seems to be unknown to those who might otherwise persecute her. Certainly, Priscillian's estates in Lugo are long gone, and his people, scattered. Claudia therefore claims her as cousin, until, of course, if she wishes, she returns to Lugo. She will have friends there at least. But most of that, too, belongs to them now, and the estates of those who openly followed her father. May they all rot in hell!" He caught himself short: "Forgive me, I know such things are meaningless. They are in hell already."

I sought out Galla, and made pains to try to tell her of my love, but either I was not clear enough, or she was too affected by Procula's own experience, or, and this is what I have told myself, she felt nothing for me and never would, I realized that now was not the time. So I went to the east. And there found an astonishing woman. But do not misunderstand me, for she represented herself, and was received, only as one who has traveled well.

Her name was Egeria.

"In the previous six years," she said, "I have traveled the length and breadth of the world: to India, and Egypt, to Syria and almost to China. Searching for Truth amongst the monks and the peoples. And Herenius you will not believe what I am about to tell you: almost all said exactly the same! Oh, there were variations of course, and none more so when generations had passed, and sects had split. Though I have become conversant in some languages, I am proficient in none other than my own, and Greek, and a little of Coptic, from having lived in Alexandria—but at base: Herenius! God is God. God is strong, and loves us all. He or she—now I confess I do not know—cares for us all equally! Every single person on this earth, regardless of his or her status. And God perhaps regrets that we were given the seeming illusion of free will: for we have very little unless we recognize our own strength. This world is all but

conquered, Herenius! We war against our own species. We kill in the name of God and each of us thinks we are right. And it is only for power and monetary gain that we do so. Daily, we kill our brothers and sisters, our nieces and nephews, and they kill us and our children! And God mourns and weeps, for it is a lesser god we heed, and no-one dares to say otherwise! I fear that it will always be so."

"You say you went to the East. A woman, alone. Surely this is dangerous, even for a Roman citizen?"

"I went to find my husband, Ausonius, although perhaps I did not love him as well as his ideals." Egeria said. "Before I left, I met a man with whom I entrusted his belief: a Book of Jesus, long since lost, for Ausonius had entreated to me to do so, before he disappeared. Now I hear they have killed that man too. And my sister. Strange, is it not, the way the loves of God work, if indeed it is He?"

I felt as one stung. Surely this could not be? I continued to probe: "This man with whom you entrusted the book. May I be so bold as to ask whom it was your husband entreated you to seek out?" I feared the answer.

"His name was Priscillian. Perhaps but for me, he would be alive today. They called me Agape then, but I have become aware that I, as a human being, perhaps did not deserve the name. Though I have tried hard to live to up to it."

"And your sister?"

"Half sister: Euchrotia. My mother was born in Galicia, as was I, on the western coast, but she died when I was born. My father returned to Aquitania. He was a druid, and a poet. He was heartbroken. I remained with my grandmother, but once he had another child, there was little contact: Euchrotia came to us on occasion. You see, no-one ever expected my father to marry again. When I met my husband, my father all but disowned me: I reminded him too much perhaps of himself, and of my mother, who was gadabout, and likely not faithful. Even after, he claimed, he wasn't sure of my parentage: but I am his child, of that I am certain. I saw my sister perhaps twice or thrice. I was the black sheep and I married a black sheep. Pity, there is much in my father that I feel akin to. I have no doubt as to who to call father. But that time is long gone. They say, my sister married his clone. Yet fell in love with someone else entirely. Tell me. I met him but the once. Did you know Priscillian?"

*   *   *   *

We closed up upon a hillside. The night before had promised a full moon, but she has whispered to us: "not yet." It was too late to continue and anyway, we were leagues yet from Lugo. Galla had become more and more sequestered with the women of our growing entourage. We rarely saw one another. And never intimately.

That night, the Moon was at its fullest. Those of us most close to the casket convened in an inner circle. We were on top of a hill and had been two day's slow journeying since Iria Flavia. With so many accompanying us, we had made frequent stops.

Galla, and six other women, entered the hilltop clad in simple white sheaths. She held a rose above her head, nothing more. A single white rose, in the fullness of its bloom. It was spring remember, early spring, and I wondered where she had found such a thing. An elderly wolfhound ambled along beside.

She began to speak:

"My father grows weary of his journey. As to where or why, I cannot tell. You can understand, I would have brought him to Lugo, his home, and my own. Yet, last night, I dreamed of a white rose, atop an oaken-clad grove, and today, despite the season I found such a rose, only a short distance before we broke our journey, and now we are on a small hilltop, and what do we see around us, protecting us? Truth to tell, I know little of what he believed in, but this makes of little mind. There are many of you around me in the darkness. I can see very few. But perhaps, that is likened unto our beliefs. We can see a little which is revealed to us: the rest, we accept as faith. I have been told to look to the heavens as a sign as to where my father's remains should be. And to look with care, as many will come through the ages, even though they may not know what it is that they seek. For this reason, I beseech you, tonight, search the skies; we will know if this place is right.

We began to think of our sleeping places, for all were weary, yet ...

She had not a second to cease speaking, for at the closure of her last syllable, a streak of light flew across the sky from right to left, and in all honesty, before it burned itself out, we waited for the explosion which must follow, as it hit the earth, it was that bright.

Not a sound was heard, until Galla said: "God has spoken. Here will be Priscillian's resting place. And may those who follow him remember his name"

✳   ✳   ✳   ✳

And many did. Many came in place of Pilgrimage to that Saint who never was, many may come later, and their reasons may be legend, and now, as I am dying, I ask only that my remains be placed beside his, and Donatus, who left us 5 years ago. For a while they called us Bishops. But who is to place their minds there. For me it is of no importance. Suffice it to be said, I attempted at least to keep his name and what he believed, alive, even while the "Orthodox" (they with no other choice, I say), sought to silence us. I never conquered my love for his daughter. I have wanted her until the day I die, and it may be soon, but I do not doubt that love, and lately as I grow older, I tell myself it does not matter—though only part of me believes it, and the other part now is powerless to act. Perhaps we will be reunited elsewhere, in soul and in spirit. I know I would have lived my life in no other way.

I am old now, and the century is a new one and I have little faith in it. I reflect on the atrocities they have committed against us in Jesus' name, beginning with the stoning of Urbica, the daughter of Urbicus, who had sheltered Priscillian's party as he sought refuge in Burdigala. Urbica, believing herself safe (and without Urbicus' knowledge), had gone to the market in Burdigala. On her way home, she was stoned to death, just before approaching her home. Whether Priscillian or Euchrotia had ever learned of this, I don't know. Since then there have been hundreds, and history will never give you their names! If this story has intrigued you, only slightly, even if you are 100 years away from the story I tell, I urge you to find out for yourselves. So many of our persuasion have been killed—so many estates and property expropriated, in the name of "God". In all honesty, the extent of what has happened to us, because of our beliefs, so close to their own yet denying them ownership and control, is beyond my capacity to tell you. And no doubt these will continue, at least for one hundred years after my death. All I can say is as Jesus said: Let those who have ears to hear, let them hear. And, forgive me, all, for I would add: Open your eyes to deceit. Your reward is the world of God where you are yourself, as you were ever meant to be.

EPILOGUE

▼

Miranda's note: Dublin, 2000
Kieran and I married on the 31st of October. Felix was the Best Man, and never stopped reminding us of the fact, or the date. Laura was my maid of honor and quietly wore a pretty blue diamond, small, but significant. I tell you this perhaps only because perhaps you wanted to know. But there is more.

Having walked to Fatima, and disliking it, but deciding they liked each other intensely, Catherine and Kevin are planning to marry in Mauritius at Christmas. "It's sort of half way," Catherine told me by e-mail. We are invited, but given Kieran's chemo appointments are not likely to be able to. The last we heard, Alex had found someone special in the south of France, and we all wish her special love and luck. That's about all we can tell you, except that Mary went from Santiago to Los Angeles and is working in a jewelry shop selling designer clones on Rodeo Drive. As to Peter and Josje, I don't know, but have a feeling they might turn up sometime. Dominic last wrote to us from Norway. It seems there are Gnostic connections there too.

Kieran's book was rejected by his first potential publisher as "too controversial" and he and I are in search of another. We are aware the big publishers won't touch it. But perhaps someone out there will be willing to take a chance. I've heard that stories about Jesus' life, the Gnostic Gospels, even that Jesus married and had children (Hey, and why not, Kieran just interjected from the kitchen: he is hopeful and I am ready) are likely to become quite popular and even read by a few people who wouldn't formerly have considered such things. Though I can bet equally, there will be some who will claim such things as the 'Works of the Devil'. Oh well, you can't please everyone.

As for me, I have a sick husband to love, with little hair these days, (his not mine) it must be said. But we take the days as they come to us, and we are optimistic. The Irish climate is not so bad, certainly not so extreme as Canada, and I have made friends. I even have a part-time teaching job. I have hung my Compostela on the wall, in the kitchen, but truth to tell, I don't pay much more attention to it these days than I do to the cookbooks on the shelf: them ... well, I just peruse them and look at the pictures, and make it up as I go along. I have found that that is a good way to approach life.

We're having Felix and Laura to dinner tonight. They at least I know, will accept this philosophy.

And Felix'll tuck in anyway.

Appendix:
The Apocryphon of Jesus the Christ

Whoso seeks the interpretation of these sayings
will not experience death.

*　　　*　　　*　　　*

We were gathered together, that last night, the twelve and Mary Magdalene who loved the Savior. We were to eat well in our upper chamber, and had drunk of the sweet juices of the last grape harvest. But all knew that the events of the most recent days were portents of things to come. We knew that we were assembled maybe for the last time. And so I perhaps in particular knew the importance of keeping those things which were to pass that night, though why this task should have come to me and not the others, remains a mystery to me. Perhaps I knew they would take less notice of me. These, then are the secret sayings of our Master which I wrote down as I was listening to them talking with one another. I hope and pray that they will come to the notice of those who will question and understand them, for they are the way to truth and everlasting life.

*   *   *   *

We asked him: 'Master, when shall the kingdom come?'"

And he answered us straightways: It will not come by waiting for it. It will not be a matter of saying, Here it is ... or There it is ... Rather, the kingdom of the father is spread upon the earth, but men do not see it.
If those who lead you say to you, 'See, the Kingdom is in the sky." Then the birds of the sky will precede you. If they say to you, 'It is in the sea,' then the fish will precede you. Rather the kingdom is inside you, and it is outside of you. When you come to know yourselves, then you will become known, and you will realize that you are the sons of the living father. But if you know yourselves not, you will dwell in poverty, and it is you who are that poverty.
You must become passers by.

Those who say they will die first and then rise are in error. If they do not first receive the resurrection while they live, when they die they will receive nothing. They say: baptism is a great thing, because if people receive it, they will live, but they are in error. There is more to learn, but ...

The world came about through a mistake. For he who created it wanted to make it imperishable and immortal. But he fell short of attaining his desire. For the world never was immortal, nor, for that matter, was he who made the world.
And the Lord paused as we pondered his words.
For things are not imperishable, but his sons are. Nothing will be able to become imperishable until it becomes a son.

The cup of wine and water is appointed as the type of blood for which thanks are given. It is full of the Holy Spirit and it belongs to the wholly perfect man. The living water is a body. And it is necessary that we put on the living man; therefore, when he is about to go down to the water, he unclothes himself, in order that he may put on the living man.
In perfecting the water of baptism, we empty it of death.

Those who were gathered asked him: 'Lord, what is the fullness, *and what is the deficiency?'* (The word here is *pleroma*, and this is closest translation I can make. K)
He said to us: You are from the fullness and you dwell in the place where the deficiency is. And Lo! His life has poured down upon …

And the Lord said: Blessed is the wise man who sought after the truth and when he found it, rested upon it forever and was unafraid of those who wanted to disturb him.

Judas asked: 'Why for the sake of truth, do we die and live?'
And the Lord answered him, saying: Whatever is born of truth does not die. Whatever is born of woman, dies.

I was disturbed, and asked: 'Lord, is there a place which is lacking truth? I want to understand all things, just as they are.'
He answered me straightway: The place which lacks truth is the place where I am not! He who shall drink from my mouth shall become as I am. I shall become as he, and all things that are hidden shall be revealed to him.

But Peter said: Let Mary leave us, for women are not worthy of life.

But Jesus said to him: I myself shall lead her in order to make her as male, so that she may too become a living spirit. For every woman who will make herself so will enter the kingdom of heaven.

But Mary was afraid of Peter for he knew that he hated her race and believed that they were incapable of telling the truth.

The disciples said to him: 'We know that you will depart from us. Tell us who will be our leader then?'
He said to them: You are to go to James the righteous, for whose sake heaven and earth came into being.

Jesus asked us: Compare me to someone and tell me whom I am alike.
Simon Peter said to him: 'You are like a righteous angel.'
Matthew said to him: 'You are like a wise philosopher.'
Thomas said: 'Master, my mouth is incapable of saying whom you are alike.'
Jesus said: I am not your master. Because you have drunk from my words, you have become intoxicated from the bubbling spring which I have measured out.

The disciples said to Jesus: 'Tell us how our end will be?'
Jesus said: Have you discovered then the beginning, that you look now for the end? For where the beginning is, so then is where the end will be. Blessed is he who takes his place at the beginning; he will know the end and will not experience death.

His followers said to him: 'Lord, when will the repose of the dead come about? When will the New World come?'
And he answered them: What you look forward to has already come and you still do not realize it.
'Should we fast upon the Sabbath day?'
The lord said: If you do not fast as regards the world, you will not find the kingdom. If you do not observe the Sabbath as a Sabbath, you will not find the father.

His disciples asked him: 'When will you be revealed to us, and when shall we see you?'
Jesus said to them: When you disrobe without being ashamed and take up your garments and place them under your feet like little children, and tread upon them then you will see the son of the living one, and you will not be afraid.
Whoever comes to be as a child will be acquainted with the kingdom.

Jesus said: He who has come to understand the world has found only a corpse, and who ever who has found a corpse is superior to the world.
It is to those who are worthy of my mysteries that I tell my mysteries. Do not let your left hand know what your right hand is doing.

There was a rich man who had much money. He said: 'I shall put my money to use that I may sow, reap, plant, and thus fill my storehouse with produce. The result will be that I shall lack nothing. Such were his intentions, but that night he died. For those who have ears to hear, let them hear.
The harvest is great, but the laborers they are few. Beseech the lord, therefore, to send laborers to the harvest.

Peter ever was the practical one of the followers and he asked:
'*Lord, you have taught us to forsake the world and everything in it. We have renounced those things for your sake. But what concerns us now is how do we find food for a single day? Where will we find the needs that you ask us to provide for the poor?*'
The Lord answered: Peter have I not already told you that if you ask, it shall be given to you, if you seek, then you will find. I am telling you, do not worry about your life, what you will eat, about your body, or what you will wear. Isn't your life more than about food, and the body more than clothing? Think then of the ravens. They do not plant, harvest, or store grain in barns, yet God feeds them.
Do not carry money, or a bag, or sandals or staff ... whatever house you enter, say 'Peace be upon this house'. And if a child of peace is there your greeting will be received.
Peter, it was necessary that you understood the parable. Do you not yet understand that my name, which you will teach in, will surpass all riches?
And he gave us a pouch of medicine and said to us: Heal all of those who believe in my name.
And Peter was afraid for he signaled to John who was beside us and he indicated that he should talk this time. John began: 'Master, forgive us for our doubts, but we have not been taught to be physicians. How then will we know how to heal bodies as you have instructed us?
And Jesus answered him: "John, rightly have you spoken for I know that the physicians of this world heal what is of this world. But remember this: the physicians of souls heal what the heart needs and craves. Heal bodies first: but afterwards, heal the sicknesses of the heart also.
Thomas said: 'You have certainly persuaded us, Lord. We realize in our heart, and it is obvious that this is so and that your word is sufficient. But these words that you speak are ridiculous and contemptible to the world since they are misunderstood. So how can we go and preach them since we are not esteemed in the world?'
Jesus answered him: They will cling to the name of a dead man, thinking that they will become pure. But they will become greatly defiled and they will fall into the name of error, and into the hand of an evil cunning man and a manifold dogma that they will be ruled heretically. For some of them will blaspheme the truth and proclaim evil teaching. And they will say evil things against each other.
Many others will oppose the truth and are the messengers of error. They will set up their error and their laws against these pure thoughts of mine, as looking out from one perspective, thinking that good and evil are from one source. They do business in my word. And they will propagate harsh fate ...

And there shall be others of those who are outside our number who name themselves bishop and also deacons, as if they have received their authority from God. They bend themselves under the judgment of the leaders. These people are dry canals.

The disciples asked him, 'Lord where shall we find you?'
The Lord said: I am the light which is above all. Split a piece of wood, I am there. Lift up a stone, and you will find me.
Light and darkness, life and death, right and left. These are brothers of one another. They are inseparable. Because of this, neither are the good 'good', nor evil 'evil'. Nor is life 'life', nor death 'death'. For this reason each one will dissolve unto its earliest origin. But those who are exalted above the world are indissoluble. Eternal. Names given to the worldly are very deceptive for they divert from what is correct to what is incorrect.
He gave us pause to ponder his words:
The names which are heard are in the world and they deceive. If they were in the eternal aeon *they would at no time be used in the world. Nor were they set among worldly things. But truth brought these names into existence in the world for our sakes because it is not possible to learn it without those names. The* archons *wanted to deceive man since they saw that he had a kinship with those things which are truly good. They took the name of those that are good and gave it to those that are not good so that through those names they might deceive him and bind themselves to those which are not good. Thus, they take the free man and bind him to them and make him a slave forever.*
Some will say: the Lord died first and then rose up. They are in error, for he will rise up first, and then die. If you do not attain the resurrection, you too will die.
And again, we thought upon his words.
And he explained to us: God is like a dyer. The good dyes dissolve with the things that are dyed in them, so it is with those whom God has dyed. Since God is immortal, they become immortal by means of his colors. But all of the colors come out white. Even so has the son of man come out of as a dyer.
Faith receives, love gives. No-one will be able to receive without faith. And no-one will be able to give without love. Because of this, we believe, in order that we may love: we give, since if one gives without love, he has no profit from what he has given.

The disciples asked him: 'How then shall we move forward into truth?
And Jesus answered us as a parable—the type of story we had often seen him use to help the people understand his message: An ass which was tied to a millstone did a hundred miles walking. When it was loosened, it found it was still in the same place. There are men who make such journeys; they make no progress towards any destina-

tion. When evening comes upon them, they see neither city nor village, nor human artifact, nor natural phenomenon; neither power nor angel. In vain have the wretches labored.

Wretched is the body which is dependent upon a body. But more, wretched is the soul which is dependent upon these two. And it was clear to us, his deeper meaning.

And they said to Jesus, 'Come let us pray today.'

Jesus instructed us: When you pray say, 'Father, let your name be holy. May your rule take place. Give us each day our daily bread. Pardon our debts for we will pardon those who are indebted to us. And do not bring us to temptation.

The disciples entreated him: "Lord, how shall we know truth from falsehood?"

The Savior answered us thus: Woe to those who are captives, for they are bound in caverns. In mad laughter they rejoice in what they think you see. They neither realize their perdition nor do they reflect upon their circumstances. They do not realize that they have dwelt in darkness and death! They are drunk and full of bitterness. Their mind is deranged because of the burning that is within them. Darkness arises for them as the light, for they have surrendered their freedom for slavehood. They darken their hearts, and surrender their thoughts to folly. They baptize their souls in the water of darkness.
Woe to those who dwell in error, heedless of the light of the sun which judges them and looking down upon them, circles all things. Woe to those who dwell in error, heedless that the light of the sun which judges and looks down upon all will circle all things so as to enslave the enemies of light.
But when the light appears, man comes to recognize that the fear which took hold of him was nothing. Thus men were in ignorance of the father, whom they saw not. This ignorance inspired in them fear and confusion and left them uncertain and hesitant, divided and torn into shreds ... like sleepers who are prey to nightmares. But only down to the moment when those who have passed through all this have woken up ... Thus they have cast their ignorance far away from them, like the dream which they account as naught.

Matthew said: 'Lord, I want to see that place of life, where there is no wickedness but rather there is pure light!'

The Lord said: Brother Matthew, you will not be able to see it as long as you are a carrier of flesh.

But Matthew persisted: 'Lord, even if I will not be able to see it, at least let me know it …

And Jesus answered him: Anyone who has known himself has seen this light: everything has come to him in his goodness. If you know yourselves then you will be known, and you will know that you are the sons of the living Father, as I am.

The Lord said to them: Whoever believes in me, believes not in me but in he who sent me. I have come as a light unto the world so that no-one who believes in me will remain in darkness. For I have not spoken on my own authority, but the father who sent me and gave me a command, what I should say and what I should speak.

"*What are we to learn from this?*" *we asked.*

The sun and the moon will give a fragrance to you together with the air and the spirit and the earth and the water. For if the sun does not shine upon these bodies, they will wither and perish just like the weeds and the grass.

And the Lord continued: Watch, and pray, that you come not to be in the flesh, but rather that you come forward from the bondage of the bitterness of this life. And as you pray, you will find rest, for you have left behind the suffering and the disgrace. For when you come from the sufferings and passion of the body, you will receive rest from the good one, and you will reign with the king; you will be joined with him and he with you from now on.

Amen.

THE PRAYER OF THANKSGIVING:

AND THIS IS THE PRAYER THAT THEY SPOKE:
We give thanks to you.
Every soul and heart is lifted up to You, undisturbed name
God, and praised with the name, 'Father',
For to everyone and everything
Comes the Fatherly kindness and affection and love
and any teaching that may be that is sweet and plain,
Giving us mind, speech,
and knowledge: *nous,* so that we may also understand You;
speech, so that we may expound You;
knowledge, that we may know You.

We rejoice, having been illuminated by knowledge.
We rejoice, because while we were in the body
You have made us diving through Your knowledge.

The thanksgiving of the man who attains to You is one thing: that we know.
You—intellectual light. we have known You.
Light of Life—we have known You.
Womb of every creature—we have known You.
Pregnant with the nature of the Father—we have known You
Eternal permanence ...
Thus we have worshipped the nature of your goodness.
One petition only we ask: that we be preserved in knowledge.
One protection only we ask: that we not stumble in life.
AMEN

And once they had said this prayer, they embraced each other soundly, and they
went to eat of their holy food which had no blood in it.

    *   *   *   *

I have copied this one discourse. Indeed, very many have
come to me, and also I have not hesitated to copy them
though the matter may burden you. Since the discourses
which have come to me are numerous ...
(*and here the copyist's note ends abruptly,*
and why?)

Tarantella

Do you remember an Inn,
Miranda?
Do you remember an Inn?
And the tedding and the bedding
Of the straw for a bedding,
And the fleas that tease in the High Pyrenees,
And the wine that tasted of tar?
And the cheers and the jeers of the young muleteers
(Under the vine of the dark veranda)?
Do you remember an Inn, Miranda,
Do you remember an Inn?
And the cheers and the jeers of the young muleteers
Who hadn't got a penny,
And who weren't paying any,
And the hammer at the doors and the din?
And the hip! hop! hap!
Of the clap
Of the hands to the swirl and the twirl
Of the girl gone chancing,
Glancing,
Dancing,
Backing and advancing,
Snapping of the clapper to the spin
Out and in—
And the ting, tong, tang of the guitar!
Do you remember an Inn,
Miranda?
Do you remember an Inn?
Never more
Miranda,
Never more.
Only the high peaks hoar;
And Aragon a torrent at the door.
No sound
In the walls of the halls where falls
The tread

Of the feet of the dead to the ground,
No sound:
But the boom
Of the far waterfall like doom.
Hillaire Belloc

Afterword

Pilgrimage to Heresy is first and foremost, a work of fiction.

It hopes to give compelling reasons why the object of the pilgrimage to Santiago de Compostela may not be St. James at all.

Dan Brown has been repeatedly criticized, even vilified, for the content of The Da Vinci Code. I wish to avoid this at all costs. The *raison d'etre* of this book is to entertain you and, I hope, to make you think: perhaps question. It is not intended to teach you history, and most emphatically, **not**, to teach you theology or trample on your idea of the Divine.

Yet Priscillian was very much a real person, and was executed in either 385 or 386 CE much as described here. Where he was born, where he lived, where he was educated, whom he married (if anyone), how he came to believe in his ideas–very Gnostic ideas–I leave these questions to the historians. And good luck to them. With the exception of the admirable Henry Chadwick, to whom I owe the prince of all debts of thanks for his book Priscillian of Avila: The Occult and the Charismatic in the Early Church, there is really surprisingly very little written about my main character. Although, having said this, when I first tried to research Priscillian back in 2001 there were very few links indeed on the Internet (especially in English), whereas now there are thousands, mostly drawn in some way or another from the Catholic Encyclopaedia, the writers of which, we have to admit, are not likely to be particularly open-minded or sympathetic in this case.

To the other characters in this book, most existed, and most with some connection to Priscillian. Euchrotia, for example, was married to Delphidias, had a daughter of about Procula's age, and followed Priscillian to Rome. She was one of the six who were executed along with the bishop. Procula, her daughter, did become pregnant, although by whom is unknown. Priscillian was implicated in the death of her child.

I have let my imagination and an obvious sympathy for the unavoidable plight of my character to absolve him from any physical connection with her pregnancy. As for any love affair between him and Euchrotia, this is strictly romantic fabrication on my part, although one thing is certain: Priscillianism (perhaps the man himself) had an irresistible fascination which brought both women and men flocking to his side, especially in Galicia where it remained for many years following his death. I have made a case for the alternative idea for "celibacy" which, given the fragility of human passions, I think is perhaps not so far from the truth. Not to be born is the ideal of the Gnostic understanding. Priscillian may have realized that his own ascetic ideal would have been impossible for most. Egeria's travels and her diary still make fascinating reading, but although it has been conjectured there is no mention of a direct connection with the Priscillianists. However, it seemed to me that she may have been a character very much like "Agape" and so it is Egeria who brings the book to Priscillian. And perhaps she did. The bishops mentioned—his interlocutors and persecutors—are all documented fact, as is the presence of St. Martin of Tours who was persuaded to act against his conscience, and who ever after regretted it.

The giant Herakles simply refused–like Priscillian's dog–to remain outside the narrative but simply forced his way in, as Giants do. There is a story connected with St. James of a rider and a horse covered in seaweed and cockleshells which is where the pilgrim symbol originates. I have simply woven it into the Prologue.

The Sacred Gospel is my doing. While writing it I half-expected a lightning bolt to strike me at any time. It didn't. Anyway, although I have woven together fragments of the Gnostic papers, very few of the words are mine but are taken from a diverse set from the Nag Hammadi Library, in particular the Gospel of St. Thomas. As to the narrator and author of the "Secret Gospel", I'll let you figure it out.

Some "characters" from the Camino are real enough, but they are mentioned in so many guidebooks that I do not feel I am imposing myself too much for mentioning them. Many of the actual events are reflections of my own pilgrimage and very many of Miranda's thoughts, doubts, misgivings, fears, and ultimately joys are mine alone. To this extent I acknowledge a certain "biographicalness" of the modern day sections of the book. The pilgrims themselves are fictitious, but one cannot walk on the Camino as I did in 1999 and not become absorbed in the personalities of those who choose, for whatever reasons (and sometimes for no reason at all!) to go on Pilgrimage, in this case in the (2nd to) last year of the Twentieth Century. All are either composites or are completely taken from my own imagination. Those I walked with: you may remember certain places, certain events, certain individuals: but you are none of these, although there are a few who will remain forever in my heart as angels along my way.

Who is buried in the cathedral in Santiago de Compostela? St. James? Most tourist and pilgrim literature will have you think so. And perhaps it is one of the Sons of Thunder after all. Then again perhaps not. As Alex wisely says: It doesn't really matter.

And as for Priscillian—it is time to tell his tale.

Tracy Saunders
Benahavis and Benamahoma, Spain
August 2007

Suggested Reading List

This is by no means an exhaustive list. I have included some favorites which gave me the historical and spiritual background for Pilgrimage to Heresy. Some of the following, inevitably, contradict my thesis that Priscillian was guilty of no crime. Some I have found inspirational and reflect Miranda's experiences and self-doubts (and mine).

Priscillian of Avila: The Occult and the Charismatic in the Early Church.
Henry Chadwick, Oxford University Press, 1976
Indispensable. I waited for two years to get a copy. It was worth the wait.

The Nag Hammadi Library Revised Edition
James M. Robinson, General Editor, Harper Collins, 1990

Gnosticism: New Light on the Ancient Tradition of Inner Knowing
Stephen Hoeller, Quest Books, 2002

The Gnostic Gospels
Elaine Pagels, Penguin Books, 1982
The standard reference book on Gnosticism

The Early Church
Henry Chadwick, Pelican Books, 1967

The Oxford History of the Roman World
Edited by John Boardman, Jasper Griffin, and Oswyn Murray, Oxford University Press, 1988

A History of God
Karen Armstrong, Mandarin Paperbacks, 1994
She doesn't mention Priscillian, but it's still worth a read

Secrets of the Code
Edited by Dan Burnstein, Orion Books, 2004
I bought this in a supermarket! Some good background reading on some controversial religious issues generated by Dan Brown's The Da Vinci Code

Off the Road
Jack Hitt, Simon and Schuster, 1994
I've read it a dozen times, both before and after the Camino. Perhaps the only true "Pilgrim Guide" in its honesty. Great fun.

The Pilgrimage
Paulo Coelho, Harper Collins, 1992
Neither my Camino, nor Miranda's. But a classic.

Egeria's Travels
John Wilkinson, Amazon.com

El Camino de Santiago a Pie
El Pais Aguilar, 2004
Don't Leave Home Without It! In Spanish, but never mind

Running From Safety
Richard Bach, Dell Paperbacks, 1994
Arguably my favorite book. I have worn the spine out on each of the three copies I have purchased.

The Re-Enchantment of Everyday Life
Thomas Moore, Harper Collins, 1996
A gentle guide on living a more "mindful" life

Travels in Catholic Europe
Colm Toibin
(Vintage Departures)
Encountered on the Camino in Azofra: I am too disheartened by the author's singular lack of understanding of what a Pilgrimage means to make a comment on his published work, but here I cite him, nonetheless, as mentioned in the text.

On the Web:

The Poems of Hillaire Belloc
http://www.poemhunter.com/i/ebooks/pdf/hilaire_belloc_2004_9.pdf
Free download e-book

On the "Hiberi"
http://www.britam.org/hiberi.html

An interesting site on comparative religions put out by the Ontario Consultants for Religious Tolerance
http://www.religioustolerance.org

A History of the Church by Phillip Hughes
http://mafg.home.isp-direct.com/book/v2toc.htm

The Library of Iberian Resources Online
http://libro.uca.edu/payne1/payne1.htm

Paganism and Pagan Survivals in Spain up to the Fall of the Visigothic Kingdom
http://libro.uca.edu/mckenna/paganism.htm
(Both of the above are excellent resource material)

Wikipedia: The Library of Alexandria
http://www.en.wikipedia.org/wiki/Library_of_Alexandria
Wikipedia: Priscillian
http://en.wikipedia.org/wiki/Priscillian

The Twilight of the Celts by John Patrick Parle
Origins of the Celts by Michael Wangbickler
http://www.realmagick.com

The History of the Pilgrimage to Compostela
http://www.gosantiago2004.com/santiago-pilgrimage-history.html

The Individuality of Portugal by Dan Stanislawski
http://www.libro.uca.edu/stanislawski/Chap6.htm
Good background on the spread of the Celts

On St. Martin of Tours
http://www.ewtn.com/library/MARY/MARTIN.htm

On St. Ambrose
http://www.newadvent.org

The best site for information about Gnosticism
http://www.gnosis.org

and much more.

Made in the USA
San Bernardino, CA
18 February 2014